Deborah Jean White

SEEN AND NOT HEARD
Deborah Jean White

Seen and Not Heard

Deborah Jean White

SEEN AND NOT HEARD

WAS FIRST PUBLISHED IN GREAT BRITAIN IN 2021.

This is a work of fiction. Names, places, event and incidents are either the products of the author's imagination or used fictitiously. Any resemblance to actual persons, living or dead, is purely coincidental.

A CIP record for this book is available from KDP Books.

ISBN: 9798648049192

Also available as an Ebook & Audible (2022)

Printed and Bound by KDP Books.

Seen and Not Heard

Deborah Jean White

For my daughter, Abigail Rose McCann, who surprises me every day

Seen and Not Heard

ONE
MOLLY

I grimace at the quivering hammer in my hand and notice on my forearm dripping blood.

It's done. What should I do next?

To admit remorse would be welcoming the crazy notion: objects can feel. Ridiculous. I refuse to project my emotions onto things that don't matter. Not anymore.

I turn away in a single spin. It's so hard to breathe. I lift my head to the sky filled with puffed up, dull-grey clouds. Are they forming the shape of a house? I need to pull myself together. I'm falling apart like the apple crumble I shared an hour ago with Matthew. I should have stayed there with him. What compelled me to leave the welcoming music, comforting gingham cushions and... and... and his wonderful, perfect company?

A crow descends with a hard thud upon the scrutinising school building.

"What the heck are you doing here?"

Grandad used to say, "Crows aren't a good sign, Molly-Moo. Linked to death, they are. Linked to death. A warning. Best to avoid 'em like the plague." I don't need this right now.

Hopping from one tile to another, the mocking crow mimics the thumping of my beating heart.

Aware of my cold bare feet, I try to stand tall and avoid seeing Grandad's face raising the alarm in my mind's eye.

The sky opens. Rain pelts down and down and down. Like the marble paint we used in the classroom; the rivulet of scarlet on my arm fades now to pink. The blood dollops onto the meddling ends of my long hair; the harsh red contrasts dramatically with my natural flecks of golden blonde. Saturated. It dyes my ends and flattens the curls. The crow, with pride, stretches out his perfect ink-coloured wings.

"Bloody show-off."

I hear the sirens getting closer. I stumble forward leaning on the railing. How the heck would I explain this?

The crow gawks at me, pointing his razor-sharp beak at the weapon still in my hand. I drop it. The crow knows what I did.

"I had to do it… for the children…"

The words plummet like the bricks of a demolished house. I am losing my mind.

The crow cocks his head at me.

"I know they won't believe me." With one peck, he agrees. The rain slows down dripping alongside the chip-chop thoughts in my head; full of random, unconnected details. Bible verses, bullying, play-based learning … death.

I try to stay calm.

"If a blue house is made of blue bricks and a red house is made of red bricks. What is a greenhouse made of?" With one piercing alarm call, the crow abandons me. "It's glass. The answer is glass. Ack, it doesn't matter… It really doesn't matter." I watch him soar away and I *wish* to follow in his flight path: escape. Deep down I know only houses can make wishes and Harry has gone on without me.

Houses can make wishes? What am I thinking? Houses are like fat, flightless birds: grounded. How the hell can houses make wishes? I shouldn't swear. I really shouldn't swear. I'm without a doubt losing my mind.

The darting rain stops.

I stand tall, as if I had just finished a one-foot spin for the clapping spectators down at the ice-rink.

But dizziness surrounds me.

I begin to hiccup. My light dress clings to my shivering body. I don't feel good.

Leaning against the cold gable wall, my head continues to whirl.

I contemplate telling them the truth.

Two things are certain: I know I need to get my story straight and a story isn't a story without a beginning, a middle and an end.

I take a calm deep breath.

When did this craziness start?

To tell the truth, I need to understand where and when. Put together the jigsaw of madness. But I have always been pathetically rubbish at doing puzzles. Do I even have a beginning for this bizarre story?"

Maybe.

I close my eyes and with a brand-new perseverance, I picture myself standing in the fortune-teller's cul-de-sac.

Falling sideways, I slide down the wall. I feel different. Something inside me has changed.

I am a girl.

I am.

I am.

***

As we made our way towards his building, we bumped shoulders. Anita and I couldn't be any closer. We scanned it up and down. The flat looked cheap: the roof was flat, the walls were not yet painted, even the windows seemed small and thin. The slight garden on the way in was covered with weeds; long dandelions and out-of-control buttercups. I pulled my hand over my stomach. My nerves were out of control too. I started to hiccup.

"I don't know why I let you talk me into doing mad things with you," I said hovering my finger over his doorbell. My hiccupping nerves began to Irish dance; stiffening my stomach and making fast precise movements. Anita leaned over and pressed my finger onto the doorbell.

"Ow! That was sore."

"Sometimes Molly ye just got to take the bull by the horns."

An annoying Christmas song played out even though it was the end of April. We stood and waited and waited some more.

Anita popped the hedgehog necklace I bought her three years ago into her mouth as she rummaged through her skinny-fit, combat tracksuit pockets for his phone number.

"Are you sure you made the appointment?"

"Yes, six months ago. He's so good you've to go on his waiting list... Don't worry. He's clairvoyant, he *knows* we're coming..." she said digging my ribs and tossing her long, red hair behind her shoulder.

"I don't want to be here."

"You'll be chuffed to bits if ya find out how things will work out between you and Matthew Stewart. That is, if ya ever get around to introducing yerself." I stared into Anita's enthusiastic brown eyes and smiled. My dancers slowed down and tapped gently.

There was a noise behind the door. A large stone hit the pit of my stomach and my dancing nerves scattered.

"Someone is coming," I whispered and did one more hiccup. Anita's face became serious and she spat the hedgehog out of her mouth. I gripped her wrist and squeezed it. "Can't believe you're making me do this," I whispered and the door opened.

He was large. I didn't expect that. A fat ostrich. He was about fifty and had a walking stick in his hand. His beige trousers were hauled right up above his waist, providing a place for his flabby chest to rest.

"Hi," he said with a sharp, feminine tone, "Come on up."

The corridor was narrow and the stairs were steep. A strong smell reminded me of the damp clothes I had dragged out of a forgotten ice-skating bag that lived under my bed for at least a month.

I whispered, "What do you call a fat clairvoyant? A four-chins-teller!" Anita belted out a loud, fake cough. The ones that always make a bad situation worse. She used to do those a lot in school to cover up one of my terrible jokes or the crap answers I gave to teachers in class.

I smirked at her as I stepped inside.

On the first stair, there was a large basket filled with pieces of brick and round, smooth pebbles. Some he had probably painted himself like a big kid. We had to squeeze past to make sure it didn't topple over. Every part of the wall was covered with items, mainly brass, ugly things: horseshoes, bowls, two swords and a shield, and three ducks in a row. They were arranged haphazardly and some knocked against our arms as we trudged up the stairs behind him. He tolerated one step at a time and stopped at every third step for a rest. Sometimes he leaned on the bannister with his stick in the same hand and rubbed his leg with his free hand.

Anita made small talk.

"So, have ya been doing this long? The fortune-teller stuff."

"Yes, the four-chins-teller stuff," I said behind her. Anita coughed again and with the back of my hand I slapped her thigh.

"Have ya been out much?"

Next, she would be asking him for a date!

"Hopefully it'll be barbecue weather soon."

As if he cared. Did Anita see his out-of-control garden out there? Not really barbecue ready.

The houses in his cul-de-sac had all looked the same. No personalities rendered; grey and dreary. Like a row of lifeless mockingbirds. Boring, inane birds; territorial, hostile and malicious. They mimicked each other in rapid succession. There was no way this guy or his neighbours even considered having barbecues.

"Do ya think the sun will shine again soon?"

He didn't reply to any of her questions and I didn't blame him.

At the top of the stairs, he led us into a small living room and mumbled, "Wait here and I'll set up the kitchen for you both."

He disappeared down the hallway and through a door to his right. Anita stood with the hedgehog back in her mouth. Her back straight and her neck long and high. I put it down to our ice-skating training. I did a double-check of my own posture.

My focus went to the walls. My eyes traced the strange hangings there and they stopped on the first picture of a cross in front of a stormy-looking sky: John 14:6.

"I am the way, the t…r…u ruth?"

Anita stood behind me and whispered, "I am the way, the truth, and the life: no man cometh unto the Father, but by me. John…"

I glared at her and then looked back at the picture. A thick layer of dust covered the frame it hung in.

I hated when Anita jumped in and helped me. Not that being helped was beyond me. Needing help every day with reading and writing properly wore me down to willingly acknowledge: this was how it was going to be for me.

To *ask* for help was a different matter though. I could endure help then. I got the same feeling when someone corrected my reading. It was when I was wrong and didn't know I was wrong. When dyslexia crept up on me like the wolf in *Little Red Riding Hood* and tapped me on the shoulder to remind me it's lurking, ready to pounce on any foolish *I can read or write this on my own* inkling I might be gripping onto in my tiny brain. A little reminder might be easier to handle if it ended there, but *my* dyslexia wolf would never stop there. Oh no, too easy. Instead, it would grab me, hold me down, start pulling me apart before pigging out on me with its razor-sharp vowels and word-puzzling teeth, and only then walk away with a grin on its face. So that's when it bugged me.

Doing a side-step, I bulldozed my word wolf to the side of my mind. I came to the next picture. Only slightly more pleasant, showing a lonely house in an unkempt field. I looked closely at the house.

Hebrews 3:4. Anita whispered this verse too, "For every house is built by someone, but God is the builder of everything." Did Anita consider herself to be *my* Woodcutter? Was *I* Little Red Riding Hood?

As I continued the floorboards creaked. I glanced down at the faded purple carpet with dirty brown swirls that may at one point have been golden. The next picture was another storm cloud, lit up by a brass overhanging light: Matthew 7:25. "The Rain came down—"

"Don't!" I held my hand up to her face knowing this woodcutter was now being *too* helpful.

Spitting out the hedgehog, Anita protested, "I was trying to read it for ya."

"I'm fine. Your creepy-ass voice was freaking me out."

"It stinks in here," Anita moaned.

"Don't even think about complaining. *You* made us come here," I snapped as I peered behind her at the wall with a window overlooking the dreary street. The wall here had more brass items but this time the fortune-teller had interspersed old photographs amongst his odd items and pictures of crosses. I stepped over to the wall.

"Molly... Oi! Molly, did ya apply for any of those jobs?"

"Look at all this stuff," I said ignoring her.

I stepped towards one black and white photograph that stood out.

"Well?" she asked, throwing her metaphorical axe down onto the ridiculous carpet.

"Well, what?"

"Did ya get around to applying for those jobs? Ya better get a job soon or yer mum is going to go ape-shit."

"A couple," I answered, leaning down to look closely at the photograph. It was a family outside a tall house with net curtains in each of the four windows. On the left-hand side of the house roses grew. The door looked out of place as if it belonged to a grand house and it shouldn't be on this plain-looking terrace. There was a woman holding a cigarette with shoulder-length hair standing by a man in a uniform; his arm around her waist. His face tan and weather-beaten. His eye lines made him look like someone who loved to smile and I knew he loved his family dearly. Two children stood in front of them: a boy, half off his bicycle, and a shorter girl with a doll in her arms.

"Which ones? Did ya apply for the one in the school?" Anita asked still determined to be the hero in my odd fairy tale.

"Weird pic."

"I know, it's beyond weird," Anita whispered at my shoulder, making me leap away from the photograph.

"Ha, made you jump," she continued, picking up a Tiny Tears doll from a basket filled with other eerie-looking dolls. Its dirty face and hair made her look a little insane. Anita wiggled it in front of me. "Ya still need to answer my question... Did ya apply for the one in the school?"

"Mum made me. I'll not be going if I get an interview. A dyslexic working in a primary school... Ridiculous." I was stuck. I never wished to be stuck, I just was. I needed to soar high, achieve something to impress *her*. But my dyslexic-clipped wings held me down; controlled my every move.

"It's not ridiculous. This is."

"Get off. It looks like the doll in the photograph."

I shoved my word wolf and the doll away from my face, and the thing landed on the floor. Its head rolled off.

"Oh crap!" I said and lifted it, trying to shove the head back on. Too late!

"Right girls, in you come."

I hid the doll behind my back. From my mouth came a heavy breath of relief, followed by a hiccup, when I realised he was back in his kitchen.

"Surely, ya don't need to worry about that dyslexic thing now you've left school?" I couldn't believe the words fell out of her mouth. Surely, she was the one person who got how hard it was for me. It was worse more than ever now that I was out of school: form filling, pressure from Mum to pay my way, and the fact *all* jobs involved some form of reading or writing. I sighed as I looked at my carefree friend.

Scouting around for options, I chucked the doll, head and all, behind a velvet green cushion on the settee. I fired Anita a dirty look, which she returned with a smirk and a shrug. His shadow appeared in the hallway as he beckoned for us to follow him into the kitchen.

The room was smaller than the living room. There was a cheap, white camping table too big for the area it stood in. He had lit a candle on the table and positioned beside it a deck of cards. They had angels on the top.

He directed us to sit and we squeezed beside the white cooker on two wobbly chairs like contestants on a horrific game show. The window ajar and two wind chimes knocked against each other occasionally. Anita had her hand mirror out pressing on a tiny spot on the side of her jaw as if she was squeezing bubble wrap. I forgave her quickly.

I did what I normally do when I wanted to forgive someone or tried to avoid answering awkward questions. I brought in the *real* woodcutter. The one who would make everything all right; provide me with a warm electric blanket and cosy me up. I brought in my sense of humour and told one of my notorious jokes.

I leaned towards her, "Anita, what's a teacher's favourite nation?" Anita shook her head but willingly waited for my punchline, "Expla-nation."

"Not funny, Molly."

"I know, I know… But *this* is going to be fun-knee," I said, smelling the incense in the air and pinching her knee.

"Who's first?" he asked as he ran his fingers through his matte comb-over hair that barely masked his receding hairline. No doubt a wild turkey. The ugliest bird I'd ever seen.

Anita surprised me when she said, "I'll go first." She leapt up and he pointed to the chair at the table. She eased down and he positioned himself opposite her. In the candlelight, he appeared even bigger. His round face lowered down to the table and he closed his eyes. The light flickered over his face and disappeared again; he groaned. Anita pleaded with her eyes for me to pull her ass right out of there.

I smirked. *Suck it up, Buttercup.* In a way, I was still reeling from the doll incident five minutes ago. I guess I hadn't forgiven her after all. *Suck it up, Buttercup? Where did I get that from?* It must have been from Grandad. I missed him terribly, and my dancing nerves slinked back into my stomach.

The fortune-teller lurched forward; his chestnut eyes wide, "You're going to be married soon."

Anita sniggered, clutching at her necklace, "Not that soon, I hope. I'm only seventeen."

I sat up straight. *Oh, maybe he'll say that to me.*

He reached out and grabbed her arm forcefully, nearly breaking the chain of her beloved necklace and I chirped in with a loud hiccup. He turned to me as if he was noticing me for the first time and I whispered, "Sorry."

"He'll have dark hair and dark eyes," he continued and stared back at Anita. Unblinking. Anita shifted her frightened eyes to me.

"Should I be writing this down?" I asked as I rummaged through my rucksack for a pen and paper. Luckily, I found a pen but only a long shopping receipt. I scribbled over the top to make sure the pen worked. It did. I turned it over to the blank side and I wrote down: *bark hair bark eyes*. Then scribbled through the bs and changed them to ds.

"You'll have two children. Both girls." He let go of her hand and stared into the candle. "One will bring trouble to your household but it will all be okay in the end. You've an amazing bond with your father... Your mother... Your mother isn't in this picture. She's not here..." I cringed a little. When she was born Anita's mum had died. I knew about it but we never touched on that subject. We avoided it the way I fended off reading, spelling and writing. Instead, we talked about everything else: life in general, family problems and ice-skating.

"But your father is in the vision. Your bond with him will continue throughout your life."

"You're right. I *do* have a bond with... with my dad... already," answered Anita leaning towards him. Hooked; taken in by this weirdo and I ecstatic another conversation about her mum was dodged. A squeak of a sigh escaped from my mouth and with my eyes I apologised; girls with peculiar green eyes can do that.

He leaned over, grabbing Anita's hand again making us both jump and I let slip a spontaneous snigger. He continued with his eyes closed.

"Your marriage will not be a happy one. He'll control you and you'll allow him. You'll agree to his suffocating demands. He'll tell you to not wear makeup and he'll take away your friends. He'll make you... miserable." He squeezed Anita's hand and the colour changed from pink to white. She pulled back and I liberated the breath I had been holding for too long.

"Can you tell me something good, please?" Anita said in a wavering voice.

He glared at her and hummed with his eyes closed again. He opened them and I moved back a little as if he had thrown a dagger at Anita.

He said softly, "You'll be a fantastic mother and an even better grandmother. Your first grandchild will always have a special place in your heart and no one will take that love away. I'm seeing the letter L. Your husband will have an affair and he'll break your heart. But you're a good person and you'll gain the happiness you deserve."

Anita leaned towards him again, "Happiness? What kind of happiness? Tell me more."

"It's going."

"What's going? My happiness?"

"The vision has gone," he said and he lowered his head. Anita jumped up and rolled her eyes.

"It's yer turn, Molly. I'm clearly going to have a crap life. A husband who's going to break my heart and happiness that fades away. Just brilliant!" she said sarcastically. Her face went red as she paced up and down the small kitchen. She glared over at me shoving her hedgehog back into her mouth and I ignored her.

I began to panic. What would I say if he started ranting on about my inability to read and write, or that I would never be able to work and have money to buy my own car or house? Do fortune-tellers know your inner thoughts? I only wanted to absorb a load of my future with Matthew and hear about how my figure skating would improve. I didn't want any doom or gloom.

I heaved myself up hoping he wouldn't bring up my relationship with *my* mum and made up my mind to escape if he mentioned my dyslexia. I swapped places with Anita.

His eyes were closed when he lifted his head back off the table. He opened them and let slip a haunting groan, plonking out his hand. I reluctantly placed my hand onto his; my palm facing up. His hot sweaty hand made me grimace. He seized my wrist and jumped up.

He flung my hand down on the table and snatched a small bell that sat behind him near the sink. He began ringing the bell as he stretched out around the kitchen, muttering to himself. I flinched back as he rang it straight in my face. He grabbed a bundle of dried herbs tied with string with his other hand.

"I need to use sage. I need to use sage."

He stopped suddenly, throwing the herbs in front of me. He put down his bell, struck his matches and lit the sage. Taking it back up in his hand and with wide eyes he yelled, "We're done here!"

Was he kidding me? There was no way this guy was serious right now.

As I stood up he clutched for the bell again and clung to it as if he needed it for protection. He grabbed his walking stick that was leaning on the radiator and he tramped out of the kitchen avoiding eye contact with me.

"You can both go."

"What do you mean?" I asked. He turned and from the doorway rang the bell again around the room. Anita stood up and lifted my rucksack.

"Just brilliant. Let's go," she said.

"Why? Have you nothing to tell me?" I asked keeping my eyes on him.

"Children should be seen and not heard. Children should be seen and not heard. Children should be seen and not heard," he repeated and Anita bustled me out of the kitchen.

"Do we need to pay for this?" Anita asked.

"No payment. Just go," he answered. Anita turned and sprinted down the stairs. I went to do the same but he grabbed my wrist, "You must not enter that school. Don't go. Whatever you do, don't go!" he spat in my face.

"What do you mean? What school? Tell me. What's wrong?"

His eyes glazed over and he dropped my hand and said, "Children should be seen and not heard. Children should be seen and not heard." His nose bled and it dripped onto the carpet.

I flew down the stairs. Anita was at the bottom frantically trying to turn the key in the door. I tripped over the basket filled with stones and rocks, and snatched a small red brick to put back in the basket but instead, I held onto the thing. I clambered behind her.

"Get me out of here. Hurry up!" I wanted to scream, laugh and shout all at the same time but all that came out was a hiccup.

I glanced back and he was standing at the top of the stairs, shaking his head. He shouted down, "Stay away from that school! If the children stop speaking, it will damage them in ways you will never understand. Think about the children!"

Anita opened the door and we both nearly fell down the two broad steps on the way out.

We bolted, leaving the door open. It was at least five minutes before we both stopped. Anita handed me my rucksack.

"That was beyond weird."

"Not as weird as this," I said, showing her the piece of brick.

"Is that from the basket?" Anita asked as she glanced over her shoulder.

"Yep," I said as I chucked it into my rucksack, and suddenly felt again like Little Red Riding Hood.

TWO
HOUSE

I am House and there are two sides to every story; just like there are four walls in every room.

I have an inner voice humans will never hear. It used to rise from the deep depths, within my foundations, through my plumbing and it made me choke on my own spit.

Now I shout out an uncontrollable "Run!" as I look down at the screwed-up faces of the people who stride through my door.

Ridiculous.

They can't run.

I need to give up on trying to make them leave as I've lost interest in how long they stay. Now I want them to leave me alone.

I can't make their children's lives better. I can't protect the children from the pain they will inevitably experience. Was that ever my job?

The adults bore me. All have this desire to try. They must try to decorate me to their own liking, set in furniture that looks right and makes them feel good. And more importantly, they must try to form relationships with those they chose to live with.

Unfortunately, the children don't have that choice and I don't have that choice either.

I must accept all who have my key, turn it and enter.

THREE
MOLLY

"He didn't say anything about you," Anita said, taking out her hand mirror and wiping one of her long eyelashes off her pale cheek.

"I know. Saying that, there's nothing exciting about me that he could have said."

"Nothing exciting? Don't talk rubbish. You're funny, ya always think outside the box and ya make me smile. I thought at the very least he would have mentioned your ice-skating ability and how humble y'are about it."

"Humble? I'm hardly humble about it."

"Do you remember when ya came in second at our very first serious competition? Ya didn't even go up for yer prize. I had to run after ya in my boots to give ya yer trophy."

"That's hardly humble."

"Think what ya want but if that had been me, I would have been straight over to the judges, gathering my roses, holding my trophy up for all to see and posing for the photographs." I watched my friend in full-blown imaginary mode and I shook my head.

Anita left me at the lamppost and I watched her as she skipped off home. When she turned around, she still had her hedgehog in her mouth and I wanted to tell her that she could choke on that thing. She stuck up her arm and kicked her leg out to the side and I smiled.

Friends like Anita were as scarce as hen's teeth. The first time we met we just clicked the way my skate guards clamp onto my boot blades. The spring design made it the best fit and we were the best fit for each other. We met in school. We sat together in class and she leaned over me and pointed to a word I was struggling with in my reading book. She whispered the word and then went back to her own work. That one gesture made me feel safe and I smiled at her and said, "Thank you."

She simply said, "I like your hair. Your Goldilocks."

From that day on we stuck together like jam on toast. We even started ice-skating together. Our first competition was one to remember.

I knew why I hadn't gone up for the trophy though and it had nothing to do with being humble. Throughout the entire competition, I had scanned the rink looking for Mum. She had promised me she would be there. She didn't show. When I stepped onto the ice, I became the ice itself. When I got into my starting pose, I scanned the rink one more time.

No Mum.

Instead, Dad and Josh were performing Mexican waves in the spectator seats. Dad's mop of dark hair contrasted dramatically with Josh's blonde. Dad had called out over the silent rink, "Go for it, Molly-Moo!" He made me heat up like a kettle.

When the music started, I forgot about Mum not being there and I performed, remembering every trick, step and jump I had up my sleeve. At the end, I lowered my head and heard the applause. When I looked up, I saw Mum just arriving and I knew she had missed my entire routine.

I didn't care about coming in second. I didn't care about my trophy. I just wanted Mum to see me. Really see me. When I asked her, "What did you think?" she lied as if she had been there the whole time.

"It was good, love. Really good."

I barely remember Anita running up with my trophy. I do remember it being cold in my hands and it remained on our car floor for several weeks before it made its way into our house.

I turned to go home and stopped. A goldfinch. I froze. Using its sharp fine beak it teased out small seeds from a dandelion. Grandad used to call me his "little goldfinch" when he sat with me in his kitchen, pulling me through my reading book.

"Your face is as red as a goldfinch. You don't need to be worrying now. Life is too short to worry through it. Now let me help ye with the words."

When he died of "old age", I knew at just fifteen: life was too short. The whole way through his funeral I had hiccupped and moved about in the wooden seat as my black tights were a tiny bit too small. They kept creeping down on me; I yanked them up during each hymn. A good strategy, I thought, but Mum had given me her death look. I remember thinking: if Grandad was here, I wouldn't be wearing this stupid outfit. We would be up a mountain or on a hill happily taking notes and bird-watching. But he wasn't here. He was dead and my bird-watching had died with him.

As I watched the goldfinch a little longer, my heart ached inside and I was glad when it flew away with a song in its heart. At least her heart was whole. I sauntered around the corner and then moved at a fast pace to my house. I fumbled in my rucksack for my keys attached to a spongey, green avocado with plastic eyes. Where had Anita found such a hideous thing? I know I liked avocados but one attached to my keys was beyond ridiculous.

I turned my key, entered and ran up to my room. My bed was a crumpled mess; I had to tiptoe through my clothes to get to my bedside cabinet and I threw my keys back into my rucksack. Inside, I saw the odd brick from the fortune-teller's place. I threw it into my open top drawer and flopped down on my bed.

After a while, I slipped into my pyjamas and pulled out my black book. I looked at my old sketches of a variety of birds in flight and then flipped to my goldfinch page. I wrote down the date and then my phone dinged. I closed the book and shoved it back under my mattress. A message from Anita:

That was beyond weird A. x

Very, M. x I replied and waited.

Maybe the school he was talking about ws the 1 ur mum made you apply for!

Hardly

Ha, Laters A. x

I sat in silence wondering why I let Anita drag me to those creepy things. Maybe because an ice-skating blade always needs a cover to prevent the skates from piercing the shoe pocket and I always needed Anita to make my life seem more exciting, more worthwhile and refreshing.

I googled the verse I remembered on my phone: John 14:6.

Jesus saith unto him, I am the way, the truth, and the life: no man cometh unto the Father, but by me.

I popped on my glasses with the green tint and read it out. It sounded unnatural reading the words out loud and I had no idea what they meant. I flicked through several articles on different websites but still didn't understand it. I gave up and clicked my phone into its charger.

FOUR
HOUSE

People start with that awkward hug that forces me to look away. I cringe at their stupidity. Then they live in me. They usually end with a shrug or a deep sigh that assures me I was right all along. They shuffle away and I never see them again.

I've stopped caring.

A voice interrupts my thoughts, "Stephanie, Stephanie. Come and see. It's big and roomy, just what you wanted. I hope you're going to be happier here!" These words mean nothing because I have heard similar words throughout the years, and I now know the words are lies. They may play house for a little while, but it will not end with the happiness they chatter about on that first day.

When I was first built, in 1961, I was different. I cared then. I watched eagerly as my occupants arrived, made plans and remained within my walls.

Three families lived with me and this is my fourth.

Over the years, I have come to a sad conclusion. It is their children who become their biggest burden and their intermittent crying makes the adults turn on them.

I can't bear to watch their cruelty anymore.

They are either cruel or they leave.

They will desire a bigger house and move. They might grow old and be forced to leave within an odd, wooden box. Did they die? Do houses die?

Even children change over time. They grow up and sadly become adults themselves. Then they move. I look different now. Am I growing old? My wallpaper has faded and my carpets are fraying in some of my rooms.

My new occupant bends down and lifts part of my carpet and announces, "That'll be easily sorted." I know by his tone he will indeed sort it and I will look new again.

No, houses don't die.

He plonks the end of the heavy carpet back down on my wooden floor and I groan.

My breath is quick and frantic, and yet I'm not sure if I can breathe at all.

"Come and live within me," I hear myself say, but it's as if my voice is miles away now. The way you feel in an odd dream where nothing makes sense and voices speak out but the words mean nothing. Pointless. I don't care anymore. Do what you want. Live here or go somewhere else.

I stare at him as he chews his gum and I know I am apathetic.

His wife appears holding a baby. It is a girl. Her soft, plump cheeks glisten with a purity, brightening my living room. A few sprigs of soft, brown hair escape from her crisp, white baby cap. A calmness envelops me as her light green eyes meet mine and she smiles a toothless grin up at me. Babies know I am here. They know I exist and they make me feel I belong.

"Stay quiet, little one!" I scream as I put out my invisible hand and steady myself with a sigh back into the walls, which create rooms where secrets lie.

My inner voice sounds frantic now and it screams to the top of my chimney pot, "Stay quiet, little one, before it's too late." It pauses and my inner voice whispers in my roof, "The adults will not put up with your incessant crying."

My inner voice falls silent as the little girl sticks out her tiny hand and I long to take it. My inner voice knows I don't want them to run away anymore. The baby and I greet each other and a joy sings out of my whole being. It is a song that sings louder than my whimpering inner voice, which gives up with a sigh and clangs back down into the pit of my foundations. Disappointed. Silenced.

Don't run. I want you all to stay now.

I can barely take my eyes off this little baby who has won me over completely, but when I do, I see the man of the house lifting and dropping items within my being. The look on his face tells me exactly how he feels. He is going to make changes. It's as if he had waited his whole life for this one single moment. He is now a proud owner of a three-bedroomed house that needs work. A corner terrace house set amongst similar, tall houses. My only distinguishing feature: a number fifty-one at the side of my door. I know I am tall as from my back door, in the distance, I can see a row of short houses. I look down upon them daily. From my front door, I can see up the lane to my right. My view interrupted only by a few, unkempt hedges. To my left, just beyond the park, I see the wooden bridge I know leads into the city.

I will always need work. Yet the people don't know they are the ones who need the *real* work. They *need* to be kind to their children. They *need* to not raise their voices to tell them what to do and they *need* to hide their anger from their little ones.

It is fun to sit back and observe, now I know a baby will live within my walls and I want to capture this moment in my memory forever.

Stephanie shouts out from my master bedroom, "Oh, look at the storage in here. Perfect for all my clothes. Jack, come and see." I know their names now. I had told myself I wouldn't care but now I know their names, I have to care once more.

Jack and Stephanie believe I'm the one with issues and problems that need to be sorted, but alas, it will be them. Humans have the worst problems of all.

Glancing back down at the sweet baby who wiggles her chunky, short legs happily in her Moses basket, I smile. It is going to be a good thing to have a baby to watch, protect and love again. Watching the other two will not be good.

I take a calm, deep breath.

I am House.

I am.

I am.

It is indeed wonderful to have a baby here. I will be happy now... but only for a short while. I will be happy until they raise their voices at the little one.

FIVE
MOLLY

Perched on the end of my bed, wearing my pink, snake-print top and my high-waisted jeans, I began to hiccup. My hands gripped the mattress as I willed them to stop. That was the last thing I needed. Matthew Stewart would not want to talk to a hiccupping teenager.

As I waited for the doorbell to ring, I considered changing my trainers. Pink Adidas trainers might not be his thing. I licked my thumb, threw my leg up onto my knee and tried to wipe the dirtiest trainer clean. The letters of the word "Adidas" danced about in front of me and I widened my eyes, trying not to blink. I knew they would settle soon and form the word. I had to wait. Being dyslexic enticed words to jumble in front of me. That's why reading hurt my brain; my personal nightmare for seventeen long years. Dad encouraged me to see it as a quirk rather than an actual disorder but that's slowly wearing thin, now I've left school.

I tutted out loud and lifted my mobile. I checked him out again on Instagram: MattS21. Matthew with his guitar. Matthew with his beloved German Shepherd. Matthew reading a book. Matthew with his guitar again; this time in front of an audience. Matthew and his new tattoo. I missed that one? I zoomed in and snapped a screenshot of the three birds on his tan shoulder.

The doorbell rang out at 6.45pm as expected: Josh's guitar lesson.

"Finally," I said as I propelled myself off the bed and bolted downstairs like a professional sprinter, "I'll get it," I screeched.

Be brave, Molly. You told Anita you would do this. Be chatty and brave. Not too chatty. Just enough to make him fall for you.

As I hit the fourth stair from the end, my brother appeared out of nowhere and opened the door.

"I got it," he said. I slumped against the wall and remained there imagining myself knocking my brother out of the way with one spectacular roundhouse kick.

Sunlight flooded into our hallway and I stifled a random hiccup.

All I needed was a hoover or a hammer and a nail. It wasn't easy looking busy on the stairs. It wasn't as if I could be dancing a jig, painting my nails or watering a plant. I counted the stairs from the bottom. Being caught on the fourth stair is the worst place ever.

I peeked over at him and then pretended to pick a fleck of dust off our clean, white wall.

Matthew Stewart. Perfection. His brown hair swept over his left eye as usual and his tan hand held the handle of his beloved guitar case; books wedged under his armpit. Mum described him as "the overweight guitar guy, who needs to lose some beef", which didn't make sense to me. His size made me feel as if he would protect and look after me. I never did like any of the skinny guys at the ice-rink or the tweebs who followed me around when I was at school. He was everything I wasn't: organised, self-assured and most definitely not dyslexic. My face reddened; heat from my cheeks travelled down to my neck.

"Alright, mate," Josh said as I tried to look normal, hating this stupid fourth stair.

Today was lesson number seven. Three more to go. Today had been the day for me to introduce myself and come across as the mature seventeen-year-old that I was. Ruined.

"You ready for your lesson? Did you get much practice in this week?" Matthew asked Josh, and I held my breath. His voice like hot gravy on my Sunday dinner.

"Yes and no. But I did nail that new song. Had to flex my skills on Finsta. Did ya see me?"

"I'll check it out later. I'm sure ya slayed it."

"Come on up," Josh said and bolted up the stairs past me in a flash. I imagined myself stepping to the left and blocking Matthew's way. It would make him notice me, force him to have a conversation with me and maybe, just maybe, he would ask me to be his girlfriend. But my feet didn't budge. I was destined to remain on this side of the stairs forever.

Matthew closed the front door and dropped his books.

"I'll get 'em," I said in a louder tone than was necessary. He looked up at me, then shifted his eyes to our white tiled floor. He didn't respond. Not a good sign. I wanted him to say something. Anything.

I flopped down the four stairs as if I was practising some bizarre ballet moves and my arms dangled round like a scarecrow. I stared at his books. I tried to read the title of one but the letters jiggled around and I couldn't put them together quick enough to make sense.

Matthew said nothing. Instead, he swooped down and scooped the books up. He did it so quickly; I didn't even get a chance to bend towards them. I could've bumped heads with him and he would've helped me, held me or at least offered me a glass of water.

Trying to hide the disappointment that must have registered on my face, I hiccupped. But it didn't matter as Matthew had already bolted after Josh, taking two steps at a time. He didn't even look at me.

The only positive to come out of this ridiculous meeting was his soap-scent filling my nose as he clambered past. I made up my mind there and then: I'd talk to him properly on lesson number eight.

SIX
HOUSE

Jack makes a cup of tea and as I watch the new baby a bit longer, my memories flood back to the time when I first met a family. It was in 1961.

* * *

Abigail and Walter resided within my walls.

After the first three days, I learnt men and women were very different from each other. Men shouted a lot and women tended to whisper. Women talked a lot too but only when they were alone together. Our neighbour, Sadie, would call to have what she called a "chat". This could occur at any time of the day. Females tended to say a lot of words in their sentences whilst males would be short and snappy.

One day, Sadie called again and bored me with her long spiel to Abigail. Sadie always bored me. I could hear her next door continuously talking about anything and everything.

"It's yer stunning blonde hair. Just look at it. The shine is unreal. And don't get me started on yer blue eyes. Men are drawn to eyes like that... and he knows it. You're stunning."

"I'm not stunning. Don't say that," Abigail whispered as she lowered her head. Was she stunning? I examined her pale skin and freckles. Her face and body were delicate but was she really stunning? I agreed with Abigail. Sadie shouldn't say anything. She should stop speaking. Women talk far too much after all.

"Just look at ye. Innocent ye are. Ye haven't a clue what way men think. He's jealous and it's written all over his face. That's why he treats ye the way he does. That's why he h—"

"Stop, Sadie," Abigail said, her eyes wide. I couldn't agree more. Sadie's chat was continuous and boring; women talk far too much.

"I know he did. I saw the..."

A silence followed and I was thankful. I liked it when adults were calm and controlled. I would listen to their shallow breaths and wonder why they never breathed in and out at the same pace.

In and out.

In and out.

I loved the rhythm.

I tutted when Sadie boosted her large body up and joined Abigail on the settee. Was she going to start her babbling again? She stroked Abigail's shoulder.

"Just look at yer hairstyle: the perfect bee-hive. Not a hair out of place. Ye look like a film star, and don't get me started on yer clothes. Everyone can tell they're expensive."

"They're not expensive. Just clothes I bought in Australia. People notice them because they are different. That's all."

"Yer makeup is the same. Yer stunning. He's not and that's what his main problem is. He's controlling and bad-tempered because he knows other men are looking at ye—"

"Stop it, Sadie. This is not helping."

"Ye can't let him get away with it. Do ye hear me?"

"He has no reason to be controlling. I am happy to stay indoors and be... be with my family. He just doesn't want me in bars or clubs and I am happy not to go."

"He shouldn't be telling ye what ye can and can't do. Ye mustn't let him treat ye that way. Ye must stand up to him. Are ye listening to me? Tell him to go."

"I can't. Where would I go if he left me? I don't work. I have no money. I can't tell him to go." Abigail stood up, yanked off her apron and rolled it up into a ball.

"I just can't." Still holding it, she slumped down again.

"Ye can. Ye stand out, Abigail. You'll meet someone else. Ye don't need to put up with this shit."

"The kids will hear you."

"I'm sorry, but it's true."

"I do not have a choice, Sadie. I have been married twice now. I could not face a third husband. I have seven children for goodness sake: six with my first husband and one on the way." She placed her hand on her stomach and I wondered what she meant by "one on the way". "No man will take that on. I cannot ask him to leave. I have to put up with him. I have to."

Sadie hugged Abigail and left. Her final words bugged me: "I'm here for ye and we'll chat again soon." I was glad she left but dreaded the day when she would return to "chat" again.

Women talk far too much. Children, on the other hand, talk a lot too but some talk to me, so I didn't mind them.

Abigail loved every one of her children. Her eldest boy had remained in Australia. Two had left to set up their own homes and one escaped to the Merchant Navy at the age of sixteen. Only three remained with Abigail now: one teenaged boy with a sour face, D.B., one excited four-year-old, Sarah, and it wasn't long before I met the "one on the way". A perfect little baby.

I had never seen a baby before. When Abigail and Walter paraded in with her, I was immediately fascinated. She was so helpless, so vulnerable. Her bright blue eyes found mine somehow and her little face shone with an inner light. I needed to be seen and this baby knew it. I whispered sweet things in her ears and I knew I would always care for her.

When she was born, she had been wrapped in a blanket and rushed away from Abigail as her purple skin made the midwife panic. The big doctor had sorted it out and the midwife returned her little baby back into her arms. Seven pounds three ounces, and her mum called her Emily. Sarah, her big sister, insisted on the Brooke. Hence, Emily-Brooke.

Abigail told this story many times. Each time, I would hold my breath until she said the words, "She was fine. The big doctor fixed it." After the fifth telling of the event, I felt I had been there myself and witnessed it all.

Emily-Brooke was a dear little thing. She gained weight fast on Abigail's milk. She became chubby and fat folded at her wrists and ankles. Abigail dressed her up like a dolly. Walter ignored her. D.B avoided her and Sarah rolled her eyes at her. I observed her every move. I loved her every second, every minute, every hour over the next three years, and I was happy.

She knew God and God knew her. She babbled daily about Him to anyone who would listen. He was simply all around her and there was never a doubt in my mind it wasn't so.

Who was He? I could not see Him, but I knew He was there with Emily-Brooke. He surrounded her daily and Emily-Brooke would speak to Him. Sometimes referring to Him as God and other times as Jesus.

At the age of three, Emily-Brooke said to me, "Jesus said, I am the way, the truth, and the life: no man comes to the Father, but by me."

Do I have a Father? I was House and that was it. No beginning and no end. Emily-Brooke quoted the Bible and yet there was no Bible in me. In fact, the word "Bible" was never mentioned within my household. I didn't know this Jesus. It was strange.

Abigail found it strange too.

"I do not get it. We do not go to church and Emily-Brooke has never been to Sunday School. Yet there she is, always talking about God," she said to Walter one evening before sunset.

"Who cares?" said Walter with a yawn.

"I do. Don't you think it's weird?"

"Maybe she heard about God from someone outside. It's no big deal."

"She knows Bible verses, Walt. And we do not even have a Bible. If that is not strange, I do not know what is," said Abigail.

"Go back to sleep."

"But—"

"Now!"

In the beginning was the House, and the House was without God, and the House was... House 1:1.

What was I? Was I a voice that could not be heard?

Yet children knew I was here. They spoke to me daily.

I loved children. They made me feel as if I belong.

* * *

Interrupting my thoughts with one loud desperate cry, the new baby makes me yell out, "Lift her up. Stop her cries. Lift her up. Stop her cries."

Stephanie holds her close. Her cries change to sobs and then small grunts. Then silence.

Stephanie walks into the kitchen with the baby snuggling into her chest.

"This is our new kitchen, Sophia. We are all going to be happy here. I am going to concentrate on us now. I promise."

Her name is Sophia. I look down at her. The happiness I had once felt with Emily-Brooke pours over me and more memories of Emily-Brooke flood into my mind...

* * *

One bright sunny day, Abigail stood in my kitchen contemplating the dishes. The dog barked and she opened the back door to let her out.

"Get out, Trixie," she said. Trixie ran and lay down beside Emily-Brooke.

Abigail closed the door and opened my little kitchen window that faced out into the garden.

Emily-Brooke, nearly four, was sitting in the garden playing with her favourite doll, Beanie. A doll in a pink romper suit with a white frilly bib, wide unblinking eyes, and fingers chewed down into small stubs.

The sun shone all around Emily-Brooke and her doll, and this made the ground warm.

Sadie's daughter, Lisa, called in and tapped at my door. Abigail's older son, D.B., sat on the pavement outside my gate lifting cigarette butts out of the gutter with his dirty fingers, watching Lisa. His eyes were like slits.

"Hey!" shouted D.B., "Don't knock, you'll wake Walter."

"Emily-Brooke coming out?" she asked, chewing her lip and scratching at her hand.

"She's in the back. Go on round."

Lisa opened my side gate and Emily-Brooke looked up.

"Yea, Lisa! Come on over. Look, I've Beanie and Trixie with me." She was a loving child and everyone was welcomed into her little world.

Sadness engulfed Lisa as she had been told off by her mum next door. The pointless argument had made me moan.

"Don't touch the fire," Sadie had shouted. Ten minutes later, a horrifying cry shattered the silence by the mum's sharp words, "I told ye not to touch the fire. Why did ye not listen?"

My walls became solemn and I made my first promise to myself: children should never be told off.

Emily-Brooke put her little arm around Lisa to comfort her; wiping her tears with her thumb.

"Oh, don't be sad, Lisa. You're going to be okay. You'll be all right in a little bit."

Abigail, from my window, watched in wonder.

"How lovely," she said. I had to agree. It was nice to see a child caring for others at such a young age. Emily-Brooke hadn't even started school yet and there she was, comforting a friend in such a mature way.

Then it happened. Emily-Brooke began talking about God. Her mother leaned towards the open window to make sure she was hearing her right. I knew I could not lean towards her but instead, I listened carefully. I was silent.

Emily-Brooke said, "You know God, Lisa? Even a little bit?" Lisa shook her head. "Well, He has loads of love and it goes all around people if they ask Him for it."

"Do ye ask Him for love?" asked Lisa.

"All the time," she answered as she clutched Lisa's burnt hand in hers, "You can ask God to fix this for you too."

"Do ye think He'll fix it if I ask Him?" asked Lisa, her eyes wide.

"Yes! God's love will fix it. Ask Him into your heart and you'll see," Emily-Brooke said.

"Okay, I will."

Emily-Brooke stated with a tone of authority, "Just ask God to make you happy and He'll do that for you." Her mother's mouth opened in surprise and if I had a mouth, I would have done the same. My head buzzed with thoughts of how and when. How did she know God? How could she speak with such certainty? When did she hear about God?

God was not mentioned in my household and yet here was Abigail in her kitchen listening to her own daughter preaching the word as if God was her best friend.

Emily-Brooke stood up and raised her little arms to the sky. Lisa copied her. Both looked up. Trixie lay on her side and stretched out. Emily-Brooke's mum found herself leaning out the window further and looking up to the sky herself. I scanned the sky from my chimney pot. It was a hot day and only one or two clouds floated in the sky. I didn't know what to expect but I unexpectedly expected something.

Abigail saw nothing. I saw nothing too. I was only a house, after all, and houses only feel and hear what goes on around them. Yes, my hot-press holds my memories, my wiring expresses my emotions, my plumbing protects my deepest darkest secrets, my bricks hold my desires and fears, my skirting boards are my nerves and my floorboards is my voice but I can't possibly see everything.

I gazed over at the two small figures. Their hands remained in the air. The sun continued to smile down on the two. Their backs were turned away from us. How did their little faces look? I instinctively knew they were both happy. Smiling.

Abigail closed my window and flicked on the kettle to heat the water to do the dishes. I was disappointed. She leaned wearily on the counter with her hand clenched. She toppled a little and steadied herself. She stared down at her engagement and wedding rings, running her forefinger over them both. I was surprised a tear fell abruptly from her left eye. She wiped it away firmly and stood up straight. She lifted the kettle and drowned the dishes with its content. Steam rose and condensation covered my window. Emily-Brooke and her friend could still be seen; still with their arms in the air and looking upwards. But the condensation made the little scene like a dream. Something in the distance.

Emily-Brooke's mum did the dishes and left them drying on the drainer. They were not very clean.

SEVEN
MOLLY

He hadn't noticed me and there were only three more lessons to go. I slumped down on our settee beside Dad.

"What's up, baby girl?" he asked.

Oh Dad, please don't ask. I have been ignored by the one and only: Matthew Stewart.

"Why was the scarecrow promoted?" I asked.

"Don't know, Molly-Moo."

"He was outstanding in his field." Dad laughed and I leaned my head on his broad shoulder.

"Are you ready for your big interview tomorrow?" asked Dad.

Oh shit, I had forgotten about that stupid thing.

"I think so," I said, "I can't see myself working in a primary school though, Dad. I'm not good with kids." The idea of working with kids scared the living daylights out of me. What if one asked me to spell a word? Or even worse: what if I had to read to them? I closed my eyes and listened to Dad's breathing. Hopefully, Mum would forget all about it and I wouldn't have to go to the interview.

Dad's arm gently rose and fell with each breath. My worries disappeared like rainwater rushing down a drain as brisk as a sneeze. My body relaxed; no longer reacting to my dyslexia storm. It wasn't as if I needed a job. I didn't have a place of my own and had no intentions of pursuing one. I was happy here. Calmness sifted into my bones.

"Go for your mother, Molly-Moo. She wants you to make something of yourself."

The drain spluttered out the dirty rainwater and my word hurricane forced me to open my eyes and sit up straight. I turned to face Dad. Such a hard worker. A dentist. Spending his days filling cavities and mending teeth. Every morning he power-walked to his private practice around the corner and in the evening he plodded back. He had met mum whilst training at dental school. Mum was doing admin and he fell for her organizational skills and her lean, long legs. When they married she stopped working and became one of the ladies who lunch. Dad made sure she had a wardrobe of clothes and when we arrived the same for us. I was so proud of dad. Passionate about his job and all of us. I loved his passion and wondered why passion only knocked at my door down at the ice-rink.

I was letting him down.

"How can I make something of myself if I don't know what I want to be?"

"Maybe you shouldn't have been so rash to leave school then."

I wanted to throw a full-blown tantrum; stand up, stamp my feet and yell out. I couldn't make something of myself. I couldn't be anything because of my dyslexia: every job involved reading and writing.

Dad heaved himself up and reached for his newspaper sitting on the other chair.

I allowed the dirty rainwater to trickle back down the drain as I inhaled several deep breaths.

I must not become annoyed. I must not become annoyed.

I searched Dad's eyes for his twinkle. Nothing.

I was annoyed.

A whirlwind of questions made my head thump. Was he disappointed in me? Did he feel the same way Mum did? Did he really think I should have stayed on at school? It was heart-breaking. Why did being dyslexic make everything so difficult?

"School… it just wasn't my thing. Boring. Mum is—"

"She's not, babes," said Dad, folding the newspaper with a sigh.

"Not?" *Please don't say disappointed. Please don't say it.*

I wanted to scream out to stop this conversation. Cry like a child and then feel okay again but instead I said nothing. I scanned Dad's face and waited for the large plug to drop down. To stop this ocean of pain.

Dad opened his mouth and said, "Mum is not disappointed. She doesn't want you hanging around the house wasting your life away. That's all."

The word rang out loud and clear. The dirty water on top of the drain spiralled around and around, and my stomach hurt. My head turned hot. Mum *was* disappointed. I stood up and moved to the chair where the newspaper had been. I hated that word. Even the length of it made me mad. I plonked down hard on the chair.

Dis... a... point. What was the *point* of such a long, boring word?

"Mum doesn't get me. She's making me go for a job I'll suck at. What if I can't do it?" I asked Dad.

"Molly-Moo, you're very capable." His half smile brought back the twinkle in his eyes and I swallowed hard.

He thinks I'm capable.

Dad went on in his positive rant and I allowed his words to flow over my body. "Whatever job you take, you will be able to do it. You'll be grand. You're a smart girl. You just have to believe in yourself." But then he added a line that sent a sharp knife through my gut, "Although, you know your mother and I need you to contribute to your ice-skating. It's too pricey now you're in the professional group." He opened his newspaper with a sharp snap that felt like a twist of the knife. Contribute to my ice-skating? Were they struggling to pay my fees? Did I need to land a job to continue to ice-skate?

"You're a capable girl. I believe in you and I know you'll do the right thing."

"Okay, Dad," I whispered, wanting to believe maybe, just maybe, I *was* capable of doing a job.

"You know your mother. She wants you to be more..."

"More?" I asked and immediately wanted to kick myself for doing so.

"More helpful around the house and more independent."

She still thinks I'm lazy. I tried to calm the pain that continued to churn in my stomach.

"Dad, what kind of exercises do lazy people do?"

"I should just call you the joker-lolly Molly."

"Do you want to know the answer? Do you? Do you?"

"Yes, hit me with it."

"Diddly-squats."

Mum came out of the kitchen, walking past us both with two cokes and two glasses half full of ice on a tray. Thoughts of Matthew made my whole body react.

"Mum. Where are you going?" I asked and jumped up.

"Upstairs," said Mum, flicking her bobbed blonde hair, recently cut in a blunt style. Since the cut, she would choose an interesting clip to keep the thicker side of her hair in a controlled position. Today, three rows of pearls.

I was glad she got it cut. Before we looked too similar; both with long, blonde hair down to our waists and weird pale green eyes that everyone and anyone would have to comment on. Strangers would even stop us in the street and comment on how our eyes were so unique, so different. One guy even said, "enticing" in a dreadful, creepy voice.

"Molly, move out of my way," Mum made me jump and bashed my inner thoughts right out of my head.

"Mum, I'll…"

"Molly, get out of my way. I'm taking these drinks up to Joshua and that guitar guy."

"Matthew… His name is Matthew," My face burned again.

"Yes, of course," said Mum as I jerked the tray off her.

"I'll do it," I said banging into the door as I turned around.

"Well, that's a first," said Mum with a groan and she sank down beside Dad. I peeked over at them both and caught her rolling her eyes.

"What do you mean?" I asked and immediately wanted to kick myself again for caring. Dad reached out and touched Mum's hand and narrowed his eyes. She gave away a long, exaggerated breath and I left the room.

Every step down our hallway was a struggle.

My legs were heavy and my stomach still hurt. I needed to help pay for my ice-skating. There was no way I could give up my beloved hobby. I really did need to land a job. But with my dyslexia, I knew that this interview to work in a primary school was not for me. I'd have to find another job; one where I didn't need to read and write.

I can do this.

I'm not lazy.

The day I started school, Mum called me lazy. She didn't get why I struggled to read or write. When I was diagnosed, she went insanely quiet. Worse for me. Mum thought I was useless then and still does now.

I tried to move my focus onto Matthew when I hit the fourth stair, but Mum rolling her eyes played over and over in my mind. I imagined what I would say to Matthew to make myself forget: my name is Molly. Josh clearly forgot to introduce me the seven times you've been in our house. But let me do it for him. Oh, nice tattoo. New? Three birds. Where did you get that done? Sorry, what was that? You want to meet up for a coffee, a drink… yes, I'm eighteen. Well, almost eighteen.

I reached Josh's door and gawked at it. I hiccupped. Oh shit. Matthew's deep voice penetrated through the door, explaining to Josh where to put his fingers to learn a new chord.

"Ya see. Ya slayed it. That's great, mate. Ya know what I mean now?"

Pushing the door open with my foot, I coughed.

"Coke?" He looked up and his blue eyes met mine. He wore a light blue, short-sleeved shirt with the top button open, skinny blue jeans and Vans with no socks. It looked great.

"Sure," said Matthew as he stood up and reached out to take the tray off me. My fingers wouldn't let go. My grip was frozen. "Eh, thanks, eh?"

"Molly," I said and hiccupped again.

"Molly?"

"Yes, my name is Molly."

Joshua blasted in with, "Leave it down, Molly. We're in the middle of a lesson and I'm finally getting the hang of this."

"Oh, yer name is Molly. I got ya now," Matthew said with a laugh and threw himself back down on Josh's bed, hugging his guitar. Once again, I felt my face redden. Josh pointed to the top of his bedside cabinet and I placed the tray down. The ice clinked in the glass as loud as my heart beating at a fast rate. I started to make my way back to my brother's bedroom door.

"Blondie, hit the door on the way out," ordered Josh. *Hit the door on the way out!* Thanks a lot, Josh. I literally had two seconds in Matthew's company.

My heart still pounded as I moped down the stairs, confused why my fingers didn't let go of the stupid, bloody tray. How could I convince him to see me, like I saw him?

Mum met me on the stairs.

"Molly, aim to tidy that room of yours before the end of the week please. I can't bear to look at it anymore." The flood gates opened wide and my entire body went weak under the pressure. It's me she can't bear to look at and not my room at all. "Oh, and I've asked your father to iron your white blouse for your interview tomorrow."

Nightmare! I did a loud hiccup. I knew there and then I would have to go to that stupid interview and when I glanced down, I was stuck on the fourth stair again. What the heck was going on?

EIGHT
HOUSE

Jack appears in my kitchen and looks down at Sophia in Stephanie's arms. Jack didn't look very strong; his arms were long and lean with no muscle definition. His grey eyes were cushioned far into the hallows on his face and sat above two dark bags just above his rosy cheeks. His chin small with no clear definition. I don't know why but I didn't trust him. To me he was a weak man. Someone who could fall apart at any moment. That made me despise him.

"Do you want me to put her to bed? It's been a long day."

Maybe my opinion would change over time. Time would tell.

"Yes," whispers Stephanie, holding Sophia up to Jack, "I do like it here. We will be happier."

Jack smiles and I notice a fat wad of gum in between his teeth on the left-hand side.

He answers, "I hope so... We just need to stick together. I couldn't handle another—"

"You won't need to. As you said, we just need to stick together," Stephanie says putting her hand on Jack's arm, "I'll make us a late tea."

I watch him as he places Sophia in her basket, noticing his balding spot right at the top of his light brown head. I follow his long, dangling movements as he strolls back downstairs. His weakness makes me shudder as he enters my living room.

Jack turns on their television with a small box and I watch in wonder. It is in colour! He flicks through the channels. I remember Walter going on and on about wanting a colour television to replace his grey box. He never got one but Jack has one. I know I will learn a great deal with this high-tech television. Maybe Jack is stronger than what I first thought. He has a colour television after all.

As Jack continues to flick, I think back to memories of years ago; stored in my mind like the towels in my well-kept hot press. They unfold as energetically as children on Christmas Eve.

***

I found myself on full alert. Abigail had set a flame under a mixture of plants from outside on the device they called the "cooker". I felt a knock on my door and Trixie barked like a crazy thing. I was glad Abigail heaved herself up off the settee to see who it was as I was too busy watching the cooker. It was about 10 o'clock and yet a strong smell of what the children called "Irish stew" wafted from the kitchen and dived into every orifice of me.

Abigail deliberately got up early and prepared the stew which shocked me as I normally attended the cooker at 5 o'clock when dinner was being prepared.

She opened the front door and a gypsy woman stood with a large box of wares to sell.

"Top of the morning to you," she greeted Abigail with a strong Irish accent, "I'm selling some goods around the neighbourhood. Would ye care to take a look?"

"Oh, yes, I'd love too" said Abigail, "I like your notebook with the letter A on it. I need a book. I want to write things down you see. You know ... things that happen. Maybe writing things down makes things more real. Stops the maybes. Things that happen to me. I'm called Abigail so that would be perfect for me."

"Yer name is what?"

"Abigail."

"I'm called Abigail too."

"No."

"For sure to be sure." They laughed together. It was lovely to eavesdrop on their happy chat from my kitchen.

"Have you any pictures for the house? Maybe one with 'Home, Sweet Home' on it? I always wanted a sign like that in my house."

"No. Sorry, love. I have nothing like that. It must be nice to decorate a house like yers. Plenty of room in it. I don't live in a house like you. I live in a caravan drawn by horses. It's a bit on the small side."

I was immediately interested. Are there houses drawn by horses?

"How lovely," Abigail said and I had to agree with her. It was hard for me to imagine more outside the avenue in which I sat. I wished I was a house that could travel around. It suddenly made me sad that I could not see more and I would remain in one place forever.

They chatted for about twenty minutes. Well, until Abigail remembered about the Irish stew simmering on the stove. I was glad she did. The pot was bubbling. Abigail turned the cooker knob to one and I was relieved.

From my hallway, I marvelled at the brightly dressed woman with her bangled arms and flowing skirt. Her dark skin, eyes and hair made me ask, "Where is she from?" I had never seen the likes of her before.

When Abigail returned from the kitchen with her purse in her hand, she rummaged through the box and lifted out a new scrubbing brush for my sink. Then she saw a large, brown book with red writing on the front: the Bible.

"Oh, I will buy that too for my youngest. She is always talking about God." The words slipped out of her mouth; her cheeks went a rosy pink and then a red colour when she saw the curious look on the gypsy's face.

"Oh? Why's that then?"

Abigail found herself telling the story of the little incident she had witnessed from my kitchen window. I was surprised she stood there retelling the strange event to a complete stranger and even more surprised when the gypsy smiled and said, "God is all around us. Yer little girl knows about Him because she can feel Him all around her."

The words were simple, and yet left me uneasy. I didn't feel God all around me. I didn't talk randomly about God. Did other houses feel God all around them?

"It must be lovely for her ... to feel that protection. She'll love this."

A most unexpected event occurred. This dark-haired woman spoke to me.

"House, House. Ye are seen. Ye are loved," she stepped into the hallway and Abigail immediately backed away.

"I am sorry. Who are you talking to? You need to go. Look, I am going to buy these," she said holding up the Bible and the brush.

The woman overlooked her and continued talking to me, "Children must be heard. Children must be heard."

"You are going to wake my children and my husband. And you will not want to hear what he has to say if you continue this strange rant. You better go," said Abigail.

I wanted to shout out, "Stay! Talk to me some more!" But my floorboards remained silent.

"Ye will hurt many with yer stupid notions," she yelled.

Only children knew I existed, not strangers who do not belong here. I, like Abigail, wanted her to go.

Abigail shoved money into the woman's hand. The woman catapulted backwards out my door. It was as if I had pushed her myself.

"I know what you're going to do! I know what you're going to do!" she yelled. Abigail closed the door and left the Bible sitting on the hall table. She carried the scrubbing brush into my kitchen and threw it into my sink.

"Crazy gypsy..." she said and I agreed with her. She turned around to the stove, stirred the stew and flicked off the heat.

"They can warm that up later for their tea," she said out loud to herself and it made me smile. I liked it when people talked out loud when no one else was there. I pretended they were talking to me.

I was loved and I belonged.

But only children knew I existed. Not adults and not crazy gypsies.

"Oh no, I forgot the notebook. I needed that. I really did. It means nothing if I don't get to write it down," she cried. Her sadness surprised me. It lingered in her eyes; sucking out an emotion from my pipes I couldn't explain.

NINE
MOLLY

"How old are you again?"

"Seventeen," I said as I rubbed the back of my neck and flicked out my foot, banging it off his desk. I clenched my teeth down tight as the pain spread through my foot and I was glad Mr Cardwell was still consumed by his paperwork.

Thoughts of Matthew Stewart entered my head. Twenty-one and perfect. Why had he picked a bird tattoo? Very fitting for me. I've loved birds all my life. My grandfather had me addicted as soon as I could hold a pair of binoculars. The pain deep down in my stomach, the one I had when I was told Grandad had passed away, appeared again. I placed my arm over it and squeezed hard. I missed Grandad terribly.

I scanned Mr Cardwell's overpowering desk. I couldn't picture myself working here. Far too much reading and writing going on. I avoided the temptation to bite my nails.

I thought of Grandad's happy face. His whole face would glow when I appeared at his front door every weekend. He used to say, "People are like birds." Even today, I still imagined people as certain birds.

This guy was a magpie. He collected weird crap. Why do principals need so many things? Business cards, sticky notes, pens, a calculator, a stapler, a pencil sharpener and a nameplate. My eyes traced over the letters jumping around his nameplate: C. R. A. W—

"You look younger," interrupted Mr Cardwell as he peered at me over his glasses.

"Everyone says that," I mumbled and heat explored my cheeks again.

"Let's see now. You did not obtain any qualifications?"

Stop stating the obvious. Just say I'm not getting the job and let me go.

"Did you do any exams?"

"No," I said. I glanced down and coughed.

Swans stay together forever. Matthew and I are swans.

"Well, the job entails the usual: helping the children who need a little boost, photocopying, assisting the teacher when she needs it, checking a few books..." As he rambled on, I noticed his thick, black-rimmed glasses were perched on the end of his nose. A few random hairs sprouted from his nostrils, sticking out like spider's legs.

"You will have to do playground duty, but your teacher will explain all the minor details." Should he pluck those out or would that make several more hairs grow in their place? "Have you any questions?" Mr Cardwell asked.

I shifted my eyes to his. Questions. . . I didn't have one question in my head. What was I going to ask about a job I wouldn't be able to do? My hands began to sweat and I tugged at Mum's long, silk scarf; the one she had stuck on me before I left the car. Somewhere deep inside, a question popped into my head and I was thankful.

I cleared my throat and asked, "If I got the job, which age group would I work with?"

"You will be with Mrs Craig, so you will be working with the five and six-year-olds."

Why did he sound as if I had already gotten this stupid job? Oh, great! I'll be with little kids. The dopey chicks that are so needy. I'd end up having to spell loads of words for them, wiping noses and cleaning up sick. What a nightmare.

"Would I be working with one child or all the children?"

Please say one. I could deal with one.

"You will work with all the children. You will be the general assistant for the class. Special needs classroom assistants work with individuals. I can show you a list of duties. That will give you a better idea of what you will be doing each day. Come with me and I will fetch a copy for you from the secretary."

What was a group of chicks called? I should know... A herd, a library, a flock? Surely not. Chicks didn't fly. A clutch? No, that was a handbag.

I followed him out into the corridor and he opened another door. I could make out the repetitive drone of the photocopier as he bustled inside. He turned and said, "I will only be a minute. Wait here." I stood, not sure what to do with my arms. Was it just me or were arms meant to be this length? My arms were surely too long for my body.

I stepped over to the wall. There were several framed diplomas and a full-blown display board on *The Lion, the Witch and the Wardrobe.* The snowy scene made me long for another trip to the ice-rink; the only place I truly belonged. Who wrote that book? I remembered reading it years ago and stopped at the part where Lucy met that freaky fawn thing in the woods. I watched the film after or did Anita tell me the story? I couldn't remember.

The next noticeboard had a sign above it: Pupil Voice. When I finally worked out what it said, I wanted to shout out, "Boring. Who would want to hear what kids have to say?"

A small child sauntered past me, stopped and walked backwards arriving at me again. Ridiculous. He stood as close to me as he could. He smelt of pepperoni and I stepped back.

He gazed up at me and asked, "Are you a teacher?" His eyes were squinting and they were tiny compared to his moon-shaped face. He was like a little Weeble doll I had owned years ago. Where did Mum put that thing? Always getting rid of my stuff telling me it was time to grow up.

He asked me again, "Hey, are you a teacher?"

"No, I'm not," I said and wished he would go away. What would I do if he was still here when the magpie returned?

The kid didn't move and I asked, "Don't you have to be somewhere? Go... Go!" I was surprised at my own high-pitched voice. The kid stuck out his tongue and remained. He stood with his hand on his hip determined to stand his ground. He was definitely a seagull. Those annoying ones down at the beach that pestered you when you bought a bag of chips.

A phone rang in the secretary's office and a murmur of voices came through the wall of a nearby classroom.

"Do you work in this school? Are you a school nurse? Are you a parent?" As I stared at him, mad thoughts entered my head. Why was I here? Why was I going for this job? I was flipping dyslexic for goodness sake! And why was I listening to this odd, little seagull?

I glared down at him as I started to bite my nails. I knew I should stop, but I just couldn't. Moon Face interrupted my nail-biting session, "Hey, you don't listen good. Are you a school nurse or a parent?"

"No, I'm not. Now go away," I snapped and shooed him away with my hand.

"Do you know my name?"

"No, and I don't want to know it. Go away."

An empty bomb hit the pit of my stomach. I tried to relax, so I took a deep breath and let it out slowly. I couldn't believe this little nightmare was still standing in front of me. What did he want from me?

Beads of sweat formed on my forehead and I wiped them off. Makeup was all over the side of my hand. I wished with all my heart I'd taken the hanky Mum had tried to hand me in the car.

Suddenly, the principal was behind me like a wasp landing on my shoulder. He not only interrupted my thoughts, but he nearly made me jump out of my skin.

"Oh good, you have met James. He will be in your class. James, this is Miss Jolliff and Miss Jolliff, this is James."

I bent down and became aware of a quiver in my voice when I said, "Hello James. It's very nice to meet you." I stupidly held out my hand. He ignored it. I silently prayed inside.

Please don't tell Mr Cardwell I told you to go away. Please, please, please, little gull. His fat face frowned and I could hardly see his eyes anymore.

He turned to the principal and said, "I've already met her and I don't like her."

"Eh, James we do not speak to people like that. Please apologise." His booming voice of authority made me stand up straight. Mr Cardwell's fist clenched and I wanted to apologise for the boy.

"Sorry," he said with the ending going on forever. He didn't mean it. He was one I'd have to watch, I decided.

If I ended up working here, I would personally kill Mum.

"It's okay," I stuttered, "I'll see you in class." I forced a smile on my face.

"Anyway, James, why are you back in school? School is over."

"Mum sent me back in. Forgot my coat. She said I'd get soaked if I don't get it. Dad said I better not forget it or else."

"Hurry up and fetch it then," said Mr Cardwell.

James skipped off down the corridor. He stopped in front of a noticeboard and became a boxer, jabbing the wall with four punches. A laugh forced its way out of my mouth and I tried to stifle it.

Mr Cardwell continued talking and awkwardness rummaged through my body. He was speaking to me again and I hadn't heard a thing. He was standing too close to me; close enough to smell the coffee on his breath and see dandruff on both his shoulders like the fine grated cheese I sprinkled on my avocados. Ew, I had no idea why I was thinking about dandruff and food at the same time. My stomach churned.

"… so, he just needs a little bit of tender loving care. You should keep an eye on him. Anyway, five-year-olds are unpredictable. Don't take what he said to heart. Once he gets to know you, he will be fine. Now, come with me and I will introduce you to Mrs Craig."

What was he droning on about?

He turned, marching down the corridor and I followed him. We passed the toilets and the smell was woeful. I had to jog to keep up with him; his strides were massive. My feet hurt. Mum made me wear high heels and I wished I had practised on them before this interview. Another great suggestion from Mum. I didn't think I would be gallivanting all around the school. My underwear was stuck up my butt, too. I wiggled a little in my tight pencil skirt to try and sort it out, but that just made things worse.

At the end of the corridor, he clicked open a door. Did he seriously want me to follow him out there? Not only was it windy outside, but there was also that rain that soaked you right through and I had no umbrella.

"Run for it," yelled Mr Cardwell and he ran out into the rain. I ran after him wobbling on my ridiculous heels. My hair stuck to my face like spaghetti on a plate. My legs could hardly run due to the stupid pencil skirt.

Trust Mrs Craig's room to be in a mobile classroom and not the first or the second mobile either. No. Why would she be in the closest one? That would be too easy for this interview. Yes, she was in the furthest mobile in the whole school.

By the time we arrived at Mrs Craig's door, my hair was all over the place. My clothes were soaking wet and my underwear was now wedged totally up my ass. Unreal!

Lovely weather for ducks.

"Well, here it is. The children are all away home and Hazel is having her non-contact time, so I am sure she would love to meet you."

The rain pelted down on my back and I held my coat closed with my pink, freezing cold fingers. Why was he not going in? Why was he explaining this to me out in the pissing rain?

I managed to say, "Oh, good." But I wanted to shout, "Get inside! The sky is falling!"

He knocked and used a black round thing to open the door. We were in a small corridor and Mr Cardwell reached out to open the door into the classroom. I shook my head to fling the rain off it. I must have resembled a drowned rat. Whatever would Mrs Craig think of me?

"Hello, Hazel. I am here to introduce you to your new general assistant," Mr Cardwell announced happily.

TEN
HOUSE

Distracted by the words of the crazy gypsy, I didn't notice Abigail leaving the house to spend time with her chums.

But Walter did. Walter was pissed off. He paced around me, roughly handling objects, grinding his teeth and narrowing his eyes. Everyone ignored him as he strutted around me in his chequered flares and dull, orange shirt. His muscles rippled under his clothes and sweat patches formed under his arms.

"D.B., where's ya ma?" he yelled upstairs, clenching his fists. That would turn away any male who dared to challenge his authority. Everyone knew it.

D.B. turned the knob on his radio down. The music died. He emitted a deep sigh and yelled back, "She told ya yesterday!" D.B waited, picking at a scab on his arm.

Trixie looked up at him and whined. "Shush, Trixie," he whispered to her, before shouting back downstairs, "Remember?"

"No, she didn't," Walter yelled taking a deep breath and holding it in.

"Did," said D.B. letting out a short dismissive laugh, "Ya were too drunk at the time to remember," he grumbled under his breath.

"Get down here and tell me where she is!"

D.B. fetched his screwed-up packet of cigarettes from under his mattress and jammed them deep into his jeans pocket. He sauntered down my stairs shaking his head. He didn't like Walter, and Walter didn't like him.

"She told ya she was meeting her friends in Belfast and she was going to buy a new dress."

Walter ran to the jar on the top shelf of their bookcase. He flicked the pale pink and white ornament of a girl that Abigail loved to the side, and reached out with his big hand. He grasped the top of the jar and pulled it out. He yanked the lid off and snatched at the money inside. He parked himself on the settee and counted the money out onto my carpet.

"There better be fifty pounds in here."

D.B. watched him and slunk down on my bottom stair and leaned his head against my wall. His face hot.

After blowing out a noisy breath, he called in, "Mum told ya she was taking ten. Why don't ya remember?"

"Ten, twenty, thirty—"

"She was buying a new dress... remember?" D.B. said standing up and unbuttoning his top shirt button.

"She took more than ten. Bitch!" he yelled, throwing the lid at the jar. It delivered one solid clang.

"She's not a bitch," said D.B. stomping towards Walter and facing him head on.

"She is if she's out spending ma hard-earned cash," he said and made his way into the kitchen pushing past D.B. The teenager flinched and ran a hand through his hair.

"I'm going out," D.B. whispered and Trixie ran down the stairs and looked up at him.

"Not til ya pay yer way. Rent!" Walter called out from the kitchen. D.B. tutted and ran upstairs and smoked one of his cigarettes out my window; taking small, short puffs and glancing every now and again at his bedroom door.

Walter lifted the lid of the pot.

"She's left cold stew on the stove. What the hell am I to do with that?" he yelled as he slammed the lid back down, "Ma head bloody hurts and I need another nap," he rambled to himself, putting both his hands onto his forehead. He scanned the whole room. His eyes settled on his empty cider bottles standing in a row on my kitchen floor. He kicked in their direction and one of the bottles toppled over. Trixie barked four loud barks.

Sarah called from her room, "I'm hungry! Who has sweets?"

"The last thing I need is the kids to start nagging me over and over for food. Stuff this…" Walter mumbled. He went up to his bedroom, put on his shorts and slathered sun oil over his chest, arms and legs. He marched out into the garden with a blanket under his arm. It was sunny.

Emily-Brooke ran down the stairs. She jumped down the last two and I wanted to stop her. I was glad when she landed safely. In my hall, she stopped in her tracks and kept her eyes on the brown book not daring to look away. She reached out her hand and with a finger traced over the red writing.

"Beautiful. Oh, please, God, make this book be for me. Make this book be mine," she whispered with her eyes closed. I longed to tell her it was indeed hers. Your mother bought it from a gypsy woman who tapped on my door.

Trixie ran up to Emily-Brooke and licked her hand. "Thank you. I love you, Trixie," Emily-Brooke said in a bubbly tone.

She skipped into my kitchen shouting, "Mummy! Mummy, where are you?" She heaved herself up on the sink and from my kitchen window she spied Walter lying on a blanket in the garden. She called out, "Daddy, Daddy. Who owns the book in the hall? Is it for me?" Her dad didn't answer. Fast asleep.

Emily-Brooke ran out into the garden still shouting to attain her dad's attention, motivated by the mysterious brown book situated in my hallway. She skipped over to him; the big man sprawled out on the blanket. "You smell of sun oil and sweat," she whispered.

Her relationship with her dad was limited. He rarely spoke to her. In fact, he was usually out at "work" or spending hours out in his pigeon shed and it was uncanny for us to see him here at all.

"Daddy, wake up. I need to ask you a question," she said and waited, twiddling her thumbs. Walter didn't move.

"Daddy... I need to wake you up... I'm going to nip you to wake you... just a little bit. Don't be mad when I do." In a small whisper she added, "Where will I nip him?" She reviewed his immense body and pointed at his inner thigh.

Emily-Brooke stretched over her dad and pinched her fingers around the selected area of skin. I wanted to shout out to her. She dug her nails in hard with a look of determination.

I wanted to stop her, hold her back, warn her. But alas not a sound could I produce, except for the creaking of my floorboards that Emily-Brooke failed to catch from the garden.

Walter jumped up, kicked out his legs and smacked his youngest daughter in the face. She toppled backwards in shock, reeling in pain. Not a sound uttered from her throat. Instead, her nose spurted out blood that landed on her dad's leg. Once the blood started, it didn't intend to stop. It flung out of her nose, spread everywhere and finally dripped all over her pink jumper and matching shorts.

Trixie started barking from the kitchen.

"What the hell are ya doing?" Walter yelled at Emily-Brooke. She still didn't utter a sound. I suspected the pain of the belted nose was all her little body could handle right now. She rolled on the grass in agony as her dad marched into the house in disgust muttering, "Bloody kids."

Trixie ran off into my living room and hid in the far corner.

"Can't nab a minute's peace about this place. Children should be seen and not heard. Where the hell's Abigail? Unbelievable. Stupid kids!"

Everyone knew Walter was pissed off that evening and no one had dinner. The Irish stew remained in the pot, cold and untouched on the stove.

Abigail arrived back home at 8pm and I was sure she felt the awful atmosphere that hung in the air.

Shocked to see Emily-Brooke's face she demanded, "What in God's name happened here?"

Walter stayed quiet. He didn't explain.

"Well? I'm waiting..." Abigail turned to Emily-Brooke and continued, "Who did this to your face?" She glared at Walter.

"I nipped daddy when... when he was asleep. I made him jump up."

Abigail listened to her description of the event. When she heard Emily-Brooke confess that she had nipped her dad intentionally, she calmed down.

I wanted to punch Abigail on the nose. Why was she not angry with Walter? Why was she accepting this abuse?

She took a deep breath, stood up and flicked on the cooker to heat the stew. She said, "Yes, Emily-Brooke, the book is yours, I bought it this morning for you from a gypsy. Now, is anyone hungry?"

D.B and Sarah nodded in silence.

Emily-Brooke smiled despite her swollen face and her fat nose.

E L E V E N
MOLLY

Oh shit, I'd landed the stupid job. There was no way I'd be happy working in a school. My head began to pound. All my worries came upon me like a riptide. No stopping it now. No plug, no drain. Just me in a strong, offshore current caused by my inability to read or write, pulling me helplessly along a narrow band of water ready to fling me out into an ocean of words.

The dark-haired teacher, with a pale face and red lips, looked like Snow White. Maybe she'd be kind and understanding like the real Disney Princess. Maybe she would reach out her arm and pull me back in or was that wishful thinking? Perched behind her desk like a lifeguard at her tower she smiled. She stood and moved towards me.

"Oh, you have no idea how glad I am to meet you. We have been looking for a general assistant for... goodness knows how long."

"About four months, I reckon," added Mr Cardwell.

"And here you are. I'm Hazel. Hazel Craig. In front of the children, you can call me Mrs Craig. All other times, just Hazel," she held out her hand and I grabbed it. There might be some hope with this woman. A mother hen, making sure everyone knew what they were supposed to do. Maybe she'd understand if I told her I was dyslexic. Grandad's words boomed in my head, "Never be ashamed of what you can't do. Always put yer best foot forward and try yer best."

I took a tiny step forward and said, "Nice to meet you, Hazel. I'm Molly."

"Well, I will leave you two to it. Hazel, once you have shown Molly the ropes, ring over and let me know. As for you, Molly, I am looking forward to seeing you here tomorrow morning bright and breezy. You can fill out the necessary paperwork with me then. You start at 8.15am sharp."

Paperwork? Not the dreaded form filling!

My hands began to sweat at the thought of it and the riptide pulled me in once more.

I forced the word "ocean" to the back of my mind and scanned the classroom. All the hexagonal tables were dark green with different coloured, plastic chairs around them like large gifts around a Christmas tree. Each desk had a pot filled with colouring pencils in the middle, and a tray with red and blue scissors and thick yellow pencils.

Memories of my first years of school were still ingrained in my head. Words didn't make sense to me. They moved on the whiteboard and they moved on the white page. I remembered the teacher tapping my page as I read.

"Track your words, Molly. Remember to track your words." I couldn't track them; they floated all over the place. I remembered trying to avoid the teacher's stern face and I started my many trips to the toilet. My only escape.

I lifted my head and looked at the boards covering the walls like the advertisements down at my ice-rink. Every board backed with pink paper.

One noticeboard had the title "Friends" in bubble writing. I sounded it out, starting with the fr. That had been a nightmare too in school: phonics. All my friends figured it out. I never did.

When they tested me for dyslexia, they had taken me out of class, led me down a long corridor and brought me into a small room that smelt of new carpet. Nervous beyond a doubt. I was in my third or fourth year at school. Dad and Mum had agreed to the test and Dad tried to prepare me for it the night before.

"Just do your best, Molly-Moo. If you become stuck on something, just give it your best shot, baby girl." Mum had rolled her eyes and left the living room.

I heard her say, "She's not dyslexic, Brian. She's just being stubborn. Lazy." My young heart had crashed and burned that day. Mum had called me lazy.

The test itself lasted an hour. The longest hour of my life. Sheets and cards of words were presented to me and I floundered like a fish out of water trying to sound out each one. Coloured sheets were placed over sentences. When the green sheet landed on the stark white page, I remembered doing a double-take. The sentence stayed still. I didn't have to move the words around any more like a mismatched jigsaw. I read the sentence. It was decided I would work best with a green sheet over my work, work printed on green paper and Dad purchasing green-tinted glasses on Amazon. I read at a slow pace and Mum stopped calling me lazy for a while. At times, she would do my homework for me to speed me up a bit.

Way behind my friends, I acquired help from a classroom assistant who followed me around like a lost, unwanted dog. Vivid memories of her leapt into my head. Unwelcome. She had lank brown hair, dead eyes and she wore beige. When she leaned over me, every day without fail, her damp hand would land on mine and the smell of her sweet perfume would fill my nostrils. I remembered thinking: happy people should wear a perfume like that. Her face never appeared happy. Her attempts to help me made me squirm.

"Learn the strategy, Molly. Learn the strategy. Stretch the word out, Molly. Stretch it out." Her stage whisper could be heard around the class and made others snigger. My face would burn. I would try and stretch out the word to make her leave but she remained beside me. A sticking plaster; brown and lank. She made my life miserable. I was glad when I left to attend the big school. I never looked back when I marched away from that woman and that school. Education wasn't for me.

I glanced over the display board. Right in the middle was James. He got his moon face exactly right but I wasn't so sure about his arms. They weren't even connected to his body. Where were his friends? All the other pictures had two or three people in them and some had labelled their friends with large, ridiculous writing. James obviously had forgotten the aim of the project and drew only himself. Weird kid!

"Cup of tea, Molly?" the mother hen asked.

"Yes, that would be lovely. Thank you."

***

"Well?" Mum asked when I opened the car door. I said nothing. I was disgusted. Mum repeated the question again, "Well?"

"Are you crazy? Can't you see I'm soaked, Mum? Let me get in first," I said adjusting my skirt before I plonked myself down.

"Oh, don't worry, Molly. You can't expect to get the first job you go to. Your father and I are just glad you went for an interview. It is good experience," said Mum as she rubbed the back of her neck.

"Hardly," I answered as I undid the top button of my shirt and imparted a loud tut.

"It *is* good experience and you will become better over time and then you will achieve your dream job. Just you wait and see." Mum tapped on the steering wheel and gazed straight ahead.

"I got the job," I said with a huff, avoiding eye contact with Mum.

"What was that?"

"I said, I got that stupid job," I answered, taking her scarf off and throwing it onto the back seat.

"Are you winding me up?"

"Nope. I went in, he asked some stupid questions and I got the stupid job. I met the teacher, she's called—" Mum threw herself at me and I banged my head on the car window, "Mum, get off me!"

"Oh my, I am so proud of you. You have no idea how happy I am. I would have put money down you wouldn't secure the first fifty jobs you applied to, never mind your first one."

"Nice to see you have confidence in me, Mum. Thanks a lot." I snapped down the mirror and checked my makeup. Still intact.

"Wait until your father hears about this. How exciting," Mum said. She closed her eyes for a few seconds.

"It's not exciting, Mum. It's boring," I said to make her open her eyes.

"I am so proud of you." Mum hugged me again and I was a little overwhelmed. It was so unlike Mum to hug me like this. Yes, she would hug me on certain occasions like my birthday or Christmas morning, but never in a spontaneous way. Like the way she hugged Josh when he cracked a joke and made her laugh. Maybe now she would see potential in me. If I could do this stupid job. Doubt crept all over me and I shuddered.

"Mum, please drive."

"You see, that dyslexic thing was a load of rubbish. I told you that ages ago. No one listened to me. I knew you would do something with your life. We should celebrate," Mum said as she turned the key in the ignition.

"Let's not," I said, feeling a headache coming on. So, she never even believed I had dyslexia. All this time she thought it was an excuse. An excuse to be lazy. A rough stone hit the bottom of my stomach and bile splashed up into my mouth.

"When do you start? Will it be permanent or are you on trial to see if they like you?"

I swallowed hard.

"Tomorrow morning at quarter past eight and no mention of a trial," I answered as I rubbed my mouth.

"Oh good. I'm beyond happy. Molly, you've made my day."

"I'm starting at eight fifteen. Don't you think that is a bit on the early side?"

"Darling, that is normal. Don't worry, I will have you up at seven. You will have plenty of time to get ready."

"Great." I scratched at my cuticles.

"You know I can't give you a lift over."

"Oh, do I have to walk?" I whispered wondering how far the school was from home.

"Darling, I leave your brother off to school each morning in the opposite direction. You will have to walk. The walk will do you good. Keep you fit and that is good for your ice-skating," said Mum in an easy-going manner.

This job just got worse. The constant windscreen wipers and my wet clothes were annoying me. And the fact I had a job that would involve a lot of reading and writing just made me want to throw up.

"Really good for your ice-skating... beneficial," Mum repeated.

"Mum, drive faster."

"I'm driving at the speed limit."

Mum turned on the radio. She loved music. She would hum along and move her head left and right like a little doll as she did. Today her hair clip was brown. Her brighter than bright green eyes danced to the music and she reached up to look at herself in the mirror. Her features were fine and her makeup always perfectly applied. Nude lipstick, her main choice and occasionally red when Dad would take her out on a surprise date. Maybe now I was working, she would plan days out with me. I couldn't see that happening anytime soon. The rain was miserable. The journey took forever.

When we arrived, Mum couldn't wait to step into the house and tell Dad the good news. Dad's hawk eyes were wider than usual.

"Dad, don't look at me like that, you're freaking me out."

"My baby girl has gone and got herself a job." I tried to hide my smile with my hair. I lowered my head. Too late. Dad ran towards me and lifted me up, swinging me around. "I'm so proud of you. Well done, you."

"It's no big deal, Dad," I said as I struggled to get down.

"No big deal. Indeed, it is. Saying that, I never thought I'd see the day. My babes. You'll need to start organising yourself now you've got a job."

"Thanks for your confidence, Dad," I said, wrinkling my nose, "And I am organised!"

"Organised chaos, you mean, baby girl," laughed Dad, "One look in your bedroom would tell you how organised you are."

"Don't listen to your father. You will become more organised and tidier now you have a job. You should check out Joshua's room. It is always perfect," said Mum with a smile.

"Did I hear someone mention my name?" My brother sauntered into the kitchen, looking as if he had just woken up. I always pictured Josh as a little dove. Now that he was taller than me and his voice was deeper, it didn't really suit him. But he'd always be my little brother. I couldn't believe he slept the day away while I was out seeking a job for myself.

"Spill the tea?" he said as he rolled his eyes at me.

"Speak English, Joshua," snapped Mum.

"Spill the tea means 'What's the gossip'. Doesn't it, son? Your big sister has just landed herself a job," said Dad.

"So what? And mother dear, I am speaking English."

"Eh, should that not be congratulations?" barked Mum.

"Yes, where's my congratulations, Josh?" I asked sarcastically. I jumped up and checked Charlie, my plant.

"Where's the job, Blondie?" he asked as I poured half a glass of water for my gorgeous plant.

"I told you this morning. Mum was dragging me to an interview at the primary school on May Avenue. Remember?" I said as I punched him lightly on the arm.

"Nah, I wasn't listening to you," he replied, smirking down at me, "I can't imagine you working in a school. You hate reading and writing and now you're gonna be teaching kids how to do it."

My face went rosy red. I liked the fact Josh was a straight talker but not when he was referring to my dyslexia. The sad thing was, he was right. How was I going to help kids to read and write? A dyslexic helping non-readers. Horrific!

"When do you start?"

"Tomorrow morning at eight fifteen," I answered, pouring the water slowly around Charlie's soil. If I was a plant, life would be so much easier. No need to read or write in the world of greenery.

Josh doubled over as if he was in pain. He screeched a painful, gurgling laugh as he scaled upright and burst out laughing in my face.

"Did you say eight fifteen? Hilarious! No more lie-ins for you, Blondie. Good one, sis. Well, you could always do some of your bird-watching on the way to work." He punched me on the arm, full force, scratched his head as if he had nits and strolled to the fridge.

"Be careful, my glass nearly hit Charlie there," I snapped, "And I don't bird-watch anymore."

"You don't need to hide the fact from me. I know you do it. What's for tea, Mum?"

As soon as Grandad died, I stopped bird-watching and I had hidden my obsession with birds. I no longer carried his old binoculars around with me. I still had our little, black book under my bed and would record in it from time to time: descriptions and sketches of birds and sayings my grandfather used to say about birds, mainly proverbs. Surely Josh didn't know about that.

"Well, I was hoping we were going to celebrate. Brian, do you fancy ordering Chinese?"

"On a weeknight?" moaned Dad.

"Yes, on a weeknight. To celebrate Molly securing a job," Mum said pausing in between each word.

"It's Tuesday. It just doesn't feel right having Chinese," moaned Dad again, and Mum fired him a killer look, "Okay, hand me my phone. What do you guys want to eat?"

"Sweet!" said Josh.

"I'll have a beef curry with extra peas and boiled rice," I said as I clapped Dad on the back.

Josh slammed the fridge door closed and asked, "Do we have a menu?"

"No, Joshua," said Mum, "We don't keep those in the house. This isn't a hotel. Brian, order me my usual."

"Chicken satay and chips?"

"Yes, and order a big bottle of Diet Coke."

"I'll have sweet and sour chicken and chips," Josh said as he strolled over to me and flicked my ear, "Can't stay long though as I'm meeting Willow laters."

"You two are getting close," I said with a smirk.

"We're just friends. Anyway-"

"You will have to cancel Willow tonight," Mum interrupted.

"I can't."

"You will and you can."

"She's picking me up at eight. We've to leave stuff over to her sister's new house."

"I don't feel comfortable with Willow driving you all the way into Belfast, son," said Dad.

"Dad, don't start. Willow scored her driving test last year, Dad. She's a sweet driver, you know."

"Well, you can go tomorrow. Tonight is all about Molly-Moo," Dad said.

"Fine. Well, in that case, order me a side of onion rings." Josh lifted up his mobile to cancel his night with Willow, "Just remember, sis: I'm doing this for you."

"Auk, I'm honoured." I knew he was still indeed a little, caring dove.

Dad placed the order and ordered special fried rice for himself.

It was nice sitting down and celebrating my victory. Mum's eyes sparkled. It was lovely that the reason her whole face was smiling was down to me. Something I never saw down at the rink as she managed to avoid every competition I was entered in.

After she served out the dishes, she placed her hands on my shoulders and lightly squeezed them. Something about that gesture made me feel the same joy I experienced when she stopped lying about seeing my performances. Dad could stop making excuses about why she couldn't make it. I never wanted that to be his burden. My ice-skating had nothing to do with Mum.

I looked up at Dad tucking into his special fried rice. Happy.

"Dad, what do you call a Chinese man with one leg?" He looked up. "Tie won shu."

Dad laughed, Mum tutted and Josh said, "Racist." I ignored him.

Mum shook her head and smiled.

It was a good to know they were proud of me.

Maybe things were going to be okay.

TWELVE
HOUSE

Emily-Brooke pulled the rose petals out individually; as close to the core of the flower as her chubby, little fingers could manage. She gently removed each thorn one by one and placed them carefully into her brother's old brown, leather school bag. She had found the school bag discarded carelessly behind the settee. She claimed it as her own.

"In a little bit, I will start school and I will need it for myself," she said to justify taking it. The leather stench forced her to pull back, but the familiarity of it drew her towards it once more. "I'm going to put those sharp things in the bin. D.B. calls them thorns. They're dangerous," she said as she carefully traced the silver buckles, "I'm going to pick pretty flowers for Mummy."

I imagined Abigail hugging and smiling down at Emily-Brooke but my ideal vision went awry and blurred due to the anger in Walter's voice.

"Where's Emily-Brooke? She didn't tidy away her bloody dolls. Emily-Brooke!" Walter went from room to room looking for her and my wiring sparked with every heavy movement. He stepped out into the garden and my bricks were like crumpling sand.

"You... Ya destroying Abigail's roses."

"Oh, come on, Walter. She is grand. Don't you be worrying Emily-Brooke," Abigail said running behind Walter and putting her hand on his shoulder.

"Yer kids are let off too lightly."

"*Our* kids," whispered Abigail, still behind him.

"In my day, ya were seen and not heard," Walter ranted, pushing Abigail to the side who bounced lightly off my wall. Walter stormed back into the house and into my living room.

"Are you hungry, pet?" asked Abigail, rubbing the side of her arm and kneeling in front of Emily-Brooke.

"A little bit."

"Now, would you like a butter and sugar sandwich?" Abigail asked her daughter as she touched her head.

"Yes, please, Mummy," she replied and Abigail went into my kitchen to make it. D.B. was sitting at the table polishing his shoes.

Walter paced in behind Abigail.

"Get those shoes off the bloody table. Bringing bad luck into my house," he said as he whacked the shoes onto the floor. Bad luck. What was that? I listened closely in case I gleaned the answer.

"For God's sake," said D.B., lifting the shoes and the polish. Then stepping out into my back garden.

"Abigail, speak to him. In my day, ya never spoke back to yer parents."

"I am sure you occasionally did," said Abigail leaning against Walter. She reached up and planted a kiss on his lips.

"He's bloody spoilt! He's too many pairs of shoes. What's he polishing them for anyway? It's not as if he's got a job to go to!"

"We all have shoes, Walt. He is trying to keep them good."

"We all don't have shoes. I only got one pair of shoes a year. It didn't matter if ma feet grew over the year. Ya just squeezed yer feet into them if they did. And when I was his age, I had no shoes for a whole year."

"What do you mean, for a whole year? You must have had shoes, Walt," said Abigail taking the bread out of the bread bin.

"My da lit a fire on the farm. And when we were heading to school, a burning cinder fired out onto the path we were walking on. I tried to stamp it out and it burnt right through my shoe. The rubber of the sole stuck to ma sock and burned right through it too. It did."

"Walter, stop. That is a devastating story!" said Abigail, roughly buttering the bread.

"I screamed, I did. All the way back to the farmhouse. Donna and Minnie started screaming too. My ma heard us and came running towards me. My da stepped out of nowhere and caught me just before I reached her," he said his eyes wide and wild.

"What did he do?" Abigail paused as she asked. Silence. She turned and sprinkled the sugar onto the butter.

"He threw me onto the ground and tore my shoe and sock from ma foot. Tore half ma skin off with it too. My ma nearly fainted."

"Oh, how awful," said Abigail, putting one piece of bread on top of the other and lifting the knife.

"My da told me to get up and get to school. He threw ma shoe in the bin and I never got a new pair."

Abigail put the sandwich onto a small plate and said gently, "You must have got a new pair, Walt. Tell me you did."

"I walked to school on ma bare feet for three days before I went back to ma last year's pair. Cut out the toes of them with ma aul pocket knife. I suffered those for about a month and then my ma made me wear her Wellingtons." Walter jumped up and left the kitchen.

Abigail held her breath and put her hand to her head.

Seconds later, she handed Emily-Brooke the sandwich. The little girl skipped off; a tranquil cloud enveloped her as she ate her sandwich and played chip shops with mud and dock leaves.

I was happy to know all was well again; content. My floorboards eased.

That evening on the way up the stairs, Emily-Brooke slipped by Sarah. Sarah snatched her sister's hair, shook it, and banged her head off the stairs and cried.

"She bit me," Sarah yelled with a sneer. I was as stunned as Emily-Brooke. Walter appeared from nowhere.

"What ya doing biting yer sister?" Before he heard Emily-Brooke's answer he pulled off his belt and belted her legs. Sarah took a pew and watched. A wildness appeared in Walter's eyes I had never seen before. Emily-Brooke screamed in pain and curled up in a ball. I hated him. It made my whole being feel small and tight.

When Walter finished, Trixie wandered over and licked her hand. Emily-Brooke remained still except for her trembling chin.

I wanted to rewind time like a sudden change of the wind. But I too remained still. Weak. I could do nothing. I was only a house after all.

Emily-Brooke's jealous sister smiled and slinked off into the garden. No remorse. Sarah didn't see me. She was like the adults. She stayed quiet. I hated her too.

Emily-Brooke stole too much attention away from her. Sarah was four when the baby was born, shipped off to that house called "school". Emily-Brooke remained within me with her Mummy.

"I know," I heard her mumble, "I'll say I've sore feet and I'll stay at home with Mummy too." However, new expensive boots were bought with fur inside and the next day she was shipped off to school again! Anger grew in her little heart; Emily-Brooke's face, with her cute dimples, became a face to despise and resent. She wanted Emily-Brooke to go back to where she came from.

At the bottom of the garden, Sarah seized a buttercup in her hand and twisted its head off with her fingers.

"I want Emily-Brooke and her stupid doll, Beanie, to pack up and no longer be part of my world." A burning sensation delved into the pit of my stomach and a nagging pain dug into my entire being. I decided to keep an eye on her. I needed Emily-Brooke to be part of my world. I never wanted her to leave. I would be nothing without her. Empty.

"Emily-Brooke, stop trying to be her friend," I rattled through my windows.

The next week, Sarah grew bored of her friends from the street. She hunted down Emily-Brooke. *Trouble again.*

Walter had made part of the garden into a vegetable patch. Two large mounds of soil had been created either side like a ditch. Sarah and Emily-Brooke loved jumping from one clump to the other. Their confidence grew with each jump. They loved my garden and all it had to offer. I watched them and waited for trouble to arrive.

It was growing dark and fatiguing now to see the two small figures as they jumped from one mound to another. Sarah stood and examined me and I thought for a split-second. Did she see me? She turned and stuck her foot out, just as Emily-Brooke was about to jump. Down in the ditch she tumbled, and once again her parents didn't respond to her scream.

Sarah went down on her honkers with Trixie beside her and said, "You all right down there?"

"Get Mummy," Emily-Brooke cried, "I need a little bit of help."

"Help yourself," said Sarah and waited. I was beyond livid. I tried to stay calm. I really tried.

Walter watching football on the grey square thing, boxed in with shiny wood and operated by chunky silver flick-buttons on the side of it; Abigail talking to D.B. in his room about asking Walter for a new guitar. Why didn't they help? Why were humans so unobservant? Why weren't they listening?

It was a full hour before D.B. helped Emily-Brooke out of the ditch.

"Stupid kid," he said.

Sarah repeated his words, "Yea, she's stupid, isn't she?" and skipped behind him.

"Isn't she?" she repeated.

D.B. said nothing, turning a plectrum in his hand.

"Isn't she?" Sarah asked in a weaker voice.

*

Christmas came and I loved the row of Christmas cards on the mantelpiece. The majority had houses covered in crisp, white, fluffy blankets. Standing with a grandness, I admired. I knew these houses and cottages were warm and cosy. Glad for them, I hoped one day someone would be so kind to do the same to me; wrap me in a blanket.

Emily-Brooke had her own wooden desk. She said, "It is perfect." The lid lifted off and she stored all her important books inside: her Bible, a book on fairy tales, and several blank notebooks. "I'm just like a real teacher now!" she said and I knew she was happy. The four, bright red, shiny legs of the desk stood firmly in her bedroom beside her stack of board games and books.

Abigail had been making apple pie earlier and Emily-Brooke had managed to save the sour apple peelings from the bin without her knowing. She sneaked them inside her desk.

"I am going to eat those later," she said. Emily-Brooke loved the sour taste that made her whole face screw up and bestowed her a tummy ache. Days passed and the forgotten peelings fermented in the desk. The smell wound its way into the fibres of the wood, clinging to it with determination. That desk never lost the smell of apple peelings.

Emily-Brooke said, "Dad smells of smoke and he drinks a funny drink that smells just like my desk. His breath stinks."

*

Emily-Brooke was someone special. Very special, especially now she owned a light pink, plastic digital watch, and rode her bicycle without stabilisers.

I knew Emily-Brooke loved her bike. A Dawes Newpin. A hand-me-down from Sarah. I watched her daily doing her circuits around the street. Emily-Brooke rode from the top of the lane at top speed, making a sharp left to the top of the tarmac hill which led to my front gate. She made the journey at least a thousand times.

Up again. My drains choked. I was sure her legs ached as she peddled back up that hill. I was right. Before she reached the lane, she dismounted the bike and pushed. She leaned heavily on the handlebars to take a much-needed rest.

Walter and Abigail didn't notice her tiredness. But I did. Surely it was time for Emily-Brooke to come back inside. They remained indoors. Abigail cooking in my kitchen and Walter playing with his new toy: his pipe. He poked and picked at that thing for hours. Both oblivious.

Emily-Brooke chattered away merrily to her bike, believing it heard every word. It made me laugh and my wiring sparked.

*

It was Sunday and sunny. Emily-Brooke, keen to get an earful of the ice-cream van that regularly appeared in our little avenue.

"When the ice-cream man comes, I'm going to buy a poke," she sang at my gate, twisting the money D.B had given her.

She grabbed her bike and dragged it to the top of the hill. She started the journey up the lane and stopped for a second to pick up the two pence shining on the grass. She turned it over and over in her grubby hands, slipping it into the pink, plastic bag slung over her body.

When Emily-Brooke reached the top of the lane, she calmly told her bike, "Bike, take me to the house! I know you can do it without me turning your handles!"

My wiring sparked! She believed the bike knew what she was talking about. Beyond ridiculous. Emily-Brooke got on the bike confidently and started to pedal. The bike went off at top speed as usual. I knew Emily-Brooke had made the decision to not help her bike. There was a lightness in her little chest. I knew as she titled-back her head and smiled. Fear hit me. She would not operate the handles; it would turn itself. I couldn't warn her.

It didn't turn itself!

Faster and faster went the wheels on the Newpin and bang! She went straight into the lamppost at the end of the lane. Emily-Brooke went over the handlebars and she banged her nose hard on the lamppost. She shot onto the ground and a sharp stone went into her back.

Screams launched their way out of Emily-Brooke's mouth; drowned by the music from the ice-cream van that trundled into our little avenue.

All the children ran out of their houses only to find poor Emily-Brooke on the ground by the lamppost. My heart broke for her that day.

THIRTEEN
MOLLY

"Molly! Molly! This is the last time I am calling you. Wake up! Are you winding me up?" *This must be a dream.* There was no way I racked up eight hours of sleep!

Buried in snuggly sleep, I couldn't associate my mum's emergency with anything serious.

"One more hour," I murmured. I pulled my knees up towards my stomach and hugged myself, gripping selfishness.

The door swung open and I opened my eyes wide, "Mum, get out!"

"Oh my, just look at the mess of this room."

Why didn't I clean my room last night? The last thing I needed right now was a lecture.

"Mum, I'll clean my room tomorrow."

"It is a disgrace. Are those your ice-skating tights?" she asked as she seized them off the floor, "Do you know how much these cost?"

Why did everything have to be about the cost these days?

"Mum, leave them alone. I'm up, now go," I said and heaved myself into a sitting position, lifting my mobile to check the time, "It's only seven. Why so early?" I asked Mum who was now prancing around my room picking up more clothes, smelling them and cradling them in her arms.

"Mum, I might need those clothes."

"They need to be washed. As do you! Go and have a shower. You smell of teenager."

"What do teenagers smell of?" I asked as I sniffed my armpits.

"Wolf," said Mum leaving my room.

Wolf? Awful. My face burned red. I was never the wolf. I was Little Red Riding Hood.

I dragged myself into the hall and staggered towards the bathroom. The shower was on inside and I tried the door.

"Mum, Josh is having a shower," I yelled.

"You should have got up when I told you then," Mum yelled back from downstairs.

"Josh, hurry up in there. I'm going to be late for work." I stood and listened.

I knocked several times and waited again. "Josh! Josh!"

"Molly," he answered.

"What?" I said as I put my head onto the door.

"Dry your eyes," he said and I knew he was smirking. I kicked the door and ran back to my room, flinging myself onto my bed.

"I can't go to work. My reading and writing are woeful. How am I going to help children to read when I struggle myself?" I said into my pillow.

I reached my hand under my mattress and pulled out my bird book. I sat up and flicked through the pages, stopping to look at a photograph of Grandad. I missed him terribly. Without fail he always made me feel better, especially when I was worried about doing something new.

His words filled my head, "Never give up on yourself, Molly. And give yourself breaks when you feel frustrated."

My tears fell onto the photograph. I quickly closed the book and placed it back into its secret place.

I had no idea how I dragged myself into the shower, picked out clothes to wear, ate breakfast, *and* checked Charlie my plant, before stumbling out our front door. But I did. As I rushed to work, I knew I would need to find a quicker way.

When I arrived, I tugged on the straps of my rucksack wondering if I should enter the main entrance or if I should find another way in. I had no other option but to go in through the big doors. The same ones I had gone through for the interview. I picked my phone out of my back pocket and glanced at the time.

Eight o'clock.

Was time slowing down? What time did he say for me to be here? Oh crap, I was too early. I couldn't be early. That was worse than being late.

My nails were bitten down to the quick. I should have painted them last night to make them look half decent. I had eaten my Chinese, chatted on the phone to Anita for three hours, and caved in to sleep. I missed Anita and suddenly wished my best friend worked here too. She'd be having a normal day at school, sucking on her hedgehog necklace and spitting it out when a thought popped into her head. I smiled. Anita always made me smile. Even when she wasn't with me.

"Good morning. You must be Catherine," a voice said from behind me.

"Molly," I said.

"Yes, yes. The new girl for Mrs Craig? I'm Mrs McCann. I am the vice-principal. Come with me and I will let you in," she said opening the main door with the same thing Mr Cardwell had used yesterday, "This is a fob. You use it to gain access about the school. I have one already for you. Come with me, Catherine."

"Molly," I repeated and she rolled her eyes at me. Not a good start, but at least I was in. She directed me into her office and I wondered for a split second if I should just call myself Catherine here. It would make me sound more... more sophisticated.

"You better put that away," she said raising an eyebrow at my mobile, "We have a strict, no mobile phones policy."

No phones? Was she kidding? How would I keep in touch with the real world? I swung my rucksack off my back and struggled to pull the stupid thing open. I slipped it into a side pocket and looked up, taking in her office. A smaller version of Mr Cardwell's office but notably tidier. She ran her finger over her grey, A4 folders and selected one. She leafed through an organised folder.

"Ah, here it is." She slipped out a booklet of A4 paper with jumbled up letters written on the front, "Catherine, I will photocopy this and leave it over at Mrs Craig's for you. I have some forms I will need you to fill in too. In the meantime, you should make your way to your class. Mrs Craig is expecting you. Here is your fob."

"Oh, okay. Thanks," I mumbled trying to back out the door before she asked me to fill out the forms in front of her.

Forms again. Nightmare. It was going to be fun working here. The vice-principal didn't even know my name. A forgetful finch.

I marched down the corridor past the toilets. I wanted to punch the wall the same way James did yesterday, but I thought better of it. I opened the door and wandered around to Mrs Craig's mobile classroom.

I used my new fob to get in.

"Hello... Hello, Mrs Craig," I said as I opened the second door into the classroom.

"Call me Hazel," Mrs Craig said with a massive smile. I smiled back.

"I'll run through our plan for today with you. I put up a visual timetable for the kids, you can use it too so you know what is happening. We start every day on the carpet. We call it 'carpet time'. We sing a morning song and welcome the children. Today, we go to assembly and then we have R.E., followed by break," Mrs Craig started putting the timetable up on a washing line that ran from her storeroom to a hook above her desk, "Then we do number work, then lunch and then P.B.L."

"P.B.L?" I asked.

"Play-based learning," she explained.

Oh good, no reading or writing. Maybe I would survive my first day after all.

"Oh, and I better explain our reward system. This is our circle and all the pupils' names start here at the beginning of the day. This is our star. Every time you see or hear a child being good, you tell them to move their name up to the star."

"It looks simple enough."

"Yes, it is. And the children love it. Feel free to move any child to the star at any time throughout the day," she said. The bell rang out like a fire alarm and made me jump, "Oh, I better go and collect the wee darlings. Ask any questions throughout the day, and Molly—"

"Yes?"

"Have fun."

Fun in a classroom? I didn't think so. I smiled.

As soon as the children tramped in, uneasiness crept over me. All the chicks stared at me. Each lifted a stone out of one basket and threw it into another. Then, they all settled down on the carpet with their legs crossed and their arms folded.

Mrs Craig introduced me, "P.2, this is our new classroom assistant. Her name is Miss Jolliff."

I wished they would all call me Catherine; my new school name. There was something creepily formal about being called Miss Jolliff. Not only that, but it sounded like my mum. I could picture her in my room collecting clothes off my bedroom floor and I shuddered.

Mrs Craig interrupted my memory, "Now, let's see how many children are in today. Lucy, can you count the stones for me?" I forced a smile on my face as Lucy, a plump short girl with brown eyes and long blonde hair, sprung up and marched up to the front. She counted the stones in the second basket.

"Twenty-nine stones, Mrs Craig."

"Well done, Lucy," said Mrs Craig and she glanced over at me, "Lucy loves to count. She can count all the way up to one hundred."

Great. And she could probably read and write better than me too. I forced another smile on my face.

"So, who is off today?" she continued, taking out the only stone left in the other basket. She looked at the stone. Each one had a name on it. "Oh, it's James."

Typical. Moon Face scored a lie-in.

"Now, let's sing our song, P.2." They all sat up straight and sang the most ridiculous song:

> *How many stones are left alone?*
> *How many stones are left alone?*
> *How many stones are left alone?*
> *Who is still at home?*

It continued:

> *One little stone is left alone.*
> *One little stone is left alone.*
> *One little stone is left alone.*
> *James must be still at home.*

Mrs Craig filled in the dinner book and sent Lucy off to the office with it. The next fifteen minutes consisted of Mrs Craig droning on about the daily news from the children and I switched off. This was going to be a long day.

There was a knock at the door. Mrs Craig got up off her seat and opened it.

"Oh. Hello, James," she said in the same sing-song jolly voice she used at the carpet with the children.

A man behind James said, "Sorry he's late. He was playing up at home and I couldn't get him into the car."

"No problem," answered Mrs Craig. James slipped into the room. He had a massive bruise above his left eye. He must have bumped into something.

He glared over at me and said, "Hey, not ye again," and plonked himself down on the carpet. He picked threads out of it, glancing up at me each time he yanked one out, daring me with his eyes to say something.

I was glad when Mrs Craig entered the room and said, "Okay, P.2, line up for assembly."

Assembly was worse than the classroom. I had to mumble and bumble through songs I didn't know. To make matters worse, I had to take three kids to the toilet.

Waiting outside in the corridor, a woman in her late thirties marched towards me. She had bobbed, poker-straight, light brown hair with one-centimetre black roots. Her brown eyes were open wide and she click-clacked towards me in high heels.

"Eh, sorry. Do I know you?"

"I'm Molly. I got the job in Mrs Craig's class. I'm now her classroom assistant." I explained as I wondered if she had eyelash extensions. A peahen. Maybe a little on the short side for such a bird. I guessed about five foot without her heels on.

As I continued to examine her, I realised she was examining me and my cheeks began to burn.

"Oh, you're the new girl. I'm a classroom assistant too. I'm Nicola and I work in the P.5 room," she said, throwing her hand towards a nearby classroom, "You need any advice, come and find me. I've been here seven years. I know all the comings and goings in this place." She turned on her heel and wiggled her way back down the corridor. I didn't know what to think about her and I was glad when Ben came out of the toilet. I returned to the assembly hall before anyone else appeared.

When we returned to the classroom, I found out R.E. consisted of the children writing a line from the whiteboard into their books. Interactive whiteboards were not my thing. Words didn't stay still on them when I was a kid and even now as an adult the words still danced about. I stared up at the thing and wondered how I ever survived in school with all the ridiculous movement.

I was glad Lucy read the line out to her friend, "Jesus loves the little children." They had to draw a picture of Jesus with the children at his feet. I ran from one child to another, sharpening pencils, trying to encourage some of the kids to start working, and allowing kids to go to the toilet.

By the time the break bell rang, I was officially wrecked and my head hurt. Despite the thumping head, I could honestly say the activity hadn't been too bad.

"Oh, you are on break duty," said Mrs Craig with a smile.

"Break duty? What's that?" I asked, dreading the answer.

"You walk around the playground and make sure the children are behaving. If anyone falls, you can use the first aid box." She stepped to the back of the classroom and handed me a green box.

Now I'm a nurse? Great! Blood and gore. Surely, I didn't sign up for this.

Grace, a little tanned-faced girl with big brown eyes, toppled over and grazed her knee. I patched her up.

With tears in her eyes she said, "Thank you, Miss." I flinched and realised that being a nurse wasn't as bad as I thought it would be.

Looking over her head, I saw James beating the crap out of another kid. I nearly tripped over Grace to reach him.

"James, what are you doing?" I asked as I hauled him off the other kid.

"Hey! He said, I wet the bed!" James said as he tried to punch the kid again.

"Did you say he wet the bed?"

"He did when he had a sleepover at my house. He did, Miss, he did!"

"Hey, I'll bust yer face," James yelled as I held onto his arm tight.

"You go and play in the sandpit. James, you stay with me."

I knelt, parallel with his fat face, "James, don't take things to heart." He jerked his arm away from me and booted me full-force on the leg, "You wee..."

Just as well I didn't say that last word. When I turned around, there was Grace.

"Can I hold your hand?" she asked.

"Of course, you can," I said, giving my leg a rub and watched James heading straight to the sandpit.

The bell rang. Stopping him in his tracks. Nice one.

When we arrived back in the classroom, we started number work straight away. Mrs Craig had several stations set up like a car-boot sale.

The first table had pegboards out and the children had to make patterns with the pegs. The next table was covered in whiteboards where the children had to write the numbers zero to twenty. The table I had to sit at was decorated with paints and large A3 pieces of paper.

"The children will paint the numbers zero to twenty. They can change colours as they go," Mrs Craig said in the same sing-song voice she used with the children. I nodded and looked down at all the paints in horror.

The last time I painted was with Grandad. The common crane. Grandad had just come back from a bird-watching trip to Somerset. He had picked up his photographs from the chemist and was overly excited to show me his developed pictures.

"Only one hundred and sixty of these cranes in Britain now," he told me as he set out his watercolours, "The dance of the cranes is famous worldwide amongst us bird-watchers, ya know. A real privilege to see. Heads thrown back, wings flapping, tail feathers fluffed and feet stamping. Just like you on that ice-rink of yours." We had laughed that day as we drew several sketches of the majestic bird, attempting to fix the wing span exactly right, and the white patch below its eye and on its neck.

"Right, class," said Mrs Craig and I was back in the classroom. I scanned over at the other tables embarrassed by my day-dreaming. Another one had booklets spread out on it and Mrs Craig called out the kids' names and directed them around the room.

"I'm mixing up the groups into different abilities, so they will help each other," she said to me and I found myself shrugging. I had no idea what she was doing or why she was doing it.

James was at my table with Grace who smiled up at me. I also had a kid called Freddie who had a fascination with his shoes the entire ten minutes. Two other children, their names I didn't ask, kept poking each other so I separated them.

James snatched two paintbrushes and I put my hand over his.

"Stop, we haven't started yet," I snapped.

"Oi, ye hurt me there," he said.

"I didn't," I said shocked and I looked around for Mrs Craig who was busy with her group, "Now, listen to what we are going to do," I said in a calm, controlled voice.

"Hey, we already know what to do," said James squinting up at me.

"What then, Smarty-Pants?" I asked.

"You said a bad word," said Freddie glancing up from his shoes.

"Smarty-Pants is not a bad word."

"You said it again," said Freddie sticking his finger up his nose.

"It's not a bad word. Now, James, what is it that you think we have to do?"

"Paint a picture of a house, sun, and grass," said James grabbing the paintbrush again.

"No," I said, prizing the paintbrush out of his hand.

"Oi, ye hurt me again. I'm telling."

Why was he being so cranky? This was a nightmare!

"Right, we are going to paint the numbers zero to twenty. I will show you all on my page," I said as I painted a circle with the red paint, "Look, I have zero on my page and now I am going to change the colour and make the number one. Watch me." I lifted the bright yellow paint and painted the number one.

This was fun. Gliding my paintbrush over this page was like gliding over the ice-rink ready to do the performance of my life.

"Miss," said Grace, interrupting my thoughts. I smiled down at her.

"Yes, Grace?"

"You have yellow all over you now."

I looked down and the yellow paint somehow had splattered all over my top.

Maybe not the same at all.

Freddie said, "When can we start?"

One of the kids who remained nameless said, "Where do we paint the house?"

I wiped the paint down my top and made it worse.

I occupied a seat and said, "Off you go, kids," and vented a deep sigh.

I had no idea what they painted, but I dragged the pictures over to the drying rack.

I was pissed off when Mrs Craig shouted out, "Class! Class!" and the kids all called back, "Yes! Yes!"

Mrs Craig said, "Move to your next station." All the kids moved. I was faced with five more kids ready to do the same activity.

I looked down at my table. Paint everywhere.

I stole a deep breath and said, "Right, we are going to be painting the numbers zero to twenty on this table. Now go for it!"

They all painted random things.

This went on for forty-five minutes and I longed to be back in Grandad's warm kitchen with his watercolours and his photographs spread out all over the table. I was glad when the bell rang for lunch. I welcomed it like an unexpected hug from Mum.

FOURTEEN
HOUSE

"Bloody woodchip!" Jack is in my master bedroom stripping wallpaper, still chewing gum.

I temporarily close the door to my memories and stop them from unravelling from my hot press.

As each strip is torn down, I relax; going into that space where all is well. Memories of Emily-Brooke make me happy. I allow my whole being to recall when she was here. I open my memory door once more and ignore Jack.

* * *

It was September and the roses at my door were wilting; their petals were browning but a slight pink tinge still lingered.

Emily-Brooke was nine and at school. Life was exciting and full of lovely possibilities, and my garden filled with crispy leaves of orange, red and brown. I watched the school children with their shiny school shoes. In the evenings, they ran up to doors, knocking and then running away as fast as they could. Unexpected adults would come to their doorways and scowl. It was a game and I liked it. One kid shouted out, "Stop, drop and roll!" and I burst out laughing as I watched them roll into a nearby garden. I wanted them to call at my door.

D.B. explained one day why they didn't, "All the kids in our street are scared of him. I'm not afraid. I'll show him one day."

Emily-Brooke ignored him and skipped off to talk to me, "School is fun. I love getting a new reading book. I am in the red group." This meant she snapped up lots of books to read. "It is the top reading group," she announced to me as she turned the book over and over in her hands. Her eyes sparkled. She would put her finger on the shiny cover, drifting it over the title and then she would smell the pages.

Emily-Brooke would run home. I would always scan for her at 2.15pm. I kept watch on the bottom of the lane and there she would appear. Running through my black swinging gate and tapping at my door. I never grew bored of waiting for her. I truly loved her.

Sometimes, D.B. met her in the garden. He hugged Emily-Brooke and spun her around. Their never-ending stories of adventures and hopes and dreams echoed around me followed by the sound of laughter.

Other times, Abigail opened my front door and welcomed her.

Emily-Brooke would read her entire reading book to her mummy from cover to cover. Her mother would lie on the settee with her eyes closed whilst Emily-Brooke happily read. At times, Abigail dozed off but she never told Emily-Brooke, and so I would take over and listen. The stories were short but I always found them interesting. Most of the stories had a house in them and I always wondered if they were like me. When she finished her book, she would skip happily off into the garden.

*

It was October and the big brother, Samuel, arrived home from the Merchant Navy. He entered my door where the roses were soft and brown. Walter asked, "When are you going back?"

The kids moaned when he said, "In a couple of weeks."

Sam was big and strong. He lifted Emily-Brooke up and spun her around. D.B. eyeballed him with total admiration. His suitcase held many treasures, like playing cards. Emily-Brooke, Sarah, Walter and Abigail were not allowed to see. Only D.B. hustled a peak at them. There were brown bags filled with gifts, and Emily-Brooke and Sarah received a wooden Pinocchio each. D.B. got a brown leather digital watch. Samuel brought laughter and fun into me but it was short-lived. He had to return to the Navy, and his big smile and booming laughter disappeared.

Walter smiled when he left.

*

It was November and Trixie had puppies. Three were like her; brown and white Jack Russells. And one like the chocolate poodle that lived three doors down. The puppies were squidgy to hold and smelt strange; like wood and stale rain which had seeped into the little wooden playhouse where the puppies were kept. Sarah picked up the one that resembled a chocolate poodle.

"The best one is mine. It's called Cuddles!" she announced proudly to Emily-Brooke.

Emily-Brooke smiled and nodded her head. Her tummy stuck out at the bottom of her T-shirt. Was her top too small for her?

Sarah held the puppy close to her body and buried her face in its curls. Its warm, pudgy tummy stuck out and leaned on her shoulder cosily. It was so small Sarah held it with one hand. I knew she experienced an amazing love for that little, helpless puppy. I knew as she smiled and stole Emily-Brooke's hand, squeezing it happily. Emily-Brooke smiled too and so did I.

Sarah looked down at Emily-Brooke's face and said, "You know you have cute dimples." She squeezed her cheeks and then she said, "I love you, you know. You're my little sister." She placed the little puppy back into the cardboard box beside Trixie. "We'll share Cuddles," she said kindly. I was so pleased.

A daddy long-legs suddenly flew wildly around the playhouse, and both Sarah and Emily-Brooke screamed.

Their dad called them: "Sarah. Emily-Brooke. Dinner!"

They were both happy to leave the shed with the daddy long-legs swirling around like a mad thing and entered the house laughing.

Sarah leaned towards Emily-Brooke and whispered, "He smells funny again. He must be drinking." They watched him staggering around the kitchen, dishing out the Irish stew and uncomfortably buttering bread on his big hand through bleary eyes.

Walter planted himself down and examined his two girls eating their stew.

"Ye know what I got for Christmas?" he said with a slur, holding his head up with his large hand.

"What?" asked Sarah.

"An orange."

There was a long silence.

"I said an orange. Did yas hear me?" He leaned over and grabbed an orange from our fruit basket. He held it up to their faces.

"Daddy, you're joking," Emily-Brooke said.

"Nope, I'm not joking. I got an orange. I used to look forward to it every year. Ye kids want everything these days. Too greedy."

"We're not greedy, Daddy," said Emily-Brooke.

"Well, we'll see when Christmas rolls around," said Walter, throwing the orange back into the basket and leaning back on the kitchen chair. The two front legs of the chair rose a little.

"What you mean?" asked Sarah.

"We'll see how greedy yas are then. When ye write yer list." He banged the two front legs of the chair down hard and glared at the girls.

There was a long silence. Emily-Brooke began to eat her stew. The clink of her spoon echoed through my kitchen.

"Yousons think I'm a… a good father?"

"Yes, daddy. You're the best daddy ever. Best in the whole world," said Sarah who jumped up and ran to hug Walter. He simply ignored her and stood up. Sarah's face fell.

"Good," he said and wiped the side off his hand across his mouth. He left them and made his way up my stairs. Emily-Brooke got up and moved to Sarah's side. She reached out with her small hand and their fingers laced together for a split second.

Sarah snapped her hand away and said, "Shut up!" Odd as Emily-Brooke had not uttered a word.

Walter crawled onto his bed keeping all his clothes on.

That night, Sarah climbed down from her bunk bed and slipped in beside Emily-Brooke. In the darkness, I could see her wrap her arms around Emily-Brooke. She broke the silence with a whisper, "I love you, Emily-Brooke. I really do. I love you." Sarah drew small circles on her sister's back with her fore-finger. Gentle. I watched until she fell asleep.

*

It was December and the roses were dead. Some lay on my path like disregarded leather boots. The kids from the street changed their rapping-on-doors game to pinging the windows with stones. They fumbled about the ground trying to pick stones with their pink bare fingers and got ready to run when one was found. Egging each other on to be the one that threw the first stone. They dared to do it several times to my windows. I was as livid as were the adults inside, especially Walter. I didn't want cracked windows. I didn't want to feel that pain.

Emily-Brooke was a constant smiler and a people-pleaser at home, and I knew she would be the same at school; popular and loved by her whole class. She enjoyed school immensely. I loved listening to her teaching her teddies on my stairs.

"Okay, class. Get your books out. Do your work. I want no talking." I pretended to be one of her bears and I enjoyed doing the simple sums that she would write out on scraps of paper torn from her notebooks. She told us, "I'm the teacher. We are going to have fun today." School must be a wonderful house.

Walter and Sarah rarely talked to her. Her sister's love for her in the shed faded over the weeks and she fought daily with Emily-Brooke. Sarah's violence towards her escalated. She squashed her hand under her foot, took sweets off her, and locked her in the small cupboard under my stairs and left her there.

Abigail stayed in bed each day longer and longer. She didn't eat much and cried every time Walter spoke to her with a raised voice.

Emily-Brooke lost her smile. It only appeared when she entered her pretend world of being a mummy herself or when she worked hard at being a teacher. She looked after her baby dolls: changing, feeding and nursing them. She started making small books out of pages using a stapler her brother Samuel entrusted to her on one of his visits.

"Go after him!" her mum cried desperately, interrupting our made-up world. Emily-Brooke ran into the park where she often pushed her Chatty Cathy doll in a second-hand pram. She followed him slipping constantly on the black ice.

The always angry, always drunk dad.

How was Emily-Brooke going to coax him back to her mum? He was staggering on ahead determined to go back into the city to the nearest pub. She, a skinny, ten-year-old and no match for a man with hands like shovels. A man whose only communication was either a grunt or a yelling match when in this state.

He crossed the large wooden bridge and disappeared into the darkness. Emily-Brooke stood forlornly and pointlessly.

Abigail didn't say, "Wear your coat, pet." The cold air must have stabbed her like mini knives. I observed her, far away in the distance. She waited for ten minutes and returned to her irate mum.

Emily-Brooke ran up my stairs and into her bedroom. She cried and I cried too.

FIFTEEN
MOLLY

After another playground duty, it was finally lunchtime.
Mum had made me egg and onion sandwiches, and had
cut up fruit for me. I loved when Mum made my lunch.
Her detail always amused me, especially when I was in
primary school. My mum was the one who pressed a
cookie cutter onto the bread and made star shapes one day
and snowmen the next. When she found the bird cutters in
her home catalogue, she really upped her game. I was
beyond delighted. She would leave little notes too telling
me that she loved me. I had saved them all; placing them
carefully into my black book in the pocket at the back.

I fetched my lunchbox and, following Mrs Craig's
precise directions, I made my way over to the staffroom.
This twenty-minute slot was for all the classroom
assistants.

I knew I'd struggle to get on with these people. Any
person who loved working in education would struggle to
be a friend of mine. I took a deep breath and opened the
door.

"Oh, hello Molly," said Nicola, who I had met earlier,
"Sit here and I will introduce you to everyone." Glad to
see a familiar face, I edged my way along the back of the
chairs and took the weight off my feet. I opened my
lunchbox and unwrapped the tin foil.

"Stinky-linky," said Nicola as she leaned over and
sniffed my sandwiches, "Move. I hate the smell of egg."

"Sorry?" I said, feeling a bit sick.

"Move. Sit over there away from me," she barked in my face. She was serious and I was shocked. I got up and moved over to the other side of the table. I knew I was in a school, but surely bullying stopped at the children. I kept my head down. She was not a peahen. She was a bloody emu! Those things attack and like the sound of their own voices.

A brown-haired girl with doe-eyes and a pretty face strolled in, settling down beside me.

"Hi, I'm Pauline. Are you enjoying your first day?" Her voice high-pitched and child-like and she continually blinked her eyes.

"Yes," I said, taking another nibble out of my sandwich.

"I'm in P.4. I'm a special needs CA. I work with a little girl. She's a sweetie."

Working with one child would be much easier. I looked at her and noticed she had a constant smile on her face. A little lovebird.

Nicola did most of the talking in the staffroom and the rest listened. It was clear she was the alpha-female and what she said was law.

"Pauline, pour me out a tea there," she demanded.

"Oh, okay. No problem," said Pauline leaving her seat and lifting the teapot for Nicola. Her eyes blinking fast now.

"So, Molly, where did you work before this?" Nicola asked.

"I didn't. This is my first job. I'm seventeen," I answered.

"You're only a baby. Why did you leave school? Did you not want to go to college?"

"Eh, no. I was sick of school," I said, wanting the questions to stop.

"So, you went and got yourself a job in a school? Are you stupid?"

"Come on, Nicola. Be nice," Pauline said weakly and with a nervous laugh.

"She said she didn't want to be in a school. Now she's working in one. Crazy," Nicola said with a short, dismissive laugh. A burning sensation splattered through the pit of my stomach and I struggled to eat the rest of my lunch.

I didn't stand up for myself. What should I have said? I couldn't say I wasn't stupid when *clearly*, I am. I looked around the staffroom at all the other CAs and calmed my churning stomach by telling myself that they weren't all emus like Nicola.

The bell rang and everyone stood up, including the emu. Great, I didn't even meet the others properly. I only knew Nicola the bully, and Pauline the blinking-smiler. I made my way back to the classroom.

When I stepped in, I entered the world of P.B.L.

Nightmare.

Children were everywhere! The side door was open and children sauntered in and out willy-nilly. There were kids in a role-play area, a box they called the "TinkerBox": a place to tinker with nuts and bolts and screwdrivers and hammers, a pretend sweetshop... Some were playing with playdough at a round table, others were doing jigsaws on the ground, some had tablets and were taking photographs or short videos of the chaos. Who would want a recording of this?

Mrs Craig was over in the block area and the children around her were building a tower that looked as if it could crash any minute.

"Oh, glad to have you back, Miss Jolliff. Would you watch the children outside for me please? Mrs Fulton is out there. She's a parent volunteer. She will show you how the children play outside. There are different play zones," she explained.

I stepped outside. Just as chaotic. Vehicles zoomed around a road made with white paint. Children moved here and there with balls or hula-hoops in their arms. A whole crowd of children dressed up in ridiculous costumes pranced around the entire playground as if they were at a carnival. There was even one child blowing bubbles directly in my face. I was totally out of my depth here.

Mrs Fulton was a tall lady with short dark hair. Overly kind to the children who followed her about as if she was the Pied Piper. She had a permanent grin on her face and wild flowers in her hair. I zig-zagged over to her, avoiding the children.

"Hi, I'm Molly. Is there anything you need me to do?"

"Oh, hello Molly. I'm Mrs Fulton, I'm Grace's mum. It would be great if you played hopscotch over in the number zone," she said as she pointed over to the left.

Hopscotch: my favourite game as a kid. I used to spend hours on a hopscotch grid Dad painted for me in our back garden. There was a faded outline still there today.

"Okay, no problem," I said and skipped over to the area deciding this might be fun.

SIXTEEN
HOUSE

Christmas came and went, and Emily-Brooke acquired a blackboard. The one she had been admiring dearly for several weekends while looking in the shop window of Cameron's: the greatest toyshop in Ballymena. Wow! Her dream to be a teacher set alight once more as she eagerly opened the new box of chalk and made the first green mark on the board. She drew a rectangle, then a triangle on top with a chimney. Tears flowed through my plumbing as she drew my windows. Yes... she was drawing me. Above her picture, she wrote the word "house" and I was complete. My wiring sparked and my floorboards creaked with happiness. Emily-Brooke loved me and I loved her.

*

It was January and the snow was on the ground. Nothing prepared me when I realised the warm, fluffy blankets I had seen on the Christmas card houses were really cold, sharp sheets of wet seeping into my roof. I was disgusted. It was freezing. The disappointment scared me. I still knew my foundations were strong but something changed in me that month and I was different. Weak and unsteady. Yes, the snow melted from my roof but it left with it an

107

uncertainty that rose its ugly head regularly to throw me off tilter.

The children were at school and Walter at work. Abigail alone in the living room watched something on the box: *Columbo*. She had taken up knitting and was knitting a long scarf.

"In, over, pull through the loop and slip it off. In, over, pull through the loop and slip it off. In, over, pull through the loop and slip it off," she said, blowing out a long breath and smiling. This went on and on, and I tried to ignore her. But her voice echoed through my walls and I was forced to listen.

"In, over, pull through the loop and slip it off. In, over, pull through the loop and slip it off," she said with a set jaw.

The grey box didn't drown out her words and time dragged that day.

"In, over, pull through the loop and slip it off. In, over, pull through the loop and slip it off," she said as she crossed her legs and leaned back on the settee.

I remembered feeling relieved when someone tapped on my door. A man with a parcel. Tall and lean. His grey hair tied back in a ponytail showing off his haggard face and hazel eyes. When Abigail opened the door, Trixie slipped past her.

"Parcel for Walter Williams?"

"That's my husband," Abigail said as she tilted her body towards the man.

"Sign here, love," he said. Abigail signed the page attached to the clipboard and accepted the parcel from the man.

The delivery man bounced back into his van and Abigail closed my door.

I heard the bump. I heard the yelp. I heard the screech and so did Abigail. The parcel slipped to the floor.

"Trixie," she called as she reopened my door. Her hand went to her stomach.

"I'm so sorry. I didn't see him," he said from his window; his cheeks burning red. His voice wavering. Abigail backed into my outer wall.

"Trixie! Trixie!" Abigail called as the man slid out of his van and made his way around the back where Trixie's little body lay. Abigail's face turned white and she stood with her hands jammed under her armpits.

"I'm so sorry. I'm really sorry," he said as he tugged at the collar of his black jumper. Abigail moved behind his van, flinching at a car horn in the far distance. Abigail threw herself onto her knees sobbing.

"No, no, no, no…" she cried.

"I didn't see him. I'm so sorry," he said, putting his hand on her back. Abigail shrugged him off.

"It's a her, you stupid man. You killed her," she said lifting Trixie into her arms and staggered back into the front garden.

Walter was at work and I saw Edward's father running out of his house, three houses up the lane. He ran over to Abigail.

"What happened?"

"He killed Trixie. He killed Trixie," she screamed in a hysterical voice staring at the man in the van. Her shoulders quaked and her posture stooped. Trixie lay lifeless in her arms.

Edward's father dragged his hands over the legs of his trousers. He inhaled a deep breath and looked at the bewildered van driver.

"Don't worry it was an accident. Abigail is in shock. It's better if you just go… Go."

"I'm so sorry. I didn't see him. I mean her," he said jumping back into his van and driving off.

"Where's Walter?" he asked but Abigail didn't answer. Edward's father prized Trixie out of Abigail's arms. "I'm going to fetch her a blanket. I'll be right back." He carried Trixie, the way you would carry a sleeping baby, out of my garden and advanced with heavy steps into his own garden.

Abigail stood on her own, hugging herself and repeating over and over,

"No. It didn't happen. It didn't happen."

Edward's father was back within seconds but he didn't come back with Trixie. He put his arm around Abigail.

"She's gone, Abigail. Trixie has gone." Abigail sobbed in his arms and I longed for her to return to her knitting.

By the time, Emily-Brooke came home, Abigail had three neighbours in the house: one making tea, and the others sitting and comforting her. Emily-Brooke ran into the living room and her eyes studied her mother's face.

"What's wrong, Mummy?" she asked, blinking several times, "What happened, Mummy?"

"Oh, Emily-Brooke, something awful happened," Abigail said standing up and running to her daughter.

"What?" asked Emily-Brooke. I didn't want to listen to the answer.

"Trixie got knocked down," said Abigail, closing her eyes and pulling her youngest daughter towards her.

"Oh no, is she hurt? Where is she?" asked Emily-Brooke, pulling away and looking behind her mother.

"She died," said Abigail, tears falling down her face.

"No, Mummy. Not Trixie. Not Trixie," she cried, her chin trembling. She reached out and her mum hugged her again. This time Emily-Brooke stayed close and whispered the name "Trixie" over and over.

My heart broke for Emily-Brooke that evening.

*

It was February and D.B. proudly announced he had gotten into the Cadets. He stopped polishing his shoes and changed them to boots.

"I'm getting out of here," he told Emily-Brooke and her face crumbled.

"Why, D.B?" she asked, "I don't want you to go."

"Him. I'm getting away from him," he said polishing his boots harder than before.

"Who's him?"

"Walter," he answered as she tilted her head to the side. She went into the garden and watched her mummy cutting the rose bush down, leaving five buds at the bottom.

"What you doing, Mummy?" she asked.

"I'm pruning, pet. Cutting away the older roses to make way for the new. We all have to make way for the new, Emily-Brooke. We all have to," Abigail answered.

*

It was March. The roses sprung from their dormant state and children played in the garden most days now the weather was warmer. It wasn't long before the street became more enticing. All the children in the street grouped together like the leaves now growing on the trees.

Lisa and her big brother, Stephen.

The snottery-nosed twins, Ellen and Claire, lived directly opposite. Always with candles of snot dripping from their nostrils; the top half of their hair darker than the bottom half. Walter used to say, "Ye could fry chips on those kids' heads."

Edward the tall boy, who hung about with D.B., lived in the well-presented house to the right, and Stacey, the pretty bully, lived to my left.

It was Easter, and Stacey had convinced everyone to bring an Easter egg to her garden. She had made a sign saying: join my Easter egg gang. She placed it on her garden bench and stood at her gate, waiting for her victims.

Her hair in long blonde ringlets caught a glimmer from the sun and held onto it, dangling below her waist. Her father called her, "my little Princess" but I knew no royal blood flowed in those veins. The pain behind her light brown eyes cried out as she leaned over the gate and stared up at me to see if Sarah was going to join her gang. She tilted her head and allowed her ringlets to fall to the side. When she stood upright again, a thick strand was in her mouth and she sucked at it hard, before spitting it out.

I tried to blank out the information her house had told me; the horrors of what occurred within his walls. He would creak the information through his floorboards and unnerve mine in the process.

Stacey's cruelty to others was self-preservation. Her affection and love had died in her father's arms on that first night. Now this cold, numb, little girl spent her time making other children miserable. Stacey would never be as harsh as her father during those long miserable nights she had to endure. But at least it gave her something to recall when he entered her room. And that must have helped her to blank out the unthinkable.

Sarah ran past Stacey's house and read the sign. She snuck back to me, found Emily-Brooke and seized two Easter eggs from my kitchen sideboard. They joined the other children in Stacey's garden. I guarded their every move from my top window. I never trusted Sarah around Emily-Brooke, and I never liked Stacey around her either. Too cruel. She kicked our Trixie once; when she was alive. She pinched a little boy's cheeks, and she wrote bad words on the ground with coloured sticks. I was glad when the rain came and washed away what she had done.

To be part of Stacey's gang, the first rule was simple.

"Rule number one. You've to give me yer sweets from yer Easter egg," she said with an intense, penetrating stare.

Edward tutted and marched off back to his house with his Easter egg intact under his arm. Sarah nudged Emily-Brooke.

"Open your egg and give your sweets to Stacey." The sweets looked amazing in their shiny, brown wrapping. Emily-Brooke turned the sweets over and over in her hand the way she did her reading book. Paused. Then handed them over.

Stacey's face lit up. "Now, yer sweets," she said glaring down at Sarah.

"No chance," Sarah said holding her egg tight, "You've got hers so we both get in your gang."

"Not a hope," said Stacey. She caught Sarah by the hair and battered her face off her wooden gate.

Sarah grabbed Emily-Brooke and trailed her back to me. Emily-Brooke replaced her egg on the sideboard of my kitchen. We both knew inside the treasure was gone.

***

Jack coughs and the memory fades. I'm glad. I am happy to fold up the memory towels once more and close the door of my spick-and-span hot press. I know I need to remain in the present. Look after Sophia. That must be my priority.

He throws the wallpaper scraper onto the ground and sinks to my floor. He doesn't move. His head is in his hands. New wallpaper lies on their bed. Pink. Stephanie likes pink. She smiled when she brought it home with her.

"You're going to love this colour, Jack. Trust me."

"Pink? Pink in the bedroom? Are you sure?" He shook his head. I know he didn't like it then, and I know he still doesn't like it now.

His misery is clear. He jumps to his feet; his face red. Jack pulls my wallpaper off at a faster rate and it is clear he can't hold his temper. He reminds me of Walter.

"Stephanie should be helping me. She's always out with her so-called friends. What about Sophia? She needs to spend more time with Sophia," he rants and I don't trust him. Maybe he will turn to drink like Walter did. Maybe he will grunt at Sophia, stomp around my house and take out his frustrations on his wife or little Sophia. Time will tell. Time will tell.

***

"Can we just talk without you cutting me off?" said Abigail standing up and stepping towards Walter.

"No, ye can't because I'm sick of yer nagging. I'm sick of yer kids and I'm sick of y-"

"*Our* kids."

"One is," said Walter pounding into my kitchen and eating a cold piece of ham from a plate on our sideboard.

"Walt. What did you say? What did you say?" repeated Abigail following Walter into the kitchen.

"I said one." He threw the plate onto my floor and as it crashed into many pieces, he grabbed Abigail's neck. He propelled her up against my wall and her face changed to purple. "Do ya want to ask me now what I said?" His hand eased and Abigail slid down and sat on the floor. She choked over and over, and D.B. appeared at my kitchen doorway.

"You okay, Mum?" he said, throwing himself onto his knees and turning Abigail's face to his.

"I will be," she answered.

Walter opened the fridge and took out a bottle of beer. He opened it with his teeth and the crack of air escaping filled my kitchen. He spat the cap onto the ground and took a long gulp.

"Clean up this mess," he said as he left my kitchen and turned the grey box on in my living room. He selected ITV this time: *Hong Kong*. He relaxed down and threw his feet up onto the coffee table. My thirst for knowledge forced me to watch it with him. I had discovered that this odd box could improve my vocabulary, make me laugh and entertain me. So, I spent many hours watching and learning here. After *Hong Kong*, we watched *The Best of Morecambe and Wise* and then *Hawaiian Eye*. Walter fell asleep and I continued watching *The News*. Halfway through, Abigail yanked out the plug and Walter was left in the dark until morning.

***

My head hurts. These memories refuse to remain closed in.

Jack leaves the master bedroom and walks into the baby room where Sophia is sleeping. He kneels and kisses her on the cheek. Good. He cares. He smiles down at his daughter and I like his smile despite seeing the blob of gum still in his mouth. My headache eases, and my roof soothes my entire building. Jack rarely smiles, but when he does it reminds me of Emily-Brooke. He too has one dimple on his left cheek that I see occasionally. Maybe that's why he reminds me of Emily-Brooke and my hot press door remains open.

SEVENTEEN
MOLLY

I slipped into bed and hugged myself, glad I didn't need to set my alarm for tomorrow. I closed my eyes and drifted off to sleep.

I dreamt that I was back in the fortune-teller's house in his living room. I stood and looked at the photograph on the wall. I put out my hand and was stabbed by the thorns on the roses that grew on the left-hand side of that house. I realised I was inside the photograph. I looked down at my bleeding hand and wondered why it didn't hurt.

I nudged the door and it opened. I stepped inside. A child's Bible lay on the hall table. A small dog ran up to me in the hallway and followed me as I ran up the stairs. A man painting a wall in one of the bedrooms turned slowly to me, I saw he was writing the words, "Children should be seen and not heard" with pink paint.

He started banging the paintbrush on a large dressing table covered with bottles and makeup brushes.

Thankfully, I woke with a start.

Josh was banging on my bedroom door.

"Molly, Molly, can ya lend me a couple of quid?" he said in a grating voice.

"Josh, I just had a mad dream."

"Molly, can ya lend me a couple of quid?"

"Go away," I mumbled, still freaked out.

"Blondie, please. Ya work now. Do ya not rack up cash for what ya do?"

"Josh, go away. I'm sleeping," I moaned and turned over towards my bedroom wall, bringing my knees up to my body. That trip to the fortune-teller had affected me more than I thought. Josh ignored me and marched into my room. The first thing that hit me was the strong smell of his cheap aftershave.

"Get out!" I yelled.

"Flipping heck, Blondie. Ya need to tidy this place. Where's your purse? How do ya find anything in here?"

"Josh, get out. You sound like Mum. Clear off." I turned over and forced my eyes to open. He pranced around my room, looking for my purse.

"I really need this cool Xbox game and my mate on Finsta has it. Technically, he's willing to sell it to me for half the price it is in the shops." He picked up random items from my floor and threw them back down again.

"Josh, my room may look disorganised but really, it's an organised chaos. Stop moving my stuff," I said swinging my legs out of bed and pushing my feet into my fluffy, grey rabbit slippers.

"Ah, I found it. Nice one," he said holding my purse out in front of my face.

"Josh, I've nothing for you," I grabbed my purse off him and stood up. He followed me downstairs begging the whole time, trying to convince me this game was the best game ever.

"Josh, I've money to get to the rink on the bus, buy a Coke and take the bus back. Nothing more and nothing less," I said as I tugged a withered leaf off Charlie, "Good morning, Charlie. You're looking good."

"Did ya not rack up cash from your first week at work?" Josh asked again.

"No and I only did three days. I get paid at the end of the month, not at the end of the week," I said with a sigh, "Go and ask Mum."

"Mum said no, why do ya think I was asking you?"

I ignored him and nabbed a banana, strawberries and raspberries from our fruit bowl, and a yogurt from the fridge to make my Saturday morning smoothie.

"Josh, how do you make an apple turnover?" I pressed the button on the blender and watched his lips move but heard nothing.

Joshua looked animated as he spoke; he threw his arms in the air and spun around to add punch to his words. Words that I didn't even hear. All my life I had found him entertaining; he had a way with words and always gave good advice. I smiled at him and removed my finger off the blender button.

"Push it down a hill."

"Is that a yes then?" he said with a smile that showed the gap in between his two front teeth.

"Eh, no."

"How many times do I have to tell ya? Your jokes are not funny."

I ignored him.

I had to meet Anita at three by the bus stop, so I knew I had plenty of time to do my hair and makeup. I poured my smoothie into a tall glass and looked up in time to see Josh walk off in disgust.

All he cared about was his stupid Xbox. I was not his sponsor now I was working.

Mum wandered in and stole a sip of my breakfast.

"Oh my. Nice! You see, you are not just a pretty face."

"Morning, Mum. Do you want one?"

"Sure, darling," Mum said with a smile, "So, do you feel like a working woman?"

A working woman? Was that what I was now? A woman? I suddenly felt grown up.

"Yes, I do."

"Good."

I might have been a working woman but how long would that be for? There was no way they would keep me on once they found out I was dyslexic.

I inhaled and said, "Saying that, I'm not sure if it's for me."

"Now, what about the ice-skating? What time is your lesson? Do you need a lift?" I hated the fact Mum managed to ignore the important things I said. Did she even pick up when I said, "I'm not sure if it's for me?"

"I don't think the job is really me, Mum," I repeated.

"You have to work. We can't pay for your hobby now that you are nearly eighteen. It's way too expensive. There comes a time in everyone's life when they need to grow up and pay their own way," Mum said leaning close to me and keeping her piercing eyes on mine.

"So, I'm working to pay for my ice-skating. Is that what you're saying?"

"Are you winding me up? Yes, that's exactly what I'm saying."

"You're the one who made me go in the first place."

"Oh my... Made you go? Made you go? Hardly! We sacrificed a lot for you, Molly. Once we found out you had learning diff... dyslexia, we were advised to find a sport for you. Essential, they said. You needed us to build up your self-esteem. Maybe ice-skating wasn't the best choice money-wise. Your father nearly had to take a second job."

"You sent me because... because I was dyslexic?" I asked. I never knew that! I thought Mum had sent me because I was good at it. Mum lifted her glass to her lips and pressed against it for a couple of seconds before she drank more of the smoothie. She then gently placed the glass back onto the counter.

"That was not the only reason. It was one of them. I wanted you to go initially as I wanted you to have a hobby. If I had known how expensive it was, I would have encouraged you to take up a cheaper hobby... like chess," Mum said in a slow, steady pace.

"Surely, it wasn't that expensive."

"We missed out on several holidays for you, Molly. I hope you realise that. Your costumes and lessons were not cheap."

So, this was a ploy to hide my learning difficulties!

"I know that, Mum, and I thank you both for that," I said really thanking only Dad as he worked and Mum didn't.

"Well, the question you need to be asking yourself is: do you enjoy it? If you don't enjoy it then leave, darling. It's not as if your dyslexia is holding you back anymore. You've secured a job now. Things have changed."

She knew I loved it. I was hardly going to leave. I had just moved out of the intermediate level. Why would I leave now? Mum knew ice-skating was my passion. When I performed, I was in control of my life and free. Ice-skating helped me express myself. Why would she ask me if I enjoyed it? Maybe she didn't have a clue about how I loved ice-skating. She only sent me there because she was advised to, after all.

"I enjoy ice-skating. Of course, I do, but I won't be able to afford it on my own."

"Your father and I think you should pay your own way. I know how expensive it is, Molly. We have been paying for it since you were eight,"

What if I didn't make that much money? I needed ice-skating in my life. It was what I was good at. Probably the *only* thing I excelled at, in fact. It made me feel calm and serene. Where I needed to be.

"I can't imagine earning much in my wages, Mum. Will you and Dad carry on helping me with the expenses if I land a rubbish wage?" I asked.

"Well, we'll see. It depends on how much you make. In the meantime, enjoy us paying for your hobby, darling." She drank down the rest of her smoothie fast, stepped to the sink and filled the glass with hot water. She swirled it around to rinse it out and with one splash emptied it into the sink.

I sipped my smoothie and stayed quiet. I was not giving up ice-skating now I was in the higher league. I watched Mum leave the kitchen and I rinsed out my own glass.

I went upstairs, had a shower and sauntered into my bedroom. I plopped down in front of my mirror. I pulled my hair up into a high bun, and selected out a blue and silver butterfly clip from my jewellery box. It suited my blonde hair. I put on my footless skating tights and my pink and black leotard, and focused on myself.

Ice-skating helped me to stay fit. I couldn't imagine not having it in my life. I grabbed my tracksuit bottoms and jerked them on along with my Adidas top.

I sent Anita a text:

Mum doing my head in. She said I have to pay for my ice-skating now I'm working! See you at 3 at the BS. M.

Two seconds later, I got a message back:

Don't worry. See you soon, A.

At three, I met Anita at the bus stop. She too had her hair in a tight bun, ready for action with her hedgehog necklace in her mouth.

"Hi, chick," she said when I arrived, pressing the hedgehog onto her bottom lip, "What's going on with yer mum, then?"

"Oh, she's doing my head in. Banging on about me having to pay my fees for ice-skating and that includes paying for all my outfits," I said, leaving out the fact Mum had sent me to ice-skating because of my dyslexia and, now that I had a job, she believed all my reading and writing issues had magically disappeared. So, ice-skating had become pointless.

"That's going to be crap. Have ya checked out how much the fees are now we're working within the professional group?" asked Anita.

"No, but I can imagine," I said.

A loud scream came from a rough-looking house behind the bus stop. The front door opened and a kid came flying out. Tears streamed down his round, red face. I knew him.

I registered that it was James from my class. I stepped in front of Anita.

"He's from my class. I don't want him to spot me. The last thing I want to do is meet someone from my work," I whispered.

"He looks upset," said Anita as she stared over at James.

"Not my problem," I said, as our bus turned into our bus stop. I grabbed my purse out of my rucksack, paid the bus driver and went to the back of the bus. We always sat right at the back. It's what we called "our happy place".

Once we settled down in our seats, Anita turned around and said, "That was creepy at that fortune-teller's flat. What was his name again?" she asked.

"He never flipping told us his name. He just kept yelling at me, 'Children should be seen and not heard, Children should be seen and not heard'," I said, opening my eyes wide, pursing my lips and throwing my arms into the air as I said it, making Anita burst out laughing, "Not only that but I had a horrific dream last night that I was back in his flat and I went into that creepy photograph."

"Which photograph?"

"The one with the house with the net curtains. I was chased by a dog. Not good."

"Not good. At least the fortune-teller didn't tell ya that you'd get married one minute and divorced the next. Ridiculous…"

I stifled a giggle.

"Never again," I said and Anita nodded. We both stared out the window and relaxed. I suddenly felt guilty for not speaking to James. I wondered if I should get off and go back to make sure he was all right. I started to bite my nails.

A few hesitant minutes passed and Anita chirped into my thoughts.

"I was watching this mad YouTube video last night and apparently, there are two types of people out there."

"Out where?" I asked convincing myself that James would be okay.

"Here in *this* world," she said. I snorted and that made Anita laugh. The old woman three seats in front of us turned around and fired us both a dirty look.

"There *is* only one world, Anita. Have you lost your tiny mind?"

"I know. I know. Anyway, where was I? Oh yes, apparently the first type is people who have an internal monologue."

"What do you mean?"

I loved Anita's obsession with YouTube and how she relayed it all back to me. Even though half the time I hadn't a clue what she was talking about.

"Well, as ya are sitting here now, is there anything going on in yer head?" Thoughts of James' face were the only things in my mind.

"Like what?"

"Well, is there a voice going on inside yer head?"

"Do you mean my thoughts?"

"Yes," she said, bouncing on her seat. Rewarded by another dirty look. "Sorry," said Anita and she stuck out her tongue when the woman turned away. Then she popped her hedgehog into her mouth.

"Go on," I said.

"Oh, yes," she said and spat out the necklace, "Where was I before I was rudely interrupted? Oh yes. What were ya thinking there?"

"Just how crazy my best friend is, but I love you anyway," I said with a smile trying to ignore the fact that I should have got off the bus but didn't.

"Well apparently, there are other people who don't have that voice in their head. If they wanted to think of something they wanted to say in their head, they couldn't do it. They'd say it out loud. Isn't that mad?"

"I don't get it," I said.

"It's simple. Some people can't speak in their brain."

"Anita, you're the craziest person I know because you come out with conversations like this," I said squeezing her arm, "So, how do these people read?"

"Which people?"

"The people who can't speak in their brain."

"They see the sentence structure and they move their lips when they read. They don't see the setting in books. They just see the words."

"Anita, you talk crap," I said.

I had no idea what she was on about half the time but I loved my cockatiel friend all the same.

"I'll send ya the link and ya can watch it for yerself," she said as she looked out the window again playing with her necklace.

"So, do you think inside your head?" I asked.

"Yes, I daydream all the time. Apparently, people who don't have an internal monologue don't daydream. Imagine that," said Anita.

"I can't," I said letting out a short snort as Anita pulled out her phone and connected her earphones to it, handing me one. I stuck it in my ear and Megan Trainer blasted out a song about love.

Just before our stop came up, we both jumped up. I stuck my rucksack on my back and lifted my skate-bag. We both made our way down the bus.

When we arrived at the ice-rink, I waved over at Victoria and Janice and they waved back. Victoria went onto the ice with the grace of a swan and immediately admiration glided over me like when I first met her. I was only nine.

Now she looked like a condor. She built up speed, turned and did a back spin, followed by a Lutz jump as she soared over the ice.

I stretched down, held my position and then unzipped my skate-bag. I saw James' face in my head. I rose up and slipped off my tracksuit bottoms, put on my socks followed by my skates. Anita did the same. I tied my laces tight right up to my ankles. I stood up and unzipped my Adidas top and folded it as Victoria flew around the rink.

Definitely, a condor! Was she floating or skating over this frozen cloud of water? Was I now the type of person who didn't help a crying child?

I stepped onto the ice and built up my own speed. Victoria and James were forgotten and I became a bird myself, gliding through the air. Ice-skating, the only thing that worked. That stopped me from being swallowed up by words flowing from a large building with the word "library" over the doorway. Ice-skating, the release, the missing word that tripped up on my tongue from an unfinished sentence. Ice-skating, the bath filled with shiny bubbles just for me. An unexpected ice cream. The happy flutter when I first fell in love. My escape. I was in my perfect place where all my worries about reading and writing couldn't catch me.

Cool air swirled all around my body and fired short blasts on my face. I was free. Free. A bird. Not a happy duck on the ice. Something special, something unique. A bird of beauty and perfection and yet I didn't know which bird I was.

It didn't matter, I flew over the ice the way I read a card with a one-word greeting.

Swift.

I skated to a short, sharp halt and I knew I should have gotten off the bus for James.

EIGHTEEN
HOUSE

Jack takes a stick of gum from the yellow packet. He pulls the silver sleeve out of the wrapper the way he pulls items around me. He flicks open the silver paper and rolls the stick of gum up in his fingers before placing it in his mouth. The sweet, mint escapes from his gaping mouth for a second and disappears quick. A food humans don't swallow has always been a boring concept to me. Jack lifts his mobile up and paces my living room.

"Where is she?" His monotonous tone is sharp and the words echo through my house. It is late. Stephanie is not in. We wait. And as we wait, I take out a memory towel and recall when Abigail was out in my garden.

***

It was April and Abigail sprayed the roses with insecticide. Insecticides destroyed insects. Was there a spray that could eliminate me? Houses were strong and secure. There was no need to worry.

"Get inside and stop fussing around those roses," yelled Walter, and Abigail entered the house, "Ya never make time for me."

126

"I do," whispered Abigail, "Do you want some tea?"

"Oh, so I do exist," he said. Abigail rushed into my kitchen and made the tea. She stepped back into my living room and handed the tea to Walter.

"Did ya put in sugar?"

"No, I forgot. I'll fetch it now," Abigail turned to walk back into the kitchen. Walter crashed his mug of tea and the hot liquid scalded down my walls. My wallpaper changed colour and I knew that it would have to be changed. More work needed within my walls. My floorboards creaked.

"Walter," whispered Abigail, and he grabbed her wrist, pushing her against my soaking wet wall. He was making the stain worse and my wires sparked.

"Ya forget everything. You'd forget your head if it wasn't screwed on. You're useless." He rammed his fist against her chin and tears crept out of Abigail's eyes. I was surprised. Why would she cry now and yet she didn't cry when he had kicked her on the leg last week? Her leg had bruised.

***

Jack's phone rings and he answers it.

"Where are you?... No, I want you to come home... You can. Don't do this, Stephanie. Sophia needs you... I'll come and get you... What do you mean? Where are you?... Don't hang up! Don't you dare. Stephanie!" Jack throws his mobile against my wall and it breaks.

He's frantic now.

I ignore him.

Thoughts of Abigail and the children re-enter my mind.

***

They were leaving. Finally, Abigail had had enough.

127

"I should have divorced you years ago," she said to Walter who remained silent on the stairs.

"Say something," I screamed but his unemotional face said nothing.

They were moving to Bangor: a bright seaside town. Abigail promised it had all they would ever need or want.

"It never rains in Bangor," Emily-Brooke explained to me as she packed her books into a cardboard box. Maybe they needed to decamp. Emily-Brooke would be much happier away from Walter.

Abigail called the two girls and D.B. into my master bedroom, and held onto all their hands: D.B.'s hand in one, and Sarah and Emily-Brooke's in the other.

"Sarah, you will move in with Aunt Mabel. You need to finish your schooling here and work on your exams."

"I love Aunt Mabel. So, I don't mind, Mum," said Sarah pulling her hand away from Emily-Brooke and hugging Abigail.

"D.B. and Emily-Brooke, we will go together to Bangor. I have rented out a house."

D.B. smiled. I couldn't remember the last time I saw him smile. Was this his first time? His whole face lit up like the street lamp in front of my gate. His eyes sparkled and he looked different. He looked like a little boy. I was pleasantly surprised. "Sarah, you will come and visit each weekend. It is all going to work out. Don't worry."

Emily-Brooke smiled too. A sinking storm whirled deep down into my foundations. This smile tore me up inside; bouncing from brick to brick. She ran upstairs and packed Beanie into her "going away" box. She was glad and I tried to be happy for her.

Life without Sarah would be easier on Emily-Brooke too, I reasoned with myself.

But what about me?

What about me?

On the day they left, Emily-Brooke turned and said, "Bye, House," and a tear slipped from her eye.

I watched them leave and retired to the cupboard where she had written with green marker upon my floorboards:

John   14:6.   Jesus   saith   unto   him, I am the way, the truth, and the life: no man cometh unto the Father, but by me.

I felt a sadness I had never felt before. Emily-Brooke was gone and I had no one. No family. If Jesus is the way – how can I find him? I must know him to have a father? My heart fluttered. Did a house have a heart? Someone on the television referred to my kitchen as the heart of the home, but this pain affected my entire being. It just didn't make sense.

*

It was May and the roses burst out in full bloom whilst I recoiled down deep into my walls.

NINETEEN
MOLLY

After my warm-up, Terrance appeared in his pink and black shell suit. He insisted his father wore it in the eighties, when his dad was an ice-skating champion in London. Terrance, always in his father's shadow, had entered every ice-skating competition since he was six years old. Apparently, Terrance had "settled" for his present role: teaching our ice-skating group to move our skills up a notch or two.

Terrance wasn't likeable. He was short for a start, and he would shout instructions until you did exactly what he said. A proud peacock. Each year, before the end of summer, his stunning plumage would gradually fall off. His moulting reduced his popularity each year and he became less significant at the rink. His rival peacocks at the ice-rink would excel at competitions and Terrance would be left in their shadow. Refusing to accept this, Terrance became an annoying bird who bossed everyone else around and now that I had joined this group that included me.

His white platinum hair folded over his head, perfectly symmetrically, like a little Lego man's stick-on hair. He would look up at you when he shouted and had this annoying habit of clicking his fingers in your face as he did.

Fiona, his sidekick, accompanied him to every lesson. Everyone would try and guess their relationship with each other. Were they boyfriend and girlfriend? Were they married? She wore a wedding ring. He didn't though. Was Fiona his P.A? She was tall and slim with a thick head of chocolate brown hair that always looked perfect. A perfect crane.

She wore a thin headband that changed colour on a weekly basis. This week it was yellow.

She carried Terrance's skates, helped him to de-robe from his hideous shell suit, and even tied up his laces. The whole time, Terrance barked instructions at us.

"Victoria, gorgeous as usual. Have you been talking to Phil about pairing up?"

Oh, she was going to have a partner? How exciting!

Victoria glided to the edge of the rink and said, "I've just been talking to him on the phone, Terrance."

"That is not going to get you anywhere. Meet up on the ice at least three times this week or you are off the team."

Victoria nodded. Terrance, well-known for throwing ice-skaters off his team and everyone petrified they would be the next victim.

"Molly Jolliff!" he shouted.

Oh, crap. Me next! I stumbled as I made my way to the side of the rink and my cheeks roared red.

"Yes?" I said.

"You know you have only been with me three weeks."

"Yes, Terrance," I agreed.

"How many times have you been on the rink since you joined my team?" he snapped as he elbowed Fiona to the side and stormed over to me.

"Three Saturdays," I whispered.

"What was that? Did you say three? Three..." he snapped his fingers three times. "Not good enough, Molly. I want you on this ice at least three times a week. Do you understand? Over three weeks that will be nine visits. Who do you think will remain on my team? Someone who performs once a week or someone who performs three times a week?"

"I've started a new job and—"

"Irrelevant," he said and slid onto the ice; his head held high, "Did you all warm-up? Let me see you fly, little birds."

The lesson and Sunday passed in a blink. Monday morning arrived too soon. My alarm went off several times but I just pressed the snooze button. Tossing and turning, I couldn't erase that creepy fortune-teller man out of my head or the haunting house with the net curtains in the photograph.

Maybe I shouldn't go back to school. He did yell at me several times not to. I'd love to see Mum's face if I told her I wasn't going back because a fortune-teller told me not to.

I stuck out my arm and reached over to find my phone. I blindly knocked against nail polish bottles, my deodorant and my desk lamp. My loose change clattered to the floor. Finally, my hand found my phone and switched off my alarm. I rolled over and went back to sleep.

The sunlight shining through my window made me open my eyes.

"Oh crap!" I said. Eight o'clock!

I threw myself out of bed and picked random clothes from my wardrobe that were scattered all over my floor. I spotted my half-full energy drink and slurped a slug.

"Flat!" I said tossing it into my already full wastepaper bin. It balanced beautifully on top. I wrestled with myself to pull my trousers on, before I realised I needed to change my underwear and I stripped the trousers back off again. I could face work without a shower but I couldn't live with myself knowing I had the same knickers on for two days in a row. I lifted my underwear out of my top drawer and paused.

There lay the brick. I needed a stone today for the stupid song Mrs Craig insisted we sing each morning.

How many stones are left alone? How many stones are left alone? How many stones are left alone?

The crap song danced about in my head.

Who is still at home?

Perfect!

Dad yelled from downstairs, "Molly! Babes, I hope you're up and away. If not, you're mega late."

"Stop stating the obvious, Dad!" I yelled back, tripping over my own feet. Reminder to self: don't try and put trainers on whilst trying to leave my bedroom.

"It's five past eight, baby girl," Dad yelled back.

I was impressed with my own speed. That took me five minutes.

Well done, Molly!

I ran back to my drawer and grabbed the brick and placed it on my dressing table. I should take that for the song.

I looked in the mirror, wetting my forefinger and wiping off the black mascara that had managed to create panda eyes and flick itself all over my left cheek. I tied my long hair back and thought better of it, throwing it up into a messy bun.

"That'll have to do," I said out loud. I ran out of my room and into the bathroom to brush my teeth.

Dad shouted up, "Do you want breakfast, babes?"

"No time, Dad."

I closed the front door with a slam. I picked a leaf from our hedge and tore it up as I power-walked.

I had worked out a shortcut last week; down an alleyway. I was so glad I had put on trainers and I ran down it. Take-out chip paper and cigarette butts littered the whole area. I avoided the potholes that were filled with dirty rainwater.

A jet black cat appeared from behind an empty box and stopped me in my tracks. His crazy coat warned me he was wild.

"Go away. Scat," I said. I noticed to my left strange graffiti. The cat meowed and I turned back to it. It ran off past me and I put my hand on my chest to steady my breath. I focused on the graffiti, carefully reading out the words, "Children should be seen and not heard."

I stepped backwards and my foot went straight into a pothole. "Crap!" I said as I shook the water off my foot and the water seeped deep down into my sock and onto my foot. "What a shit start to the day." My words echoed through the whole alleyway.

Behind me, the hiss of the black cat again made me jump. The light of the exit ahead flickered, so I kept my eyes forward and ran.

I literally threw myself through the door of the classroom. Empty. A note was on the table addressed to me.

It read: *Molly, photocopy these for me for the whole class. Thanks, Hazel.*

My worries split like air escaping from a deflating balloon and I lifted the colouring-in page of *The Princess and the Pea*. With a quick walk, I went out of the classroom to make my way to the photocopier.

That was a close one. I joined the queue of teachers chatting happily in front of me. Birds of a feather flock together. I half-listened to their conversation.

"I'd just made us all a chicken salad and Dave came in with Chinese food. Needless to say, my diet went down the pan," said Mrs McEwan, the P.4 teacher.

"Did you go to Slimming World last week?" asked Ms Perry, and Mrs McEwan spouted out a cackling laugh.

"No, and I missed it the week before. Dave doesn't understand that I am trying to be good. What did you get up to, Emily?"

"Aaron was called into work so Jae and I went up to the church. There was a good preacher visiting. Pastor James McConnell. He did a sermon on 'Is your tongue productive or destructive?' It was interesting," said Mrs Dunkan, the P.1 teacher.

The conversation continued amongst the boring pigeons but I zoned out. Instead, I listened to the repetitive drone of the photocopier and watched as the digital numbers counted backwards.

I jumped when Ms Perry shouted in my ear, "You're next. Enjoy."

"Oh, thanks very much," I said with a weak smile. I stuck my page down and closed the lid. I typed in twenty-eight and pressed the green button.

The machine spat out three sheets and stopped. "Crap!" I said out loud and peeped behind me to make sure no one had heard. I yanked out the bottom drawer. Typical. A paper jam!

When I returned to the classroom, Mrs Craig was starting the morning song already. She nodded at me when I walked in and I went over to my rucksack, taking out the piece of brick. I selected a permanent marker from Mrs Craig's desk and scribbled my name over the surface of the brick: Miss Jolliff. It looked ridiculous but I didn't care. I moved over to the two baskets by Mrs Craig. I popped my stone into the basket with the sign: I am here today.

I plopped down and sang the woeful song. Everyone out of tune. I scanned the room. I hadn't bonded with any of them. They were all so needy.

James sitting picking his nose. Gross!

"What do you think, Miss Jolliff?"

I wasn't listening as usual. I pored over the teacher carefully for some prop or clue as to what she was referring to.

James managed to take a second to remove his finger from his nose and shouted out, "Aye, what do ye think,

Miss Jolliff?" He had a huge smirk on his face. Did he know I wasn't listening?

Mrs Craig saved me with, "Do you think it will rain today with those huge clouds in the sky?"

I glanced outside and rambled, "Yes, I do. They look dark and heavy. I reckon it is going to be a miserable day." My phone dinged at the end of my sentence and the whole class laughed.

Dawn shouted out, "Oh, Miss Jolliff, is that your mobile phone?"

Mrs Craig clapped her hands and said, "Right class. Settle down." I wanted to kick myself for not turning my mobile off; I was made aware of the school's strict policy of no mobile phones on day one. Mrs Craig didn't look happy. Suddenly, the clouds broke and the rain pelted down. It was indeed a miserable day.

How I hustled through my first Monday, I had no idea.

As I hiked home, I pictured myself on the ice gliding over nothingness. I'd have to wait until Saturday before I could skate again. I tutted as I wandered past the tunnel. Police tape was covering the entrance. Nightmare I would have to walk the long way home.

I marched on. I thought of Matthew again.

At least I had Matthew's weekly visit on Wednesday. Hump day. This was the week when I was going to have a full conversation with him. I slipped out my mobile and flicked onto Instagram, gazing through his photographs. Another photograph of him in front of an audience. I did a quick screenshot and zoomed in.

Whitewell Church.

He played his guitar in a church? I wasn't expecting that. He must be very brave to play in front of a full congregation. I admired him even more for being able to do that.

When I arrived home, I made myself some avocado and toast with a sprinkling of cheese and pepper, and went to my room. I made myself comfortable on my bed and switched my television to YouTube. What was that crap Anita was talking about on the bus on Saturday?

I typed in *i n t e r n a l* space *m o n*... oh, there it was. I ate my sandwich as I watched three clips about it. Intriguing.

The doorbell rang out interrupting my thoughts; Anita's voice and Mum's inviting her inside in an overly friendly way. I ran down the stairs missing the last two, nearly banging into Anita.

"Hi, chick! I was just thinking about you," I said, glad to land a chance to speak to someone who wasn't my family member or five years old.

"Hi, I hope ya don't mind. I thought I'd pop by. I've a surprise for ya," said Anita, her face beaming.

"What?" I asked as I prodded her in the ribs.

"Well, ya know the way I've been getting those driving lessons?" said Anita starting to catch the giggles.

"Yea?"

"Well," Anita announced, bouncing from one foot to the next, "Look!" she squealed dangling a bunch of keys with a large, fluffy hedgehog attached to them in my face.

"Oh, congratulations. How exciting," said Mum giving her a big hug.

"What? What do you mean? You didn't tell me you had your test coming up."

My insides were doing somersaults, "You haven't bagged a car, have you?"

Mum let go of Anita and said, "Well done, you. Health to enjoy. Do you both want a cup of tea?" She sauntered off into the kitchen.

"I'm fine, Mrs Jolliff." She then turned and looked into my eyes. "I wanted to surprise ya. To be honest, I didn't think I would pass the first time so I didn't tell anyone but Dad."

"That's amazing!" I screamed.

"I can drive us to the ice-rink anytime we need to go. In fact, I was hoping we could go for a drive now," said Anita jingling the keys in my face. I snatched them from her.

"Of course. Let's go. I want to see the car."

"Yes, let's go. It's a used car. A Skoda. Dad bought it for me," Anita said jumping up and down again. I ran to the door and down our garden path.

"Unreal, Anita. We've wheels," I said throwing up my arms.

"Well, I do, but ya can come along for the ride," she said as she squeezed my waist.

Dad came to the door, "Molly-Moo!"

"Dad, come and see Anita's new car."

"Oh. Nice, Anita," said Dad, narrowing his eyes like a hawk.

"We're going for a spin, Dad," I said.

"Eh, baby girl. I'm not into you going with Anita. She's just passed her test. You should wait a while," said Dad and he cleared his throat.

"Dad, I hope you're joking," I said, emitting a short snort, "Terrance said we've to show up on the ice at least three times a week. Having a car means we can go in the morning."

"Wait a couple of months. I'm sure Anita will understand," said Dad looking at Anita and letting out a heavy sigh.

"Dad, I'm not getting the bus to the ice-rink if Anita is driving. We go everywhere together. Anyway, I'm an adult. I have a job for goodness sake. I can make my own decisions," I snapped, "Come on, Anita." I looked back at Dad. The look on Dad's face said it all. My whining comment made me sound like a child. A hundred miles away from being an adult.

"I'm a very safe driver, Mr Jolliff. It'll be handy to deliver us to all our ice-skating lessons on time too. We're only going down to the beach and back again. I promise

I'll be safe," said Anita making strong eye contact with my dad. Anita was the adult here. I wasn't sure if I was proud of her or... jealous.

"Dad?" I said.

"It looks like rain, girls. Maybe the beach isn't such a good idea." He was ignoring me. I, the annoying child and the jealous friend.

"We're not going to be out long," I continued.

"Well... If you're only going to the beach..."

"Thanks, Dad," I said flinging my arms around him and giving him a kiss on the cheek, "I'm sorry, Dad. I love you..."

He was surprised and I suddenly awkward.

"Oh, and Dad, why did the dog fail his driving test?"

"No idea," he chuckled.

Anita opened the passenger seat for me and I slipped in. I leaned out the open window, "Because he's a dog. Dogs can't drive."

Dad smiled and my stomach lurched. The smell of vanilla hit me.

"What's that nice smell?" I asked Anita as she drove away from Dad, wondering if I was jealous. Anita's pale face was shining like a cleared ice rink. She really was going places. Was I? *Oh, shit that sounds like jealousy. What was going on with me?*

"It's an air freshener," she said and flicked a little tree that dangled from her rearview mirror. I flipped down the mirror and looked at my own face. My green eyes looked dull today and I closed them tight. Of course, I'm not jealous of my best friend. I'm proud of her. We compete on the ice rink but never in real life. I opened my eyes and smiled.

"I can't believe you're driving, Anita. It's amazing." We arrived at the beach and parked in the carpark. Anita turned the key in the ignition and pulled it out.

"I'm so happy I passed the first time," she said, leaning back and stretching her arms out, "Ya know wha?"

"What?"

"Tomato ketchup is a standalone ingredient we add to food. Right?"

I rolled my eyes.

"No hear me out. Nothing, and I mean nothing, has been added to ketchup to make it more interesting. It simply doesn't need anything added. On its own, it is at the top of its game."

"Anita... where do you learn all this crap?"

"I pick these things up in my... my journey through life," she answered shrugging her shoulders. "In a way, we're ketchup: we're happy just the way we are. We don't need anything added to our lives to make us happier. We're simply ketchup."

As I watched her I wished I could be like that: carefree and full of knowledge that could be plucked out from the deepest, darkest part of my brain and brighten my day; make life a little easier, happier. I looked away and suddenly wondered if I was happy. What was stopping me from being ketchup?

Anita began to hum.

"You say the maddest things." I said and glanced again at her animated face. I knew she was indeed ketchup but I wasn't. I wasn't complete. There were so many things I needed to put right in my life before I could proudly say, "I'm ketchup."

Anita continued as if she had read my thoughts, "People can be like ketchup and decide that they like themselves the way they are or people can try and add things or parts to their personality and mess up their real being. It's like at school in art class. Ya do a fantastic picture; one that ya are so proud of and then ya add to it. You know ya shouldn't but ya can't help yourself. Then it's ruined. Too late. We've all done it. Well I'm sure we all have."

Silence. I could almost hear her brain ticking. Then she continued, "That's okay if it's a picture. Ya can always start again. But it's not okay if it's your personality. Ya should love yourself for who ya are. We do that." She looked over at me and smiled. "We are content with what we have. Molly, we are ketchup."

I looked at her with total admiration. "You've got it all sussed," I said.

"All sussed? What do ya mean?"

"Life... you have it all sorted." I focused out of the window. Two big splashes of rain landed on the windscreen and I followed the track of one, whilst the other stayed still.

"Me? No... I'm still at school. Now you, you have it all sussed. You've a job, for goodness sake."

"A job I can't keep. That's hardly me having my life sorted. If anything, I've made it worse taking that stupid job." I watched more raindrops kiss her car.

"What do ya mean, a job ya can't keep? Yer mum said ye were happy."

"When did you start listening to what my mum says? You're still at school. You're going to go to university and now you've your driving license and a car!" I started to hiccup and I tried to hold the next one in.

"Molly, what's going on? Why do ya think that ya can't keep yer job? Are ye regretting leaving school?"

"No, I know it was my time to leave. I just didn't think I'd end up in a job that would need me to read and write at a high level," I said as the rain washed the windscreen.

"Ye worried about yer dyslexia? If ye are, ya should tell them. I'm sure they'll understand. It's a good job, and think about the money you're going to have at the end of each month," Anita said turning back on her ignition, turning her windscreen wipers on.

"Do you really think they would understand?" I whispered and hiccupped again.

"Yes, they're teachers for goodness sake. They know about those things. They'll know how to make it easier for ya. Just tell yer boss. You're working with kids. Every day is different when ye work with kids. It's fun. Don't give it up because of dyslexia."

"I do think I could start to enjoy it," I said, knowing I couldn't lose this job.

"Have ye had two days that are the same since ya started?"

"No."

"Exactly, every day is different. That's a good thing. What about the kids? What are they like?"

"I haven't got to know them yet," I replied suddenly seeing all their small faces in my head.

"Molly, if you're worried about the reading and writing, tell them," Anita said. I shook my head and witnessed the sudden downpour slowing down.

"Molly, promise me you'll speak to yer boss," Anita said, switching off the wipers and playing with her hedgehog necklace.

The rain stopped.

"Let's talk about you," I said looking at my Ketchup friend.

"Promise me first."

"I'll try."

"Good. Don't give up on yer first job. They could end up helping ya," Anita said, "Now, look. The rain has stopped. Let's go for a walk and talk some more."

"I said I'll try, so I'll try. If we are going to walk and talk, can we change the subject?"

"I wonder what my mum would have thought about me driving?" Anita clicked her seatbelt and allowed it to run through her fingers. A look creeped onto her face I had never seen before. A sadness that made her pretty face fall for a minute. Her rosy cheeks disappeared; paleness took over. A face that called out for answers. I, the blithering idiot, stuttered,

"But... but we don't talk about your mum."

"Ye mean, you don't. I talk about her... sometimes."

"I've never heard you..."

"I think she would be proud of me," Anita said, popping her hedgehog back into her mouth and opening her car door. I wanted to say her mum would have been *so* proud of her but no words came out. Anita had answered her own question. I had failed my friend. I knew she needed reassurance but it was too late. I sat for a minute. Then took off my own seatbelt and opened my door.

"It's cool you have a car," I said closing the door, "It's going to change your life."

"Our lives. Think of all the places we can go and all the people we can see."

I moved around the back of her car and reached over and took Anita's hand in mine. "Anita, your mum would have been so proud of you." The pink in her cheeks reappeared and I reached up and took the hedgehog out of her mouth and moved her hair behind her shoulder. "She would have looked at her beautiful daughter and hugged her." I hugged my best friend and we stood for a minute until Anita coughed awkwardly.

"So, when's our first road trip?" Anita said stepping back.

"Maybe we could check out Whitewell Church up in Belfast?"

"Whatever for?" asked Anita, her eyebrows raised.

"For one reason and one reason only: Matthew Stewart. He plays there every Sunday." And just like that everything was okay again. Everything back to normal. The way things should be.

"Sure. Why not," said Anita with a smile, "Anything for my friend and her need to speak to the wonderful Matthew Stewart."

TWENTY
HOUSE

There is no laughter with this family, and I pine for it like my radiators pine daily for warmth. The only being who laughs is Sophia and so I smile down at her. Stephanie concentrates on her makeup and her clothes each day. Jack trudges from room to room starting projects and leaving them half-finished.

Stephanie had designed a beauty station in one of my rooms and she scans her precious purchases daily. She reaches out her hand and hovers over each item. A woman obsessed with her own reflection. She pats an odd, brown bottle into her hand; the same way Emily-Brooke did when she tried to extract the sauce out of the bottle to add to her chips. The *thud, thud, thud* had bugged me and I was glad when D.B. demonstrated how to poke a knife up and twirl it around to force the sauce down.

I wonder why Stephanie doesn't use a knife. The liquid stuck in her bottle finally comes down and lands on her hand. Selecting out a brush, she applies the brown gooeyness to her face. It spreads like smooth peanut butter on bread. The one without the nuts.

In the past, I noticed Abigail applying the same stuff. Except hers had a slight tinge of orange. Abigail stopped at the top of her neck. Stephanie works it down her neck until it looks even.

Stephanie, concentrating on her eyes, transforms the colour of her eyelids; matching them according to her outfit for today. She plucks out something that looks like spider legs from a white box, and with a little bottle of glue she applies these to her eyes. Disgusting!

Lipstick is next: red. She has twenty-four sticks of the thing. She insists to Jack they are different shades of red. And she needs them all.

"Oh, just leave me alone," she snaps at Jack after he complains about the money she spends on makeup and she storms away from him.

Their love for each other isn't as apparent to me as the love of the two who moved into me after Walter left: Rab and Gillian.

* * *

After Abigail, Emily-Brooke, D.B and Sarah left, Walter stayed for another month and I barely checked on him. He stopped eating and drank more cider instead. The bottles mounted up in my kitchen.

When *he* left, I was pleased.

I remembered the loneliness I endured when Walter closed my door. Cars entered the avenue where I resided and lights from their headlights would dance a waltz across my empty floors. I only watched.

The House next door would harangue me about Stacey's father over and over again to distract me from my sorrow; my only meaningful connection with the outside world.

Some people busted into their house in uniform and led the father away; Stacey's mother clung onto her.

She repeated over and over, "Why didn't you tell me, darling?" and "I'm so sorry."

Their House remained silent; I missed his daily rants. Stacey was different from that day on. She smiled more and made up games that were less cruel and more fun. Her mother kept her in the garden and checked on her regularly.

I was left alone for two weeks. The only heartbeat belonged to me and yet I wasn't sure if I had a heart.

Was my heart my kitchen?

My lights were out the whole time and I remained in the darkness. I didn't like it. There was no warmth inside me. I was lonely.

The beginning of the third week brought with it a blue bottle fly. He appeared in one of my rooms unexpectedly. At first, I ignored his wildness to locate an open window and escape. After the third day, his buzz rang out and his many taps on my windows drove me mad. I loathed his fat, light blue abdomen with its metallic glaze.

Whilst in mid-air, I followed his zig-zag movements and cringed when he bumped around my rooms. His erratic movements surprised me more than Walter's outbursts when *he* lived within my walls.

I found him at the end of the week on my window sill in my bathroom. On his back; his legs crookedly reaching for my ceiling. Exhausted by his flight, did he choose to die?

The next week, I observed that his wing had fallen off. It lay slightly away from his unmoving body. Only then did I savour a tiny sprinkling of sympathy for this bumping intruder. Like me, it had no way of fixing broken items without the help of humans.

When Rab moved in, I wondered if he would fix the blue bottle's wing. He moved in first on his own. I was too big for him; I watched him move from room to room aimlessly.

His friend, Ken, arrived and Rab babbled happily about a girl he had met in a tearoom.

"She avoided me totally, Ken."

"Surely not. Imagine someone ignoring our handsome Rab," he said ruffling Rab's hair and punching him lightly on the arm, "Did you not tell her you have this lovely house and a car *and* you received your acceptance letter from the Navy? Girls are impressed with that sort of thing."

Ken described me as a lovely house. Was I lovely? Were girls impressed by houses?

"Not this girl. I have practically pleaded with her to go on a date with me. She's only interested in meeting her chums and smoking cigarettes. She sucks on them the way you suck on your beer. She even makes smoke rings."

"What a girl," said Ken with a smirk.

"No, mate. I'm serious. She is beautiful, Ken. The perfect girl for me."

"What's she look like?"

"She's about five foot and slim. And Ken, she has one of those bodies that just… well, you know what I mean. She's a redhead and has bright emerald green eyes."

"You have *really* fallen for this girl," said Ken, interrupting his description.

"I have. She was wearing a short red dress. I have a real thing for curves, man. She had those go-go boots on. The same ones your Maggie has."

"Bloody hell, Rab. We all have a thing for curves but you've taken in every detail. You sure do like this girl. Is she easy to talk to?"

"No, Ken… She makes me turn into a bumbling idiot."

"When was the last time you saw her?"

"I smashed right into her at the corner of May Avenue."

"You're taking the mick. What do ye mean *smashed*?"

"I was flying around the corner and she was coming in the other direction and we literally bumped into each other. She knelt down on her honkers with the pain. At first, I hadn't realised it was her. The blow to my own head nearly knocked me out."

"Trust you to bang right into the girl of your dreams," said Ken with a chuckle.

"Of course, I was the perfect gentleman. I helped her to her feet, Ken. A big red bruise was developing right in front of my eyes on her pretty forehead. She was gorgeous. I drew her in close to me. Her small frame was quivering from the shock of the bump. I felt protective over her. It was enchanting. I wanted to sweep her up in my arms and do everything in my power to protect her."

His desire to protect this girl was the same way I was when Emily-Brooke lived within my walls. As he said the words, I immediately felt a secure connection with Rab. The way I felt when all my doors were locked and my sash windows slammed shut.

"Did she fall for you then?"

"She yelled in my face, 'What were you thinking? Look what you've done!' She put her hand up to her head and felt the large bump. She was horrified. I found myself begging her for a date inappropriately. Maybe bad timing on my part but I knew the traditional way the day before hadn't worked. She pulled away from me. She removed her little hand mirror from her red and white leather bag and looked at her reflection. She was livid."

"Well, did you bag a date or not?"

"She called me a muttonhead. I kept repeating 'sorry' over and over as she applied some makeup to the bruised area… I should have had my Merchant Navy uniform on."

"Yep. Rab, I told you that. Girls can't resist a man in uniform. So, you didn't bag a date with her then?"

"I did," Rab said with a smile.

"You didn't."

"I did. I remembered I had a scrambler race today and asked her to come and watch me. I found myself waffling on about how exciting it was to drive through fields, over mud, through streams and how I had built my own scrambler out of a regular road bike. And how my bike was now stripped down to shave weight for speed and how I had made the suspensions taller and the exhaust pipes higher and changed the tyres... She gazed at me in total wonder. She was well into it."

"There's no way she was into your scrambler. Are you taking the mick?"

"She was and she is coming to watch me ride my scrambler today down in the north field."

"She's probably never seen a motorbike, never mind an off-road bike. You better impress her today. A first date in a field filled with bikers rambling around the earth bumps. Well, I never. Well done, you."

Over the next three months, I rarely saw Rab. Out every day with his new girl who he called Gillian. He arrived back one day with her up in his arms. He carried her over my threshold and she moved in.

She cleaned me. She swept the blue bottle fly into the bin without a thought. She didn't fix his broken wing.

Rab spent more and more time in the Merchant Navy, and Gillian continued to clean me, wandering wearily through my rooms.

After a short visit from Rab, she called her friend on the phone.

"Yes, I'm pregnant. I really am. Rab doesn't know. I'm going to wait until he comes home so I can tell him... Yes, I'm happy."

Another baby. I hoped this baby would help me to fill the gap within my walls that was created by Emily-Brooke when she left.

* * *

My thoughts of times gone by are interrupted by Jack stomping around my living room.

Yelling out, he repeats over and over, "My mother told me Stephanie wasn't right for me. Why didn't I listen? Why didn't I listen?"

He goes to my back door and stands on my step. He takes his chewing gum out of his mouth and moves it about in his right hand before going to the bin and throwing it in. He lights up a cigarette. I had never seen him smoke. I observe him in total wonder.

Seconds pass and he flings the half-smoked cigarette onto the ground and says, "What a bitch. Out shagging a guy while I stupidly doing everything in my power to try and keep her happy. She won't be happy when I sling her whoring ass out of my house." He pulls his motorbike down my path. He puts on his helmet, starts his bike and is away.

Time slowly ticks by.

Stephanie appears with Sophia in her pram. She leaves Sophia in the hallway and I watch over her.

Stephanie paces around the house shouting, "Jack! Jack! Are you home?" She shuffles into my living room, sits down and places her head in her hands.

Jack returns. He parks outside, near my gate, and I hear him say, "Spoilt, little brat..." as he marches up my path and opens my front door. I know he's still angry as he slams my door shut. My glass holds on to the pane.

Stephanie immediately jumps up, "I know you know. Let me explain."

Jack yells out, "Get out. Get yer stuff and clear off!" Shock falls upon her face. She slides past Jack and moves towards the doorway. She mumbles something about taking her clothes and disappears upstairs.

Sophia starts to cry.

Jack ignores her and so does Stephanie. Jack strides outside and drags his motorbike around my back garden. Stephanie packs her clothes. I try to reassure

Sophia all will be well but she ignores me and continues crying.

Stephanie leaves her clothes and walks down the stairs and moves the pram slightly. She notices a chip on her fingernail and tuts. Sophia continues to cry. When Jack storms in, Stephanie shuffles over to him.

"Let me explain…"

Jack shakes his head and points to the door. She stamps back upstairs, packs the rest of her clothes and slinks back down holding two bags. "I will pick up Sophia when I secure a place to stay," she says as she opens the front door and slowly leaves.

My heart breaks for Sophia and I wish for Stephanie to return. I didn't wish hard enough as Stephanie didn't return. I am disappointed.

Jack rips open a stick of gum and throws it in his mouth. He leaves Sophia in her pram and concentrates only on his chewing on the settee all night.

Time passes.

Anger grows all around me and I want to shake Jack and say, "Care for your baby." Sophia eventually falls asleep and so does Jack. I attend to Sophia and wish harder throughout the entire night for Stephanie to return.

In the morning, Jack stands up, ignores Sophia once more and strides up to his bedroom. He stands there and puts his hand on his head. He leans down and takes off his boots and socks, standing weakly on my cold, laminated floor. The floor he had put down last month but had left unfinished over at my window.

Anger twirls up inside him. I know as he punches my bedroom door three times. His knuckles bleed and Sophia cries.

He sinks to my floor and puts his head in his hands. I continue to wish for Stephanie to return to Sophia.

TWENTY-ONE
MOLLY

The next day, I was up bright and early. I had a shower, washed and straightened my hair, and put on a dress.

"The early bird catches the worm," I said, remembering Grandad saying this to me on one of our bird-watching adventures.

I stared in the mirror. My hair always looked beautiful. Straight at the top and perfect, ringlets from my shoulders down to my waist. Easy to keep it that way. I would dampen it each night and whirl it up into a bun and each morning I would allow it to fall like a blonde waterfall. But my face was a different matter. I studied my skin. I looked far too young. I spent the next half an hour applying more makeup over the top of my usual daily routine. I was a crimson-bellied parakeet.

When I went down for breakfast, Josh's eyes nearly popped out of his head.

"Hello, stranger! Do we know you?" Mum nudged Josh. Dad looked up from his newspaper.

"Oh, welcome to breakfast. We gather, at this time, every morning. It's nice to see you are part of our family."

"Very funny, Dad," I said kissing my beautiful plant and plonking myself down, helping myself to some toast.

"Tea, darling?" asked Mum.

"Yes, please," I said.

"So, what's the occasion? Is there someone at work who ya fancy?" asked Josh.

"Nope. I don't have a thing for someone the way you do for lovely Willow. I've just decided this is the new me," I said with a smile and I sipped the tea Mum had placed in front of me.

"Willow and I are just friends. How many times do I have to tell ya? Anyway, you do have a thing for someone."

"Who?"

"You're sweet on Matt. Are you not?"

Mum raised her eyebrows and I spluttered tea all over myself.

"How did ya miss a mouth that size?" laughed Josh.

"Shut up."

"I'm only stating the obvious."

"Well, don't."

"So, what was that mumble about the new you? Have ya lost your mind?" said Josh stuffing half a slice of toast into his mouth.

"Yes, the new me. I'm getting up at this time every morning, walking rather than sprinting to work, eating healthy food and enjoying life," I said holding my head up high.

"We'll see how long that lasts," said Josh, rolling his eyes.

"Joshua! You should be encouraging your sister," said Mum.

"Joshua," Dad said from behind his newspaper, glancing up for the first time and looking at me closely. Always the hawk.

"What?" I asked, jutting my head back.

"Nothing, nothing. Don't you think the makeup is a bit much, baby girl?"

"No, Dad. I'm an adult. Adults wear makeup," I barked.

Josh jumped up and wiped the crumbs off his trousers.

"Technically, you're not an adult until you turn eighteen, sis."

"I'm eighteen in two weeks' time. I'm an early developer," I said.

"Blondie, I'm glad that you have decided to change your lazy couldn't-be-assed ways and I wish you all the best," said Josh, trying to open the dishwasher with his foot.

"I'm hardly lazy. And what do you mean by couldn't-be-assed ways?" I asked, opening my eyes wide.

"Ha, you don't think you're lazy? You're the laziest person I know," he said, managing to wedge the door open as he threw his plate inside.

"Go to school, little boy," I snapped.

"Go to school yourself," he replied as he put on his blazer and flicked my ear.

"Clear off, you," I said trying to whack him but I missed because he jumped back.

"Mum, take him away," I moaned.

"Come on, you," Mum said to Josh, "Maybe you should take a leaf out of your sister's book and start walking to school. It would be good for you, Joshua."

"Aye, Josh," I said and I wanted to kick myself for not sounding like the new, mature person I'd become. When Mum and Josh left, I leaned over towards Dad.

"Dad?"

"What is it?" he said looking over his newspaper.

"I need something," I said.

"What is it, babes?"

"I need driving lessons," I said, smiling my wonder smile.

"Too expensive."

"Could you not teach me?"

"No chance."

"Please," I begged.

"We'll see," he replied.

"Thanks, Dad," I said and jumped up, grabbing my handbag before he changed his mind.

Dad glanced over at me. "Where's your rucksack?"

"I told you: this is the new me," I said as I skipped out the door.

I rambled to school at a slower pace today and repeated over and over again, "This is the new, positive me."

When I arrived, Nicola was standing outside my classroom.

"What you all dolled up for? Have you got your fob?"

"Oh, nothing," I said suddenly feeling self-conscious, "I have my fob. Why?" I asked.

"I forgot mine. Hand it over so I can get in," she snapped.

"Oh, will I not need it for myself?" I asked.

"No. You're already at your classroom," she said, flapping her hand towards the door. "Open this door first and let yourself in. Then give me the fob so I can get into my room."

"Oh, okay," I said, opening my classroom door and holding out my fob for her to take. Being positive and happy, I smiled down at her. She snatched it off me and click-clacked away down the ramp. Charming!

I forced myself to shout after her, "Nicola!"

"What?" she said spinning around on her heels; her eyes squinting up at me.

"Have a nice day," I said with a smile. She grunted and marched off.

I was in the classroom before Mrs Craig, and I decided to remain positive and upbeat. I started at the door and made my way around the room tidying. I opened a few windows too and sprayed the air freshener around the room. I filled the kettle with water and leaned down to grab two cups.

In strolled Mrs Craig.

"Oh my, Molly. You are here nice and early," she said, looking around, "Have you been tidying up? It smells lovely in here."

"Good morning, Hazel. Would you like a cup of tea before we start?"

155

"Yes, please. That would be lovely," she said turning her head a little and nodding.

When the children arrived, we sang our lovely song:

> *How many stones are left alone?*
> *How many stones are left alone?*
> *How many stones are left alone?*
> *Who is still at home?*

This was great. It continued:

> *Five little stones are left alone.*
> *Five little stones are left alone.*
> *Five little stones are left alone.*
> *Five must be still at home.*

That seemed like a lot to me. Five children off. Mrs Craig said nothing so I forced it to the back of my mind. After registration, we started with number work. I sat with the yellow group: Aaron, Dawn, Caroline and the delightful James.

"I'm bored," said Dawn. We hadn't started yet and she was bored already.

"Come on, Dawn, this is going to be fun," I said in a cheery voice. Determined to remain happy and positive. Five kids were off today so the stations would not be as hectic.

"You won't be bored in a minute, Dawn. We are going to have some fun with maths," I said and smiled, "Now, everyone. Have you all got a number line?" They all reached over and snatched a number line from the middle of the table. I leaned over towards Aaron.

"Look, Aaron, the sum says one add four. Can you find one on your number line? Good boy. Now, jump forward four. Count as you go," I said in my best teacher voice.

"One... two..."

"Keep going, Aaron," I encouraged.

"One…"

"No, don't start again."

He couldn't be that dumb, surely!

"Three?"

"Wait, you jumped at one there and then… Let's just start again. Find one."

"I can't find my pencil," said Dawn, throwing herself under the table to look for it. How could she lose a pencil in two minutes flat?

"I handed you all a pencil before we started. Does anyone know where Dawn's pencil is?" Everyone shrugged. Of course, no one knew. Why did I ask?

Caroline looked as if she was about to cry, "Are you okay, Caroline?"

"No. I need toilet," said Caroline, standing up and doing a little jiggle.

"Go then. Go quickly, Caroline," I said in a sharp tone. Caroline stared at me with her eyes wide. I jumped up. "Quick, Caroline. Go… go. Go!" I said ushering her in the right direction.

By the time I returned to my seat, Dawn had found her pencil and had put the number two in all her boxes. Why was she so obsessed with the number two?

"Dawn, did you work those out or did you just guess?" I asked, beginning to sweat. I reached up and grabbed an eraser from the shelf and rubbed out all her answers. Dawn cried.

"I was finished. I was finished."

"Dawn, you were not finished. You didn't use your number line. Let's all do this together. Now, what does the first sum say?"

"One add four," said Aaron with a grin.

"Yes, good. It says one add four. Oh, hold on a minute. Where's Caroline? I'll go and fetch her. You all work out that sum with your number line."

"What sum?" asked Aaron, and James picked his nose.

I stared at my group in total despair and James said, "I'm done!" and showed me his work.

"Yes, James you got it all right!" I said, clapping my hands.

"You pleased, Miss?" he asked.

"I sure am," I said and I meant it. James reached up and threw himself on top of me, giving me an unexpected hug. "Oh, thank you," I said, taking his little arms off my neck. I lowered my head, a little embarrassed. James had a massive bruise above his wrist. "Oh, James how did you do that?" I said, pulling his school jumper up seeing the bruise didn't stop but continued up his arm.

"Get off, Miss," he snapped and I rocketed up, stepping back.

"Oh, okay," I said, a little hurt by his sudden change in behaviour.

"How's this table getting on?" Mrs Craig asked in her happy-clappy voice.

Aaron piped in with, "James got all his work done."

I joined in, "Yes, and he got it all right."

"Great job, James. You can go on the star." James skipped over to the star and put his name on it. Caroline arrived back with her dress tucked into her knickers. I jumped up and fixed her.

I liked the new me: positive and happy.

By the time lunchtime came around, I was wrecked and starving. I lifted my lunchbox, sneaking a peek to make sure Mum didn't make any smelly egg and onion sandwiches. Good, cheese and tomato. Now Nicola wouldn't give me a hard time.

I practically skipped around to the door that led to the main school. When I arrived, I searched in my handbag for my fob.

"Where the heck is my fob?" I said bending down and lifting each item out of my handbag, placing everything onto the ground. My lunchbox tumbled onto its side and my sandwiches rolled out into the muck.

"Crap. Nicola, the emu, has my fob. Crap!"

TWENTY – TWO
HOUSE

As I watch over Sophia, memories of Gillian and Rab's baby flood into my very being.

* * *

The baby was cute. He had a mop of red hair and a round face like a plump cushion gobbling bottles of milk daily. He giggled a lot and Gillian loved him. They called him Harry.

Another baby arrived two years later: Susan. Rab brought back gifts when he found out Susan was born. He bounced into me and I smelt of strawberries.

"We are going to sort this place out once and for all, Gillian," announced Rab happily and I knew he was going to make changes.

Pink carpet was put into my box bedroom. All my blinds were taken down and replaced with clean, white curtains that moved when the wind blew in through my windows. And Rab surprised Gillian with a brand-new washing machine.

"Oh, Rab... That is just what we need. It was getting a little bit hectic in here with three bundles of clothes to wash every week."

Susan giggled in her pram and she made everyone laugh. Gillian turned and sang a strange song. I listened carefully.

Humpty Dumpty sat on a wall
Humpty Dumpty had a great fall

My heart sank. Humpty fell and I wanted to know if someone would help him. I listened carefully again.

All the king's horses and all the king's men
Couldn't put Humpty together again.

No one could fix him? Was Gillian serious? I looked at Susan still giggling and I was shocked. That poor guy.

***

Sophia bawls. As I try to soothe her, I realise that I love all babies. I smile at Sophia.

***

Over the years, I realised that Emily-Brooke would never walk through my doors again. She would never play on the stairs with her dolls and teddies. Would never draw my portrait on her blackboard.

All I had left of her was the scribbled Bible verse. Even her brown Bible with the red writing on the front was gone.

When Harry started to crawl, he struggled to lift his tummy off my floor. When he turned five, he liked to sit in the cupboard and trace over the letters of Emily-Brooke's verse.

He called Gillian in one day and asked, "Who wrote that, Mammy?"

"Goodness, I've never noticed that before. Let me see now. What does it say?" she asked, scanning over the green words herself, "It's a Bible verse, Harry. It looks as if a child wrote it. I'll read it out to you. Now let me get comfortable."

She chose a green velvet cushion from Harry's bed and sat inside the cupboard with Harry right beside her. I made myself comfortable too, longing for the words to be read out loud once more.

"It says 'John 14:6'. That's the book in the Bible. The book is called John. This one stands for the fourteenth chapter and this one means that the words are on the sixth line in the book of John," She pointed under each word as she read them, *"Jesus saith unto him, I am the way, the truth, and the life: no man cometh unto the Father, but by me.'* It's a lovely verse, Harry. It means that there is a way to God. And if you know God you can live on with him when you die. Look, it says the way to God is through his son – Jesus. He is the way. If you learn about Jesus you will learn the truth. He gives you life. What do you think of that, Harry?"

Harry put his arms around his mum and hugged her, "You're the best mammy ever. I love you."

* * *

I feel a drip on my floor upstairs and I check. It is blood dripping from Jack's knuckles. He wipes his face. Blood is pouring from his right hand and yet he just stares down at it. I don't understand why.

He blinks.

He stands up, holding his hand with his other hand, and strides into my bathroom. He takes a deep, pained breath and closes his eyes. He presses his hands onto the rim of the cold sink and shakes his head in disbelief. He chews on his gum at a fast rate. Blood continues to flow from his knuckles. He runs my cold water over his hand and takes a white towel from the towel rail. He pats his hand and wraps the towel tightly around it.

He takes some toilet roll into the bedroom and awkwardly wipes up the splashes of blood from my floor with his left hand. He sprints down the stairs, grabs his biker jacket and flies to my door. Sophia lets out a whimper and he stops in his tracks.

My whole being cries out for him to lift Sophia.

He pauses.

I make a wish, "Lift Sophia."

He lifts her and I am delighted.

As I watch him holding Sophia with tears in his eyes, I remember back to Harry and Susan.

* * *

New children now lived in my street: Fran, Phil and Nick.

Phil was Harry's mate. He sat on my stairs with Susan who played with her doll. Her beloved Tiny Tears she called Kimmy.

She turned and looked at Phil and said, "You're a plonker."

Suddenly, Phil grabbed Susan's hair, shook it and banged her head off my wall. Susan cried. Harry was in his bedroom. He ran down the stairs, twisted Phil's arm and bit down on it hard.

"He bit me," Phil yelled and Harry's mum came out of the living room to find out what all the commotion was about, "Harry bit me." Phil yelled again. Gillian's face fell when she saw the mark on Phil's arm.

"Why would you do such a thing? Say you're sorry, right now."

"Mammy... Ma... Phil gr—" protested Susan.

"No, I'm not sorry," said Harry.

"Harry, you're grounded," said Gillian.

Phil slinked off home, hopefully feeling bad for what he had done.

Harry wasn't allowed out on his bike. He had to remain in his bedroom. Did he regret what he had done? He clenched his teeth as he lay on his bed.

Susan came into his bedroom and said, "You'll be Mr White and I'll be Miss Pink." Harry frowned.

"Why do your games always involve dolls and sitting down pretending to have tea?"

"They just do."

He humoured Susan for a while and I could see he was glad when Gillian called Susan downstairs.

Susan and Harry slept in separate rooms but they devised a secret knocking code to send messages to each other when they were told to go to bed. I tried to work it out but it only confused me and made my roof sore.

The next day, Nick came over with his broken bicycle.

"Harry, you reckon you can fix it for me?"

Harry grinned. He stood with his hands tucked into his armpits, listening to Nick's bike troubles. Harry gave out a long and satisfied breath.

"I know what the matter is," he said.

Within minutes he was down on his honkers fixing the bicycle. Nick stood back in amazement. When the bike was tested out, it worked perfectly. Nick was delighted. Harry waved off his compliments but stood tall with his shoulders back.

*

Flowers grew everywhere. Rab had insisted on building a greenhouse and regularly grew tomatoes and cucumbers. He would leave strict instructions to anyone who would listen, as to how they were to be looked after when he was at work. Harry and Susan loved my garden and all it had to offer. However, it wasn't long before the street became more enticing as I knew it would. My life was repetitive and I liked the routine of my daily life.

The new children in the street played outside every day with Harry and Susan. They loved meeting up and playing "kerby", "clap hands" (Susan's favourite), "football" and "hunts".

It was Easter. Fran gathered everyone around her outside my gate.

"Go and get your Easter eggs and we will share them."

Harry skipped back to the house with Susan and lifted two Easter Eggs from the living room unit. They joined the other children in Fran's garden. Fran's mum had prepared a nice picnic with fruit slices and little ham and cheese sandwiches cut into hearts. Susan was smiling from ear to ear.

Harry helped Susan open her egg. All the children shared their sweets. The sweets looked amazing in their shiny, purple wrapping. When they were handed over, Fran's mum helped them to divide all the sweets so everyone received the same amount. It was a lovely day.

Harry was happy because his little sister was happy. She poured the lemonade into everyone's plastic cups and Harry said, "Great job, Susan."

Harry always fixed things. He babbled daily about how things worked and he was constantly taking things apart to work out how to put them back together again. I watched him for hours.

He wasn't a keen reader like Emily-Brooke but he loved non-fiction books on cars, bikes, planes and anything on his dream job of becoming a mechanic.

Gillian would allow him to tinker away in her kitchen. If he wasn't with her talking about bikes, he was away out on a bike. I missed him when he left the house; sometimes away for hours.

* * *

Jack, still holding Sophia in his arms, whispers to her, "Don't cry, little one. Don't cry, and all will be well."

There is something magical about the words Jack says and I repeat them in my whole being, "Don't cry, little one. Don't cry, and all will be well. Don't cry, little one. Don't cry, and all will be well."

TWENTY-THREE
MOLLY

It was Wednesday: Matthew Stewart day.

Terrance was going to kill me. I hadn't managed to hustle my way to the ice-rink since Saturday. Would Anita take me tonight after Matthew left or maybe tomorrow?

When I arrived in school, I met Nicola in the corridor.

"You look a right mess," she snapped and click-clacked down the corridor. Great, another day in paradise. No, I needed to be positive and thoughtful.

"Like water off a duck's back," I said out loud, remembering my grandad explaining this phrase to me in his kitchen.

Mr Cardwell met me at the end of the corridor.

"Good morning, Molly. How is it going in P.2?"

"Great," I said with my wonder smile.

"Oh, good. Are you enjoying it?"

"Yes, loving it," I said and watched him disappear into his office.

When I arrived in the classroom, Mrs Craig greeted me.

"Good morning, Molly. Are you looking forward to another day in P.2?"

"Yes, I sure am," I said, accepting the positive vibe off Mrs Craig.

"I received a phone call from Ben's mum yesterday evening after you left. Apparently, he has stopped talking. He must be a little bit under the weather. Probably caught a bug."

The bell rang before I could discuss the woes of catching a bug. Mrs Craig went off to collect the children from the playground. I considered the timetable. We were starting with P.B.L. All the kids trooped in and lifted their stones from the basket.

Lucy asked me, "Miss Jolliff, are you moving your stone over?"

"Yes, of course," I said and stretched over. I lifted my stupid stone and flipped it into the "I'm here" basket.

When we sang our song, there were ten stones in the basket that had the sign "I am not here".

Mrs Craig started calling out the names of the children who were absent, "Grace, Ben, Jill, Freddie, Victoria... hold on a minute. Maybe there is an issue on the road. Let's give them a few more minutes."

We gave them an extra ten minutes as Mrs Craig came up with the bright idea of singing a few songs, starting with *The Wheels on the Bus*. Of course, it was pointless; no other children arrived. Mrs Craig completed her registration and started the children playing.

Grace was off, so her mum didn't turn up to volunteer. I was outside on my own the whole time.

"Dawn, can you help me open up the sandpit?" I asked. Dawn stared at me with her mouth open, "Dawn, did you hear me? Can you help me open up the sandpit?" She stood, gaping at me.

"Dawn? Dawn? Are you choking?" Dawn shook her head and tears filled up in her eyes.

What the heck? Was this child choking? I ran over to her and banged her on the back, I grabbed her upper arm, swinging her towards me. "Dawn? Are you okay?"

Still nothing! I lifted her and ran inside to Mrs Craig. "Help, help. Something is wrong with Dawn!"

Mrs Craig's face turned white. "What do you mean? What happened?"

"She's not talking and she's crying. I think she's choking," I spurted out and I began to hiccup. Mrs Craig lifted Dawn and sat her down on a chair.

"Dawn, are you okay?" Again, Dawn said nothing. "Open your mouth, Dawn," Mrs Craig demanded, and Dawn did.

"There is nothing there. Dawn, can you speak?" she asked and Dawn shook her head and silently cried. "What is going on here?"

Mrs Craig strode over to the class phone, "Hello, Mr Cardwell, I'm sorry to disturb you but we have had an incident in P.2 and I need you now," her voice quivering a little, "No, it's an emergency... yes, thank you. I would appreciate it," she hung up, "Miss Jolliff, can you go outside and ask the others to come back in?"

That was easier said than done. Eighteen kids ran around the playground like head-the-bins.

"P.2," I called out. Nobody responded. I tried again, "Line up, P.2." Again nothing. How the heck was I going to encourage them in?

James skipped over to me and squinted up at me because of the strong sunlight.

"What you doing, Miss?" he asked.

"I'm trying to get everyone to line up. Mrs Craig wants everyone in."

James took a deep breath and shouted out, "Everyone line up now!"

As if by magic, all the children stopped and made their way to the line. I was in awe.

"Well done, James."

"Can I go on the star, Miss?" James asked standing up tall.

"Yes, of course you can."

When I marched the children back into the classroom, Mr Cardwell was in the room. He was down on his honkers in front of Dawn and she had her mouth open; tears were streaming down her face. What the heck was wrong with her? Maybe if I had a younger brother or sister, I would understand what I was working with here! The three years between Josh and I didn't help me in this situation.

"Let's go over to the carpet, P.2. And I will read you all a story," I said as I went over to the library and selected a random book.

All the kids settled down and concentrated on me. I was impressed with myself. Even James, who was as happy as punch that his name was now on the star, sat right at the front at my feet. His arms folded.

"Look, James is sitting really well. He's a good boy. Well done, James." I took my green-tinted glasses out of my zip-up pocket and slipped them on. "Now this story is called *Can we go ice-skating, Mum?* by Rick Barnes. That's an interesting title, P.2. Believe it or not, I ice-skate," I said turning the book over and looked at the photograph of the author on the back: dark hair and a handsome face.

"Do ye wear those funny boots?" Katie asked.

"Yes, the boots are called ice-skates," I said, feeling comfortable that I was talking about a topic I knew everything about. Mr Cardwell and Mrs Craig tiptoed past me.

Mr Cardwell said, "You have them all eating out of your hand. You don't mind if I steal Mrs Craig for half an hour until we get to the bottom of this."

Was Mrs Craig leaving me alone with eighteen children? My dyslexic storm rose its ugly head and I wasn't sure if I could do this. I nodded at Mr Cardwell, and Mrs Craig smiled a nervous smile at me before they left the room.

"Miss, do you wear one of those princess dresses when you skate?" shouted Jill from the back row. I took a deep breath and got comfortable in my seat. I could do this. I wanted to be positive and thoughtful. I repeated the words over and over in my head.

"I wear tights and a leotard with a short skirt over the top," I said as I reached for the whiteboard marker and drew a sketch of myself onto the flip chart.

"Cool," said Jill and I smiled looking at my drawing. I really should look into doing Art again.

"Any other questions?" I asked. I was maintaining good control over the children and I was glad they were impressed by my artwork. Everyone had their hand up and I touched my throat.

"Tobie?"

"When do you go ice-skating?" he asked.

"I used to go three or four times a week. Now I go once a week. I go every Saturday."

"How does it make you feel?" asked Katie. I paused and glanced up at the ceiling. I took a deep breath.

"It makes me happy. I'm free like a bird when I step onto the ice."

"My mummy ice-skates and so do I. I don't like it," said James. The classroom door opened and there was Nicola.

"Oh," I said, looking up at her.

"Mrs Craig sent me over. She didn't want you being on your own. You being new and all. So, P.2… what are we all up to?" she said snapping the book out of my hand. She was a bully!

My stomach flipped as she glared down at me. "I'll read the story. You're new here and I'm not. I know what I'm doing. Let me sit there," she said leaning towards me in an aggressive way. I reluctantly stood up and moped to the back of the classroom. She read the title again to the children, "*Can we go ice-skating, Mum?* by the author, Rick Barnes."

I dragged down the hem of my skirt and stumbled over to the sink. I filled the basin up with hot water and started throwing the milk cups in one by one whilst trying to stop my chin from trembling. I ignored her words and washed the cups, leaving each one to dry on the drainer.

When I had finished, I continued looking at the back wall. I wrapped my arms around myself like a stupid, scared canary!

TWENTY-FOUR
HOUSE

Stephanie stomps up my stairs and enters Sophia's room. Beginning to pack Sophia's clothes, tears flood into her eyes. I'm devastated. Sophia is downstairs on her mat. She too starts to cry and I shout from my chimney.

"Don't cry, little one. Don't cry, and all will be well. Don't cry, little one. Don't cry, and all will be well."

Jack is pacing up and down my kitchen still chewing on his gum. Stephanie stops for a while and waits.

She continues to pack Sophia's items: her socks, her baby-grows, her nappies, and the little gloves she wears to stop herself from scratching her face.

I yell from my chimney pot again, "Don't cry, little one. Don't cry, and all will be well. Don't cry, little one. Don't cry, and all will be well."

Stephanie walks downstairs to the living room with the suitcase buckled. I regard her warily. She lifts Sophia off her mat.

"Come, little Sophia. We can't stay here," she says, and my wiring sparks.

I refuse to take it in. I don't want her to leave.

Memories of Rab, Gillian and their two children come into my being and I allow myself to remember them to ease the pain. I open my hot press door and unravel my memory towel.

* * *

Work was on the phone and Rab wasn't obtaining his promised two weeks' leave. He had to return to the dock on Friday. Only three days. Ridiculous.

"How am I going to explain this to Gillian?" he said as he slowly put the phone down.

Gillian had popped into Belfast to meet up with her chums and grab lunch. He looked as if he wanted to call the kids in from their play in the back garden but held back when he heard their happy-go-lucky cries of laughter.

He went up to the bedroom, put on his shorts and smoothed sun cream over his chest, arms and legs. He strolled out into the garden with a blanket under his arm. It was sunny.

Harry raced up to him at the doorway and flung his arms around him. Rab ruffled his red hair and stepped out onto the patio. Susan waved from the garden swing and asked for a push. Harry dashed to the rescue. Rab stopped in his tracks and kept his eyes on his two lovely children.

"I could not feel any prouder of my happy family. This is the perfect way to live," he said out loud. Rab unrolled the blanket and lay on the grass watching his children. Susan yelled over, "Dad, how do you get a baby astronaut to sleep?"

"I don't know, Susan. How?"

"Rocket!" Susan laughed louder than her dad.

Rab shouted out, "Did you hear about the monster who ate his own house?" I suddenly became interested and listened carefully.

A monster ate a house? Were monsters real?

"No," shouted Susan.

"He was homesick."

"I don't get it," said Susan. I didn't get it either but I worried about that conversation for months.

Susan skipped around the garden. She continued to shout to capture her dad's attention and he willingly provided it to her. She skipped over to him and surveyed the big man sprawled out on the blanket. She had a close bond with her dad and she happily threw herself down beside him, chatting merrily about her friends at school. He was usually out of the house at "work" and so Susan and Harry made the most of their time with their dad and vice versa.

Susan leaned over her dad and hugged him, "I love you Daddy!" Rab went red and I knew he felt a guilt that covered his very soul as he considered his happy daughter's face. Everyone was expecting him to stay for another twelve days.

He jumped up, seized his daughter by the waist and spun her around. She screamed with joy.

Harry bolted over and shouted, "Me! Do me now!" Rab lifted his older, much heavier child, and with the same determination spun him around too. All lay on the blanket afterwards out of breath.

Rab asked them what they wanted for lunch and they hungrily announced their requests for food.

"Your wish is my command," he said and went into the kitchen. The fridge was full and so it wasn't long before he served delicious food to his two children sitting around the garden table: hamburgers, mini pizzas and chips, and another plate filled with cut-up fruit.

Gillian arrived back home at 3pm. Rab broke the news about work and Gillian flopped down with a sigh.

She took a deep breath and called out, "Kids, come in. We have some news for you. Daddy can't stay. He has to go back to work."

Susan cried, and Harry sprinted off up to his bedroom, "We never get to see Daddy," he cried into his pillow.

* * *

I feel my front door open and I remove myself from my hot press of memories and stare as Stephanie and Sophia leave. Stephanie closes my door and my floorboards groan. I want Jack to go after them. But Jack sits down at the computer and I know he won't. He's too busy chewing on his gum.

"She's deleted all our documents," he murmurs and I look at him in disgust, "Where the fuck is my 'recover me' file?" He rummages through the drawers on his desk. He finds what he is looking for. He pops the disc into his computer and pops open a bottle of wine. He slugs on it the way Emily-Brooke used to slurp on her weekly milkshake.

He sits on his own, staring at the computer screen. He sips the red wine and swirls it around his teeth. He stares into Stephanie's little hand mirror and rubs his lips red with the juice.

"I need this new lipstick. I really do," he mimics Stephanie's voice and flings the mirror onto my floor. The mirror breaks and I feel the sharp edges cut into my bare floorboards.

I glance at the clock and it is midnight. A ding sounds on the computer; a file has been recovered. Jack stands up and looks at the screen, "That's mine," he says. He presses the delete button and sits on the floor.

He opens another bottle of wine and drinks it down in gulps. It is late and I'm surprised he doesn't long for sleep.

He pulls himself up onto the chair and rests his head on the arm. He tucks his legs under a cushion and closes his eyes.

Another ding sounds. He lazily gets up and checks the computer again. "Another one of mine. Why did she delete the files? What else is she hiding?" he asks and returns to the chair and falls into a deep, discontented sleep.

He wakes up with a start. Several dings come from the computer, then some more. He glances at the clock; it is two o'clock. He walks over to the computer and leans down.

"Eighty-four items! So, she was a snake," he says.

He flicks through the first five standing. He then sits down to look through the rest.

"She was having several affairs," he says as he shuts down the computer. He spits his gum out onto my floor and I look at the disgusting, distorted greyish blob and wonder when he will pick it up. He doesn't. He walks up stairs and climbs into his bed. I know he sleeps well as he hardly moves.

* * *

The feelings inside me now are the same feelings I experienced when Susan and Harry grew up, left me and moved on. Gillian, Rab and I were left alone.

Rab eventually retired from the Merchant Navy and landed a job in the local chemist delivering prescriptions to people's houses.

Susan and Harry would occasionally call but Harry was busy being a mechanic and Susan was busy working at a hairdresser's.

One day in October, when the leaves were on the ground about my garden, one of them died. It wasn't inside my walls and so I had little interest in the news. They were adults now and my interest in them had waned.

Gillian smoked when her husband was at work and hid them from him when he arrived home.

It was a lonely time.

*

One strange day in December, Gillian found it difficult to breathe. Her husband rubbed her back in the living room.

"I will have to phone an ambulance, Gillian," Rab said in a serious voice.

"No... no... I'm okay. Leave it, Rab," Gillian said and with great difficulty she stood up and shuffled across my floor. Rab ignored her and phoned the ambulance. When they arrived, they settled her with oxygen but said, "You should go to the hospital to get this checked out," advised the paramedic.

When they left, I was left alone. With each day that passed, the less I cared.

Rab returned on his own and he spent the next seven days clearing out Gillian's clothes.

Rab stayed in the house for five more years pottering about his garden, growing tomatoes and cucumbers. He moved with a slowness that made me sigh with sympathy. He no longer ventured up my stairs. Harry had turned up one day with a friend and brought Rab's bed downstairs.

"I miss your mammy," Rab said with Harry perched awkwardly on the bed.

"Time's a healer, Dad."

"It's just not the same without—"

"I know. I know."

"This house might be too big for you now, Dad. You need a bungalow. Something easier to manage. Here, take this," he said handing Rab an odd stone.

"I don't want any of your mumbo-jumbo. Take it out of this house."

"It's not mumbo-jumbo. It's a crystal, Dad. It will protect you. Make you feel better."

Months dragged by. Rab moved out one day in August and I never saw him again.

* * *

I watch Jack sleeping and I wonder if I will ever spend time with Sophia again and my inner voice calls out: I will never see her again. Emily-Brooke, D.B., Harry, Susan and Sophia will never be back within my walls.

It is finished.

I am House!

I have an inner voice humans will never hear. It used to rise from the deep depths, within my foundations, through my plumbing and it made me choke on my own spit.

Now I shout out an uncontrollable "Stop!" as I watch people leave.

Ridiculous.

They can't stop.

I need to give up on trying to make them stay and yet I don't want to be left alone.

My main focus has always been on the children. I try to make the children's lives better; protect them from the pain they inevitably experience. This was and is my job.

The children are the adults' biggest burden. The children's crying makes the adults turn on them and I can't bear to view the cruelty anymore.

I feel different now. I know what I must do.

My breath is quick and frantic and yet I am not sure if I can breathe at all.

"Children should be seen and not heard," I hear myself say and it's as if my voice is solid now. Alive and real. My words mean something because now my words are magical.

A calmness envelops me as the words ring out once more, "Children should be seen and not heard."

They know I exist and they make me feel like I belong. They don't deserve the cruelty they receive from adults. I will help the little ones.

I will.

I will.

I put out my invisible hand and steady myself with a sensation of relief running down my walls. A joy sings out of my whole being. It is a song that sings louder than the whispering inner voice which clangs back down into the pit of my foundations. Louder than Emily-Brooke's cries. Louder than Walter's shouting. Louder than Harry's sobs in the dead of the night.

I will not disappoint the little ones.

It was fun to sit back and watch; now I know I can sort it all out.

I smile.

It is going to be good.

I take a calm, deep breath.

I am House.

I am.

I am.

TWENTY–FIVE
MOLLY

When I arrived home, Josh was in the kitchen with his guitar. I listened to him playing as I flicked on the kettle and put bread in the toaster. He was playing surprisingly well.

"'As the deer panteth for the water'? I've never heard that song before. It's lovely."

"One of Matt's favourites," Josh said.

"It's great. You're playing well. Your singing could do with some work though."

He plonked his guitar down and stuck his tongue out at me.

"I'm only kidding. It was really good. You should ask Mum and Dad for more lessons with Matthew," I said lifting up Charlie, my beloved plant, lacing my fingers in between his leaves.

"I might," said Josh and I smiled.

I plonked down beside him and thought about my crazy day. Thoughts of Nicola marching into my classroom and snatching the book out of my hands played over and over in my head.

"What's up, Blondie?" asked Josh, setting his guitar down and leaning towards me.

"Oh, it's just work…" I said, taking a bite out of my toast and chewing it slowly.

"Care to talk about it? Spill." I shook my head. "A problem shared is a problem halved," he continued, imitating Dad's cheery voice and my stomach tensed. He added, "Something's bugging you. Come on, ya can tell me."

I took a sip of my coffee and gave away a deep sigh.

"It's this woman at work. She's a right pain in the ass," I said as I placed my mug down with a thud.

"Does she work in your classroom?"

"Josh, I don't want to talk about it." I added more milk to my coffee.

"Technically, you've started so ya might as well finish."

I sighed again.

"She's in with P.5 but yesterday she came over when I was left with the kids on my own and I was about to start a story. She snatched the book out of my hand and took over," I said. Josh stared at me without blinking and yowled out a freaky cackle.

"I can't imagine ya in the classroom reading books to children, Molly," he said.

"I didn't get to read to the children. As I just told you, she took over. Are you even listening to me?"

"Why did you let her? Have ya lost your mind?" he asked.

"I don't know what it is about her. She's so intimidating. She's been there seven years and I've only been there a week."

"That doesn't matter. Technically, if it's your classroom, they're your kids. You should've told her to piss off and read the book yourself," he said lifting up his cereal bowl and rinsing it out at the sink, before putting it into the dishwasher, "Talking about books, I bought something for ya. Maybe it will help you to dry your eyes."

"What is it?" Sometimes, Josh impressed me with his advice and his unexpected surprises. He still was a wee dove. He bolted upstairs to fetch my surprise. He was right, I should have ignored her and read the book myself.

When he returned, he put a brown parcel down on the table in front of me.

"What is it?" I asked again.

"I got it for your eighteenth but I want you to have it now," he said, his blue eyes dancing.

I tore open the paper. It was a book.

Josh read out the title, *"The Complete Illustrated Encyclopaedia of Birds of the World: A Detailed Visual Reference Guide to 1600 Birds and Their Habitats, Shown in More Than 1800 Pictures."*

"Thank you," I whispered, delighted with the thoughtfulness of the gift.

"I presume you are still obsessed with birds and I know this was on your wish list on Amazon so—"

"I'm not obsessed. I just like them," I said, running my hand over the front cover, "I love it. Thank you, bro."

Someone tapped the window and I glanced up. There was Matthew. I froze. Josh opened the back door.

"Yer ma was in the garden and she sent me round. She thought ya were in the back garden. Ya know what I mean?"

"No, I'm in here. Sweet. Hit the door on the way in. Check out the book I got my sister," said Josh and my hands started to sweat. Matthew leaned over me and I immediately smelt his fresh, clean smell. He flicked the book in his direction and lifted it up.

"Oh wow. Ye guys are not going to believe this. I have this book."

"Really?" asked Josh.

"Really?" I repeated, then hiccupped and Josh rolled his eyes at me.

"Ya," said Matthew looking down at me, "I take it ya like birds."

"Yes, yes I do. I love birds," I said looking up at him. His eyes appeared bluer today and he had a little overlapping tooth on the left-hand side of his mouth. My heart was beating fast and I wanted Josh to disappear and leave Matthew and I alone.

"I'm obsessed with birds. When I was younger, I used to bird-watch with my da. Actually, sometimes I take myself off with ma bins and check out the hot birding sites, if ya know what I mean. And look, I even have a tattoo," he said pulling down his T-shirt, flexing his arm in my direction. I stared at the tattoo on his broad shoulder.

Matthew Stewart: a bird-watcher? Unreal.

"I love it. I mean the book. And yes, well, the tattoo too. I used to go bird-watching with my grandad. That tattoo is perfect," I rambled.

"I had it done last year to remind me of ma dad. His favourite song was *Three Little Birds* by Bob."

"Bob?" I asked and I hiccupped again.

"I like when ya do that."

"What?" I asked.

"Those little hiccups. If ya know what I mean. It's cute. It's Bob Marley. Here, I'll play it for ya." He swung his guitar case off his shoulder and unzipped it on our kitchen table.

His brown hair flopped over his eyes as he examined the instrument. His broad shoulders moved every time his fingers flew up and down the guitar as he tuned it; his large hands made me want to reach out and touch them.

He pulled out the spare chair beside me and squatted down. His eyes still focused on the top of his guitar. His thighs were muscular and wide; his jeans strained to cover them.

"Got it," he said. I coughed and didn't know where to place my hands. He sang.

"That's cracker, mate. Pure skill," Josh commented. I fired him a dirty look. There was no way he was going to ruin this perfect moment. A man in my kitchen singing a song about my favourite thing: birds. He was beyond amazing. The song itself was lovely. As he played, the first bird at the top of his shoulder appeared and disappeared several times.

"What did ya think?" he asked.

"Brilliant, mate," Josh answered and I opened my mouth to respond but my phone dinged. It was Anita.

Fancy a trip to the rink tomorrow? I can pick you up at five, A.

Matthew placed his guitar back in his case and zipped it up. He focused on me.

"It's cool ya like birds. Later."

Josh and Matthew were about to leave the kitchen and I called after them.

"Josh!"

He turned around and said, "Yep?"

"Thanks," I said. He winked and left the room, "And Matthew, I'm glad we finally managed to meet." The words sounded odd and as soon as I said them, I regretted them. I hoped he didn't hear me. He had left the room with Josh so I wasn't sure.

I leaned forward and banged my mobile off the side of my head. Matthew popped his head back into the kitchen.

"Me too," he said and disappeared again.

Me too? Did he say, "Me too?" I hiccupped, giggled and threw my phone down on our kitchen table. I hugged my bird book.

On the way to work, I was walking on air.

TWENTY–SIX
HOUSE

When Rab left, I was empty for only one day before two more arrived to live within my walls. They were like the gypsy I had encountered many years ago. Muhammad and Nadia wore bright clothes and had tan skin. I watched them both carefully. Intrigued.

They were both young and were determined to make friends with my neighbours quickly. I knew because on their first day they talked to each other over the fence.

"Yous aren't from around these parts," said Tom who had moved in next door the year before.

"No," said Muhammad.

"Where did yous live before?" asked Kate, Tom's wife.

"Driouch in North Morocco."

"Morocco? Is that where those Muslim people come from?"

"Our religion is Islam. Yes, we are Muslim," Muhammad answered starting to collect rubbish from my garden.

"Do you always cover yer hair?" Kate asked and I was glad. I too wanted to know about the scarf on Nadia's head.

"Yes. We cover our head from the age of thirteen. It's a sign of respect for our husband and our God." Her chocolate brown eyes had a little twinkle that made me like her. Muhammad smiled and joined Nadia again, putting his arm on his wife's.

Muhammad was of a slim build, like Walter, with a full head of dark, curly hair. He was about five foot seven. Nadia was small, barely five foot, and plump.

Muhammad looked Tom straight in the eyes before he spoke.

"Let's unpack. It was nice to meet you both." Tom and Kate watched them as they went through my back door.

Weeks turned into months. Kate and Nadia spoke daily. Tom and Muhammad didn't. They would work in their gardens; Tom in his and Muhammad in mine. Seeing each other but never speaking to each other.

I enjoyed listening to the conversations between Kate and Nadia.

"I love yer tan skin," said Kate, handing Nadia a cup of hot tea, "But what's with the tattoos? Women here don't get tattoos on their faces."

"I've had them since I was ten. I remember lining up with all the other women in Driouch. I was so scared."

"Why did you get it done?"

"To show where I belonged. All the girls in Driouch get these marks. My father held my head still as the man tattooed my face. I choked out a small whimper and my father fired me a look that made me stop. It was best not to cry. My friends all stood in the line and copied my bravery. My mum cried when she saw the marks on my face."

"Yer ways are so different from ours. The way yous pray five times a day, cover yer hair and now yer tattoos."

I had to agree with Kate. I found their ways strange too. Yes, they talked to God but it was different from the way Emily-Brooke talked to God. Emily-Brooke talked about everything and anything. Nadia and Muhammad repeated the same words during each prayer. One minute they were standing and the next minute they were on their knees on a mat. Did they pray to the same God? Surely not.

"Did you go to school?" asked Kate.

"I wasn't encouraged to go to school. I can't read or write."

"Really? Do you not miss that?"

"No, what would I miss? I've never done it. I love my life." Innocence surrounded her. She was like a child rather than an adult. She didn't wear makeup like Stephanie, or smoke like Gillian, or carry a sadness with her like Abigail. Nadia was happy.

She was a great cook and knew it. All our neighbours asked for Nadia's bread and she loved seeing the joy on their faces as they munched merrily on her baking. She smiled regularly.

"I'm delighted when Muhammad is kind to me. Every day I would feel butterflies in my stomach just before he would arrive home."

"That's so sweet," said Kate.

"I love him, you know."

"I know ya do. Ya can't stop talking about him."

Nadia talked about Muhammad regularly and when he strolled in my front door, she fell into his arms joyfully.

One year after moving in, she discovered she was pregnant.

Kate rejoiced with her when Zara was born. Nadia had her first baby and the baby saw me. I greeted her.

She didn't stay long like the others. She died at the age of three months. Nadia found her in the cot and her little heart had stopped beating. She listened to Zara's chest. Nothing. She didn't hear her own scream as it hauntingly woke up Muhammad in the next room.

My heart broke in two with that scream. He raced to her and despair gripped me as he saw the cold body of Zara in the little cot. Nadia clutched her chest and slumped to the ground in total fear. Her baby was not alive.

When she woke, her baby had already been washed and wrapped, and she could no longer hold her little body in her arms. Tears flowed uncontrollably.

The Imam spoke in whispers to Muhammad. They bowed their heads and Nadia cried even louder for her Zara.

Her friend held her and hushed her. She must be quiet. Crying was not the way.

The Imam spoke sternly to her, "You must not mourn for Zara. She belonged to God and God acquired her back. He simply took her back. God will be angry if you mourn."

She couldn't stop crying and her constant sobbing upset Muhammad. He told her the same as the Imam but in a sterner voice.

"You were told not to cry. Stop it!" Nadia hid her sobs, but her tears continued to flow.

A year later she was pregnant again. Another baby girl was born. She called her Zara after her first baby.

When Zara reached the age of three, Nadia went to her little bed and Zara was not breathing.

"If only I had not cried for my first baby. God is angry with me." She stifled her scream. She pushed the tears back; away from her eyes. She calmly told Muhammad their baby was dead and went back to Zara, holding her close.

When the Imam arrived, Nadia calmly handed over her second little Zara.

She went into my kitchen and made bread.

A year passed and Nadia never shed a tear for her little baby. She refused to visit the burial area when Muhammad asked.

When she became pregnant again, she explained to Kate, "I know God has forgiven me. I know this baby will grow old."

"I hope so for yer sake," agreed Kate, "Tom thinks the whole comings and goings are odd. He said it makes him uneasy."

When she was told the baby was a girl, she called her Zara. She was healthy and strong.

Muhammad wanted a male child to inherit his farm back in Morocco and so the babies kept coming. They had three more girls and I was full of happiness and joy once more. Her children were always perfect: dark-haired, tanned, plump with good Moroccan food, and immaculately clean.

Women stopped by the house and complimented the children. Nadia always smiled politely and offered food to all who entered.

Men were not allowed in her company, especially Tom. Muhammad was the only man she was allowed to be with. He made her laugh daily and loved her food.

When she was pregnant again, she gave birth in my kitchen. The first male was born and everyone rejoiced.

Adil had his mother's smile and his father's curly, dark hair and brown eyes. He was spoilt from the day he was born in the kitchen, and he was loved immensely by his whole family. I loved him too.

I loved all the children.

TWENTY–SEVEN
MOLLY

The next day when I arrived at my classroom, Mrs Craig was talking to a girl with long, blonde hair like mine, caught back in a high ponytail. She was wearing a grey Adidas tracksuit.

"Oh, Molly. Let me introduce you to Jasmine. Jasmine has worked here before and she is back again. She will stay with us initially until Mr Cardwell decides where she is meant to be."

Jasmine stepped towards me and held out her hand.

"Lovely to meet you, Molly. Oh, I love your dress. Is it from River Island? I saw it in the window."

"Yes," I said leaning in towards her.

"I'll go and pick up the children whilst you two get to know each other," Mrs Craig said and left the room.

"So, how long have you been working with Mrs Craig?"

"Just a week," I answered.

"Only a week? I thought you'd been here for months," Jasmine said with a smile, "So, how are you finding it?"

"I've only just left school, so it's been a bit weird for me," I said awkwardly.

"What about the other CAs? Have you got to know them?"

"Only a few, to be honest. Pauline and Nicola... and I think the other girl was Alex but I haven't had a chance to get to know her."

"Oh, how are you getting on with Nicola? She can be a bit of a handful."

"Well, not great. I don't think she likes me," I said.

"Nicola doesn't like anyone, so that's no big deal. Don't take any of her crap. She thinks she runs this place. Did she give you the line, 'I've been here longer than you?' She thinks she's the top dog about this place, but she isn't."

I smiled. There was something straightforward about Jasmine that I liked and I knew we were going to become friends. A little bluebird.

Maybe Josh was right. I *was* obsessed with birds.

The door opened and in came Mrs Craig; a paler colour than when she left. She was shaking her head. She stepped towards us, talking in a serious tone.

"I don't understand it, we only have twelve kids today."

"Twelve?" I repeated without meaning to.

"Yes, I'm worried. We will do our carpet time now and if you two don't mind, I'm going to pop over and speak to Mr Cardwell. I am starting to feel concerned. Maybe a deep clean is needed in this classroom. Something isn't right. Sixteen off. That's odd." She moved over to her seat at the carpet and settled herself.

"Now P.2, guess who is in our class today? Yes, Miss Ward. She is back for a visit. Let's sing our morning song. Did everyone move their stone over to the 'I am here' basket?"

All twelve kids said, "Yes," in unison. They sat up straight and sang the stone song:

> *How many stones are left alone?*
> *How many stones are left alone?*
> *How many stones are left alone?*
> *Who is still at home?*

This was ridiculous; sixteen were off. It continued:

> *Sixteen little stones are left alone.*
> *Sixteen little stones are left alone.*
> *Sixteen little stones are left alone.*

Lots of children must be at home.

Mrs Craig continued with the dinner book, and Jasmine and I set out the play equipment.

"Do you think that they have all caught something?" she asked me.

"I've no idea. Sixteen off... that is a lot," I answered.

"It's probably chickenpox. It spreads like wildfire," said Jasmine as she opened the playdough tubs.

"Probably," I said.

Mrs Craig came over and put her hand on my shoulder.

"I'm going to pop over to Mr Cardwell now. Are you sure you are okay on your own?"

"Yes, we will be fine," I said. It was nice Mrs Craig trusted me alone with the children. Being positive definitely made a difference.

When Mrs Craig left, Jasmine and I had a lot of fun. Jasmine was very much at home within the classroom. She dished out the paints and had a small group around her in seconds.

"I want you to paint a picture of Mrs Craig. She has just popped over to speak to Mr Cardwell and it would be a nice surprise if she returned and saw your pictures." Her group set to work. She moved over to two other children and asked, "Would you like to play snap?"

"What's that?" asked Pamela, a short-haired kid with beautiful grey eyes.

Jasmine opened the games cupboard and lifted out the snap cards.

"You guys are going to love it. Wait and see."

"If you're happy here, I'm going to read a story to that small group over at the carpet." I said.

Jasmine smiled, "Great idea, Molly."

I went over to the library and selected a book called *The Happy House*. I settled down and the group crowded around me. I began to hiccup. I took a deep breath and popped on my green-tinted glasses.

"P.2, I'm going to read you a story about a house. I want you all to sit up well and I want you to listen carefully," I said and took a deep breath and read:

"Once upon a time there was a happy house. Inside the house, there lived a family; a mummy, a daddy, a little boy, and a little girl. Everyone loved the house and the house loved them. The little girl was a little bit lazy. She found it difficult to keep her bedroom tidy. It was always a mess."

"My room is always a mess too, Miss," Natalie said and I glanced up.

"Me too, Natalie. But if I promise to tidy up mine, will you do the same?" Everyone laughed and Natalie agreed to the deal, "Okay, everyone, let's find out what happens next," I lifted the book back up and began reading again. A confidence swept over me like a warm blanket.

"'I need to sort out my bedroom. It is a mess,' said the little girl. 'Poppy-Lotus, are you coming down for breakfast?' said her mum."

"That's a funny name," said Tim.

"Yes, Poppy-Lotus is a funny name," I agreed and continued reading, making myself comfortable in the teacher's chair, "'I'm tidying my bedroom,' she shouted back. 'Hurry up,' said her mum. 'Your toast will get cold.'"

James had his hand up. "Yes, James?" I asked.

"My dad rushes me all the time," he said.

"My parents rush me to do things too," I said.

"Last week, my dad shoved me down the stairs and I fell and my nose was bleeding. He said I was going too slow."

I drew in a large breath, overwhelmed by what he had said.

"Oh, poor you," I said.

"Blood was everywhere but Dad told me to jump into the car. I got blood on the car seats too, Miss," he said.

"Poor you," I repeated and lifted the book up again, "Now, where was I?"

My eyes couldn't find where I had last stopped. The words swam all around. That poor little boy. I began to hiccup again.

James piped in with, "Ya were at the part where Poppy-Lotus was cleaning her bedroom."

I coughed nervously and I found the place and began reading again, "It was lunchtime and Poppy-Lotus was still tidying her bedroom. 'Lunch is ready,' called her mum."

Everyone laughed and I looked up shocked. Why were they laughing? I was so taken back by what James had told me I had just "barked at print" and had no idea what I was even reading now.

Sadie said, "Keep going, Miss."

"'Not now, Mum. I am tidying my bedroom.'"

"Hey, Miss, Miss," said James.

"Yes, James?"

"Can I go to the toilet?"

"Yes, James." As he brushed passed me, I had to push tears away from my eyes; I could hardly read on. Imagine being pushed down the stairs. By a parent.

"'Hurry up,' said her mum. 'Your soup will get cold.' The little girl continued to tidy up her bedroom. When she was finished, she called her mum upstairs. 'Come and see my bedroom,' she said. It was lovely. Her mum was happy and so was the house. Mum heated up her soup in the microwave. The end."

Mrs Craig marched back into the classroom. I closed the book and my little group clapped. Jasmine looked over from her table and smiled warmly over at me.

"P.2, did you enjoy the story? Now I want you to do something for me. I want you to draw me a picture of your house," I said with a smile. They all went back to their seats and I got to my feet and grabbed the A4 paper and asked Tanya, "Would you give these out please?"

"Yes, I will, Miss," she said. I slipped over to Mrs Craig who was now sitting at her table.

"Are you okay, Hazel?" I asked.

"Not really. It is so odd, Molly. We have sixteen kids off today and we rang home to five of them. All five said that their child is not speaking. They are the same way Dawn was with us yesterday," she said shaking her head.

"That's odd. Dawn scared the wits out of me."

"Mr Cardwell is going to ring the others and then he'll come over here. If all sixteen are off for the same reason, we will have to contact the board."

"The board?"

"The education board," she explained.

The break bell rang, and Jasmine and I went out into the playground.

When we went in, Mrs Craig was an awful shade of grey as she sipped on water.

"Are you okay?" I asked.

"Mr Cardwell phoned over. All sixteen children are off today. They have *all* stopped talking."

"Oh my word. Why is this happening? Is it only our class or other classrooms too?"

"Only one or two are absent in other classrooms so I think it's only our class. I don't know what's going on. I'm worried about it… How am I going to teach number work now?"

"Let's keep it simple and you have a sit-down. You're probably in shock. You have gone a strange colour."

"I'll give out their number booklets and they can work on those. I don't think I can stand up there and teach a lesson when I know sixteen of my kids are at home and not speaking. This is awful."

Mrs Craig handed out the number booklets and the children got stuck into their work. Jasmine and I moved around the classroom encouraging everyone to keep working whilst Mrs Craig looked devastated at her desk.

When it was our lunchtime, I was happy to walk over to the staffroom with Jasmine. It was nice to have a friend at work.

On the way past Mr Cardwell's office, he popped out and in a grave voice he said, "I'm sure you are aware of the drama that is happening in P.2, Molly. I was wondering if you could pop into my office after your lunch so we can have a quick chat."

"Oh, okay," I said, suddenly feeling a bubble of worry circling around my stomach.

"Nothing to worry about. We just need to get to the bottom of this," he said.

"Okay," I repeated as he disappeared back into his office and closed the door. Jasmine put her hand on my back.

"Molly, remember he said it was nothing to worry about. Let's grab our lunch."

"Do you think he thinks I did this?" I asked, feeling the bubble bursting into a million panic droplets. I felt sick.

"No. That's ridiculous. How could you make them go quiet? Impossible."

"Yeah, that's ridiculous."

Nicola came click-clacking down the corridor and glared at Jasmine.

"You're not back, are you?"

"I sure am, Nicola, and good to see you too," said Jasmine.

"I see you haven't lost your cheekiness," snapped Nicola. She looked me up and down, "Is it true kids in your class have stopped speaking?"

"Who told you that?" butted in Jasmine.

"Wouldn't you like to know?" snapped Nicola.

"This school is hectic. You can't keep anything quiet," said Jasmine.

"Why are you back then?"

"Oh, you know, I missed ye all," said Jasmine, opening the door and she flicked her hair as she bumped her way past Nicola, strutting into the staffroom. The classroom assistants all greeted her with a cheer.

"Yeah, you're back. You better stay longer this time," said Pauline, giving her a hug.

"Come and sit down with me," said Brenda, the P.1 classroom assistant.

"So good to see you," said Ann, the secretary.

Nicola stepped in front of me and pranced through the door next and sarcastically said, "Jasmine's back yeah. Wise up guys, you know she'll not stay long."

"Come and sit with me, Molly," said Jasmine, ignoring Nicola. I happily joined Jasmine and it was nice to finally get to meet Brenda and Ann. They were both lovely girls. Working here wasn't bad after all.

I was as happy as a lark here. Now that I had friends.

TWENTY–EIGHT
HOUSE

Mice!

It began in my garden; a family of two moved in and I was not impressed. I never minded animals, insects and bugs that passed through on their way to somewhere else. But the mice stayed and I was not happy. They blended in under the pigeon shed which used to be filled with Walter's prize possessions. Muhammad filled it now with gardening tools and the kids' bicycles.

No one seemed to notice the mice except for me. They were more active at night scurrying about. Their twitching noses, quick movements and large front teeth made me uneasy.

It got worse when one ventured up my drainpipe and entered my insides through a hole in the wall. I focused on her with her ears up high as she stalked my skirting boards. She froze and remained still when Nadia marched up my stairs. Hidden by the large pieces of furniture, it grew in confidence leaving its brown droppings in her wake.

"Leave," I cried.

It was a cry that called louder than any child who lived within my walls. My inner voice heard me and, with a sigh, woke up from the pit of my foundations. Wide awake. Ready for action.

My inner voice sounded frantic and it screamed to the top of my chimney pot, "Leave now. You are not welcome here."

It paused and my inner voice whispered in my roof, "You can't stay here. You must leave."

This matte brown intruder scorned all the reasons why it should not make a home under my roof. A soft panic fell on my walls as it made its way up into my attic. It made a nest in the far corner where clothes were stacked in a black bin bag.

It gnawed constantly at my woodwork and unsettled me. Soon, Nadia opened her eyes in the night and shook her husband's arm.

"Wake up. Do you hear that? Listen." Her husband turned over in the bed.

"It's nothing. Go back to sleep."

But the noise didn't stop and the mouse dragged out a strange item, like a pink sack resembling a wet tongue, from its backend. It yanked at it with its teeth, licking and gnawing frantically. It plucked out a pink baby mouse with blue-grey eyes closed tight letting out little chirps. It cried out for assistance.

The whole episode repeated many times until five baby mice, like the jelly babies Emily-Brooke used to eat, were in the nest.

My inner voice fell silent as the little babies quivered. My inner voice knew I didn't want them to leave anymore. The pinkies and I greeted each other and a joy sang out of my whole being. It was a song that sang louder than my whispering inner voice, which gave up with a sigh and clanged back down into the pit of my foundations. Disappointed. Silenced once more.

TWENTY–NINE
MOLLY

Twenty minutes flew by and I was disappointed when the bell rang.

"Don't forget: you have to pop in and see Mr Cardwell," Jasmine reminded me, squeezing the top of my arm.

"Oh, crikey. I forgot about that. I was having too much fun in there," I said as we marched towards his office.

"Don't be worrying now. I'll see you back in the classroom."

Easier said than done. A stone shot to the pit of my stomach. I reached out like a cautious snake tamer and knocked on the office door.

"Come," he called out and I opened the door.

"You asked me to call in…" I said after clearing my throat.

"Oh yes. Take a seat, Miss Jolliff." He called me by my second name. I immediately felt as if I was about to be told off. I took a seat and memories of the interview flooded back. Mr Cardwell let out three long sighs and I planted myself on my hands so I wasn't tempted to bite my nails.

"Molly, what do you think about the event that is occurring in P.2?"

"I'm surprised," I said rubbing the back of my neck whilst looking over his overpowering desk. Why was he asking me what I thought? I'd only just started working here. I focused on his desk again. My eyes traced over the letters on his nameplate; the same way I had traced over it when I had my interview. The letters were still muddled.

"It's probably a coincidence, but this only started when you joined the class," Mr. Cardwell said, peering at me over his glasses.

"Me?" I mumbled and I felt myself going red. Did he think I caused this creepy thing to happen? Was this magpie blaming me? One for sorrow...

"I was wondering if you might have read P.2 a story about staying quiet," he said rubbing his brow, "I know it's a long shot but—"

"No, I've only read one story and that was today. It was about... oh, let me think now... oh, yes. It was about a house and a little girl. She was tidying her room... I have no idea why this happened. I've got nothing to do with this."

"Oh, I know you have nothing to do with this," he said, crossing his arms in front of his chest, "My job is to glean information from this strange occurrence, and I need to speak to everyone involved with this class. I'm not putting you on the spot or anything like that. I just need to tick all the boxes before I phone the education board," he continued, chewing at his bottom lip.

I glanced up at his bookcase and my eyes drifted over his files. I shifted my gaze back to him. A pounding started in my head. My hands began to sweat and I asked, "Will the board think I did this?"

"No one thinks you did this. I'm trying to get to the bottom of it. There must be some logical explanation. I just can't see it at the minute," said Mr Cardwell, standing up quickly and opening his office door. I stood up and stepped past him.

"Thank you," I said and went back to Mrs Craig's room.

Was I to blame for this? I shoved the idea to the back of my mind.

Impossible.

The rest of the day was surprisingly pleasant. Having a friend in the workplace made the whole ordeal less daunting.

"I love dancing. I go to a hip-hop class downtown. It's excellent," said Jasmine, drumming her feet against the floor.

"I'm an ice-skater," I said.

"Oh cool. Do you do all of those mad jumps and wear the gorgeous outfits?" she asked leaning towards me.

"Yes," I said with a laugh, "In fact, I'm going tonight. You should come and see me skate sometime."

"I can't tonight but I'd definitely love to see you skate another time. I watch it on television and it's cool," she replied smiling widely.

When the bell rang, Jasmine and I left the school. It was good having someone to walk home with. Jasmine lived around the corner. I was surprised I had never met her before.

"I'll meet you here tomorrow," said Jasmine, and I practically skipped the rest of the way home.

Anita arrived at five on the dot, still proud as punch in her car.

When we arrived at the rink, it was packed. We both stood at the edge. Two teenagers held onto the wall as they tried to balance on their thin blades. An announcement boomed over the loudspeaker inaudible due to the shouts, cheers and constant slicing of the blades on skaters as they zoomed past.

Before we moved to get changed, I spotted Terrance on the ice. He was with Fiona and they were flying around holding hands. Fiona's hairband was gold. I nudged Anita and she saw them straight away.

"They look ridiculous," I said watching their routine. He had on black trousers with a yellow stripe down each side, and a matching silk shirt with a black waistcoat over the top. She had on a gold dress; the kind you would wear at a competition. They did a double axel jump in unison and we both gasped.

"Beyond weird... Pretty good though," said Anita touching her throat, grabbing her necklace and popping the hedgehog into her mouth.

"It's the size difference that makes it look so odd," I said opening my lip balm to apply it to my lips. My finger stopped midway to my mouth when Terrance and Fiona did a perfect throw jump and Fiona did two full revolutions. They glided around the rink and I touched my lips, rubbing the balm all over them.

How come his hair didn't move at all? It looked as if it was painted on. Fiona ended with a sit spin. From where we were, her right leg was beautifully extended and her left leg bent creating a perfect ninety-degree angle. I was about to clap when Terrance, red-faced, flew back towards her, stopping in such a way he showered her with ice. Clicking his fingers down at her, his face changed from red to purple.

"I can't watch this," Anita said, rubbing the back of her neck and looking away, "It's a train wreck just about to happen."

I had no idea what he said to Fiona but I knew by her face that it was nasty. Fiona got up and with her head down, tried to flick off the ice with her hand. She left the rink.

Terrance continued to skate around doing a sequence of jumps: two camel spins, and spirals he repeated at a fast and furious speed. He ended with a spread eagle and moved backwards around the rink.

Anita and I got changed. We said nothing about what we had witnessed. A girl strolled past me with a hot chocolate in her hand and it smelt delicious. It reminded me of the cosy nights at Grandad's bungalow after a long day of bird-watching; comparing notes and bird sketches. I smiled at the memory.

When I stepped onto the ice, I relaxed despite the crowds of people out tonight. I found my own inner space and glided happily around the rink for my warm-up. I wasn't sure if Terrance saw me on the ice and I didn't care. I began my short programme working exceptionally hard on perfecting the steps. A stray hair stuck to my lip balm and I wiped it away. After several attempts, I was happy and I moved on to my long programme: my favourite. I was me here; free and happy like a bird.

I needed a drink. I went to the vending machine to nab a Coke. As I was popping in my money, I sensed someone was watching me. Goosebumps appeared on my arms and I turned back only to see Terrance looking up at me. I began to hiccup.

"Molly, it's good to see you here. I am glad someone takes my advice. I have something I want to run past you," he said, making strong eye contact with me. A child squealed beside us and a teenager boy threw his puck onto the ground in front of me.

"Oh? Yes... what is it?" I said turning my grandmother's ring on my middle finger.

"Let's sit down," he said and directed me to the benches that spread down the middle of the changing area. I took a pew and he remained standing.

Was this proud peacock making me sit because he was shorter than me?

"Molly, I need someone to do something for me," he said rubbing his hands together.

"What is it?"

"I need someone at your level of expertise to teach my beginner class. You would be a good match," he said licking his lips in an odd way.

"Oh, I'd love to do that. I really would. Are you sure you think I'm a good match?" I asked and hiccupped again. He snapped his fingers down into my face.

"I wouldn't have asked you if I didn't think you would be a good match. Anyway, it will be a paid gig so that should make it more enticing. It is, however, an early lesson," he said.

"Oh, how early?" I asked.

"Saturday morning at 7.30am."

"Oh, that is early," I said, wincing a little.

"If you do well, there might be more work for you. I like your skating style and... well, never mind that. I was going to ask Anita too. You could do the lesson together and work out who needs an extra boost, whilst the other will work with the more able in the group. Anyway, you two would be responsible for your own organisation of the lessons. But if you need any tips, I'm happy to run through some good ideas with you both," he said at top speed. I sat there with my mouth open.

This was the perfect job for me. A job that didn't involve reading or writing. Earning money to be on the ice.

"Well, what do you think?" he said.

"I'd love to do it and I'm sure Anita would be happy to do it too," I said looking out at the rink and seeing Anita flying around the ice oblivious to the exciting conversation I was having.

"Well, don't make up your mind now. Both of you can talk to me on Saturday. Have a good think. I need reliable girls to do this," he said clicking his fingers once more as he spoke.

I stood up and said, "Thank you Terrance... for thinking about us two." He didn't answer. He just turned around, stomping back over to the ice and stepping on.

"Oh, crap!" I said, remembering I hadn't taken my Coke out of the machine. I stepped over to it. But the Coke was gone. I searched in my purse for more money but I didn't have enough.

Anita came over and poked me in my ribs, "Ha, made you jump. So, what was that about? You having a wee chat with Terrance?"

"You're never going to believe what he asked me."

"Tell me," Anita said popping her hedgehog into her mouth.

"He's gone and offered us both a job."

"A job? Where?" said Anita narrowing her eyes.
"Here at the rink. He needs teachers for his beginner group and he's offering it to us two." I took in the sights of the rink and watched as the Zamboni cruised up and down the rink leaving a slick trail of smooth ice in its wake.

"Are you joking?"

"Nope and it's on Saturday mornings, so perfect for us both."

"I'd love to do that," said Anita.

"Good because we have to tell him on Saturday if we want to do it. And at least we are not aspirin' to work in a chemist."

"Was that a joke?"

"Maybe... On another subject: can you buy me a Coke?"

"Uh-huh," said Anita with a happy smile spitting her hedgehog out of her mouth.

THIRTY
HOUSE

My happiness soared as I examined the little ones in their nest. Their mother would scurry off and, guided by my skirting boards, would make her way down to my kitchen for some treats for herself: crumbs, chicken fat and cornflakes. Always her favourites.

Nadia knew they were there. She would continue to wake in the night and wake Muhammad. He would listen and it wasn't long before he too heard them scraping.

One night, he went to the pigeon shed and fetched a spade. What did he plan to do? Why did he need a spade? He left it in the kitchen and went back to bed.

He put his hand on Nadia, "Don't worry, darling. I'll sort it tomorrow."

I worried all night repeating his words over and over again: "sort it tomorrow, sort it tomorrow." What did he mean?

The next day, I followed their every move. Nadia cleaned all day: bleaching the surfaces, brushing the floors, and carefully wrapping up food and putting it away into cupboards.

When Muhammad woke, he got the spade in his hand and he went from room to room searching for my little ones.

My whole being was furious at them both. How dare they cut off their food supply and search for them. I froze when Muhammad made his way up to my attic. My low beams appeared lower that day. Dust danced about the air here and the skylight window was dirty. Old photographs were stashed in my corners; black and white and overlooked. Unlike the photographs downstairs which were brightly coloured and kept in glass frames on display.

The mouse jostled her babies far into the nest when she heard him on the ladder. I knew she was afraid and I shared her fear.

Muhammad banged my walls and with each thud a sickness leaked into me. Something I had never felt before. The mouse jumped with every bang and ran.

"Don't run!" I yelled.

Too late. Muhammad sliced the sharp edge of the spade through her tiny body. I slunk low down into my foundations knowing the babies were now on their own.

Motherless.

THIRTY-ONE
MOLLY

I woke up to the pitter-patter of rain on my window. Another day. The "walking in the rain" thing was starting to wear off. I turned towards the wall. I snuggled down deep into my quilt, only to hear my alarm blasting beside me like an albatross around my neck. Why me? I needed to pass my driving test and land a car.

As I searched for an outfit to wear, I made up my mind that tonight was the night that I'd clean my bedroom. It was time for me to become an adult.

By the time I got downstairs, all the milk was gone.

"Joshua had the last of the milk in his cereal," Dad explained when I slammed the fridge door shut.

"What a pig. I can't even make a cup of tea before work. And have you seen outside, Dad? I've to walk in that you know," I said checking Charlie.

"Dad, Charlie looks a bit sad. Could you keep an eye on him today?"

"Sure, babes," said Dad rolling his eyes.

"Dad, I'm serious. Please help. He doesn't look good," I said before I left the house.

When I arrived at the spot Jasmine had told me to meet her, she wasn't there. The rain kept on coming. My feet were like sponges and I wished I had boots on. Was I destined to always make the wrong choices?

I stood and waited for three minutes. I timed it on my mobile. It felt like half an hour. She must have gotten a lift. I power-walked the rest of the way.

By the time I got to work, I was fed up. I was soaked through and desperately in need of a cup of tea. I made my way to the staffroom.

When I flew through the door, I bumped straight into Nicola.

"Watch it!" she yelled and we both focused on the small puddle of coffee that had spilt onto the floor, "You nearly knocked hot coffee all over me. What's with you?"

"Oh, I'm so sorry. I didn't see you there," I apologised.

Nicola brushed herself off exaggerating her motions, even though she was perfectly fine.

"Seriously, what is going on with you?"

I blinked several times. What was going on with me?

"What? What do you mean by that?" I stammered.

The corner of Nicola's mouth curled in a dissatisfied grimace.

"You... Prancing around like you own the place after only being here a week." Her eyes studied me up and down, "And your clothes. I mean, just look at you."

"I... I..."

"And do you even own a hairdryer?"

"It was raining," I said and she dragged out a disgusted sigh, "What's this about?"

"You know what it's about. You are up to something."

I stepped back, "Up to something?"

"Yes, up to something," she repeated stepping forward, going nose to nose with me, "I do not know what you did but you did something. You start here and kids start dropping like flies," she continued.

"That's nothing to do with me," I said.

"Only in your classroom. Don't you think that's a little bit odd?"

"I... um..." Again, I was lost for words, "It has nothing to do with me," I repeated, going back to the door and putting my hand onto the handle.

"Doesn't look that way from where I'm standing. Never had a problem with those kids until you showed up. If you aren't connected, I'll eat my hat!" She railroaded forward, bumping me out of the way with her hip, "Now if you'll excuse me, I have work to do."

Just like that, she was off and away before I had an opportunity to respond.

What a dirty, filthy, rotten, stinking bad egg she was! This was turning out to be the morning from hell. I was livid. I glared at the time; I had no time to make tea.

When I arrived in the classroom, I yanked off my coat and my jumper placing them on the radiator. Steam rose off them. My blouse was damp and I rubbed my hands up and down my arms wondering where Jasmine was.

The bell rang.

Eight kids arrived today. I searched for James amongst the eight but he was missing and my heart sank. As I heard the morning song, I questioned myself. Was I to blame for this crazy nightmare? The fortune-teller did tell me to stay away from school.

Memories of that crazy man ringing his bell, stretching out around the kitchen and muttering to himself rushed into my head. Even what he did with the sage was mental.

What did he yell in my face? "We're done here!"

What did he mean? He repeated the words, "Children should be seen and not heard. Children should be seen and not heard. Children should be seen and not heard."

I scanned over the small group on the carpet and ejected a gasp. The children who were off... they were seen and not heard. What was going on here?

""You must not enter that school. Don't go. Whatever you do, don't go!" The fortune-teller's words echoed in my head and a vision of the big guy standing in front of me, with his nose dripping with blood, didn't fade.

"Molly... Molly," said Mrs Craig, making me jump, "Molly, can you give out the worksheets?"

"Yes. Yes, of course," I said getting up from my seat, taking the worksheets from her. My hands were trembling.

"Are you okay, Molly?"

"I think so," I said, feeling faint.

"Molly, you don't look too good. I'll give out the worksheets. You take a seat." I flopped down and watched as Mrs Craig handed them out. When she finished, she came back over to me.

"Oh Molly, your nose is bleeding," she said, fetching the tissues from her desk. I put one to my nose and waited. The blood covered the white tissue in splotches. "Molly, go to the bathroom in the main school. Get yourself cleaned up and have a cuppa in the staffroom. You are going to be fine."

"But—"

"No buts, just go," she said and I lifted my fob, making my way back round to the main school. When I entered the corridor, Jasmine stepped out of the P.5 room.

"Hi, Molly. Sorry, I didn't meet you this morning. My dad made me take a lift with him. Oh, and did you hear the news?"

"News?"

"I've been moved to P.5. Mr Cardwell told me this morning. To be honest, I'm a little bit disappointed as I was enjoying working with you."

"Are you working with Nicola?"

"Yes, she'll end up doing my head in but I can deal with her. Are you okay, Molly? You don't look too good."

"I think I'm to blame for this. The kids aren't talking and I'm to blame," I said feeling faint again.

"Molly, you're not to blame for this," said Jasmine, leading me into the staff toilet and handing me more tissues.

"I was told by a fortune-teller not to work here. He said the words, 'Children should be seen and not heard.' I didn't listen to him. I thought he was a nut-job but he was right: the children are seen but not heard. Now we are down to eight kids. Eight! Even James is off and although he does my head in, I miss the little critter," I said sinking down to the floor and leaning my cheek against the cold tiles. Jasmine sank down with me.

"Poor James. He's the last person you'd want to be off," she said staring into the distance.

"What do you mean?" I asked.

"James, you do know his background, don't you?"

"No," I said, suddenly feeling sick in my stomach.

"His father has been physically abusing him for years. Apparently, the school has reported it several times but child protection hasn't acted on it. Well, they did send social workers out to his house but they had no evidence it was happening. So, the case is ongoing," she explained.

"What? How do you know this? Why is nobody stopping this?"

"I was with your class last year, Molly. We were told to keep an eye on James. I didn't see any signs of physical abuse but I did notice he was angry all the time and found it difficult to make friends." A memory of the friendship board flashed up in my head. The rest of the children with friends all around them and James with no one.

"I've seen bruises up his arms and he told me his dad shoved him down the stairs," I blurted out.

"Did you tell Mrs Craig?" Jasmine asked. There was a long pause.

"No," I said.

"Why did you not report it?" Jasmine asked, looking shocked.

"I... I just didn't. I feel like such an idiot. I was so concerned about myself and my feelings I didn't think about him," I said, squeezing my eyes hard to stop tears from forming.

"This job is all about the children," said Jasmine, "Look, I better go. Sort it out, Molly. I'll see you at lunch."

How could I sort it out? I couldn't stay in work. I needed to go and make sure James was okay. I knew where he lived, remembering he lived behind the bus stop.

I left the bathroom, went to the double doors and shouldered my way through. Something inside told me to speak to Mrs Craig first but I ignored it and marched out onto May Avenue.

Once I got to the alleyway, I wished I had my coat with me. It was drying on the radiator. It was probably warm and toasty. I was freezing cold and soaked. Avoiding the puddles, I made my way to the bus stop. The rain kept on coming.

Why was I such a selfish person? How could I ignore the signs that James was being abused? How dare his parents bully him. A five-year-old. Life was hard enough without someone bullying you constantly. The memory of James running out of that house flooded my mind like the water that was now rushing down the street towards me.

Why didn't I ask him if he was okay? Why didn't I get off the bus? I was only interested in going ice-skating! I was despicable. Poor kid. I had to do something, anything, to help him now.

I was outside his house and frozen to the spot. The miserable exterior made me feel sick: an overgrown garden, a front door with black paint flaking off and a hole at the bottom that hadn't gone right through. The windows were covered with dirty, net curtains with rips that could never be repaired.

A house should be a home. It should be bright and cheerful and welcoming. My own house that stood just around the corner was charming. The cut grass, the trimmed hedge, the bright yellow door. My house even had a name: Daisy Manor. Mum had potted two large, shiny yellow pots with daisies. They sat on either side of our door. Every time that door was opened, I would be welcomed and loved. My parents did my head in at times but they never laid a finger on me. All my bruises over the years were formed by my own stupidity. Josh and I had a good family. I loved my family. Every one of them: Mum, Dad and Josh.

I scrutinised the house in front of me and knew James was somewhere inside feeling miserable.

I needed to make sure he was okay. I marched down the little path littered with rubbish that had dropped from the overly stuffed bin parked by the front door. I knocked and prayed silently inside.

"Please help me to say the right words." My whole body tensed up when I heard a noise from within. A man answered the door, his face surprised to see me. He was wearing black Adidas tracksuit bottoms and no top. He had a slither of spaghetti bolognese on his chin and his lips were dark red with the sauce. I wanted to point to his face and ask him to wipe it off but stopped myself.

"What?" he said.

"Hi, I'm from James' school. I'm checking in on the ones who are off," I said trying to sound normal.

"Aye, well come on in then," he said. He kicked several toys to the side as he advanced down the carpetless hallway. He opened the door to the left and directed me to his black, leather settee. "Ya want a cuppa and a towel?" he asked. I nodded and he headed into his kitchen.

I stared around the small living room. There was a large television in the corner with an Xbox and two controllers, all covered in dust. There was a large photograph on a canvas above the unlit fire. It was James. His round face was happy. He was eating an ice cream. His chin was half-covered with cream. The mantelpiece above the fire had random items displayed, all covered in a thick layer of dust: a wallet, an iPhone with the battery removed, a small jar filled with coins, a spanner, and a half-empty cup of cold tea.

James' dad came back. In one hand, he held a mug with a motorbike on the front and in the other, a small cream towel. A packet of Ginger Nut biscuits was tucked up under his bare armpit.

"There ya go, love," he said, handing me the cup. The heat from the tea made me wince, "Mind yerself there. It's just freshly made," he said, handing me the towel. I placed the cup down on the beige carpet and used the towel to attempt to dry my hair. The towel had a strong smell of washing powder.

He opened the Ginger Nuts with his teeth and picked the plastic covering off around the packet. He held them out to me, "Here, beat that down yea. Did ya walk here? I didn't see a car outside," he said looking outside.

"I don't drive," I said.

"Unlucky," he said chomping down on a Ginger Nut, "So, what's going on? Our James hasn't said a word since he came home from school yesterday."

"That's why I'm here," I lied, watching him dunk the other half of his biscuit into his tea.

"Aye, I see that. Do ye need to see him?"

"Yes, please," I said, taking a small nibble of my Ginger Nut.

"He's with his ma upstairs. I'll call them down," he said walking to the door. He turned around to me and said, "Help yerself to another Ginger Nut."

What the heck was I going to say to James?

"Fiona, bring James down. His teacher is here," he shouted up the stairs. I leaned towards the door.

"I'm the classroom assistant," I mumbled. I wasn't sure if he heard me.

James' dad went up every stair with his heavy feet.

He shouted down, "Miss... Miss Craig, come on up. His ma doesn't want to move him downstairs. She wants to keep him in his bed."

I opened the door and called up, "Oh, okay. And I'm Miss Jolliff. Mrs Craig is the teacher. I'm not the teacher." I tiptoed up the stairs feeling more and more nervous with each step.

What if James wasn't up there? What if his wife wasn't up there either? He could grab me and do anything to me. No one would know where I was. Anita had told me about a thirteen-year-old who was kept in a guy's basement for years. She even had a kid with the guy who captured her. Why did I come here? Why did I listen to my friend's mad stories that scared the wits out of me?

"Hello," I called out nervously, expecting him to jump out.

"We're in here," he said and I opened the door only to see Fiona from the ice-rink; a bright pink hairband in her hair. And James.

"Oh, Fiona!" I said.

"Do ye two know each other?" James' dad asked.

"Well, I don't know if you know me but I know you from the ice-rink," I said.

"Oh, I recognise your face," she said in a sweet, gentle voice.

"Yes, I saw you skating with Terrance. You were fantastic. I love your style," I said forgetting the real reason I was there.

"Don't start talking about ice-skating," James' dad said. I coughed nervously and leaned towards James.

"James, hi. I'm just checking up on you. Can you speak at all?" James shook his head.

"He hasn't spoken since yesterday. It is stressing me out. Do you know what's going on? What about the rest in his class?" Fiona said.

"Twenty are off and I think all of them are off for the same reason," I said lowering my head.

"I don't know what to do. Do you think we should take him to the doctor?"

"I don't know," I said, continuing to look down at my feet.

"Did Steve fetch you a cup of tea?"

"Yes, I did. Will I make ye one, Fiona? I'll fetch James a drink while I'm down there too. Kill two birds with one stone," he said kissing her on the head before he left the room. Wow, I thought it was just me that came out with bird proverbs!

Fiona put a wet flannel on James' head. The room was small; powder blue on the top half of the walls and dark blue under the dado rail. We were bundled in with a vacuum cleaner, three suitcases, a dinner set and three porcelain dolls. The bed was small, which would have suited a toddler rather than James. The bedcover was a faded Liverpool one with a flat pillow like a pancake where James' head lay.

It was clear James was stressed by the fact he couldn't talk and he moved this way and that. After a while, he closed his eyes and I presumed he had fallen asleep.

"Eh, Fiona can I ask you something?" I said knowing I would never forgive myself if I left and didn't ask.

"Yes, sure," said Fiona.

"It's James and his arms. I noticed he had some bruises on them," I said trying to sound informal.

"Oh those," she leaned over and pulled back the covers, "He got those from the rink. He's in the beginner class. And well, Terrance pushed him too far to try and make his group do tiny jumps but they weren't ready for it. When he came home bruised from top-to-toe, I made an official complaint and Terrance was livid. He's not allowed to teach the beginners now. He blames me, you know. I understand why. He was giving James free lessons as he knew we wouldn't be able to afford them after Stevie lost his job. I agreed to help him out in return. Steve thinks he takes the mick out of me; making me carry his ice-skates and demanding I attend all the lessons and competitions… but I don't mind. I love to ice-skate, you see."

"I love to ice-skate too. It's everything to me. I've only just moved into the professional group. And I have to agree with Steve, Terrance can be a bit much," I said. Steve arrived with the tea.

"Did ye want another cuppa, Miss Craig?" Steve asked and James sat up in the bed.

"I'm Miss Jolliff and I'm grand, thanks. I've got to go and… check on the other children. Thank you for everything. As for you James, I hope you feel better soon."

"I'll show ye out," said Steve and followed me downstairs.

"Thanks for the tea, Steve."

"Anytime," he said with a smile. He had a front tooth missing.

"Steve, can I ask you a question? It's probably nothing but James said in class when you were in a rush one day you shoved him down the stairs," I said swallowing hard.

"James is always exaggerating. Fiona said it's because of his age. Full of imagination. I remember that day too. He was on the bottom step, just where you're standing now. He was refusing to move when I came behind him. He was moaning on and on about his nose starting to bleed and I nudged him forward. He did a dramatic fall and cried. He didn't want to go to his ice-skating class, ye see. He's a bit afraid of that Terrance bloke. Any excuse not to go," said Steve.

"I know Terrance. I understand why he would want to avoid his classes," I said with an awkward smile, "Anyway, that clears that up. I can see he's in a loving, caring family."

"We sure are. Once we sort this place, we will be even more loving. This is Fiona's dad's old place and he left it to us in his will. We have big plans for this house, but it's all time and money. That's why Fiona accepted that job in the first place with Terrance. If it was up to me, she'd be taking proper ice-skating lessons and be a kept woman. It will work itself all out in the end, once I land a new job."

"Good luck getting a job, Steve. You deserve to get one," I said deciding Steve and Fiona were both snow geese.

I hoofed it down the path. I was a total idiot. Talk about judging a book by its cover! They were a loving, caring family. It was odd it was Fiona though. No wonder Terrance was yelling at her at the ice-rink.

I began to hiccup. I'd better return to school.

THIRTY – TWO
HOUSE

I couldn't listen to the desperate cries for their mother, and so I stayed away. The babies died in their nest and I knew who had killed them.

Muhammad continued to pray each day on his mat with his wife and children standing behind him. They would repeat this five times a day and not once did I hear them mention the little mouse. There was no doubt in my whole being; Muhammad was a sinner. Muhammad: a sinner with no remorse. A creepy, heartless murderer with no repercussions. His reputation still intact with his magnanimous family. They chose to turn a blind eye to his debased, profane, contemptible villainous decision to kill my mouse. I was sickened. Aghast.

The girls laughed in their bedroom as they put on their head scarves. Why didn't Adil or Muhammad cover their heads? Surely, Muhammad was the one who should cover up his hair, his face and those cruel hands. The hands that held that spade on that frightful night.

I no longer responded to Muhammad. I chose to ignore him. Punish him. Isolation was all he deserved. Even during Ramadan; their special month. There was always an excitement in the air before it arrived. I only paid attention to Nadia and her children.

"Tomorrow is the big day," said Zara.

"It sure is," said Yasmine.

"My first year doing it properly," said Adil.

"It sure is," said Yasmine again.

"You are going to be fine," said Rislan.

"He was born in the kitchen, remember. He might find it hard to stay out of there," laughed Zara.

"I'm dreading tomorrow," said Jamila.

"You'll be fine. The second year is always easier," said Rislan.

Nadia joined her children in the living room and plonked herself down next to Yasmine.

"You okay, my flower?" she said, stroking Yasmine's arm.

"I sure am," she answered. Yasmine kissed her mum on her hand.

"Big day tomorrow everyone. I hope you're all ready."

"Are you allowed any water during the day?" asked Adil.

"None. You are not allowed any water," said Nadia jumping up and capturing Adil and holding her only son close.

"I better take a drink now then," said Adil and skipped into my kitchen to take a drink of water. Zara laughed.

"He might struggle tomorrow."

"Well, we'll see how he goes. It is his first year fasting. I will be so proud of him if he makes it through the whole month."

"You sure will."

THIRTY–THREE
MOLLY

As soon as I hit the gates of the school, regret attacked my stomach. What the heck was I going to say to Mrs Craig? I'd been away for nearly two hours! I shouldn't have had the tea and Ginger Nuts.

I strutted up to the main doors and used my fob to get inside. I decided to pop to the toilet first to make sure I looked okay.

When I arrived at the staff toilet, there was someone inside. I waited, trying to work out what to say to Mrs Craig. I knew I couldn't tell her that I'd popped round to James' house and had a cuppa and Ginger Nuts. I would have to lie to her. But what was I going to say?

The door opened and it was Nicola. Just my luck.

"Oh, look who it is," she said with a sneer on her face, "Where have you been? They're looking for you."

"They?"

"Mr Cardwell and Mrs Craig. Jasmine said you were stressing out earlier. So where did you disappear to?" she asked and I looked blankly at her.

"Can't talk now, Nicola. I need the toilet," I said and edged round her. Her face fell. I locked the door and paced the small room.

They were looking for me! I couldn't cope with this. What was I going to say? I paused and stayed still, listening carefully.

Nicola was probably still out there! I rummaged through my handbag and applied my makeup.

I could do this.

When I opened the door, I took in a blast of air and Nicola *was* still standing there.

"Well, where were you earlier?"

"I had to go home."

"Home? Did you miss your family? Did you forget to kiss your mummy goodbye?"

"No, I didn't," I said.

"Molly, why don't you face the facts? Working here is not for you. You need to go back home, phone your school and go back there to acquire some qualifications."

"I like working here. So, I'll be staying."

"Doesn't look like it from where I'm standing."

Mr Cardwell was walking briskly down the corridor and he waved over.

"Miss Jolliff, my office please. Now. Thank you," he said and turned around, pacing back down the corridor.

My heart sank.

"Maybe you won't be staying after all," said Nicola with a smirk and marched away from me.

I couldn't say I was at James' house. I would have to lie. I'd say I was sick. This was a nightmare.

I trudged up the corridor and tapped on Mr Cardwell's office door.

"Come," he said from inside.

"Hello, Mr Cardwell," I said.

"Where have you been, Molly?"

Straight to the point.

"I'm sorry Mr Cardwell. I went... I went home," I lied. What else could I say?

"That's strange, Miss Jolliff. I phoned your house and you were not there."

"Well, when I say I went home, I mean I started to go towards home. I felt sick in P.2 and Mrs Craig sent me over here to sort myself out. My nose was bleeding you see," I said throwing in a half-truth.

"Yes, yes. I know all that. You cannot just leave your workplace without either speaking to me or Mrs Craig. I am responsible for your safety. We were worried about you," said Mr Cardwell.

"I wasn't well. By the time I got to my house, I felt a little better and so I turned around and came back. I'm sorry," I said biting my lip.

"Well, that clears that up. You better go over and explain yourself to Mrs Craig. Next time, talk to someone," he said.

"I will. Sorry." I got out of there as quickly as I could. But low and behold, Nicola was waiting for me outside the office, leaning on the radiator.

"Well?" she said standing upright.

"Well? What do you mean, Nicola? Don't you have somewhere to be?"

"What's that supposed to mean?"

"You're doing my head in. Why are you following me around?"

"Listen, love, the last thing I would want to do is follow you around. I am waiting to speak to Mr Cardwell. I told you when you arrived here, madam, that you do not belong here. It is clearly time for you to move on."

"That's up to me, not you," I snapped, fed up with this woman.

Mr Cardwell stepped out.

"Everything okay, ladies?" Nicola had crocodile tears in her eyes. What a bully! "What is going on?" Mr Cardwell asked.

"It's just..." she started, then paused for dramatic flair, "She blew up at me." She added a whimpering breath for extra theatrics.

"I thought I heard raised voices," Mr Cardwell said. He turned toward me with a stern look, "Molly, we do not shout at other members of staff in the workplace."

"Eh, I didn't think I was shouting," I said.

"She was asking me why I was out here. To be honest, the way you spoke to me made me feel very uncomfortable," she said.

"Come into my office, Nicola, and take a seat. Hopefully we can get to the bottom of this," said Mr Cardwell.

"I'm… I'm…"

"Miss Jolliff, I think you have said enough. Off you go to Mrs Craig's room and hopefully Nicola decides not to make an official complaint." He closed his office door and left me standing in the corridor with my mouth still open.

Could this day get any worse?

I made my way down the corridor to my classroom.

"Molly!" shouted Jasmine.

"Oh, finally a friendly face," I said.

"Where have you been? They asked about you. I didn't know what to say. I was so worried about you, Molly."

"I'm okay, you don't need to worry about me," I said.

"Where were you?"

"Jasmine, after I spoke to you, I was worried about James."

"Oh, Molly… what did you do?"

"I decided—"

"Tell me you didn't!"

"Jasmine, I had to," I said.

"Molly, tell me you didn't go to James' house."

"I had to—"

"Molly, why would you do such a thing? Not only will you be in big trouble but you have landed me in it too."

"Jasmine, they don't know I went there. They think I went home."

"You lied!"

"Well, I didn't lie. Well, it was sort of a white lie,"

"I can't deal with this," Jasmine said and turned to walk away.

"Jasmine, wait," I said.

"I can't even look at you right now. You need to grow up, Molly," said Jasmine. She marched through the door and left me.

That's what I was trying to do! Tears stung my eyes and I swallowed hard. I hated adulthood! When would this day end?

I dragged my feet all the way to Mrs Craig's class and used my fob to enter the room. Mrs Craig threw herself on me and I was taken back.

"Oh, thank goodness. Where were you? I was worried sick about you, Molly. Are you okay?"

"I think so," I crumbled and the tears flowed. Why was she being so nice to me?

THIRTY-FOUR
HOUSE

Adil returned to the living room with a large glass of water.

"I'll not be too thirsty tomorrow if I drink all of this," he said.

"Stop worrying, Adil. You're going to be fine," said Zara.

"I'm looking forward to it. I'm not worrying."

"You sure aren't," said Yasmine taking a brush and taking off Nadia's hijab. She played with her mum's hair twisting it through her fingers for a while before she brushed it.

Rislan jumped up, "I'm going to nab myself a glass of water too. It's a good idea, Adil."

"Bring a jug in," said Nadia.

"Yes, I'd like a glass too," said Jamila.

Muhammad entered the house and I made my lights flicker.

"Murderer," I shouted but his closed ears failed to react. I blew fuses in plugs on him, switched off lights and refused to allow my water to flow when he turned on a tap. He did not deserve to live within my walls and I wanted him gone.

He laughed. Everyone was drinking large glasses of water.

"You guys all organised for tomorrow then?" I ignored him.

"We sure are," said Yasmine.

"Well, I hope you are making your lovely *harira* soup for when we finish our fast tomorrow," said Muhammad. I paid no attention.

"Of course, and I have the milk and dates ready too," said Nadia moving over so Muhammad could sit down. I froze him out.

Nadia and the children had forgiven him for what he had done to the mother mouse. I never did. I wished for Muhammad to take his family and leave. I wished and wished. A strange atmosphere fell upon my roof and swept down over my wall. It seeped in slowly through my windows and doors.

Something had changed in me.

THIRTY-FIVE
MOLLY

"Wakey, wakey! Look what I have." Josh's voice ripped me out of my bizarre dream where I was trying to put Humpty Dumpty together again, "Check this little guy out."

Curiosity got the better of me and I turned around. Josh was holding the cutest hamster ever.

"Is it ours?"

"Technically, it's mine but we can share him."

"Oh my word, can I hold him?"

"Of course." I held the cutest little creature ever! He was the most adorable little fuzzball.

"Does Mum know?"

"Have ya lost your mind? No, she would kill me. I'm hiding him in my bedroom."

"What's his name?"

"I have a few names: Butterscotch, Gingersnap or Sparky. I can't decide."

"Definitely not Gingersnap," I said seeing Stevie with his Ginger Nuts under his arm in my head, "Go for Butterscotch. He suits it."

"Yeah, okay. Sweet. Butterscotch it is," he said lifting him out of my hands, "He's a cracker, isn't he? I better get him back in his cage before Mum sees him. Don't forget Blondie, we're going for that walk." He disappeared into his bedroom.

Why had I agreed to go for an early morning walk with Josh last night?

"Come on, up and at 'em," he said marching back into my room and opening my bedroom window wide. A blast of cold air came in and I dived down into my quilt.

"When I said I would do a walk today, I meant Sunday," I mumbled hoping he would magically disappear.

"No, ya didn't. You said you were going to church on Sunday. Remember?"

"Yes. Anita and I want to check it out."

"You know that Matt goes there," Josh said.

"No," I lied. This lying thing was starting to become a habit. A habit I knew I would have to nip in the bud.

"Yeah, he's the youth pastor there. He plays in the church band. I thought ya knew that and that was why ya were going."

"No, whatever made you think that?" I said holding my quilt tight.

"Oh, I just thought you and him got on, that's all. Now, come on. It's bright and cheerful out there. Get your butt out of bed," he said and left the room. I begrudgingly heaved myself out of bed and made my way to the bathroom.

So, Josh thought that Matthew and I got on. I smiled.

Josh called in from his spotlessly clean bedroom, "Don't be caking that bake of yours with all that makeup. You look sweet without it."

I viewed myself in the mirror and smiled again. This time next week, I could be teaching the little kids at the rink so that was my last lie-in. What a great brother I had.

By the time we got to the beach, I was more optimistic and the chaos of yesterday seemed miles away.

Josh was happily chatting beside me about Willow's sister's new house and I listened to him droning on and on whilst two children with fluorescent water wings dashed in and out of the water.

"I know I'm only fifteen but I'd love to have my own place. How sweet would that be? Willow reckons that she'll move in with her sister when she's nineteen. As soon as I hit seventeen, I'm going to nail a job, like you, and score my own place," Josh said.

"I don't know why you're in such a hurry to grow up, Josh. Being an adult sucks!"

"Blondie, you're only saying that because you had a bad day yesterday. You need to dry those eyes of yours."

"I cried, Josh… on Mrs Craig's shoulder. And I confessed everything about going to James' house. You should have seen her face. She was so shocked. She told me she would have to speak to Mr Cardwell and I reckon he'll call me into his stupid office first thing on Monday morning and it will be 'bye-bye Molly'."

The crash of waves and the fizz of its foam spread across the sand, making us both run sideways to save our trainers.

"How many times do I have to tell ya? It'll not be as bad as it seems. Ya wait and see," said Josh and I stared up at him. His blonde strands framed his face. His blue eyes, brighter than the sea itself, winked at me. He looked less of a boy and more of a man. His voice had a deeper tone to it now too. I had noticed that last month. At first, it sounded ridiculous coming from the mouth of Josh with his boyish looks. Now he suited it. Josh worked out daily in his makeshift gym in our garage and it was only now I could see his muscles. He was always taller than me, but now he appeared as if he could protect me. Which was exactly what he did with his words.

"Anyway, if that job isn't for you, there are plenty more jobs in the sea. It's gonna be sweet. Wait and see," he said flicking my ear, "Do ya get it? Sea… see…"

"You may look more grown-up, Josh, but you still act like a little boy," I said bending down and lifting a pebble. I threw it into the sea. Josh did the same. Throwing his much further.

A Jack Russell dog bolted up the beach after a bright yellow ball, barking as he sprinted. A seagull darted overhead.

"I'm going to enjoy this day and forget about work," I said, taking in a deep breath of sea air.

"Sweet. Just enjoy the moment, sis. Everything will work out. Ya wait and see. You ice-skating later?"

"Yes, at three. What you at?"

"Willow is picking me up and we're going to her sister's house. We're all staying up there until Monday evening. I said I'd help paint her living room. I'll have to flex my DIY skills. It's navy and she wants it plain cream," he said, picking up more stones, "I reckon we'll need three coats of cream."

"Have you no school on Monday?"

"Nope, teacher development day. So, I'm off. Perfect. And I get to see Willow."

"What's the scientific name of a weeping willow?"

"Don't even go there, Blondie. How many times do I have—"

"Mourning wood."

"Beyond crap!"

"Willow, Willow, Willow. So, are you dating or not?"

"I told ya, sis. And I'll tell ya again, we're just friends," he said running backwards in front of me, "Anyway, what about you and the wee thing ya have with Matt?"

"Wee thing? Matt? What do you mean?"

"He likes you, you know," he said with a smile and he turned around and jogged off.

He liked me? What was that supposed to mean? He liked me? Was he serious?

Two large crows swooped down low over Josh's head and I shuddered. I spotted goosebumps on my arms as I jogged after him.

THIRTY-SIX
HOUSE

When they moved back to Morocco, I waited in the dark. I refused to react. I was cold and bored. I knew new tenants would arrive soon.

Jack and Stephanie had arrived, and after Stephanie left with her baby, it was only a matter of time before Jack left.

* * *

My house smells different now. A strange growth is creeping up my walls in several of my rooms. Its fingers spread along my scarred surfaces. My wallpaper is falling off again and I'm left waiting for someone to move in and fix me. My hot press is dishevelled now; towels tumbling onto my landing floor.

Time creeps by and no one turns the key in my front door.

I am left alone, muttering to myself.

My windows are dirty now and my front door is changing to a paler shade of red. My roof is beginning to sag and my living room door has a weak hinge.

I wait.
I wait.
I wait.

Time creeps by. Like the way Walter used to creep downstairs to drink cider in my kitchen.

I wait.
I wait.
I wait.

Another year passes and my windows are stained with yellow. Like D.B.'s fingers from too many cigarettes. Even after all this time, I miss having a family within my walls and I still long for a key to turn in my front door. I miss Sophia giggling in her cot. The Moroccan family with their strong-smelling foods upon the stove. Harry out my back fixing his bike and...

I wait.
I wait.
I wait.

And I miss Emily-Brooke.

THIRTY–SEVEN
MOLLY

Later that day, Anita picked me up so we could go to the ice-rink.

"Matthew played a song for me. On his guitar," I said with a massive grin on my face.

Anita spat out her necklace.

"And you're only telling me that *now*! When? How?"

"I was with Josh in our kitchen and Matthew came in. Oddly enough, we chatted about birds and the next thing I knew, he was playing Bob Marley for me."

"Wait! Stop! Birds? Tell me the whole thing."

"He has a tattoo of birds and—"

"Oh, that's a sign. You like birds… he has a tattoo of birds. Perfect. Go on."

"Wait, I'll show you his tattoo. It was on his Insta."

I flicked through my photographs and showed Anita.

"Nice one," she said glancing over whilst still driving.

"Anyway, Josh had bought me a bird book and Matthew said he had the same book. He showed me his tattoo and he sang a bird song that reminded him of his dad."

"Reminded him of his dad? That's beyond weird. Is his dad dead?"

"Oh, shit. I don't know. He said he got the tattoo as it reminded him of his dad. I probably should have asked him about that. I didn't think."

"Typical Molly," said Anita popping her hedgehog into her mouth. I watched my friend as she moved her head to the music playing on the radio and as she carefully took over a car on the road.

"What...? What do you mean typical me?"

"It's what ya do, isn't it?" she answered with the stupid hedgehog still in her mouth.

It's what I do? What the heck did she mean by that?

"Sorry? What?"

"Molly avoids death."

Did that just spill out of her mouth? How did anyone "avoid death"? It wasn't like death was a person you saw and suddenly walked on the other side of the road to avoid speaking to. Or the creepy guy you avoided at the ice-rink who was clearly not there to ice-skate but instead stood at the side and just leered.

I glared at Anita. She kept her eyes on the road.

"I... I avoid death? I avoid death. What a ridiculous statement. Explain yourself."

Anita spat the hedgehog out of her mouth.

"Never mind now, go on with the story."

"No, I want to know what you mean. How do I avoid death...? I don't avoid death."

"Well, you've never had a conversation with me about my... my..."

I swallowed hard. The realisation of what she was going to say popped into my head like a row of annoying cheerleaders.

"Are you going to say your mum? Are you serious?"

"Yes. Every time I brought her up, ya would change the subject and not too subtly either. At first it pissed me off, but now it amuses me *how* ya avoid the subject. Especially when ya started telling those cracker jokes."

"It amuses you?" *Cracker jokes!* Did she think I was being funny? Every time her mum came up, I really wrecked my brain to come up with something else to talk about. Did she find that amusing? "I'm shocked."

"Why?"

"I just thought you wouldn't want to talk about it. It's a... touchy subject. One we don't talk about."

"You mean one *ye* don't talk about it. I talk about my mum all the time. Just not with you. Same with yer grandad. When he died—"

"Don't even go there." Once I said the words, I knew straightaway I had just avoided death. Was my best friend right? Grandad's face appeared in front of me and he nodded.

"You see. As I said, ya avoid death. So that's just the way ye are. Now tell me about Matthew."

"That's it really. He played his song and sang."

I did avoid death. The idea of Grandad no longer existing scared me. I was scared *for* him. No more bird-watching, no more sketching and painting, no more tea-making and giving advice. He always gave out the best advice.

"Is that it?"

"I melted, as usual... And he went off with Josh to do their guitar thing."

I missed him terrible. I didn't want to avoid death. I wanted to face difficult things face on. A memory of Grandad's funeral rushed into my mind like the children rushing over to the dress-up box during P.B.L. at the school. I had spent the whole time fidgeting with my clothes and thinking about bird-watching and trying to piss off Mum. I hadn't faced death.

"Oh, and then this morning, Josh announced Matthew likes me."

"Oh, did he tell Josh that he likes ya?"

"You know Josh, it's like squeezing blood out of a stone trying to draw information out of him. I did ask but he just kept smirking at me and nodding and told me nothing."

My grandad had been taken by death. Swept away down a deep, dark hole of nothingness and I was livid.

"I'm chuffed to bits for ya. You'll have to ask Matt out," announced Anita. Tears welled up in my eyes.

"Josh has two more lessons with him." I stared out the window. In my head, I chanted over and over that I was sorry. I wanted Grandad to know that I was there for him even in death.

"What are ya going to do?"

"I'll have to do something. And soon. He asked Mum and Dad for more lessons but they can't afford to pay for them."

"What about work? How's it going?" asked Anita.

Telephone pole after telephone pole passed us by. Anita was completely oblivious to the thoughts about death in my head and my problems at work. I decided not to tell her about all the drama.

"School's fine," I lied and we drove for a while in silence.

"Nice one... You'll not believe what I saw on YouTube last night," she said.

"Huh?"

"Are you even listening? I'm talking about conspiracy theories."

"Oh, yeah right," I said. She was right, I wasn't listening. I had too much on my mind. I was nearly eighteen: an adult. I was realising there were good aspects about life and not so good.

"Apparently, there are some people who believe the Earth is flat. Does that even make sense? It's beyond weird," she laughed. I put on a fake smile trying to humour her, "They think the satellite photos of Earth as a sphere are fabrications."

"Anita, sometimes I think you make this crap up just to entertain me," I said, wondering when she had accepted the fact her mum had died and that she would never get an opportunity to meet her.

"No, I'm serious. They have evidence and everything. I'll send you the link," she said as she tried twice to back into a parking space.

When Anita finally parked, I smiled.

"This is my favourite place in the whole world. Now I can forget all about school," I said taking off my seatbelt.

"School? Why... what's happening in school? Thought ye said it was fine," asked Anita, reaching out and grabbing my arm.

"Nothing."

"Ya sure. It doesn't sound like nothing."

"No, nothing. Let's go," I said opening the car door. As we walked closer to the entrance, we both did a little run "Heaven on earth," I said with a smile.

"I have to agree with ye there," said Anita, throwing down her coat and swinging her ice-skating bag off her shoulder.

Within five minutes, I was ready and on the ice. As soon as I stepped on, I wobbled.

What the heck? I never wobbled. I steadied myself on the barrier.

I waited.

I started my warm-up. I glided with Anita and she flew into a backward skate.

"What's going on with ya, Molly? Ya nearly bumped into me there."

"Oh. Sorry, Anita. I'm going to go off and check my skates," I said.

I made my way off the ice and there was Nicola sitting on one of the benches with a guy who appeared way younger than her and two little girls. Both girls were mini versions of Nicola. But with blonde bobbed hair. They looked about eight.

"Oh crap," I said. The last person I wanted to see in my world of ice-skating was Nicola. I hoped she wouldn't see me. I kept my head down and wished I had worn my baseball cap.

"Molly? Molly?"

What a nightmare.

"Oh, hello Nicola. What are you doing here?" I asked.

"I'm with my two nieces. This is Katie and Lydia. Oh, and this is my husband, Dean. What are you doing here?" I couldn't take my eyes off Dean. Nicola had gone for the younger husband. Up close he looked even younger; wrinkle-free and handsome. He had dark hair and brown eyes that sparkled. Nicola coughed and I gaped down at the girls.

"Hi girls, are you not ice-skating?" I asked, feeling Nicola's stare drilling into my forehead.

"We will be soon," said Katie.

"We can't work out how to tie their laces. Can you help us?" asked Nicola.

"Yes, of course," I said bending down to fix their laces.

"So, you can ice-skate?" Nicola asked.

"Yes, I'm part of the professional team here," I said, "Are you not skating, Nicola?"

"No, I don't skate. I would be a mess on the ice. So, you're in the professional team here? That's pretty impressive," she said and I didn't know if she was being genuine or not.

"Can we go on the ice, now, Auntie Nicola?"

"Yes, go. Go!" said Nicola. The two girls stepped onto the ice and worked their way slowly around the rink like the hour hand of a clock.

Dean spoke and I observed him again, "Hot chocolate?"

"Yes," Nicola said and he turned to me.

"Would you like a hot chocolate?" he asked and I decided that he was gorgeous. I was surprised; Nicola did not suit him at all. If anything, he looked like her son. Which was sad. Nicola coughed again and I looked away.

"Sorry, I'm in a lesson. Thank you for asking."

Dean smiled and strolled off. Nicola ogled after him and I became aware of her wrinkled face. Pity rippled into my stomach for her. Her eyes followed his every move and I knew she was insecure. She didn't trust him. I coughed. She glared back at me.

Feeling braver I said, "Nicola, I don't think we've seen eye-to-eye since we met."

"I wonder why that is…" she said, trying to find Dean again who was now lost in the crowd.

"Exactly, I wonder why too."

"We just clashed, I suppose." She looked back at me and there was an awkward silence between us both.

"You practically put me in it with Mr Cardwell."

"Well, you were shouting at me outside his office, Molly."

"I wasn't shouting."

"You were."

"The bottom line is: you don't seem to like me. We can either start again and try a little harder to get on or stay out of each other's way."

"No, I'm happy to try and build up a friendship with you," said Nicola, but I didn't trust her. She was looking for her husband again. I could see him flirting outrageously with a much younger, prettier girl. I swallowed hard. I looked back at Nicola. Did Nicola spot him too?

"Auntie Nicola, come and see. Come and see," shouted Katie. Nicola nodded at me and stepped over to the barrier. I checked my boots and tightened up my blades. When I glanced up, Dean was back with two hot chocolates in his hands.

"So, you know my Nicola then?" he asked and my cheeks burned red.

"Yes, I work in the same place."

"Oh, she's so paranoid that she will lose her job there."

"Really?"

"It's her age," he said glancing over at Nicola who was taking photographs of Katie on the ice, "She thinks younger, prettier girls, like you, are going to make her job redundant. She does my head in talking about it."

I was embarrassed by how open he was about Nicola. In a way, I felt a little protective over her.

"I have to go," I stuttered and made my way towards Nicola. I knew he was eye-balling me. I decided there and then that I didn't like him.

When I slipped by Nicola, she said, "I can hardly wait to see you on the ice." I stepped on, unsteady, knowing she was watching me too. I began to hiccup.

I began my short programme working exceptionally hard on perfecting my steps. Out of the corner of my eye, I saw Nicola and Dean examining me and they both looked impressed. I moved on to my long programme. On my fourth jump, I hiccupped, slipped and fell.

I got up and knew Terrance was keeping tabs on me as his eyes were wide. He had just arrived with a white and lime green rolling suitcase that you would use to go on holiday. Fiona was not with him.

Oh, great! I couldn't believe he saw me falling. He would be throwing me off the team if I wasn't careful.

Anita skated over to me, "Ye okay, chick? That was beyond weird. What's going on with ya today? It's not like ye to fall."

"I'm having a bad day. Terrance saw me too. He's going to be livid."

"He's going to go ape-shit," agreed Anita and we made our way over to the rest of the team. Terrance was wearing his usual outfit: pink and black shell suit. He had new black boots on today with purple, glittery laces and I couldn't take my eyes off them.

"Molly, what was that ridiculous performance all about?" he barked and all eyes landed on me. I wanted the ice to swallow me up.

"I wasn't concentrating. I'm sorry, Terrance," I whispered covering up a new hiccup.

"Louder!" he said, snapping his fingers.

"I wasn't concentrating," I said in a higher tone.

"Beyond ridiculous. You represent my team. Therefore, you should always be concentrating. You make a fool out of yourself, you make a mockery out of me. Do you understand?"

"Yes, Terrance. Sorry, Terrance," I said louder than my normal voice; my cheeks roaring red.

"Good, the last thing I want to see is a spectacle of tomfoolery. Now, where is Tina?"

"Here," said Tina moving to the front. Terrance continued barking his orders. Nicola and Dean were on the bench taking it all in. What was she thinking? My thoughts were interrupted with Terrance's loud booming voice, "I will join you on the ice in one minute. Everyone, do your short routines. Let me see you fly, little birds."

Anita said, "Molly, go. Go!" and I followed after her.

I closed off everything from my mind; the kids not speaking in my class, Nicola and her young husband over at the side examining me, my fall out with Jasmine, my visit to James' house, me avoiding death, my fall...

My mind went to that happy place where all was well. Present in the moment. The cold air blasting in my face. I perfected my turns, jumps and twists. A warmth rose from my feet through my whole body, right down to my fingertips and I was happy. No person, place or thing could take this moment away from me. I was indeed a bird. A free bird. My dyslexic-clipped wings were gone. I was free.

When I finished my routine, I looked up and Terrance flew towards me, clapping.

"Bravo. Bravo," he shouted and my face flushed red again.

"You were truly wonderful out there, Molly. Perfection. Well done. I feel so proud," he said.

"Thank you," I murmured.

"You were amazing. Just what I am looking for. Maybe we should compete,"

"Compete?"

"Yes, yes. Together. As partners," he said skating off and doing a double axel.

There was no way I was skating with him. That would be my worst nightmare. I watched him glide around the ice with a massive grin on his face.

After the lesson, Terrance chatted to Anita and I about taking the beginner class. We were to start next Saturday. We were both excited.

On the way home I asked Anita, "Do you fancy checking out that Whitewell Church tomorrow?"

"Uh-huh," said Anita, "Saying that, I know nothing about church. I didn't even go to Sunday School."

"There's only one thing you need to know."

"What's that?"

"What Adam told his children. You see, after having children, Adam and Eve started getting a lot of questions from their kids about why they no longer lived in Eden."

"Really?"

"Yes. And Adam said, 'your mother ate us out of house and home.'"

"Don't get it."

"Never mind... Just know from now on you can talk about your mum anytime with me."

"Cool."

"And that means I can use my cracker jokes all the time and not just to avoid a conversation."

"Nightmare," Anita said and popped her hedgehog back into her mouth.

THIRTY–EIGHT
HOUSE

I wait.
I wait.
I wait.

I miss her dimples when she smiles, her love for God, her love for others, her reading, her happiness and her love for me.

My garden is wild now. More mice move in and live under the pigeon shed that is falling to one side. My floorboards sing as a little mouse moves inside; through the hole that has developed over time on my back door.

She's not like the little mouse Muhammad killed on that frightful day many years ago. She is white and less jumpy. She scuttles across my floorboards and I am happy for her to stay. More sneak in through the hole. Soon, I have many families living within my walls.

I wait.
I wait.
I wait.

Another year passes and then footsteps are on my path and a rattle of a key goes in my lock. The key turns, and two men stand in my hallway. The mice scatter and stay quiet.

I whisper in each ear, "Don't cry, little one. Don't cry, and all will be well. Stay quiet, little one. Stay quiet."

They stay still and are quiet. All is well.

I look down at my new tenants, both with white hard hats on their heads.

I am House!

Now I shout out an uncontrollable "Stay!" as I look down at the screwed-up faces of the two who walk through my rooms.

Ridiculous.

Of course, they will stay.

I can make their children's lives better. I can protect their children from the pain. This is my job. My hot press will be neat and tidy once more.

I want to care again.

A voice interrupts my thoughts, "John, what year were these houses built?"

"In the early sixties, mate. This one is in pretty good nick considering. I wonder how many families have lived here over the years," John said.

"Four," I shout out, "And you will be my fifth. Bring your families or establish your families within my walls. I will love, protect and care for your children."

His name is John. Is he the one who wrote the verse?

Jesus saith unto him, I am the way, the truth, and the life: no man cometh unto the Father, but by me.

I hope he is.

All is well.

My new occupant, John, bends down and lifts part of my carpet and announces, "Carson, whoever lived here last must have liked patterns. Look at this carpet."

They will sort it and I will look new again. He plonks the end of the heavy carpet back down on my wooden floor and I groan.

My breath is quick and frantic and yet I'm not sure if I can breathe at all.

"Come and live within me," I hear myself say, but it's as if my voice is miles away now. The way you feel in an odd dream where nothing makes sense and voices speak out but the words mean nothing.

I stare at them and I know I am excited again.

They walk outside. John bends down and writes the number three on my path.

"This will be the third one to be demolished. The sooner they get rid of this row, the quicker they can throw the apartments up."

"Pure luxury, John. Pure luxury. I'd love one myself," said Carson.

"Me too, mate. Me too."

It is fun to sit back and watch; now I know a family will live within my walls again and I want to capture this moment in my memory forever. My hot press will be clean and neat once more. All will be well.

I am House.

I am.

I am.

THIRTY–NINE
MOLLY

It was odd waking up so early on a Sunday morning and the drama of working out what to wear to church was a nightmare. I ended up picking out my black ripped jeans and I brightened it up with my pink, snake-print top.

As I applied my makeup, Terrance's words were ringing in my ears.

"You were amazing. Just what I am looking for. Maybe we should compete. Together. As partners."

Imagine Dad and Josh's reaction if they watched me skating with that nut case at a competition. I would never live it down. There would be no Mexican waves then. Just shocked faces.

"Tomfoolery…" I said out loud and laughed at how ridiculous it sounded.

Anita honked her horn outside and I flew down the stairs.

"Where are you going in such a hurry?" asked Mum.

"Church," I said as I opened the front door.

"Church? Are you winding me up? Are they appropriate clothes for church?" Mum called after me. I ignored her. How would she know what people wore in church? She'd never been.

Anita looked well in her skater skirt with a vintage Vogue top and killer black heels.

"How are you driving in those things?" I asked.

"With great difficulty," she said with a smile.

"So, what's been happening?"

"Just thinking there about objects. Do ya think objects can feel?"

"No… another ridiculous thought."

"No, I'm serious. Whenever ye were younger, didn't ya feel sorry for the toys ya didn't play with? When I played with my dolls, I had to play with them all just in case one was feeling left out."

"I don't remember that far back, Anita."

"No, hear me out. If we feel sorry for the last biscuit in the packet, the last page in a printer and the unpaired sock in the sock drawer, do we feel sorry for them because deep down we know they can feel?"

"Anita, are you telling me you feel sorry for a biscuit, a page and a random sock?"

"Yes, and maybe that's God's way of letting us know that objects have feelings. Who said ye have to believe that only living things feel? Scientists, that's who. And let's face it, they get things wrong all the time."

"Maybe you're not feeling for the object at all. Maybe you are imagining yourself as that object and feeling sorry for yourself. No one wants to be the one not picked like your biscuit, lonely like your page or without a partner like your sock. So, you start projecting your emotions on the things around you."

Anita sucked her hedgehog and shrugged, "Maybe."

When we arrived at the church, the size surprised me. It was massive. Everyone looked as though they knew where they were supposed to go and they all appeared happy. Maybe this was what they meant by "happy-clappy".

"Don't think these guys believe in a flat Earth," whispered Anita, popping her hedgehog necklace into her mouth.

We followed the majority of the crowd and found a seat near the front. I scanned the whole place to find Matthew. He was nowhere in sight.

The service began with songs and I relaxed as they flowed through the air. The words made me feel loved and cared for. There was a warm atmosphere in the air. The lyrics were all about love, forgiveness, peace and Jesus. I had been to Sunday School a few times but had experienced nothing like this. I studied everyone and it was clear they were here for the love of God. They knew Him and I clearly didn't. Memories of Anita's conversation about me avoiding death rolled into my mind. Did I avoid death because I didn't know what it involved? These guys didn't believe there was only a dark hole of nothingness. They believed in Heaven and the afterlife.

The preaching started and I listened to every word trying to face death and what exactly it involved. Where was Anita's mum and where was Grandad? Matthew Stewart was forgotten. The pastor talked about God wanting a relationship with us and I gasped.

God Almighty, who made Heaven and our Earth, wanted a relationship with me? Could that be true?

He continued, "We have all sinned but Jesus Christ, the son of God, died on the cross for our sins. We can ask Jesus to forgive us of our sins and become pure and clean of sin."

Could that be true?

The sermon continued and I didn't understand most of it, but the words, "Jesus Christ, the son of God, died on the cross for our sins" stuck in my head.

After a few more songs, a prayer was said at the end. I bowed my head and whispered, "God if you want a relationship with me, I want you to know I want a relationship with you. I don't know how to do that. Please show me."

The pastor said, "Does anyone want to give their heart to the Lord Jesus Christ. If you do, put up your hand." I was shocked. Did I need to give my heart to Him? I peeked over at Anita and her hand was in the air.

"What are you doing, Anita?" I whispered.

"I want this," she whispered back.

"So do I," I said and shot my hand up too.

The pastor said, "I see two lovely girls who want to become Christians. You can put your hands down now."

Christian? Did I just become a Christian? What would Mum think?

The service was over. Anita hugged me and I scanned her face. She looked happy. Her eyes were shining and I knew something amazing had happened to us both.

What would God want me to do with my life?

The question popped into my head like a ping-pong ball in the electronic Bingo Blower at the bingo hall Grandad dragged me to on my fourteenth birthday.

Where did that question even come from? I had spent the majority of my life wondering what exactly it was that my mum wanted me to do with my life and the mystery was never resolved. Yet here I was wanting to know what God wanted me to do with my life.

We made our way out of the main part of church and when I reached the hallway, I heard his voice behind me: Matthew Stewart.

"Molly... Molly..."

"Matthew."

"Do you belong to this church?"

"Eh, no. We just came today. My friend..." I scanned around for Anita but she was nowhere to be seen.

"Are ya a Christian?" he asked, holding his Bible up at my face.

"Yes," the word came out and I felt my face redden. I began to hiccup, "I mean, I just became a Christian. We both did. Anita and I." He grasped my hand in his and pulled me in for a hug.

"Sweet. I'm so glad. Ya slayed it. Praise God," he said and let me go. My heart was pounding and my head hurt. Was this happening?

"Are ya hiccupping again?" he asked, pointing his Bible at my mouth, "I'll give ya this Bible if ya hiccup again." We both waited and no hiccup came and he laughed, "It works every time. If ya know what I mean."

Anita's voice called from the door, "Molly, stay with me. Hurry up, we need to find my car. This place is huge."

I turned back to Matthew, a little overwhelmed.

"I'm sorry, I have to go."

"No, I understand. Go... go. Laters!"

I turned around and stepped away, but he called out after me.

"Molly, I'm glad I cured yer hiccups. I'll see ya on Wednesday. If ya know what I mean. We'll talk then."

I glanced back and smiled, "Yes, Wednesday."

FORTY
HOUSE

"Excuse me. Sorry, excuse me. My name is Emily. I used to live here many moons ago, and I was wondering if we could possibly have a quick look around," she says with her hand on my black gate.

I'm disorientated. It is Emily-Brooke! She has returned to me.

I am House.

I am.

I am.

"The whole row is getting demolished next week, love. It wouldn't be safe for you guys to go in," Carson said.

She's older now but her eyes still shine with the innocence I saw when she was a baby. Her dimples still show up on her face when she smiles.

I am happy.

FORTY – ONE
MOLLY

The next day, I woke up with a major headache. Did yesterday really happen? Did I become a Christian? Did I face death? Did I need to tell my parents?

I made my way to our bathroom. It was lovely getting up for once and seeing the bathroom was free. I noticed Josh's toothbrush on its own on the sink and I looked at the rest of the toothbrushes in the cup.

Was Josh's toothbrush lonely because it wasn't with the others? I lifted his up and added him to his friends and smiled. Was Anita making me crazy? I turned on the shower.

Josh was in Belfast with Willow. Lucky sod being off school today.

I had a lovely, long shower and applied my makeup. I selected out a pretty black dress with red flowers and slipped on my red kitten heels. I joined Dad downstairs for breakfast.

"Morning, baby girl. Your mother is having a lie-in this morning. She doesn't need to take Joshua to school as—"

"I know, Josh told me. Did Mum not think it would be nice to take me to work instead?" I asked not expecting an answer.

"Toast, Molly-Moo?" said Dad.

"Yes, please," I said, taking a seat and I turned to look at Charlie but he was gone, "Where's Charlie, Dad?"

"Oh, babes. I have some bad news."

"Dad, where is he? Oh no, Dad," I said standing up and looking for him.

"Your mother thought he looked awful last night and well... well, we can buy a new one," said Dad.

"Did Mum throw him out?" I said, looking into the kitchen bin.

"Yes... in the bin outside," answered Dad.

I rushed out and rescued him, knowing that Charlie did have feelings.

"You'll be fine, Charlie. I'll keep you in my bedroom. You'll be grand," I said running upstairs and leaving him beside my bed. I circled my fingers over his brown, dead leaves.

Memories of crying on Mrs Craig's shoulder made me cringe. I was sure I'd be called into the office to be told off for going to see James. I would take it on the chin. Face my fears and be a real adult. Was that the answer to my question in the church? What did God want me to do in my life? Maybe I could do it with his help.

"Today is going to be a good day," I said and yet in the pit of my stomach a whirlwind was brewing.

When I arrived at school, I decided I was going to be positive and assertive today, and face the music. I used my fob to get inside.

Mrs Craig said nothing to me about my mad visit to James' house and I was glad. The morning started off the same way it usually did. Only I stood in shock. Sitting on the carpet were three children. Only three!

"Okay, class. It is so odd only seeing three of you here today but let's sing our P.2 song anyway." They sat up straight and sang:

How many stones are left alone?
How many stones are left alone?
How many stones are left alone?
Who is still at home?

This was ridiculous twenty-five were off. It continued:

Twenty-five little stones are left alone.
Twenty-five little stones are left alone.
Twenty-five little stones are left alone.
Lots of P.2 must be at home.

"Fortunately, because there are only three of us in today, Mrs Dunkan has agreed for you all to join her class today," Mrs Craig said.

"I don't want to go to P.1," Tristan said, standing up and stamping his foot.

"P.2, you will be going there for the week. Hopefully, then all the rest of P.2 will return and we can get back to normal. Tristan, you can carry our stones over to Mrs Dunkan's class. Cheer up. It's only for a short while."

"I'll walk them over," I said.

"Yes, please do. Then come straight back. I need to have a word with you," Mrs Craig said and I knew by her tone this was what I had been dreading. I would take it on the chin. I would be a real adult. I marched over to the P.1 mobile.

I had never met the P.1 teacher but when I did, I thought she was lovely. She had long dark hair, blue eyes and dimples to die for. She was a little house sparrow. Her whole class was organised, bright and cheerful; her P.1 children all looked happy.

"Come in. Come in," she said welcoming me in, "Oh, good. Tristan, you brought the stones over. I made up the stone song, you know. I'm sure you are sick of hearing it. I'm Emily, by the way. Emily Dunkan," she said and put her hand on my back.

"I'm Molly," I said, "I have to pop back and see Mrs Craig but I will be straight back."

"No problem. I will see you later," she said with a smile and I made my way back to Mrs Craig's room.

"Molly… unfortunately, I have some bad news for you. Apparently, James' parents are in this morning talking to Mr Cardwell. They are not happy about the fact you pretended to be a teacher—" said Mrs Craig.

"I didn't!" I interrupted her, "I told them both I wasn't you and I was Miss Jolliff."

"Well, their story is different. Molly, you are seventeen, you are not fully an adult yet. You just have a lot to learn. When you are an adult, you need to be responsible, think before you act and know your actions have consequences."

Tears stung my eyes and my head was thumping.

"Every time I try and do the right thing, I find out I've done something wrong."

"Well, sit down and have a think about what you are going to say to James' parents. I know you will do the right thing. I will meet you over at Mr Cardwell's office," she said and left the room.

What was I going to say to Stevie and Fiona?

I jumped up, knowing I needed to apologise. I said a quick prayer. Well, I tried. I was finding the praying part difficult so my prayers were always short.

"God help me to face James' parents the way I faced death in Whitewell. Amen."

I left the room and marched over to Mr Cardwell's office. I knocked on his door and took a deep breath as I slipped in. James' parents were sitting on the black, leather two-seater settee. Mrs Craig was sitting on an orange chair with an empty seat beside her. Mr Cardwell was behind his overpowering desk. I swallowed hard.

"Come and sit down, Miss Jolliff," Mr Cardwell said. I perched on the end of the chair and nodded at James' parents.

"Why did you call around to our house?" asked Fiona.

"And why did ye pretend to be a teacher?" snapped Stevie, showing the gap in between his teeth as he clenched down.

"I'm sorry. I didn't say I was a teacher. I was concerned about James and I just wanted to clear up a few things," I said.

"Check-up, ye mean. Ye were spying on us. Ye were asking personal questions too. Out of order!" said Stevie.

"Right, let's keep calm. Let's just stick to the subject at hand, shall we? I think what is important today is that we all decide what's... what's best to move forward—" said Mr Cardwell.

"She should be kicked out," interrupted Stevie.

"Molly is new to our school and it is clear she has made a mistake here. She didn't know that she shouldn't call at houses. I'm sure Molly knows that information now," said Mr Cardwell.

"Yes, yes, I do. I am sorry," I stuttered.

"Ya will be. I'm making an official complaint to the Board of Governors," said Stevie. Fiona reached over and gripped his hand.

"How old are you, Molly?" Fiona asked.

"I'm seventeen," I said, tears forming in my eyes, "I'm so sorry. I was worried about James. It was stupid of me to call round."

"I can see that, Molly. And James really likes you. Which is a good thing. James doesn't like too many people. He's fussy, you know. I can see that you meant no harm. There's no need for us to contact the Board of Governors—"

"Indeed, we will. It's ridiculous," shouted Stevie, and Fiona looked up at him.

"Stevie, she's young. She made a mistake and it won't happen again. We've all made mistakes; some bigger than others. . . Are you sure it won't happen again?"

"No, it definitely won't. I'll be asking Mrs Craig for advice from now on. That's if I still have my job," I said as I glanced at Mr Cardwell and Mrs Craig.

"This comes down to Miss Jolliff not knowing the rules. She is a good classroom assistant and it is clear she is genuinely sorry," said Mrs Craig and I was thankful.

"Well, it better not happen again," said Stevie.

"I can guarantee it won't," said Mr Cardwell standing up, "Molly will receive a warning after you leave and she will be reading several of our policies."

"Okay, thank you," said Fiona as she reached out and touched my arm, "I know you meant no harm."

"I... I promise I didn't."

When they left, Mr Cardwell addressed me and my cheeks burned. I felt like a little girl being told off.

"Now, I want you to go home and think about your behaviour. You nearly lost your job today, Molly. You are receiving a written warning over this incident but hopefully that will be the last of it. You can go. Mrs Craig and I will chat about our other problem in P.2: children who are not talking," he said. I got up and left.

FORTY – TWO
HOUSE

"It would be a walk down memory lane. We won't stay long. Just a quick five minutes," she says and I know I still love her.

"I suppose you could have a quick walk around. This one is in the best nick. Some of these houses would collapse around you. I'll fetch you both a hard hat from the van," says John.

Emily-Brooke places her fingers on my black gate. She strolls with her male friend up my path and stops at my front door.

You are back and I'm happy. I never want you to leave again.

"You guys from around this area?" asks Carson.

"No, no. I'm originally from Ballymena... Sorry, I'm Emily's fiancé," the man with her reaches out his hand and shakes Carson's hand.

Emily-Brooke is getting married. How perfectly lovely.

"We both live in Belfast now but I teach in the local primary school around in May Avenue," Emily-Brooke says.

"Oh, my kids go there. Mya and Carol Topping. Do you know them?"

"Oh, yes. Mya is in P.7 now and Carol must be—"

"Primary four," answers Sam.

She's a teacher. Her dream did come true. All those days teaching her teddies on the stairs were worth the effort. She made it.

"Small world," says Emily-Brooke, "Talking about small, this house looks a lot smaller. I remember it being much bigger. Saying that, I left here when I was ten."

She thinks I look small. How odd.

John returns with the hard hats. "Here you go. We are going to grab a sandwich in the van so tap the window when you're finished."

"Oh, thank you."

"Enjoy."

She pushes open my door and I welcome her in.

I can barely take my eyes off Emily-Brooke who has won me over completely. But when I do, I see her fiancé lifting and dropping items within my being. The look on his face tells me exactly how he feels. He is going to make changes. It's as if he has waited his whole life for this one single moment. He is now a proud owner of a three-bedroomed house that needs work. A corner terrace house established amongst similar houses. My only distinguishing feature: a number fifty-one at the side of my door.

I will always need work.

It is fun to sit back and relax, now I know Emily-Brooke will live within my walls and I want to capture this moment in my memory forever.

They move into my hallway.

"Oh my goodness, I used to teach my teddy bears on these stairs. That's what inspired me to become a teacher. This door leads to the living room," she says, opening my living room door, "I used to read to Mum here every day after school. I miss our conversations."

I miss our conversations too!

"Alzheimer's is a horrible disease," her fiancé says.

"She thinks she's a teenager again. Poor Dad, he can't turn his back on her for even a second. The last time he did she was away."

"You're kidding me."

"Nope. She sat at the train station for two hours. If she'd had her handbag with her, she'd have been away to goodness knows where. Sarah found her. Mum didn't recognise her. Sarah still hasn't got over that," Emily-Brooke says opening the door into my kitchen.

Poor Abigail! I wonder if she ever got the notebook she wanted so badly.

"Dad used to leave his cider bottles in that corner. Awful when I think about it now. He was such a bad drunk, you know."

"I know, love. It must have been awful."

"I'm glad he stopped drinking. He's like a different person. Anyway, Dad wasn't the problem for me. It was Sarah. She was horrible to me. Imagine being abused by your own sister."

"You are well rid of her," her fiancé says.

"As I got older she got worse. Being nice one minute and horrible the next. I didn't know if I was coming or going with her."

"A narcissist. I'm so glad you are staying away from her now."

"Me too," she says and they embrace each other.

I'm glad Sarah is no longer part of Emily-Brooke's life. I steady myself within my walls.

"It's funny, I can still picture D.B. sitting there polishing his boots," she says with a laugh.

"At least D.B. is happy and his wife Catherine. His two kids, Ruth and Robert, are lovely. It was nice meeting them on Saturday. They all looked so happy," her fiancé says as he looks out my dirty window.

"They *are* happy. I am too," she says looking down at her engagement ring, "I can't wait to be Mrs Dunkan."

"Emily Dunkan. It has a nice ring to it," her fiancé says.

"I'm glad I got rid of the 'Brooke' part. Sarah picked that name for me. She's nothing to me now. Once I got rid of the name, a burden lifted off my shoulders."

"Have you seen enough, my love? The guys will be wondering why we are taking so long."

"I want to see my old bedroom," she says sprinting up my stairs. She opens up my built-in wardrobe and lets out a gasp, "Oh look, my verse is here. 'John 14:6. *Jesus saith unto him, I am the way, the truth, and the life: no man cometh unto the Father, but by me.'*

Look at my big writing. It's worse than my P.1's writing. I know I'm a Christian now but I can honestly say I always was one. Even at that early age, I always knew Jesus was looking after me. Knowing him drew me closer to God, my father-"

"Shall we go now?" he interrupts her.

"Go?" I yell. Don't go, Emily. Don't go.

Emily nods and they strut down my stairs. He turns to Emily and asks, "If you had one wish, would you ever move back in here?"

There is a long pause and I know the answer will be yes. I listen carefully.

"No... I would never move back in here."

My heart cracks in two like an Easter egg with no treasure hiding inside.

FORTY-THREE
MOLLY

I needed to go back home and get myself sorted; I looked a right mess. One thing I knew, as I marched out the school gate, was I hated being told off in work. It was worse than being told off at home. Awful!

I walked at a fast rate and a cat scampered past me with a bird in its mouth. I stopped abruptly. A small house wren. Sickness rushed into my stomach. My street curved sharply at the end of the road and a shadow creeped onto my path as I turned into it.

I saw my lovely, welcoming house from the top of the street and appreciated it for the first time. Our house was the opposite of Fiona and Stevie's house. Mum and Dad worked so hard to provide Josh and I with such a perfect home. Keeping my job had to be my priority now. I wanted to help out financially. I wanted to start paying my way.

I strolled up my driveway and stretched my hand over our hedges as I did. I picked off a single velvet green leaf.

A flock of crows flew above me. A murder of crows.

I knew something was wrong. The door was open slightly and frantic noises came from inside.

Two police officers moved down our hallway and were stunned to see me standing there. Was I in more trouble? Did Steve and Fiona report me for being in their house? They were fine when they left the office.

"Molly?" the policewoman asked, "Come inside. We have some bad news," she continued. I saw Mum. She looked awful: the makeup on her face had tracks where tears had fallen and more were flowing. Her hands were up in protest. She sped towards me and held me. Mumbling into my ear, I froze. I couldn't make out any words but I knew something awful had happened. Something unthinkable. I tried to move Mum off me but her full weight was on me and I was holding her up.

"It's your brother. I'm sorry, Molly. He was in an accident and—"

Mum screamed in my ear and the policewoman held her from behind. Dad appeared in the hallway; his face a grey colour.

He repeated, "No, no, no" over and over and my body braced itself for the terror it was about to receive.

The policeman continued, "We tried to contact you at your work but they couldn't find you. I'm sorry, Molly. Your brother was killed in a car crash. The woman who was driving, Willow Malloy, is in intensive care."

Dad shouted out the single word, "Dead!"

The word hit my chest like a bullet as if someone had slapped me up the face full force, ripping part of me away. I started to shake.

Mum dropped to her knees and clung onto my legs. Tears rolled down my face as I turned to the policeman. I choked the words out of my dry mouth.

"His name is Josh. Mum and Dad call him Joshua," I said and dropped the leaf in my hand.

FORTY–FOUR
HOUSE

The house two doors down was knocked down today. I had never seen anything like it.

They started with the roof and it crumbled like a house of cards.

I am scared.

I am.

I am.

FORTY-FIVE
MOLLY

I didn't know how we all ended up in the living room. I looked up and we were all there alongside our neighbours: Tim and Janet. Mum sobbed in the corner and Dad was sitting close to me; his elbows on his knees and head in his hands.

Janet, for something to say, said, "Shall I make tea? Sandwiches?" Tim, knowing no one was going to answer his wife, awkwardly responded with a nod.

I didn't want to move or speak. If I did, somehow it would make it real. Josh was younger than me. He couldn't be dead. I never thought of death taking young people before. Only Grandad in my family had died before this moment. Was death that uncaring and heartless? Lurking around like a serial killer waiting for its next victim.

Dad reached out and gripped my hand, holding it tighter than normal. The fortune-teller's Bible verse came into my head and I repeated the words over and over.

"John 14:6. Jesus saith unto him, I am the way, the truth, and the life: no man cometh unto the Father, but by me."

Whitewell came into my head. Did Josh know you had to be a Christian to go to Heaven? Did he know Jesus was the way? Was Josh with God?

I spoke the words out, "Where's Josh?" Mum threw her head up, shaking her head over and over. I repeated the question, "Where's Josh?"

Dad focused on me and said gently, "He's at the hospital, baby girl. The hospital."

"Why are we here? Let's go and see him," I said nearly choking out the words.

"We have to wait, Molly-Moo. We have to wait," said Dad.

"They can fix him, Dad. We need to at least try," I said my breath catching on each word. Mum howled in the background and I bypassed her, "We need to try, Dad. Let's go!"

I waited.

Time went slowly by and people entered in and out of the house, shaking their heads in disbelief. I sat quietly knowing if I moved, I would know Josh was dead; he was not going to walk through the door and flick my ear anymore.

F O R T Y – S I X
HOUSE

The house beside me was knocked down today.

They started with the roof and it tumbled like a house of cards.

I am scared.

I am.

I am.

FORTY-SEVEN
MOLLY

I moved and I knew he was dead.

Permanently dead. Josh wasn't coming back. Death didn't care. It wasn't loving. It ripped out my heart and emptied it. Returned it to me broken.

Relatives repeated the words, "I am so sorry" over and over and it made me seasick. I forced myself to stand up and walk. I wrapped my arms around myself as I tried to accept this reality. Coldness emptied every hint of warmth inside me.

Josh was gone.

A knock on our front door made me cry out, "Josh?"

My dad answered it. He touched my arm on the way to the door. It was one of Josh's many friends. Fifteen-year-olds all looked the same. He looked like Josh but Josh would not be coming through our door again. Not anymore.

I left the crowd of caring people bustling around our living room like bees around a hive.

I trudged up the stairs.

"Molly." I turned around and it was Matthew. He stepped up a couple of the stairs towards me and I stepped down one. I was on the fourth stair again.

"Eh, Molly, I'm so sorry. I came as soon as I heard. If ya know what I... I..." He reached up. He clutched my hand and held on to it. A weakness ransacked my knees and I wanted him to never let go.

"How did you hear?"

"Facebook. I'm devastated for ya all. He was so young. I'm sorry. He was a great friend. A great kid." He let go off my hand and skimmed his hand through his brown hair biting down on his lip.

"He was."

"Did he tell ya he became a Christian?"

"No," I said. Tears filled my eyes as a weight lifted off my shoulders.

"I called as I wasn't sure if he told ya. If ya know what I mean now."

"No, he didn't tell me," I said as I titled my head back and closed my eyes for a second, "I'm glad you told me. Thank you. Thank you." Josh was not in death's dark hole.

"Ma da died last year so I know how you feel, Molly. Ya see… I want you to know it will get easier," he said looking down at our carpet.

"I'm sorry your dad died," I said reaching out and taking his hand again. I held it for a second and then let go.

"Look, take ma number and call me when this is all over." He pressed a card into my hand and stepped up onto my stair, pulling me towards him. His strong arms held me. I wanted to cry onto his shoulder but I kept my tears in. He turned and was gone into the crowd downstairs.

I took a calm deep breath.

Josh was in Heaven.

Holding onto the card, I marched up the rest of our stairs. I went to Josh's bedroom door and I made myself do two little knocks. I leaned my head on his door and longed for the words, "Dry your eyes, Molly." But they didn't come. I reached my hand out and turned the knob, slowly opening his door.

A spike of pain stung my whole body when Josh wasn't there.

Plants die, not brothers. Did I have to let you go?

I placed my hand on his chest of drawers and skimmed my hand over the top. I opened the first drawer and all his socks were matched and perfectly lined up.

"Josh, why do golfers wear two pairs of socks…? In case they get a hole in one… Josh, I never told you how perfect you were. You were the best brother ever," I whispered as I closed the drawer and opened his second drawer. His T-shirts were perfectly lined up too and I lifted one out, unrolling it in my hands. It said, "I'm with stupid" with an arrow pointing to the left.

"Are you trying to tell me something, Josh?" I said with a laugh and guilt cut my laugh short. Why was I laughing when my brother was dead? I held the T-shirt up to my nose and breathed it in. It smelt of Josh.

I sat on his bed and pored over his bedside table. There was a Bible on top of a book by the author Rick Barnes and a scribbled note "batteries for Xbox".

"I didn't know you read the Bible, Josh," I said out loud, "Always a dark horse… I'm glad you became a Christian. You should have told me." I stared at his guitar and his deer song rang into my ears.

I pulled open his first drawer and there were two framed photographs. One was a framed picture of us. Both of us with our tongues out and making rabbit ears on each other.

"You framed our photograph… I love you too, Josh. I'm sorry you're gone now."

The other one was a photograph of Josh with Willow. She had her arms around his neck and was kissing him on his cheek. Oblivious as to what had happened to Josh.

I wished… I wished I was oblivious.

I looked closely at her. She was beautiful; hair in bunches and pretty, brown eyes and eyelashes to die for.

"So, you two *were* dating. I should have kept a better eye on your Finsta," I said touching the heart in the far corner of the photograph, "Josh: the dark horse."

A small knock on his door made me jump.

"Josh?"

It was Anita and my heart crashed to the floor again.

"Molly, I'm so sorry. I came as soon as I heard. I'm so sorry," she said and raced to me and held me, "I shouldn't have said ye avoided death. I'm sorry."

Anita held my shoulders and scanned my whole face. Her fingers nervously grasped for her hedgehog necklace.

"I'm sorry."

"You said that twice."

"Are ya okay? I don't know why I asked that. Of course, you're not okay. I miss him. Not that we had a close friendship but he was always in the background of us. Yer wee, annoying brother. I'm sorry," Anita said and burst out crying.

"His room is so tidy. Don't you think?"

"Uh-huh… the opposite of his big sister," Anita said with a nervous giggle.

"I need to tidy mine. I've a dead plant in there."

Josh and Charlie were dead.

"This is so strange," I whispered.

"Uh-huh, it is," said Anita.

"I was never the grown-up. Josh was," There was a long pause, "I thought piling on the makeup, carrying a handbag and wearing high heels made me into a grown-up but it just made me into a fool. Just look at how organised and mature Josh was. Not only was he dating Willow and planning a future with her but he knew the important things in life. He was always loving. Look," I said holding out his photograph, "I'm not a loving person. I work with five-year-olds… babies… and I never care. I'm not loving. The class is not talking and it's probably down to me… somehow. Why did I not stay away when the fortune-teller told me to? Because I'm selfish. I never once told Josh to be careful. Dad told us every day to be careful. I should've told him to be careful. I should've told him not to go. It was all my fault." I clutched his pillow and squeezed it.

"Molly, it was not yer fault," Anita said.

"I can smell him here, Anita," I said as I wiped the flowing tears from my face with the pillow, "It was my fault. He told me at the beach he was going. I should've cared more. I should've said, 'Tell Willow to be careful.' I didn't. I said nothing. I'm selfish. I didn't know what type of bird I was. I knew everyone else's type. I just didn't know my own. Now I do. I'm a cuckoo bird."

"Cuckoo bird? Molly, what are ya talking about? Forget birds. You're not a selfish person," Anita said.

"I am. I am. Look he was alive here and now he's dead," I said, throwing the framed photograph about. Anita grabbed the photograph out of my hand.

"Oh, is that Willow? How's she?" Anita said to distract me and my head pounded.

"Still in intensive care," I whispered, "Josh was sensible, loving and kind. Do you know he was off painting Willow's sister's living room before he... died." I choked out the last word. He was loving and kind. Was that what God wanted Christians to be: loving and kind? He was so loving He died on the cross for our sins. I did nothing for others.

"He was fifteen and he was more caring and loving than me. All I've ever cared about is myself... and a plant I called Charlie," More tears rolled down my face. Would I ever stop crying? "I haven't even spoken to Mum since this happened. Her only son has died and I haven't even spoken to her. What type of person am I?" I asked Anita, desperate for an answer.

"Molly, ya can talk to yer mum now. There are no deadlines with what ya do. You're in shock. Come here," she said as she reached out and pulled me towards her. She held me for a long time.

I whispered, "God help me."

"Ye have yer mum. I wish I..."

"Oh Anita... your mum—"

"It's okay."

"I'm so sorry."

"I know."

Dad called from the bottom of the stairs, "Molly, we're going to see your brother. We want you to come."

I stood up and straightened my clothes and said, "I don't want to be a cuckoo bird anymore. It's time for me to grow up. I'm not a child anymore. I care now. I do."

We both heard a scraping sound in the corner of the room. We both froze. "What the heck?" I said and the noise continued.

"This is freaking me out, Molly," said Anita grabbing my wrist. I crept towards the sound and it wasn't stopping. It was in the far corner of his room. Anita continued to squeeze my wrist and I could hardly breathe. What was going on here?

There were several blankets in the corner and I leaned down and ripped them away from the corner. There was Butterscotch's cage and there was Butterscotch!

"What the hell is that thing?" said Anita backing away. I kneeled and lifted him out.

"Allow me to introduce you to Butterscotch." Anita continued to back away.

"I don't like those rat things," she said putting her hedgehog into her mouth.

"I better feed the wee thing," I said as I replaced his water and food, gently putting him back into his cage.

I turned around and looked at Anita sucking her necklace.

"You're going to choke on that thing," I said. Anita spat it out of her mouth and we both smiled. We held each other.

FORTY-EIGHT
HOUSE

I reject death.

I do.

I do.

I do not want to die.

I feel the crunch in my roof and I call out, "Run, little ones." The mice scatter.

Rain pelts me in slow drips and I feel each of my walls crashing. My hot press crumples and I know I am nothing. My whole being and all my memories. Numb.

I feel grief for my own self.

I whisper: "John 14:6 Jesus saith unto him, I am the way, the truth, and the life: no man cometh unto the Father, but by me."

Death lurks in the bulldozer that crawls towards me.

I didn't know Jesus, so will the Father not know me when I die?

Will someone mourn for me?

I am afraid.

I am.

I am.

FORTY-NINE
MOLLY

I hurried out to the car because of the sudden downpour. My uncle Billy was driving, and Dad was hunched beside him at the front like a kiwi bird. Mum was sitting on the back seat. Her bent-over figure made me wince. Teardrops were on the windows.

I opened the car door. "Mum, I'm going to sit with you," I said.

I adjusted my dress before I slipped in.

"Okay," said Mum and I spotted her strained face with makeup tracks down her cheeks.

"Don't worry, Mum. We're going to get through this together," I said putting my hand on her back. Her body felt frail to me. I was going to be her fairywren; the kindest bird on Earth.

"Okay, darling," said Mum. I unbuttoned the top button of my dress and put on my seatbelt.

"Everyone ready? Let's go," said Uncle Billy tapping on the steering wheel and staring straight ahead.

"I'm sorry, Mum," I said reaching out and taking her hand. I stared down at it. I never noticed how small her hand was before. "I'm sorry," I whispered again.

"What was that?" Mum said, blinking up at me.

"I'm sorry for not talking to you," I answered.

"I know, darling. I know."

"Mum, I care. You know I care, Mum, don't you?"

Mum leaned over and hugged me. "I know, love. I know you care."

"I love you, Mum. I love you."

"I know, darling. I know," Mum said wiping a strand of hair away from my face.

"I'm sorry, Mum," I repeated.

"He was too young," Mum said and I nodded several times blinking the tears away.

"Everyone okay back there?" Dad asked. Mum closed her eyes for a few seconds.

I leaned forward and put my hand on Dad's back, "Yes, Dad," I said my voice quavering. I could do this. I could be there for them both. Josh, if you caught my thoughts: please help me to do this.

"I'm so proud of you," Mum said and I nodded.

"I'm proud of you too, Mum."

"It's so sad."

"I know."

"I miss Joshua."

"I miss him too."

We arrived and moved like four ghosts towards the funeral parlour. I grabbed Mum's hand; Dad reached out and gripped mine.

I could do this. I was a new bird.

FIFTY
BRICK

Silence.

A voice shattered the quiet.

"I used to live here. I'd a great childhood here. What are they building here now?"

Is my journey not complete?

"They are building apartments. You should see the plans. Come with me and I'll grab them out of the site office for ya," Carson said.

Silence.

"You don't mind if I take a brick. That old house held many good memories for me," the voice said.

Someone lifted me up and held me in their hand. My journey will never be complete. I did not die.

I am alive.

I am.

I am.

FIFTY-ONE
MOLLY

Days came and went. The funeral came and went. My eighteenth birthday came and went.

I was an adult for real now. But without my brother.

I opened the book he had bought me on birds and flicked to the front page. He had written something inside. I hadn't noticed when he gave it to me. I looked at it in shock. I grabbed my green-tinted glasses and took a deep breath.

"To my blister, Molly. A bird does not sing because it has an answer. It sings because it has a song. Be free like a bird, Blondie. Enjoy being an adult and stop worrying about that dyslexia thing. Love ya, sis! Now dry your eyes. Josh."

Tears welled up in my eyes. Josh may have died when he was still a child but he was wiser than any adult I'd ever known. I reread the words and dried my eyes on my sleeve. I stood up and placed the book on my bedside table beside my black bird-watching book. It no longer lived under my mattress; out in open. I pressed my forefinger onto the leather.

I would enjoy being an adult, Josh. For you. Every day would matter from now on. I was free like a bird in all areas of my life. As for being dyslexic... Yes, it was part of me, but only a small part. There were many more parts to me. From now on, I would not say I was dyslexic instead I would say, "I have dyslexia but it doesn't define me as a person." I shoved the glasses up onto my head and smiled to myself.

I carried my last bin bag out of my room. Childish teddies in one hand and Charlie in the other.

"How's the room looking now?" called Mum from her room.

Mum was different since Josh died. She didn't laugh anymore. She was quieter and remained in the house.

I remembered the conversation she had with Dad and I last night. Josh's room was to remain the same.

"I can't go in there yet," she had explained to us both and I understood.

"When you do want to go in, Mum, I will be with you," I had said and Dad nodded.

I looked at Mum sitting on her bed gripping onto two photographs. I set down my bin bag.

"My room looks great. I wanted to finish it before I go back to work."

"When are you back, darling?"

"Day after tomorrow," I said and cosied up with her on the bed and clasped her hand, "It's okay, Mum. I'll phone you when I arrive and on all my breaks."

"Thank you."

"Who's in the photographs?" I asked seeing Josh's blonde hair on the little part of the photograph I could see.

"It's you guys," said Mum showing Josh down at the beach; his eyes bright blue and his smile unreal. The other photograph was me on the ice in my dark green performance outfit. A kooky sensation crept into my stomach. The one you got when you knew you needed to confront someone about something but knew it was probably the wrong time. I had faced death, so why was I finding it so difficult to ask this question? Surely, this should not be this hard!

"Mum, why... why did you...?" I started to hiccup.

"What is it, Molly?" said Mum taking the photograph from me and looking at it, "You are so beautiful on the ice."

I sat up straight and held in my hiccup, refusing to let it out.

"Mum, why did you never come and see me skate?"

Mum turned and looked at me. Her green eyes looking into mine like a mirror.

"I did when you first started, darling. But when you fell, my heart went into my mouth. I wanted to jump onto the ice and grab you out of there. Rescue you. Maybe that's just motherly instinct. I don't know but I knew your journey was not going to be plain sailing. I knew this hobby would involve so many more falls. I just couldn't bear to watch you fall over and over again. I decided there and then that Dad would go instead of me."

My mouth was open. This whole time she couldn't face coming to see me in case I fell. If only I had known this.

"Mum, we learn how to fall. We fall in such a way that it doesn't harm us as much. And now I'm in the professional group, it's very rare if I do fall."

"Really?"

"Yes, come and see me. I want you to be there."

"I want to see you skate. I will come."

We hugged each other and a massive weight lifted off my shoulders. I did want Mum to see me skate. I was so glad she would.

"Is that Charlie?" she asked. I looked down at my dead plant.

"It *was* Charlie," I said with a chuckle.

"I thought I got rid of Charlie ages ago."

I burst out laughing, "I rescued him out of the bin."

"You are kidding me."

"Nope. I got him out ages ago," I said holding in another laugh.

Mum burst out, "That's ridiculous." We both laughed. It was lovely to hear Mum laugh again.

It was a perfect moment.

FIFTY–TWO
HOUSE

"You probably don't remember me. You used to be a house and I used to be a young boy who lived... within you. My name is Harry and my parents were Rab and Gillian."

I know immediately it is Harry and joy fills my being.

"Imagine speaking to a brick," he says with a laugh and throws me into a basket at the bottom of his stairs. I'm a little bit taken back and I hate the scratchy feeling of the basket under me.

I remain in the basket for weeks, maybe months. I listen carefully each day to Harry who calls himself a "fortune-teller". He tells others about their futures.

I am a brick.

I am.

I am.

I have an inner voice humans will never hear. It used to rise from the deep depths, within my foundations, through my plumbing and it made me choke on my own spit.

Now I have no foundations, no plumbing and no hot press filled with memories. And yet I can still remember.

I shout out an uncontrollable "Run!" as I look down at the screwed-up faces of the people who reluctantly creep through Harry's door.

Ridiculous.

Harry cannot tell you your futures.

I need to give up on trying to make them leave. I should remain quiet in this basket.

No children come and it makes me sad.

The adults bore me. All have this desire to know their futures. They want to know about their future jobs, their finances. And more importantly, they want to know of future relationships.

What is my future? Will I always be in this basket now? I must accept this is it for me. I am not House. I am a brick. My fears and desires still reside with me. Remain.

I unload a deep sigh that assures me I am right. I will never see children again.

A voice from behind my door, interrupts my thoughts, "I don't know why I let you talk me into doing mad things with you."

And then the doorbell starts to sing. I'm sick of hearing "Jingle Bells"!

"Are you sure you made the appointment?"

"Yes, six months ago. He's so good ye have to go on his waiting list… Don't worry. He's clairvoyant, he *knows* we're coming…"

He's not clairvoyant. He's Harry: a little boy in a man's body who fixes things and looks after his sister, Susan. Where is Susan now? Why does she never visit?

Harry slowly descends the stairs. Where is the young boy I remember zooming away from me on his bike? He's old and fat now. His hair is going and some of his teeth are missing.

"Someone is coming," they whisper from behind the door, "Can't believe you're making me do this."

Harry opens his door.

"Hi," he says, "Come on up."

One girl whispers to the other one, "What do you call a fat clairvoyant?" I wait for the answer, "A four-chins-teller."

I don't get it and I have no time to work it out as one of the girls takes a coughing fit.

The two girls squeeze past my basket. I catch a glimpse of them both. One with blonde hair that falls way down her back with magical clover-green eyes and a frown. The other is pretty with red hair like Susan's. But she is not Susan. Her face is different.

Harry walks up, taking one step at a time and stops at every third step for a rest. Sometimes he leans on the bannister with his stick in the same hand and rubs his leg with his free hand. He is so old now. Struggling to walk. Will he die soon? Will I be left alone in this basket? I feel a panic fall upon me. Like the first time I experienced snow upon my roof when I was a house.

I feel miserable.

"So, have ye been doing this long? The fortune-teller stuff?" The red-haired girl asks.

Who cares? No one can predict futures.

"Yes, the four-chins-teller stuff," the other girl agrees.

"Have ye been out much?" the red head continues.

She sounds as if she is going to ask him out on a date! Maybe that would be a good thing. He could marry and have children of his own. I would be happy again.

"Hopefully it will be barbecue weather soon."

Does Harry not remember the barbecues his dad used to do for him and Susan?

"Do ye think the sun will shine again soon?"

At the top, he leads them into his living room and mumbles, "Wait here and I will set up the kitchen for you both."

He disappears down the hall. I listen carefully. I hear stifled whispers.

Then, "Don't!"

"I was trying to read it for ye." I wonder if they are reading books like the books Emily-Brooke used to read. I am so restricted here in this basket. I want to be a house again. I miss being a house.

Their droning bores me and I'm tired now.

"Who's first?"

"I'll go first."

"You're going to get married soon."

I know the words are lies. Like the snow that fell upon my roof promising warmth and comfort, Harry promises nothing but lies. Harry cannot know when she will get married. Just as the snow couldn't provide any of those wonderful things. Once the snow knew that I knew, it melted away like a cat in the night. Sneaky.

"You'll have two children. Both girls."

He always tells them they will have children. I wonder why Harry never had a family. Children are everything.

"Can ye tell me something good, please?"

There is nothing good to tell.

I was first built in 1961. Four families lived within my walls. Over the years, I have come to a sad conclusion. It is the children who make the adults miserable; their intermittent crying makes the adults turn on them. This never ends. Alas, your life will be miserable.

"You're a good person and you'll gain the happiness you deserve."

Happiness? Adults are never happy. If she has children, she will become angry and upset. Her husband will have an affair like Stephanie did on Jack. All will not work out. All will not work out.

"Happiness? What kind of happiness? Tell me more."

"It's going."

Children change over time. They grow up and sadly become adults themselves. Then they move on. Of course, the happiness is going.

"The vision has gone," Harry concludes.

My breath is quick and frantic and yet I'm not sure if I can breathe at all.

"It's yer turn, Molly. I'm clearly going to have a crap life. A husband who's going to break my heart and happiness that fades away. Just brilliant!"

"You will have a crap life," I hear myself say, but it's as if my voice is miles away now. The way you feel in an odd dream where nothing makes sense and voices speak out but the words mean nothing. Pointless. I don't care about her life. It's pointless. My life is pointless too. I will remain in this basket forever.

I listen and I know I am apathetic.

"I need to use sage. I need to use sage," I hear Harry shout. This is different. I listen carefully.

What is sage?

"We're done here!" Harry shouts again and I long to know why. "You can both go."

"Why are you telling them to go?" I scream as I put out my invisible hand and steady myself with a sigh back into the basket.

"What do you mean?" one of the girls asks and I hear a bell ringing.

"Just brilliant! Let's go."

"Why? Have you nothing to tell me?"

"Children should be seen and not heard. Children should be seen and not heard. Children should be seen and not heard,"

My inner voice is frantic now and it screams throughout my whole being, "Children should be seen and not heard".

Did he say, "Children should be seen and not heard?" It pauses and my inner voice whispers in my entire being: children should be seen and not heard.

Children should be seen and not heard.

He knows I'm here. Harry knows the truth.

"Do we need to pay for this?"

"No payment. Just go,"

The red-haired girl turns and runs down the stairs. Harry grabs the other girl's hand at the top of the stairs, "You must not enter that school. Don't go. Whatever you do, don't go!" He spits in her face as he speaks.

"What do you mean? What school? What's wrong? Tell me," she asks.

My inner voice falls silent as the girl pulls her hand away from Harry and I long to take it.

His eyes glaze over and he drops her hand and says, "Children should be seen and not heard. Children should be seen and not heard." His nose begins to bleed and it drips slowly onto the carpet.

She runs down the stairs. The other girl is at the bottom frantically trying to turn the key in the door. The blonde trips over my basket and I spill out onto the carpet. She takes me.

"Get me out of here. Hurry up!" she yells. Harry is standing, shaking his head at the top of the stairs.

He shouts down, "Stay away from that school! If the children stop speaking it will damage them in ways you will never understand. Think about the children!"

The red-headed girl opens the door and they both nearly fall down the two steps on the way out.

Leaving the door open, they run.

I'm outside!

My inner voice knows I am happy to be outside. The girl with the blonde hair and I greet each other with a joy that sings out of my whole being. It is a song that sings louder than my whispering inner voice, which gives up with a sigh and clangs back down into the pit of my being. Disappointed. Silenced.

Don't run. I want to stay with you now.

I can barely take my eyes off this girl who has won me over completely. But when I do, I see houses all around me. Their roofs are flat, their walls are mouse-grey and their windows small and thin. I miss being a house.

The look on her face tells me exactly how she feels. She is going to keep me. It's as if I have waited my whole life for this one single moment.

She is now a proud owner of a brick that needs to belong to someone who cares.

"That was beyond weird."

"Not as weird as this," she said holding me up higher. I will always need work.

"Is that from the basket?" her friend asks.

"Yep," she says, throwing me into a rucksack.

It is fun to relax in the rucksack.

Now I know I belong to a girl who rescued me from an uncomfortable basket.

I take a calm, deep breath.

I am a brick.

I am.

I am.

I belong now.

I will be happy.

FIFTY-THREE
MOLLY

My last pile of clothes waited; begging me to sort them. I plucked my black cardigan off the pile and threw it into the laundry basket. A card fluttered to the floor. I picked it up and examined it. It had a guitar on the front and I knew immediately it was Matthew's business card. I flicked it over. His name was in a formal font:

Matthew T. Stewart

Guitar Coach

I wondered what the T stood for. I traced over his number. I threw the last bundle of clothes into the laundry bin and smiled.

It was time to go back to work. I surveyed my spotlessly clean bedroom. On my bedside unit, the picture of Josh and I smiled out at me. I smiled back.

"My room is still clean, Josh. And it'll stay that way," I promised as I made my way to the shower.

I was surprised to hear Mum in her bedroom. She had been sleeping in a lot since Josh died. "Morning Mum," I called in, "You're up with the lark."

"Morning, darling," she called back, "I'm driving you to work today."

"Mum, you don't have to—"

"I want to," said Mum popping her head out of her bedroom, "I don't need to take Joshua to sc—" Mum stopped herself and a stabbing pain dug into the middle of my forehead.

"The lift will be great, Mum. It means I can have a big breakfast with you and Dad."

"You can do your makeup too," suggested Mum.

"Only mascara today, I look better without caking my face with foundation. I used to use a trowel to apply it." Well, so Josh told me, I remembered and smiled.

When I reached the kitchen, Dad had his head in his hands. "Good morning Dad," I said in the best cheerful voice I could muster.

"Oh, morning Molly-Moo. I didn't realise you're going back to work today. Do you want breakfast?" He got to his feet and popped bread into the toaster.

"Yes, but not just toast. Mum is taking me to work so I've loads of time."

"Good," said Dad looking out the window. I noticed our large photograph album on the kitchen table. Three more were on the floor.

"Dad, that's a hint," I said as I feasted my eyes on Matthew's number again.

"What? Sorry, baby girl. I was thinking about—"

"I know who you were thinking about. You're allowed to say his name Dad. Josh. You were thinking about Joshua. It's okay, Dad. I promised you both we will get through this together and I meant every word of it."

"Thanks, love. Sometimes... I should have done more."

"More? Dad, this is not your fault," I said knowing since Josh died, Dad was blaming himself.

"I should've warned him more and he would've warned Willow. He would be home today."

"Dad, the motorbike came out of nowhere. Willow swerved to avoid it. She didn't see the tree. It was an accident. Nobody could've stopped it from happening."

"I know... I know. I just wish—"

"Dad, there was nothing any of us could have done. Josh would want us to know that."

"I know. I know, baby girl."

"Scrambled eggs, Dad," I said with a weak smile.

"Really?"

"Yes."

Dad made me some scrambled eggs and he began to hum. It was nice to hear him humming. It made me smile. I slipped out my mobile phone and entered Matthew's name. I typed a text.

Matthew, it's Molly here. Love to get that coffee you promised me. It wd b good to talk.

Mum arrived and slipped in beside me.

"It's nice to hear you humming."

"I suppose you want scrambled eggs too," Dad said, winking at me.

"Are you winding me up? Of course, I do," Mum said smiling over at me.

"Why should you never tease egg whites, Mum?"

"I don't know."

"They can't take a yoke."

Mum reached out and took my hand. "You are really funny. You know… I really mean that."

Dad served us the most delicious scrambled eggs with toast and melted butter. I was about to put my fork in my mouth when my phone dinged.

Gr8! Today? Matt

I smiled.

After breakfast, Mum took me to work and we chatted happily in the car. When we arrived, she reached out her hand and gripped mine.

"Thank you, Molly." I shook my head.

"For what, Mum?"

"For being so grown up about all of this. You have made it… well, you have made it easier," she said.

"Mum, we'll always love Josh—"

"Joshua," Mum corrected me with a smile.

"Okay, we'll always love Joshua with all our hearts and we'll miss him every day but the last thing Josh… I mean, Joshua would want is for us three to be moping around feeling sorry for ourselves. He would want us to care for each other and be a family," I said.

"Thank you, Molly, for being so sensible," said Mum.

"You're welcome, Mum. Now let me go, I can't be late on my first day back."

"Wait," said Mum, "Take this packet of hankies and here, wear this." Mum reached around my neck and tied her scarf around me. I leaned in and kissed her on the cheek.

"I love you with all my heart," I said before stepping away from the car.

When I glanced back, Mum was wiping a tear away.

"I hope that's a happy tear," I called back, checking my rucksack for my fob.

"Of course, darling," said Mum smiling over at me.

"There it is," I said out loud showing mum my fob to get into the school. I strolled up the corridor checking my mobile to see if I had time to make myself a coffee in the staffroom.

"Oh, look who it is…" shouted Nicola coming in the opposite direction.

"Morning Nicola," I said, keeping my head down.

"How come you were off for practically a week? A death in the family means you only get three days off. Are you getting special treatment or what?" she said.

"He was my brother. His name was Josh. Thanks for asking."

"Not my concern, Molly!" she snapped back. I opened the staffroom door and she waltzed in front of me. I took a deep breath hearing Josh's conversation in my mind when I had told him about Nicola:

"If it's your classroom, they're your kids. You should have told her to piss off and read the book yourself."

Nicola was pouring herself a cup of tea and I marched in behind her.

"You were right there, Nicola," I said.

"What's that then?"

"It isn't your concern. In fact, I'm not your concern either so stop asking me questions. Stop lurking about when I'm about and leave me alone. Don't speak to me again." I said and calmly stepped to the cupboard and lifted out a cup for myself.

"How dare yo—"

I held my hand up to her face and said, "Sorry Nicola, what part of 'don't speak to me again' did you not understand?"

She turned on her heels and click-clacked away.

I sipped my coffee and then smiled. "Dry your eyes, Nicola."

FIFTY–FOUR
BRICK

The journey stops and the top of the rucksack opens. A bright light shines all over me. The girl lifts me out and holds me in her hand. She turns me over and over in her hand the way Emily-Brooke turned over her new reading book and I know she loves me.

She opens a drawer by her bed and I fly through the air and land on soft material. The girl changes for bed and then studies her phone.

She stops and says, "John 14:6. Jesus saith unto him, I am the way, the truth, and the life: no   man   cometh unto the Father, but by me."

My whole being soars and I know I am in the right place. She is exactly like Emily-Brooke. She will look after me. She will care for me. We will find this Jesus together.

I am loved.

I am.

I am.

FIFTY-FIVE
MOLLY

I marched to Mr Cardwell's office, took a deep breath and knocked.

"Come."

I swung open his door.

"Mr Cardwell, I just thought I'd pop in and let you know I'm back," I said.

"Oh, Molly, come in. Come in. Take a seat," he said standing up, "I didn't get a chance to speak to you at the funeral—"

"You were there. I'm sorry, I—"

"No, no. I understand. My older brother, Michael, died when I was nineteen. I know exactly how you felt on the day of the funeral. That is why I provided you more time off. How are you now? Take a seat," he said going behind his desk again and sitting down himself.

It was eerie at Josh's funeral: the wrought iron gate, the paved driveway winding between the graves, the variety of headstones... granite, marble, black and white, and grey. The well-tended lawns with the decorative flower beds.

"It's hard as I miss Josh a lot..." I said, remembering the smell of the newly turned earth and the strong smell of the flowers as I gripped Dad's hand.

"If you need more time off work, I will understand."

"No... no, I'm ready to come back. That's why I called in. I wanted to say I'm sorry for calling in to see James..."

"All water under the bridge now, Molly. They are more concerned by the fact their son is still not speaking than—"

"James is still not speaking? What about the rest of the children? Did you get to the bottom of it?"

"Oh, it's been a huge drama, Molly. All the children in Mrs Craig's class are at home and the children in Mrs Dunkan's class have been dropping like flies too. The same problem. The board got involved and so the police have been here..."

"The police?"

"They suspect foul play. No one knows what is going on. They are threatening to close the whole school if it continues. Several of the children have been brought to the hospital. Even the doctors don't know what is going on."

"Awful," I said.

"Mrs Craig is off. She's stressed by the whole thing. So, you will be with Mrs Dunkan today. I hope that is okay," he said standing up again.

"Yes, that's no problem. Thank you, Mr Cardwell."

"For what?"

"For understanding about Josh," I said.

"It will get easier, Molly. I promise. Remember all the good times and hold onto your memories."

"I will," I made my way to his office door and stopped in my tracks, "Mr Cardwell, I have something I need to tell you."

"Yes?"

"It's something I should have mentioned earlier... but I was... I was a little afraid. I'm... I'm dys—. I have dyslexia." Saying the words out loud made me swallow hard and I felt faint. I could barely look at Mr Cardwell. He stepped over to his desk and fumbled about in his bottom drawer. My eyes widened. What was he doing?

"Mr Cardwell, did you hear me? I said I have dyslexia. If you need me to le—"

"Here, take this," he said, throwing me a little black box.

"What is it?"

"It's a spell-checker. Instructions are on the box. You might need it if a child asks you to spell a word." I looked up at him and smiled. He smiled back.

I could hardly believe it. My feet froze to the ground and I did what I usually do in awkward situations.

"Mr Cardwell... how do you spell mousetrap?"

"Really?"

"C-A-T."

"You are funny, Molly. You should use those jokes with the kids."

"I will."

FIFTY–SIX
BRICK

An alarm goes off. I wish with all my heart for this girl to know I was once a house. I wish and wish. There is silence and then the alarm goes off again. The pounding puts me on edge and I'm not sure if I waited eight minutes, eight hours or eight days in this drawer. My understanding of time has clearly dwindled, now I am a brick.

I hear a clatter close by and I feel afraid. Who is out there? Where is the blonde girl who rescued me from the basket?

"Oh crap!" I hear and I know the girl is moving around her room. I'm claustrophobic in this drawer. Will you ever lift me out? Remember me! The brick from Harry's flat!

"Flat!"

"Yes, yes. I'm the brick you rescued from Harry's flat. Let me out of this drawer!" I yell and wait.

The drawer opens and sunlight embraces my whole being like a warm hug. She lifts knickers from beside me and pauses, looking down. Are you looking at me?

Lift me out! Lift me out.

I hear a man yell from downstairs, "Molly! Babes, I hope you're up and away. If not you're mega late."

I know her name now. I know her name and I care for her more than ever now.

Molly. Short and sweet. I'm happy.

Lift me out! Lift me out. I wish with all my being.

My wish works!

I am more powerful than I originally thought.

Molly obeys my wish. She comes back to the drawer and lifts me out.

I am powerful.

I am.

I am.

I know I love her. I truly do. She sits me down on her dressing station, similar to Stephanie's one.

She looks in the mirror wetting her forefinger and wiping off the black mascara under her eyes. She ties her long, blonde hair back and then changes it into a bun.

"That'll have to do," she says out loud.

"You are beautiful," I reply knowing she can apprehend me the same way all the babies and children understood me when I was House.

I wish for you to take me with you, I wish again.

She lifts me up and puts me back into her rucksack.

I bump about as Molly travels.

All is good.

"Go away! Scat!" I hear her say. I listen to a cat meow and it reminds me of Harry and Susan's cat. Molly says, "Children should be seen and not heard."

She knows the truth! Children should be seen and not heard. But how can we make that happen, Molly? How can we stop the children from talking? Do I need to wish for it to happen? It is a nightmare not knowing what to do.

"Crap! What a shit start to the day," she answers and I agree with her.

We need to children, I say.

I overhear the hiss of a cat again.

My breath is quick and frantic and yet I'm not sure if I can breathe at all.

"We must stop the children from speaking," I hear myself say, but it's as if my voice is miles away now. The way you feel in an odd dream where nothing makes sense and voices speak out but the words mean nothing.

This time I know the words mean something. Children should be seen and not heard. I need you to run, Molly. Find children and I will stop them from speaking.

I know I care and I know Molly is running.

Finally, an adult who can hear my voice. An adult who understands my needs and desires and is willing to help me in my quest. If she finds children, I will make sure the children will not be heard.

There is silence.

Has she left me? Will she return?

I pick up a noise of laughing children. She has brought me to the children. I listen to their chat.

Molly lifts me out of the rucksack and writes "Miss Jolliff" on me.

Who is Miss Jolliff? Is that my name? She loves me! She has given me a name. She truly loves me. She places me in a basket. There is a sign above me: I am here today.

She knows I exist.

I am here.

I am.

I am.

I look around at the children and they begin to sing.

"What do you think, Miss Jolliff?"

The adult knows me, she calls me by my new name. The name Molly picked for me. I am loved.

One of the children says, "Aye, what do you think, Miss Jolliff?"

They all know I am here.

I am.

I am.

It is indeed a perfect day. Now I need to work out how to stop the children from speaking.

I will wish for it.

I will.

I will.

"Children should be seen and not heard," I say over and over, wishing hard.

FIFTY–SEVEN
MOLLY

When I arrived at Mrs Dunkan's classroom, she welcomed me into a class of ten children.

"Come in, Molly. Did Mr Cardwell explain what has been happening to the children?"

"Yes, it's awful," I replied, still feeling overwhelmed by Mr Cardwell's reaction to my big announcement, "Imagine not being able to talk."

"I can't. The parents are worried sick. The police say if any more children stop talking, they will put the school on lockdown."

I planted myself down and scanned the kids. What was making the children go silent?

"We are about to start our morning song. Your stone, or should I say brick, is still in our basket. Would you like to move it over?"

I reached over and lifted my brick. I spotted my name: Miss Jolliff. I turned it over.

The fortune-teller! His odd, round face appeared in my head and I knew I must go and see him. I would make him tell me why he said don't go back to that school. He must know what caused this. It was too much of a coincidence.

He kept repeating, "Children should be seen and not heard." I should go and see him after coffee with Matthew.

My meeting with Matthew... was I really going to be brave enough to go for coffee? I began to hiccup and I held my breath. Yes, I'm brave enough! One little hiccup escaped out of my tight-lipped mouth and I looked up at Mrs Dunkan.

"Molly, are you okay?"

"Yes," I said, popping my stone into the other basket.

I worked hard for Mrs Dunkan and I was glad when it was time for lunch. I knew I would need to speak to Jasmine. I lifted my egg and onion sandwiches and made my way over to the staffroom.

When I got there, I noticed there was a space between Nicola and Jasmine, and I squeezed in between the two.

"Hi everyone," I said and everyone said hi back with that look of sympathy on their faces that I had seen on everyone's faces since Josh died. I said a silent prayer: God, help me through this day. Help me to be strong. Amen.

I leaned over and whispered to Jasmine, "I need to talk to you. Do you mind if we've a chat before lunch ends?"

"Of course, Molly," she said with a smile.

I opened my lunchbox and unwrapped my sandwiches. There was a cute little envelope in purple. I knew immediately it was from Mum. I looked up and smiled over at Nicola. I opened the envelope and took out the small note. It read:

Have a lovely day, Molly. I'm so proud of you. I love you, Mum. x

"Ew," said Nicola turning her back on me, "I hate the smell of egg."

"Nicola, if you don't like the smell of egg and onion then move," I said.

"You move," she turned and barked in my face. I lurched forward slightly.

"No, *you* move. You're the one who's unhappy."

She got up and moved over to the other side of the table whilst I munched happily on my sandwiches knowing that Mum was proud of me. Win-win!

"Where do Inuits keep their eggs?"

Nicola didn't say a word. Everyone else looked at me for the answer.

"In their egg-loo." The staffroom erupted with laugher.

Just before the end of our lunch, Jasmine and I went out of the staffroom and she hugged me.

"Molly, when I heard about your brother I was devastated. Did you get my card?"

"We got so many cards. I'm sorry, I didn't read any of them. Well, I read one and it made me feel too sad so I stopped."

"Of course, I would do the same... How are you?"

"I'm okay. I'm glad to be back at work and I'm glad to see you again. I'm sorry for all the drama about James. I was foolish and I was being childish."

"Oh Molly, don't be sorry. We all do things we regret."

"You were right and I should've listened to you. I know that now. I was stupid," I said running my fingers through my hair, "I want us to be friends. From now on, I promise I'll think before I act."

Jasmine hugged me and I was happy to know all was well.

FIFTY-EIGHT
BRICK

I wish and wish. Days pass by and I continue wishing. I concentrate on five children and the same five stay away from school. Molly joins me sometimes and sometimes I am left alone.

I am happy, wishing hard and hoping for progress. Once I know the children's names, it becomes easier. Grace, Ben, Jill, Freddie, Victoria, Kim, Hannah, Carter, Nova and Terry. All ten remain at home and I listen to learn another child's name. I am making their parents' lives better.

I am.

I am.

Mrs Craig is happy and so are the other children. They sing every day to show me how happy they are with me.

Molly helps me to learn the names. She repeats them over and over.

"Dawn, if you need to go to the toilet, just go," she says and I know the next child to work on is Dawn. I wish hard with all my might.

"Dawn should be seen and not heard," I repeat it over and over. All the other children are playing but I keep my focus on Dawn. Molly has chosen Dawn and I want Molly to know we are working as a team.

Dawn walks outside to play and I am not sure if my wish is working. Then the most unexpected thing happens: Molly comes running in with Dawn.

"Help, help. Something is wrong with Dawn!" Molly screams and Mrs Craig's face turns white.

"What do you mean? What happened?" Mrs Craig asks.

"Yes, why are you confused by this?" I ask.

"She's not talking and she's crying. I think she's choking," Molly screams out.

Ridiculous! Why would you think she was choking? I stopped her from speaking. I made our wish come true.

I am Miss Jolliff!

I have an inner voice humans will now hear. It used to rise from the deep depths, within my foundations, through my plumbing and made me choke on my own spit. Now it spreads amongst the humans.

I can make the children's lives better. I can protect them from the pain. This is my job!

The adults will see their beautiful children but will no longer hear their voices. Now they will treat their children well.

Mrs Craig grabs Dawn and sits her down on a chair.

"Dawn, are you okay?"

Dawn says nothing and I am delighted.

"Of course, she is okay," I yell.

"Open your mouth, Dawn," Mrs Craig demands, and Dawn does, "There is nothing there. Dawn, can you speak?" she asks.

Dawn shakes her head and silently cries.

Of course, there is nothing there. Children should be seen and not heard... remember.

Dawn continues to cry.

Don't cry little one and all will be well.

A man arrives in the room and sits in front of Dawn. I turn to Molly and she says, "Let's go over to the carpet, P.2. And I'll read you all a story."

All is well. Molly will read to me the way Emily-Brooke read to me many years ago.

All is well.

I am happy.

"Which lucky child will I pick out next?" I wonder, looking at the nineteen faces in front of Molly.

"Molly, help me," I say.

"Look, James is sitting really well. He's a good boy," Molly says and I know who she wants me to focus on next. I work hard on James. Just as I am about to make progress, he leaves the room.

Days pass. I work on more of the children. More and more stop coming to this house.

James is hard to pin down but I want to make Molly happy and so I concentrate on him when I can.

"Molly, I will do this for you. Don't worry," I say.

"If you are happy here, I'm going to read a story to that small group over at the carpet," she replies.

Of course, I am happy.

"P.2, I'm going to read you a story about a house. I want you all to sit up well and I want you to listen carefully," Molly says and I emanate a deep sigh.

She knows I was once a house. I settle back in the basket and listen to her warm, soothing words.

"Once upon a time there was a happy house. Inside the house, there lived a family: a mummy, a daddy, a little boy and a little girl. Everyone loved the house and the house loved them…"

I am loved and I am happy.

She finishes and all the children clap and I know they are happy I am making their lives better.

"P.2, did you enjoy the story…"

"Yes, and I did too," I say and I go back to my wishing.

"Now I want you to do something for me. I want you to draw me a picture of your house," Molly says with a smile. They all go back to their seats and my heart is beating so fast I could cry. They are drawing me! Love explodes all over me. I feel the same way I felt when Emily-Brooke drew me on her blackboard many years ago.

I work on stopping James from talking and it finally works. He too is absent from this house. Molly will be happy now, but when I look at her, she has a nose bleed and has to leave the room.

It is a long time before she returns and I spend the rest of my time wishing over and over. Concentrating on each child and repeating their names over and over. Wishing with all my might, "Children should be seen and not heard."

I am tired now and Tristan carries my basket out of the room and walks over to another room. Another room full of more children.

I'm tired and yet they want me to do more.

I'm tired.

I am.

I am.

I see Emily-Brooke and I feel as if I am in some kind of dream.

"Come in. Come in," she says welcoming me, "Oh, good. Tristan, you brought the stones over…"

I am so tired but I will continue this wish for you.

"Children should be seen and not heard," I sing out.

FIFTY–NINE
MOLLY

At the end of the day, I grabbed my phone and sent Matthew a text.

Yes, let's meet today, M.

I was surprised how fast he replied.

Gr8. Do u want to meet now? I can't wait to see ya.

My fingers were tight as I sent off my next text.

Coffee shop on May Avenue? M.

Looking 4ward to it, Give me 10. xx.

I stared down at the kisses and every dancing nerve pirouetted into my stomach, joined by a couple of snapping crocodiles and rollicking dyslexic wolves. I got up and ran on the spot and made them all scatter.

"You guys *cannot* come with me for coffee." I grabbed my rucksack and ran-skipped out of the school. That ridiculous walk-run-skip people did when they wanted to get somewhere fuelled by excitement but they didn't want anyone to ask them why they were so happy.

It didn't break into a total skipping event. Instead, it became one third a skip, one third a run and one third a walk. My only failure was the smile I couldn't wipe off my face.

As I got closer to the cafe, my hands sweated a little and I grabbed one of Mum's hankies out of the side pocket of my rucksack. Mum's face appeared in my head. I wanted to protect her so much from the pain of Josh leaving us, from not wanting to leave the house and from finding Butterscotch; who was now happily living in my bedroom. I looked up at the sign on the cafe. I had never noticed the name before and I smiled up at it.

"Little Bird Cafe: the perfect place for our first date," said Matthew. He was right there in front of me. A tingling ran up my spine. The same one which ran up my spine when I was first introduced to the ice-rink. His tan hand reached out and pulled me in for a hug. I couldn't believe the words "first date" had spilled out of his mouth but I was glad they did. I hugged him and he smelt great. "Did ya know it was called Little Bird Cafe? Is that why ya asked me to meet ya here? If ya know what I mean."

"No... no, definitely not. But it is a cool name for our..." The name of the cafe couldn't have been more perfect. I'm surprised Grandad didn't know about this place. Josh would have loved taking the mick out of me for meeting Matthew at "Little Bird Cafe". I suddenly felt alone without Josh; incomplete like a sock without a partner, the last biscuit in the packet and the lonely page in the printer.

"Our?" His hand trailed down my arm and he clasped my hand. The loneliness faded a little as the electricity from the touch ran up my arm, "I would like it to be our first date. I really like ya, Molly. If ya know what I mean."

"You do?" I asked looking up into his blue eyes. There was something about him that made me feel safe, took away my hiccups and made me feel free to be myself.

"Yes, I do. Now allow me to treat ya to some lovely food," he said as he stepped towards the little duck-egg blue door, swinging it open for me. A radio was on and I could smell freshly brewed coffee and baked muffins.

"Thank you kindly," I said and we both were guided by a waiter to a table for two at the window. The wrought iron chairs had cute blue and white gingham cushions on them and there was a short, fat glass vase on the table with two white chrysanthemums inside. It was sweet.

We both ordered chicken burgers and chunky chips.

"Oh, and we will share an apple crumble," said Matthew. We snapped closed our menus and smiled at each other. It was great how comfortable I felt with him. It was so different compared to the awkward times when he called to tutor Josh. Thinking about Josh again made a pain sweep across my tummy. It was a different pain than my Grandad's-pain. When I remembered Grandad, the pain was dull and throbbing. It would bring back vivid memories of all I did with Grandad and all his tales of what he did during his entertaining, glorious life. Josh's pain was sharp and twisting, reminding me he was too young to die and he was going to miss so much in life. He would never get those exams, learn to drive, go to university or college. He would never get engaged or married and he would never have children. I would never be... Auntie Molly.

"So, Molly... I want to admit, ya make me a feel a little nervous. Which isn't like me at all."

"I make you feel nervous? Are you kidding me?" Our knees bumped against each other under the table and I knew Josh would be pleased I was finally on a date with Matthew. In my head, I could hear him.

"Dry your eyes, Blondie. Just enjoy the date!"

I looked up at Matthew and I saw sincerity in his blue eyes as he spoke.

"When I first set eyes on ya, I could barely look at ya. So beautiful, ya are. Yer hair is gorgeous and ya have the cutest smile and yer eyes... yer eyes are—"

"Green," I said with a giggle.

"Green? Oh, I got ya now. No, I wanted to say beautiful."

I blushed. "I love... like your eyes too." Our drinks arrived and I was glad. I lifted my smoothie and took a quick sip. The tart taste of the strawberries filled my mouth and I was surprised how cold it was. I really wanted this to go so well with Matthew. I needed to enjoy it. I told myself to relax and enjoy the moment.

"I only know a little bit about ya, if ya know what I mean. I'd love to know more, ya see." He reached over the table and took my hand in his. His hand was warm and much bigger than mine.

"What do you want to know?"

"Everything." We both laughed and I relaxed like Butterscotch when he was tickled behind his left ear. I took a slow breath in and smiled.

"Like what?"

"Favourite colour? Have ya a hobby? Do ya like books? Favourite movie? Favourite place?"

"Okay... okay. Ask me again... slowly."

"Colour?"

"Green."

"Hobby?"

"I ice-skate."

"Really? Wow, that's amazing. That's great."

"I can show you." I took out my mobile and showed him some clips of me ice-skating. Then our food arrived. I felt comfortable with him. I felt as if I could tell him anything.

"Do ya like books?" he asked. I swallowed hard. I reached out for my smoothie and Bob Marley played over the radio: *Three Little Birds*. Matthew put his finger up. We both smiled again.

"I like audiobooks," I said leaning towards him, "I have dyslexia, so I struggle with reading... and writing to be honest." I waited for his response. I was prepared for everything. If he was negative, I would come in hard with facts. One in ten people have dyslexia. There are approximately 700 million people worldwide who have dyslexia. Schools are becoming more and more dyslexic-friendly, but there are many teenagers and adults who struggle on a daily basis. I'm not—

"So what? Sure many famous people are dyslexic."

"Really?" He was positive. He was on my side. He understood me.

"Ya, Orlando Bloom, Richard Branson, Tom Cruise, Leonardo da Vinci and the funny guy in Dumb and Dumber. What's his name?"

"Jim Carrey? You're kidding me?"

"Nope, I'm serious. So, what's ya favourite movie?"

"Dumb and Dumber," I said and we both laughed. It was as easy as that. We worked together the way Anita and I worked together as friends. As avocado and pepper. As ice-skates to the ice.

"Now, your turn."

"That's easy. Blue is ma favourite colour. Ma hobby... ma guitar and... bird-watching. Ya got to come bird-watching with me. If ya know what I mean." The thought of bird-watching again made my whole body react with happiness. I knew there and then... Grandad would have approved of Matthew.

"I will." I wasn't the unmatched sock or the last biscuit in the packet.

"Anyone who likes birds is a friend of ours," Grandad used to say and I had to agree as I looked at Matthew's animated face.

"Favourite book... Hm, the Bible and The Great Gatsby."

"That's two. You'll have to read them to me."

"I will!" I definitely wasn't the lonely page in the printer. The bell rang above the door and a tall lady stepped in with a child following closely behind her.

"Favourite movie. Hm, that's a hard one. There are so many. All the Robert De Niro classics."

"Not a straight answer, but I'll let you off with that one."

The waiter directed the woman and her child to the table opposite us. There was something familiar about them.

"I'm done. Wait... favourite place. Did ya answer that one?" As he asked the question, I analysed the woman with her short dark hair and her smiley face.

315

"It's the ice-rink. I can be me there. Free, cheesy to say, free like a bird. You?"

He leaned over and grabbed my hand again and said, "That's easy. From today: here. Little Bird Cafe. If ya know what I mean."

Oh, it was Mrs Fulton from school with her child, Grace. I smiled over at the two. Grace's head was bowed and I immediately wondered if she was one of the kids not talking.

"Hi," I said and then looked at Matthew, "I know these guys from work." He nodded. "Mrs Fulton, it's me. Molly from school."

"Oh, Molly. How are you? It's good that you're still speaking. All the children are... well, you know. Grace is finding it hard." She reached out and put her hand over Grace's, "I just try to do things normally. And hope. Well, hope her voice will come... I'm sorry, I am getting emotional again. Can you keep an eye on Grace?"

"Yes, yes of course," I said as Mrs Fulton made her way to the bathroom.

"Is everything okay?" asked Matthew looking concerned.

"It's a problem at work. It's complicated." I suddenly jumped as when I turned around Grace was right at our table, staring blankly at us.

"Grace, Grace. Are you okay?" She held up a white page. She had written on it with orange crayon.

HELP.

She dropped it on me and I moved my chair back. Her mum arrived back and ushered her back into her seat.

"I'm sorry. Her behaviour has become so odd lately."

"No, it's okay. Grace, I hope you feel better soon."

The date was perfect and I was beyond happy but I knew I had to be somewhere else. I knew I had to go and see the fortune-teller.

When we went to leave, I glanced back at Grace. Her big brown eyes stared at her mother for answers. Answers

I had to get from a spooky fortune-teller. I held the note tightly as Matthew walked me home.

"Thank ya for a lovely time," Matthew said, "Ya looked a little distracted after that woman and her kid came in. Is everything okay?"

"Yes, it's just a work thing. Look, I had a great time too. I promise."

"Can we do it again? If ya know what I mean."

"I'd love to." He hugged me again and then left.

I didn't enter my house. I waited until he disappeared out of sight before I sneaked off to the fortune-teller's flat wishing the whole time I had gone inside and put on my trainers. My kitten heels were digging into my feet and making my skin turn red. I stopped several times to adjust them but it just prolonged the agony.

When I turned into the cul-de-sac, I took a deep breath in remembering my first visit here with Anita.

What if he didn't remember me? What if he wasn't in? I moved down his short path and noticed his forlorn garden.

I knocked on the door and waited.

SIXTY
BRICK

The children left. Molly left. Emily-Brooke left.

I am glad. I am tired. Today was hard work. I worked on all the children and I know tomorrow they will remain at home.

The door opens and three adults stand in the room. I am tired.

I am.

I am.

I don't want to wish anymore.

I shout out an uncontrollable "Leave!" as I look down at the screwed-up faces.

I am tired.

They don't leave.

"The board wants the whole school closed," the lady says in a sharp tone.

"The whole school? That does not make sense. It is only happening with the younger children."

"Mr Cardwell, there is no discussion on this. The children are not speaking. This is serious. We got the report back from the hospital and no doctor can explain this. They are bringing a specialist over from France and he should be arriving on Monday. The board is putting a full lockdown on your school."

"How exactly do we go about that?"

"Four of my colleagues from the board will come tomorrow and start the process. In the meantime, you should send out an email to all the parents telling them the school is closed until further notice."

I'm making the children's lives better. I can't protect the children from the pain they will inevitably experience unless they come here. That is my job.

I care.

A voice interrupts my thoughts, "No problem. We can send a message on our Seesaw app and the school will close tomorrow," he says. I am devastated.

"You will need to do a deep clean in the whole school too."

These words mean nothing to me.

My breath is quick and frantic and yet I'm not sure if I can breathe at all.

"Bring the children to me," I hear myself say, but it's as if my voice is miles away now. The way you feel in an odd dream where nothing makes sense and voices speak out but the words mean nothing.

I stare at them and I know I am concerned.

"The school will be closed for at least a month. No child will be allowed on the premises," the lady barks.

A panic envelops me as all three leave the room.

"Don't leave me alone!" I scream as I put out my invisible hand and steady myself with a sigh back into the basket.

My inner voice sounds frantic now and it screams to the top of my being.

"Don't take the children away from me." It pauses and my inner voice whispers, "The adults will take away the children. You are indeed on your own now."

Silence.

I take a deep breath.

I am a brick.

I am.

I am.

SIXTY-ONE
MOLLY

Finally, a noise from within told me it would be another long wait. When the door opened, I put on my biggest smile and said, "Hello, I don't know if you remember me or not but I came—"

"Hi. Yes, I remember you. Come on in," he said in his high-pitched voice.

"Oh, great. Thank you," I said and stepped inside. He started his slow walk to the top of his narrow staircase. I sounded like Anita when I started making small talk to distract from the awkwardness of the situation. "I hope you don't mind me calling again. I wanted to discuss what you said on our last visit. I was with my friend, Anita. I'm sure you remember her. She's the one you told would marry young and have two girls and then... well, you told her she would get a divorce."

"Yes, I remember," he said before he reached the top of the stairs. I stepped onto the landing and he turned to me, looking me straight in the eye, "Did you pull my doll's head off?"

I wanted the ground to swallow me up there and then. I held my rucksack over my stomach. I couldn't lie. I inhaled.

"It was an accident. I shoved her away from my face and she fell and her head rolled off. I'm sorry."

"That was my sister's doll. She died the day after her thirty-first birthday. The doll reminds me of her," he said, keeping his eyes on me the whole time.

"I'm sorry," I whispered, twisting my earring.

There was a long, awkward pause.

"How did you deal with your loss?" he asked and goosebumps appeared on my arm.

"My loss?" I asked and regretted the question as I didn't want to hear the answer.

"You brother," he said. I nodded and swallowed.

"Not well at the time but I've come to—"

"Come inside," he interrupted me and steered me into his living room, "Take a seat."

I did, trying to relax my rigid posture; not knowing what to say next. His question out in the hall had floored me. Why was I here? How did he know about Josh? Couldn't believe he knew about the doll.

"So, let's start again," he said.

"Again?" I said with a shaky voice.

"Yes, I'm Harry. I don't think we formally introduced ourselves," he said holding out his fat hand.

"I'm Molly," I said, shaking his damp, cold hand, "I'm sorry about the doll."

"It was Susan's favourite. She was thirty-one and still kept the stupid thing. Susan was a bit of a hoarder. But don't worry, I've a friend who is going to fix the doll for me... I used to fix stuff myself but I've stopped that all now," he said walking to the wall and taking down the photograph I had examined on my last visit.

"That's my daddy. He was called Rab. That's my mammy. She was called Gillian. And that's me. I used to love bikes up until Susan died... That's Susan," he said pointing to the little girl, tracing his finger over her head on the photograph.

"Nice," I said, not knowing what else to say. He uncaged a deep sigh and slumped down in the seat next to me.

"When she died, I took out my motorbike. I flew down the carriage way and at the roundabout I took the back road to Groomsport."

"It must have been awful," I said suddenly remembering how I had wanted to run away when the policewoman told me about Josh.

"Being on my bike helped me to forget... The dark trees covered the road like a tunnel. I could smell the damp leaves and I was protected by their bowing branches," he continued clutching onto the picture. I coughed an awful, loud cough and choked on my own saliva; holding it in didn't help matters. I became a barking seal. He ignored me.

"My head hurt as I repeated her name over and over in my mind... somehow my helmet eased the pain with the slight pressure. The winding road with the damp patches under the trees sparked a fiery adrenaline within me. My heart was beating so fast as I banked into the first corner. The grass brushed off my left knee; I was as low as I could possibly go," he said leaning to his left as if he was on his bike now. I couldn't take my eyes off him.

Was he serious?

"I could defy the rules of the road and yet I couldn't bring my sister back," he said rubbing the palm of his free hand against his chest, "I tried over and over but there was no breath in her," he said and tears filled his eyes. Guilt gripped me. This man lost a sister and I knew how hard it was as I'd just lost Josh. So, why was I finding it hard to sympathise with him? I didn't want to put my arm around him to comfort him. I didn't even want to say: I'm sorry for your loss. I wanted to excuse myself and leave.

He stared into the distance and in a flat monotone voice he continued, "Exhilaration mounted as I passed the little white cottage on the right and my bike leapt over the bump in the road. The sea air met me by surprise. My right hand wound the throttle fully open; I accelerated with power."

He got to his feet and replaced the photograph back on the wall. I had never heard someone speak like that before. The whole atmosphere in the room was one of heaviness and I had another annoying tickle at the back of my throat. I was too scared to cough again and interrupt his flow. I knew I should say something but nothing came into my head.

He stood facing the photograph and said, "I suddenly felt a deep appreciation and respect for the power within my motorbike."

"Motorbikes are powerful," I said and coughed again, trying desperately to clear my throat. I wanted to slap myself across the face. I must be the most heartless person in the whole world at this precise moment.

He became aware of me and nodded.

"They are powerful. I passed the tennis courts where I had played tennis badly with Susan many evenings when we were younger."

"I know those courts," I added wanting to understand his pain but I could only feel the pain for my own loss and I missed Josh terribly. We used to play tennis out in the back garden.

I couldn't make Susan come back for this odd man and I couldn't make Josh come back for myself. But I should be helping to ease his pain the way others tried to ease mine at Josh's funeral. Mourners speaking in low voices, whispering prayers and the motorised hum of his casket being lowered into the ground. Being an adult is caring for others. Being kind.

"Harry. I'm so sorry Susan died. It's awful. I wish I could take... take... take away your pain," I blurted out and he ignored me. He didn't even look in my direction. It was as if my words meant nothing, could achieve nothing. The reality was words do achieve nothing but they are kind to say. So many of my friends and relatives had spoken similar words to me at the funeral and they achieved nothing. But I knew they were being kind. Looking back now, I was glad they said them.

He continued, "Children were playing happily down at the little paddling pools separated by an arch-shaped bridge. It was too early in the season for the pools to be filled with water, but they didn't seem to care."

He sniffed and wiped his nose. His face was covered in splotchy, red marks. I lowered my head and didn't make eye contact. I wanted him to stop talking.

But being an adult didn't mean you could control things to work out the way you wanted them to. It was easy to run away from awkward, difficult situations but that was what a child did. As an adult, you had to jump on this ride called life. But on the way, it was best to be kind to others and try to make their rollercoaster journey less daunting, less scary, less sad.

He returned to his seat and with a trembling chin he said, "Their laughter rang out, and their high-pitched childish screams. It made me want to scream for the death of my sister."

I reached out and put my hand on top of his.

"That's how I did this," he said, clipping his leg with his walking stick, "It happened on the way back. The roads were wet. And when I went into the corner, the front wheel slid away from me. I crashed. My parents had enough to deal with, with Susan dying, without me ending up in hospital on the same day."

"It must have been awful for them and you too," I said kindly.

"It was. I never rode a motorbike again. Susan was gone…" There was another long, awkward pause, "She hung herself you know,"

I gasped.

"She wasn't a sad person so it didn't make sense. I found her but it was too late. I couldn't bring her back. I tried but I failed."

My phone rang and it made us both jump. In a way, I was thankful. I looked down: Terrance.

"Harry, I'm going to have to take this. I will be one minute," I said pressing one of my hands to my heart.

His sister hung herself.

"I'll put the kettle on," he said and limped out of the living room.

I let out a slight moan and pressed the green button on my mobile.

"Hello Terrance?"

"Yes, yes, yes, it's me, Molly. Have you thought about becoming my ice-skating partner? You see, there is a competition coming up and I reckon we could win it. It will mean a great deal of hard work on your part. But with dedication and time, I really do think we can do it."

"Actually, Terrance I did think about what you asked... I've decided I don't want to." My face tightened.

"Oh good. Good. I'm glad you want to. We can start tomorrow. By the way, I'm sorry about the passing of your sister. Sad news, I'm sure. Very sad," he said.

"Terrance, it was my brother and I said I *don't* want to be your partner," I said, raising my voice slightly. There was a long pause.

"Sorry, you must have bad reception there. I thought you said you *don't* want to be my partner," he said, and I could hear him snapping his fingers.

"That's what I did say."

"What? Why ever not?"

"I just don't want to," I said and my body temperature rose.

The phone went dead.

Harry appeared with a tray with two tea cups and a pot of tea.

In a cheerful, happier voice he said, "I only have Rich Tea biscuits. I hope that's okay?"

"Yes, that's grand," I said watching him shaking the teapot, lifting the lid and using a teaspoon to stir the tea bag around in the water. His sausage-like fingers struggled to not get burnt.

"So, what made you come back, Molly?" he asked.

"I started working in a school, even though you told me not to. And the children in my class stopped talking.

One by one. It spread like a virus. Now, children in another class are being affected too. I remembered that you kept repeating, 'Children should be seen and not heard' over and over and I'm now thinking there is some sort of connection."

"Of course, there is a connection. You should've listened to me. I warned you but you didn't listen."

"I'm sorry," I said.

"Drink your tea and then we'll get to the bottom of this," he said taking a sip and setting his cup down. He dunked a Rich Tea in and proceeded to suck the tea out of the biscuit just before it crumbled right down his T-shirt.

I nearly threw up.

The floorboards creaked when Harry stood. I stood up with him and stepped over to the Bible verse on his wall: John 14:6. Jesus saith unto him, I am the way, the truth, and the life: no man cometh unto the Father, but by me. "Tell me about this verse, Harry. I like it," I said.

"It was written on the floor of my built-in wardrobe when I was a child. My mammy used to read it to me. It has sentimental value."

"I wonder what it means," I said.

"My mammy explained it to me once, but I don't remember now."

"I thought about that verse when Josh died. I wanted to know if he was with God, the father. I wanted to know if he followed Jesus."

"This one here will help you with that question: Matthew 7:25. 'The Rain came down, the streams rose, and the winds blew and beat against that house, yet it did not fall, because it had its foundation on the rock.' He will be with God if he had a relationship with Him." I stared at him, confused; this guy was a total contradiction. He talked about God and was also into his creepy-ass fortune telling. "The rock here is Jesus. No one will harm him if he has God and Jesus in his life."

"I think he did. Matthew, my friend, told me Josh became a Christian. He owned a Bible. I saw it in his bedroom," I said hoping that Harry would say Josh was in Heaven.

Instead, he said, "I'll set up the kitchen and we can work out why the children have lost their voices. You can come in with me if you want," he said and I nodded.

I followed him into the kitchen. I had forgotten how small the room was. Harry lit a candle and placed it on the table. He opened a drawer and picked out his deck of angel cards, placing it beside the candle.

"Open the window, Molly," he said and I did. The wooden wind chimes knocked against each other when the breeze entered the kitchen. He opened a little bottle and a scent filled the room.

"We might need sage," Harry said.

"What does the sage do?"

"Fights against any negativity. It cleanses the room," he answered and pointed to the chair at the table, "It's better if you sit here."

His round face lowered down to the table and he closed his eyes the same way he did when Anita and I were here. The light flickered over his face. It disappeared again and he groaned. He focused on me. He reached out and grabbed my hand.

"Did you take something from my house?" he yelled and I nearly jumped out of my skin.

"What? No! I'm not a thief," I said in a raised tone.

"Are you sure?"

"Yes."

He clutched his cards tightly and then shuffled them. He turned over the first card.

"Four of wands," he said, "Are you moving to a new house? Do you have a new house or plans to buy a new house?"

"No, none at all. I live with my parents for goodness sake. This is not working. It is pointless," I said.

He stared into the candle and considered another card.

"The death card. This could mean there has been a change."

"None of this is answering why the children in the school have stopped talking," I said, wanting to leave.

Christians shouldn't listen to this stuff.

He closed his eyes, "There's a song. It's about stones."

"Yes," I said and he opened his eyes wide.

"Tell me."

"Tell you the song?"

"Yes. It's linked somehow," he said.

Embarrassing!

"Okay. Well, it goes like this... 'How many stones are left alone? How many stones are left alone? How many stones are left alone? Who is still at home?' Then it continues with... 'One little stone is left alone. One little stone is left alone. One little stone is left alone. Harry must be still at home.' It's not exactly in that tune but it's not far off."

"It's something to do with the stones. Is there a basket?"

"There are two baskets in the classroom. One basket holds all the stones and the other basket is where you put your stone if you are present. I even have a stone. Well, mine is a brick actually... oh, hold on. It was *your* brick," I said as my face flushed.

"My brick?" he said standing up.

"I took a brick from your basket at the bottom of your stairs. I didn't mean to take it. It fell out of the basket and I picked it up to put it back..." Harry shoved his chair out of the way and made his way down the stairs, "I'm sorry. I didn't mean to take it."

"I need to check which one you stole but I think I know. It's from the house I used to live in."

"Why would it matter?" I asked, confused, feeling offended that he used the word "stole".

"Because, Molly, the house was knocked down and it believes children should be seen and not heard."

"It believes? Houses don't believe," I shouted as he limped his way down the stairs. I watched, in wonder, as Harry was rummaging through the stones and pebbles in his basket.

He turned and scrutinised me and said, "You caused this. You stole the brick. The brick somehow embraces that children should be seen and not heard. Somehow, it conjured its wish into... It's like a virus."

"I caused this?"

"Yes, and now we need to sort it."

"How?"

"We need to destroy the brick."

"How?"

"Molly, stop asking me how and go get my car keys. We need to go to your school and destroy the brick. There's so much fear in that thing and even more desire."

SIXTY–TWO
BRICK

I am scared. I don't want to be alone.
I am.
I am.

SIXTY-THREE
MOLLY

"Where is the school?"

"May Avenue," I say rubbing the back of my neck, resisting the temptation to bite my nails.

I did this. I made the children silent by bringing that stupid brick into the school. I glance over at Harry who is hunched over the steering wheel, driving over the speed limit through the narrow streets. His large, shovel hands grip the steering wheel and he keeps his eyes firmly on the road.

"We must destroy that brick!" he yells. making me jump. I begin to hiccup.

"It's down there," I mumble running my hand over my head. This is as crazy as he is. Why did I agree to show him the school?

He pulls up outside the school and I am shocked to see a bright yellow plastic police barrier over the entrance. Harry grabs his walking stick from the back seat. What's next? Are we going to break in?

"I told you not to go to that school. You didn't listen. Why didn't you listen?" he asks, swinging open the car door and heaving himself out of the seat. I can sense he is nervous.

"I don't believe in fortune-tellers. I just thought it was an unusual thing to say," I answer truthfully.

He glares at me, "Come on. We need to get that brick."

My hands begin to sweat and I tug at Mum's long, silk scarf; the one she had given me on the day of my interview. Memories of that day flood my thoughts.

Meeting James for the first time in the corridor. His little moon-shaped face I had learned to care about. How he had asked me if I was a teacher or a parent or a school nurse and I told him to go away.

Now his little mouth is silent and I miss him.

I miss all the kids. The strange thought makes my head hurt.

Beads of sweat form on my forehead and I wipe them off. Makeup is all over the side of my hand. I am glad Mum had given me the packet of hankies this morning in the car.

I love you Mum with all my heart.

I follow behind Harry, watching him trying every window to get into the main school. I silently pray inside: find a window that opens. Please, please, please. I need to get away from this bizarre man.

Harry turns to me and his fat face frowns. I can hardly see his eyes anymore. Can fortune-tellers read minds?

I take a deep breath, waiting for him to speak.

"We'll have to break one."

"We?" I repeat, glad he hasn't read my mind.

"Yes, we." His booming voice of authority makes me stand up straight, "You will have to climb through, go to the classroom and find that brick. We need to destroy the brick. It's the only way the children will be able to talk again."

Harry's fist clenches and I want to run. Instead, I look around for something to break the window.

"Can we break it with this?" I say, holding up a branch. He takes it off me and after several attempts, he smashes the window that leads to the SEN room.

If the police catch me in there, what will I say? How will I explain that a house's whole essence is in a brick and it wishes for children to stop speaking?

"I'll go," I mumble heaving myself up onto the window sill, "I'll find it."

I squeeze myself through the broken window and pain sears through my entire arm.

"You better," Harry replies with a frown. I want to call him every name under the sun but decide better of it. I practically throw myself onto the floor knowing I'm bleeding. I hate that I'm wearing a dress and these ridiculous shoes. My ankles are burning red so I undo the buckles, deciding to go on my bare feet. I run off down the corridor.

All of a sudden, Mr Cardwell's words echo in my head like a strange dream.

"Five-year-olds are unpredictable. Don't take what he said to heart. Once he gets to know you, he will be fine."

Five-year-olds are not unpredictable. They speak the truth. It's fortune-tellers and old houses that are unpredictable.

I pass the noticeboard with the title "Pupil Voice" and stop in my tracks. Oh, how I wish they did. They have all lost their voices. It is eerie being in the school when it is empty. A shiver runs down my spine.

It reminds me of the church service before they buried Josh. The musty smell and the ghostly church echo. I stand still and close my eyes. I begin to hiccup again.

It's as if I am back there now: the polished wooden pews in rows, each with its own little shelf holding a Bible and a song book. The padded bar for kneeling; all I want to do is to rest my knees there and ask God to bring Josh back to me.

We had huddled together as a family in the front row with an endless supply of tissues. I couldn't look behind me but I knew the church was packed. Children speaking in too-loud whispers, babies crying, feet shuffling, heavy breathing, and the odd cough from my Uncle Sammie who sat directly behind me. They reminded me of where I was. I squeezed my parents' hands and tried to focus on the pastor speaking up at the front. His mouth was moving but I had no idea what he was saying.

I open my eyes and walk to the end of the corridor. I push open a door and think to myself.

I was just starting to like my job here.

I can't believe all the children stopped talking because of me. Why would a house think it's easier on the children if they remain silent? Do houses even think? It isn't even a house anymore. It is a stupid brick. The craziness of my thoughts makes me break into a run.

I get to Mrs Dunkan's door and my legs are aching. I need to stop and take several deep breaths. My hands are shaking as I take out the fob from the lanyard around my neck and swipe it over the keypad. I continue to hiccup.

I scan the classroom for the basket of stones. Surely this is ridiculous. My eyes spot the basket at the back of the room.

"What is the point of all of this?"

I walk over to the stones with the children's names on each one. I pick up Aaron's large pebble and run my forefinger over the top of it, tracing out his name. I move Dawn's stone gently to the side and pick up James' stone, squeezing it hard.

"I miss that kid." My own voice echoes through the deserted classroom and my heart misses a beat. I lift out each stone looking frantically for mine. Each stone represents a child, a family and the devastation that has hit each one due to this mysterious wish.

"You are a brick... How can a brick wish for children to stop speaking?" I say out loud as I find my stone right at the bottom of the pile. I lift it out and stare at it, turning it over.

It is just an ordinary piece of brick. Does this really come from a house that wants to stop children from speaking? Part of me wants to leave the brick in the basket and another part of me knows Harry spoke the truth.

In the car, he told me that because the house had witnessed so much sadness and child abuse, it decided children should be seen and not heard. Now that deep desire lived in its only remaining brick and somehow its wish got activated. Crazy!

If I could make one wish, I wouldn't wish for the children to stop speaking. I would wish for Josh to be alive. My whole heart aches as I know it is impossible. Josh is dead and there is nothing I can do about it.

I blink away the tears and look at my name sprawled with permanent marker over the brick surface. I run to the storeroom and find their TinkerBox. I take out the hammer and run outside the mobile, placing the brick on the ground.

"Children should always be heard. Children should always be heard," I yell and smash the hammer down onto the brick.

It shatters into a million pieces.

SIXTY-FOUR
BRICK

I am a brick!

I have an inner voice humans now fear. It used to rise from the deep depths, within my foundations, through my plumbing and made me choke on my own spit. Now it spreads amongst the humans.

I will be heard.

They will return the children back to me. I will make more children's lives better. I can protect them from the pain. I will never stop doing my job.

The adults will see their beautiful children but will no longer hear their voices. Now they will treat their children well.

A voice interrupts my thoughts, "What is the point of all of this?"

What is the point? What is the point? The point is to make all the families happy.

When I was first built, I was different. I watched eagerly as my occupants arrived, made plans and remained within myself. I was House and I had a purpose. I provided a shelter for the four families who cooked, slept and entertained themselves within my walls. I looked after their children and encouraged companionship, mutual support and love.

I was House. I was loved and I belonged.

What am I now?

I am a brick.

Over the years, I realised the children became the adults' biggest burden and their crying made the adults turn on them. But now I don't need to watch their cruelty anymore. I can wish now. My wish has successfully spread throughout this whole room. Eventually, it will spread throughout the town and even the whole world. The point is: it is working and I have a purpose.

The voice answers me.

"I miss that kid," and I agree.

"I miss all the kids. I miss Emily-Brooke, I miss D.B., I miss Harry, I miss Susan, I miss Zara, Zara and Zara, Adil, Rislan, Yasmine and Jamila, and the children who I met here, Aaron, Dawn—"

"You are a brick," a voice says and I know I am in a hand and no longer in the basket.

"Molly, is that you?" My breath is quick and frantic and yet I'm not sure if I can breathe at all.

Yes, I am a brick.

A brick that can make things happen.

I am a brick.

I am.

I am.

We stopped the children from speaking because children should be seen and not heard. If they are silent then the adults will treat them well.

"How can a brick wish for children to stop speaking?" she asks.

I answer her, "By wishing with my whole being, over and over again."

Tears form in Molly's eyes and I know she hears me.

"Take me with you," I hear myself say but it's as if my voice is miles away now. The way you feel in an odd dream where nothing makes sense and voices speak out but the words mean nothing.

She hears me and carries me outside. I feel love. She loves talking to me. She understands me and now she is going to care for me. She is taking me with her.

A calmness envelops me as her eyes search for mine. She knows I am here. She knows I exist and I belong. I want to capture this moment in my memory forever. She sits me down on the ground and I look up.

She yells out, "Children should always be heard. Children should always be heard."

I see a hammer in her hand and I take my last deep breath,

I am a brick.

I am.

I...

SIXTY-FIVE
MOLLY

I grimace at the quivering hammer in my hand and notice on my forearm dripping blood.

It's done. What should I do next?

To admit remorse would be welcoming the crazy notion: objects can feel. Ridiculous. I refuse to project my emotions onto things that don't matter. Not anymore.

I turn away in a single spin. It's so hard to breathe. I lift my head to the sky filled with puffed up, dull-grey clouds. Are they forming the shape of a house? I need to pull myself together. I'm falling apart like the apple crumble I shared an hour ago with Matthew. I should have stayed there with him. What compelled me to leave the welcoming music, comforting gingham cushions and... and... and his wonderful, perfect company?

A crow descends with a hard thud upon the scrutinising school building.

"What the heck are you doing here?"

Grandad used to say, "Crows aren't a good sign, Molly-Moo. Linked to death, they are. Linked to death. A warning. Best to avoid 'em like the plague." I don't need this right now.

Hopping from one tile to another, the mocking crow mimics the thumping of my beating heart.

Aware of my cold bare feet, I try to stand tall and avoid seeing Grandad's face raising the alarm in my mind's eye.

The sky opens. Rain pelts down and down and down. Like the marble paint we used in the classroom; the rivulet of scarlet on my arm fades now to pink. The blood dollops onto the meddling ends of my long hair; the harsh red contrasts dramatically with my natural flecks of golden blonde. Saturated. It dyes my ends and flattens the curls. The crow, with pride, stretches out his perfect ink-coloured wings.

"Bloody show-off."

I hear the sirens getting closer. I stumble forward leaning on the railing. How the heck would I explain this?

The crow gawks at me, pointing his razor-sharp beak at the weapon still in my hand. I drop it. The crow knows what I did.

"I had to do it… for the children…"

The words plummet like the bricks of a demolished house. I am losing my mind.

The crow cocks his head at me.

"I know they won't believe me." With one peck, he agrees. The rain slows down dripping alongside the chip-chop thoughts in my head; full of random, unconnected details. Bible verses, bullying, play-based learning … death.

I try to stay calm.

"If a blue house is made of blue bricks and a red house is made of red bricks. What is a greenhouse made of?" With one piercing alarm call, the crow abandons me. "It's glass. The answer is glass. Ack, it doesn't matter… It really doesn't matter." I watch him soar away and I *wish* to follow in his flight path: escape. Deep down I know only houses can make wishes and Harry has gone on without me.

Houses can make wishes? What am I thinking? Houses are like fat, flightless birds: grounded. How the hell can houses make wishes? I shouldn't swear. I really shouldn't swear. I'm without a doubt losing my mind.

The darting rain stops.

I stand tall, as if I had just finished a one-foot spin for the clapping spectators down at the ice-rink.

But dizziness surrounds me.

I begin to hiccup. My light dress clings to my shivering body.

I don't feel good.

Leaning against the cold gable wall, my head continues to whirl.

I contemplate telling them the truth.

Two things are certain: I know I need to get my story straight and a story isn't a story without a beginning, a middle and an end.

I take a calm deep breath.

When did this craziness start?

To tell the truth, I need to understand where and when. Put together the jigsaw of madness. But I have always been pathetically rubbish at doing puzzles. Do I even have a beginning for this bizarre story?"

Maybe.

I close my eyes and with a brand-new perseverance, I picture myself standing in the fortune-teller's cul-de-sac.

Falling sideways, I slide down the wall. I feel different. Something inside me has changed.

I am a girl.

I am.

I am.

***

Seen and Not Heard

Deborah Jean White

ABOUT THE AUTHOR

Deborah Jean White is a Primary School teacher in Northern Ireland. When writing she enjoys taking her readers on roller-coaster journeys, blurring the lines between fiction and non-fiction, creating conflict for her intriguing characters and devising plots with twists and turns.

If she isn't in school working or in a coffee shop writing her novels you will find her spending time with her daughter, Abigail and her dog Poppy. Deborah enjoys going to her caravan and taking long walks along the beach.

To hear about her upcoming releases, check out her website and sign up for her newsletter.

Printed in Great Britain
by Amazon